Salinor: The Beginnings

Book One

Revelations

Salinor: The Beginnings

Book One

Revelations

By Samuel Alexander

Copyright 2017 by Samuel Alexander
Copyright 2024 by Samuel Alexander
Publisher Samuel Alexander
Cover design by Miblart

All rights reserved. This book or any portion thereof may not be reproduced or used in any manner whatsoever without the express written permission of the author except for the use of brief quotations in a book review or scholarly journal

PROLOGUE

"Tell me why should I, Salinor, goddess of all, grant you this request? Who are you to deem yourself worthy of the favour of the gods?"

Atora, a boy of eighteen, looked up at Salinor and couldn't believe his twist of fate. Had he travelled leagues across land and sea and braved the turning of winter for nothing? And now after trekking up the mountain of the gods—the pass of Gai'n—a feat that had killed many, he was faced with this. He was even stopped from using his last bit of strength to vault himself from the top of the mountain in an act of self-sacrifice.

All this he had done to save his mother, and now he was being denied.

He was stopped from killing himself only so that she could taunt him. Laugh at him as he took his dying breaths. Could the gods really be that cruel? Even still, he came at his mother's orders, and he'd come too far even for the mother of all to deny him. As long as he breathed, he would fight for his own mother's life.

"In strength, when I was broken, in faith though doubt was certain, in hope against hope, I believed against all odds that I could save her. Even if it meant the taking of my own life," he recited the mantra.

"If I told you that even life sacrifice wouldn't ensure your mother's life, what would you do?" Salinor spoke.

"My mother, Ronilas, is a great seamstress. Let her make you a dress worthy of the gods. If it is not, then my whole family's fate is at your hands." Salinor nodded as if to say that was reasonable before replying, "She shall use the fabric of the gods and make the dress for my daughter."

Atora wasn't thrilled with this response. The fabric of the gods could only be sewn by the gods. By setting this task, Salinor was sealing Atora's family to a fate whatever torment would fulfil the Goddess' desire. Atora, for his part, showed no hint that it could not be done. So, on top of the Jargadine Mountains, home of the gods, the deal was struck. Then Atora went home to his dying mother.

The goddess temporarily healed Atora's mother to allow her to do the best work she could, and she got to work immediately. On the fourth day, she produced the impossible: A gown so beautiful that Salinor decreed anything too beautiful for words was equally comparable to Ronilas' gift. Ronilas not only gave her the dress, but also supplied two more gifts, which showcased the skills of hunting, craftsmanship, and weaponry that she had taught her children.

And so, it began. The province from which the family came was named Atorath after Atora. From there, Ronilas and her three children formed an underground alliance to overthrow the magician's rule. But first, she had to kill the magician who accidentally poisoned her and refused to rectify the mistake by healing her. Blessed with a new resistance to magic, it was a fair battle.

After almost twenty full cycles of the moon, along with the Atorathian peoples' resistance to magic, she was sure the magicians could be overthrown. But it was not enough. Neither the Alliance nor the magician rulers could overpower each other, until suddenly the magician in rule was found dead after thirteen moon cycles of war. It was rumoured that the king's brother was the one who took him down. No evidence to support this claim was ever found.

He and Ronilas met and signed a treaty that would provide equal rights for magicians and non-magicians. This allowed each province to excel in its own unique talents and provide the world of Salinor with an eclecticism that had not been seen before. This war was known as *"The War of the Beginning,"* the dawn of a new age of Salinor.

But things change.

As time moved on, old jealousies and superiorities arose in new places. Things that were true became legend. And this new equality was lost to internal politics much deeper than the mere magician versus human dilemma that started the war. In this new world, there rose a tyrant. He came to power and ruled

Revelations

Salinor with an iron fist that spawned the rebirth of the Alliance, which was now even more covert since anyone could be the enemy. The new Alliance ruler kept the destruction at bay with the help of key friends, magicians, and humans. Together they discovered a lost prophecy, one that could take down the Tyrant.

It was over one thousand years before the first sign came. No one knew when the second sign would appear, and it was ten more years before it came. The Alliance was once again on a path to save Salinor. Except this time—they might lose.

Samuel Alexander

1

DANAIS

Danais woke up on the fourth day to the sound of birds chirping outside his window. In his state of mind, it sounded more like squeaking. *The urge to throw a rock* was his first thought. He yawned and contemplated getting out of bed. Eventually, good sense won over. It was a day off, and he wasn't going to waste it away snoring in bed. He walked down the hall to find a note from his uncle on the bath. It stated that there were a few pots of boiling water in the kitchen, so he wouldn't have to take a cold bath.

He filled the tub with the hot water then went outside to the pump and gradually added cold water till he got it to just the right temperature. It wasn't that often he had the pleasure of a hot bath, so he relished every minute of it. He grabbed his towel after he was done and dried himself off as he headed back to his room. As he lay naked on his bed, the morning sun was still trying to come through the window. He stared up at his cracked ceiling and couldn't help but reflect on his misfortune.

Danais was an Atorathian, one of those blessed with a natural, albeit varying, resistance to magician's spells. However, he was what the magicians would call 'silent.' Or more commonly just 'peasant.' He didn't have any of the gifts. It was speculated that Atora requested they be given this power out of his hatred towards the magician who poisoned his mother. But just like other races could be born with no magical qualities, so could his own. He wondered how he'd survived without some accidental poisoning or stray spell doing him in, especially as a normal human.

Atorathians were arguably the best hunters. A skill Danais wished he had more of. He had minor hunting skills, but nothing a mere human couldn't match. Strategic thinking and combat were arguably some of their better talents. These were gifts from Ronilas, the Goddess of War and Wisdom—yet two more things he didn't get. He probably could hold his own against another mortal, but against a trained magician he didn't stand a chance. He had at least acquired the physical attributes of an Atorathian: muscular in proportion to height, not too slim, not too big or overly muscled. An overweight or too-slim Atorathian was usually an immediate giveaway of the 'silent' ones.

Finally succumbing to the need to start the day, Danais got out of bed and peered at himself in the mirror he had placed against one of the walls. At least he had the appearance of being normal. At his age, if his shape hadn't changed, he was bound to keep it. His ears pointed up at the top much like an elf's, except slightly rounded. The bottoms melded seamlessly into the head in a way that others usually didn't notice, as Atorathians had no earlobes without really paying attention.

Danais had a habit of doing this, looking at himself in the mirror: just to make sure that at least one physical attribute of his people was still intact. Thin, curved eyebrows, medium rounded nose, perfectly chocolate-brown complexion, full lips, and straight, midnight-black hair, which he kept very close-cut. He even possessed the unarguable Atorathian skill of lovemaking; the only skill no one could connect directly to a god. This skill was so renowned that it garnered as much money in the brothels as that of being a hunter—so much so that Atorathians always demanded top price for the 'services' of their travelling troupes during wars over the centuries.

The silent types, like Danais, were considered peasants, and no matter how good they were, they could not demand high prices. He did, however, seem to make more than a peasant should. He reasoned it was because he had the gift for real, and it was unfortunate he was otherwise a peasant. Danais sighed and prayed that maybe he was the son of a god, and any day he'd wake up with all the gifts of his people and more. But that was every peasant's dream—certainly not something that was going to happen to him.

Danais took a deep breath, put on some undergarments, three-quarter length slacks, a button-down sleeveless white shirt with a collar, worn outside the pants, and then he took one last look. He smiled in approval. He may be a peasant, but at least he was an attractive one.

Being an Atorathian peasant was the lowest of lows because the Salinor of today existed only because of Ronilas and her family's actions. Atorathians shaped the new world, so their peasants were treated lower than all the peasants if only out of spite and jealousy.

But he refused to let that thought bring him down. He put on his sandals and headed out of the house.

His uncle owned the farm he worked on. His uncle, as far as Danais could tell, was gifted but only average in the efficiency of all Atorathian skills. He had taken Danais in after his parents died. Unfortunately, he could only pay his nephew as a peasant. Favouritism was everywhere, but it had its limits. Treating peasants as favourites wasn't the same as paying them as such. In a free world, even peasants could revolt, so keeping up appearances was good for business. Otherwise, his uncle had treated him even better than his own children sometimes, Danais thought. His uncle never talked about Danais' father or mother. Danais' origins were a complete mystery. He did know that his mother was said to be as beautiful as Ronilas herself. That was a thought that Danais cherished.

His uncle's oldest child, who was an army general, had trained Danais like he was gifted; teaching him fighting and tracking skills he couldn't perform even to a small percentage of accuracy. He didn't understand the purpose of this and was easily frustrated. His obvious negative response to this did nothing to perturb his cousin, though.

He strapped his money bag around his right bicep and hurried to town as fast as he could. Miri, his cousin, was supposed to be visiting today, and he wasn't looking forward to a training session on his day off. He loved her—but not that much.

Before he had time to execute his escape plan Danais found himself suddenly cornered against a wall with her practically throwing him into the air grasping him into a hug. He was a little guy, only five foot three—small for any of the provinces in Salinor, not bad considering most Atorathians were around five foot five and probably the only race to all be so close in height.

"So how have you been, little one?" she asked.

"I was doing well when I was breathing,"

Revelations

His cousin put him down. "You've grown a lot since I've seen you last. Matured, I guess. You're still the same height. How long has it been?"

He had to think about that. "Five moon cycles since your last visit."

"So why are you running away so fast? Trying to avoid another training session?" His cousin accused with a smirk on her face.

"Can't I just be going for a walk?" Danais replied defiantly. It did nothing to waver her smile.

If the sly look she was giving him meant anything, it was that she was not convinced. "Not at the pace you were moving."

"I was just trying to get into town while the morning pastries were still hot."

Miri raised her eyebrows.

Danais refused to admit he was trying to avoid her. He could play this game all morning if he had to.

Miri chuckled. "I see."

"Besides I'm a man now. Many moon cycles past my sixteenth name day, my seventeenth even. I have to go do manly things."

"Like eat pastries?" Miri slightly raised her eyebrow again as she stared down at him. She was part Dani, from the province of Danais, so managed to be a more average height human even though she looked like an Atorathian.

"Yes."

"Should I ask who she is?"

Danais, although not really going to see someone, had considered meeting someone would be a possibility. This made his avoidance appear much more truthful in his mind. "Bye, Miri. I'll talk to you when I get back."

Danais liked the walk down the mountain known as Chibal Way. It was the main road through the mountain. It turned off to many villages in the province, and he passed some of these roads while going down. The mountain wasn't the highest in the Salinor but most of Atorath was on elevated land, so he was still up high.

The walk down was peaceful, and the farm was partly surrounded by a forest, so the path lead through the woods sometimes. The tall trees and the light shining through the leaves were extremely calming to him. On this walk he could, if only for a moment, forget who he was. Maybe one day he'd travel further into the other side of the mountain and explore the woods more thoroughly.

The town was on the water's edge of the main city of Atorath. The main street which bordered the shops on the river's edge was called Londar. The town itself was called Chin. The city was semi-circular with a grid of streets that branched off from the main road, intersecting with the roads coming in from the curved border. The market was a square section of stalls in the centre of town, full of fresh fruits, vegetables, jewellery, clothing, and the like. The bad area, if coming from the water, was a section off to the back right, and located on the circular border of the city. The slums were known as 'The Burrow,' and was where most of the town peasants and thieves lived—or, more accurately, hid. Thieves were everywhere where people had money and items to be stolen. The Burrow was merely a place to escape.

Danais didn't find it to be that bad as he walked through. He could've easily avoided the area, but he liked tall buildings. It was not glamorous. There was laundry hanging overhead somehow drying clean, in the smog. Lots of small dark alleys curving among the regular grid of streets, and people shouting and rushing to their jobs late. The Burrow was full of his kind of people, some of whom he worked with on the farm. He spoke to a few as he walked and also had to defend himself from a thief who thought he could steal his money. Nothing too out of the ordinary in this area nor for him. His cousin had trained him well, but he would never admit that.

After defeating him, Danais stole his for good measure and continued to walk on enjoying the light snack. He had a slight bruise on his hand from where he punched the thief and one on his arm from when the thief grabbed him. Neither of these bothered Danais much. He had been in much worse brawls before.

Soon the streets cleared as things like pubs and barber shops started to appear. At the end of the next block, he made a left onto Licol Road. Like all the other streets, all the streets in Chin had L names.

This particular block was the brothel centre. Both sides of

the road looked quite clean and unassuming. However, the signs on the inns were very clear as to what their product was. Usually, there was a scantily clad male or female next to the wooden inn sign, or murals painted on the entrance doors of men or women in obviously sexual situations. It was, Danais thought, rather good art, but he wondered if the artists did other conventional art as well. Surely this type of art was only a means to pay bills and not that profitable, but then again, considering how much money sex workers made, it could be profitable.

He was two blocks away from the main road in an area which held more of the usual town fare: family-owned apartments on top of family-owned inns and so on. The priciest—but not necessarily the best—shops were on the main road. It was the longest street, so they tried to lure in rich clientele and unsuspecting victims before they could get into the market, which usually held the more exciting, harder-to-find items.

The market in the centre of Chin was strategically designed to lure people into the city so that the money was spread evenly about instead of just one street performing well. A lot of front shop owners owned shops in the market, so it was all a ploy to hopefully get them to go to their own shops. Danais found this type of business dealings interesting. As a peasant, he didn't own enough to be involved in sales politics.

The Maltar River surrounded the main city, Leanor, named after the Goddess of Love, forming an island in the middle. Whether the island was in the river, or it became a lake connected to the river was partially undecided, so it didn't have a separate name and was unofficially a lake.

Danais had never stepped foot on the island before but had always dreamed of doing so. However, his mind couldn't dwell on that just yet. He had finally made it to the main road, and directly in front of him, across the street, was his favourite pastry shop. The smell of fresh goodies was overwhelming his thoughts and almost forgot it was a long journey to get here, but it was worth the walk.

The owner of the shop was Garnter. As such it was rightly named Garnter's Pastries. He was at least still early enough to get a good view on the outside terrace. He enjoyed the view over the harbour and watching the ships come in from the city.

Maybe if he were lucky, not too many of the rich would come, and he could sit outside and stare at the water all day. He stepped inside the door, and the bells chimed to signal his entrance. His ears and his nose were delighted.

"Danais! Come, come. You're late," Garnter beckoned him to the counter.

"I ran into Miri on the way down," Danais responded.

"Ah, so have the bruises from her last session healed yet?" Garnter teased.

Danais ignored him. He was too busy eyeing the expensive tarts and cakes and wanted to say, *I'll have that, and that. Oh, and two of those.* But he couldn't afford even half of that. He let out a sigh and was about to place an order when a customer interrupted him.

"Wishing beyond your means, peasant boy. Why don't you go down the street and buy a bread roll? I'm sure you can afford that with your coins. I didn't know you allowed such scum in your establishment, Garnter."

Danais would've said something but arguing with a magician wasn't wise. Luckily, he didn't have to.

"The only scum in here right now is you. I won't have none of that talk in my shop, or you will have to leave," Garnter told the stranger. The two glared at each other for a moment, and then the magician smiled and got back to reading his books and scrolls.

"Thank you," Danais said. Even in Atorath it was hard to find good, decent people sometimes.

"Nothing to thank me for. I may make you give up your table sometimes, but I won't tolerate direct hate speech. Besides, I get a lot of my supplies from your uncle. And my son is—" Danais looked up for more details, but Garnter quickly changed the subject. "So, what will you have?"

"Something boring and inexpensive." Danais sighed, thinking about how little money he could spare.

"Boring? For you? Never. Not in my shop."

"He is right, though. I can't afford anything good."

"Nonsense. You can do anything you want—gifted or ungifted."

Danais smiled. This was part of why he loved coming here. The lies just flowed off Garnter like water.

Revelations

"I've got a fresh pumpkin tart baking just for you. And an extra-large banana nut muffin. Just about ready, with extra cinnamon and brown sugar that you will love."

"I can't take that," Danais objected, but Garnter was already placing them on a wooden tray just for him, with a small glass of spiced milk.

"There you are," Garnter said, and then scoffed. "Boring? How dare you even use that word in my shop? Especially when 'you' are in the same sentence as the word." Garnter made sure to emphasise the word "you" and smile.

"And how did you have this ready at the exact moment I arrived?" Danais asked coyly.

"Well, a magician friend of mine hazarded a guess at the time you'd be here. He was a little off, but all this talk made it just right," Garnter replied rather matter-of-factly.

"That's cheating."

"Me... cheat? I'm offended at the thought."

The faux offence was hard to not find amusing. Danais laughed. Garnter was a much-needed pick-me-up after all the moping he had done in the morning. "Thanks."

"Just run along. I have paying customers to deal with. And if you tell your uncle I gave you free food, I'll tell him about the extra milk you snuck me when I ran out last week. I'm not taking your money."

"Garnter."

"Let me rephrase: If you don't take that food for free, I will tell your uncle about the milk."

"That's blackmail." Danais faked shock, but he could tell by the look Garnter gave him that it wasn't received well.

"I'm doing it out of love. Now go before I give you more food."

Danais smiled to himself and went outside on the deck and chose a nice table by the rail. He loved to look at the boats—all kinds, from rowboats to tall ships with sails. There was even a battleship heading toward the outflow of the lake. The river curved off before a waterfall and, after a slow decline, met with itself again and even further down met with the outflow of a much higher waterfall close to the farm up in the mountain. Danais pondered being a noble in Atorath, or maybe a soldier—all the things he could be if he were not silent. He had wasted away the better half of his life dreaming of how prominent he would be had fate smiled down on him.

Danais stared for over an hour, mostly at the tall ships usually privately owned by people with money. He'd acquired a certain Atorathian pride, even though he was ungifted. Some Atorathians seemed to think they were better than magicians simply because they were Atorathians and the peace of Salinor had originated there. All countries had associated a sort of pride or prejudice directly related to their skills over the years, but this Atorathian pride was the most frowned upon—ironically enough, for the same reasons the pride existed in the first place. Even so, sometimes Danais couldn't help wanting to be a part of that world. The world of the gifted.

"You have a nice voice," someone said.

Danais was in the middle of an Atorathian folk tune and hadn't realised he was singing loud enough to be heard. He stood quickly when he realised it was a magician.

"I'm sorry, sir. Would you like to sit at this table?"

"I'm just fine at mine. Admiring your singing."

"Thank you, sir. You are most kind," Danais replied with a bow.

"Still, I would like to join you. May I?"

Danais was weary of Magicians' kindness, primarily because he was a peasant, and it could just be a mean jest. Then there was the fact that one couldn't tell if a magician was working for the Tyrant. A kind invitation could turn into unwanted enslavement for a peasant. Even magicians could be forced to align with the Tyrant if they weren't cautious enough. But he was a peasant. There was a certain protocol. He couldn't say no, no matter how much the demand seemed like a question.

"Don't be alarmed. I assure you that I mean you no harm. I only want to talk."

"Yes, sir." Danais prayed a silent prayer to Miron, the God of Good Fortune, and hoped that his instincts would prove correct.

The Magician sat at the table and offered Danais some wine. It was the expensive kind, with a name Danais couldn't pronounce. This magician let him drink freely and didn't ask or try to persuade him to do anything. He wasn't working for the Tyrant, Danais thought. He wasn't a man-lover seeking sexual favours, and he wasn't trying to hire Danais to do some sort of job. Who was he? And why so generous?

"Well, it seems you've drunk the whole bottle. I'll have to order another. So, tell me about yourself, young man."

"Danais. Danais Tomal de Nera of Atorath." He introduced himself in the typical greeting: first name, title, sub-province, then main province.

"Ah. So, you are originally from this sub-province of Nera?" the magician asked.

"Yes."

"And you are not a mixed breed?"

"No. I am full-blood Atorathian."

"And silent, or just weak-gifted?"

"Definitely silent. I'm just unlucky."

The magician poured Danais another glass before continuing.

"Some say that the climb up the mountain was a tale, a legend forged because Atorath was the only province without its own god to worship. They needed a story. The poisoning was a sham and only a rumour. That the gods were always gods and never mortals."

"Jealous. Morons. It is all true. Why believe in the gods and not the story? Why respect Ronilas Goddess of War and Wisdom and neglect her mortal beginnings? To deny that would be to deny the War of the Beginning."

"Really?" the magician said with a sly yet inquiring smile.

Danais was very passionate about being an Atorathian, as most Atorathians were.

"Yes. The real reason is they refuse to believe a god would love a mortal, or that Leanor would marry Atora while he was still mortal, and that she would choose Atorath to have her main temple built. In Nera the main Province of Atorath. They refuse to give us any more importance in history, so it serves their purposes to make everyone always a god."

"So, let's hear more about you then," the magician suggested with a smile, moving on to another topic almost too deliberately.

"Parents died when I was young." Danais thought he probably shouldn't have said that, but the wine had him lowing his inhibitions and he continued inspite of this. Live with my uncle. Work on his farm. He grows some of the best fruits and vegetables, and he runs a small milk business as well. Spices and herbs. Certainly not the best in all Salinor, but the best this side of Atorath. Only the Richies can afford to import the best food from everywhere, and still, even they don't always do it." Richie was a slum term for the nobles—an insult really, and something the peasants used commonly. "Peasants like me don't get to sample that type of fruit or meat."

"Your age?"

"Seventeen. Only a few moon cycles from my eighteenth name-day."

"And the singing?"

"They say my mother had an enchanting voice. Well, my uncle says. And even though we are, arguably, said to be the most beautiful people in Salinor, my mother was said to have the beauty of Ronilas' gift to Salinor."

"Now that is a high honour," the magician offered. "It is said that when Ronilas offered the dress to Salinor, she was smitten by it. It was a shimmering blue with a sheer, flowing, top layer that always seemed to ripple like the ocean in the slightest breeze. It was laced across the chest, with a bluish-purple likeness of Salinor's own Phoenix on the front. So captivating was this dress that even she, the mother of all, could not keep her eyes off it. She decreed that anything beautiful beyond explanation should be expressed in the way you described your mother's beauty. I have an artwork by Polin that garnered the same praise."

"You own a Polin?"

Polin was by far the best artist of any art form alive in Salinor. Danais stared open-mouthed. He'd never met anyone who could afford her work.

"Your mother sounds like someone to be proud of especially as it seems she left you her vocal talents."

"Thank you, sir. I know nothing of my father. Do you believe the Atorathian legends?"

"Yes, I do."

"Then why did you toy with me?" Danais demanded in a soft tone.

"Just curious about your conviction."

"Oh," Danais replied with a nod, sipping from his he-wasn't-

Revelations

even sure-the-number drink.

"Have you been to the city before?" the magician inquired.

"No. My uncle always took his children but never me." Danais seemed to drift off as if he were remembering something, but a voice brought him out of his trance. "Did you say something?"

"My son's twenty-eighth is on this seventh day. I would like you to sing at his celebration."

"Tara's teeth! You're pulling my leg," Danais exclaimed, and then immediately realised his mistake. Calling the Goddess of the Underworld's name was common and foul language. However, it wasn't used much in front of strangers and definitely not people of extremely high rank unless they were good friends. His present situation fit all the wrong criteria. "I apologise for using the horned-tailed goddess' name in your presence." He said a quick prayer to the earth, wind, and stars before continuing. "It's the wine, I don't have a problem holding my drink but," Danais trailed off and looked to the ground.

The magician laughed heartily.

"You did what any man in your position would've done. And I was pouring the drinks. I should be the blame. Now about my offer?"

"I work on the seventh day. And it would be wrong for me to ask for payment after you've treated me to wine. However, I'm not in the position to pass up money…" Danais offered.

"Don't you worry about that. Just answer the question."

"I'll have to talk to my uncle. I am a man. But a man under his roof."

"You just tell him that Lord Vardon has invited you. And tell him I'll kill him if he says no." He smiled, letting Danais know the threat wasn't sincere.

"Vardon? *The* Lord Vardon?" Danais facial expression was that of shock. "Or just one of the family?"

"I am. It was nice meeting you, Danais Tomal de Nera of Atorath."

That was the last he said before buying one more bottle of wine and having it delivered to the farm.

Danais left the pastry shop for a walk and ended up being chased by young magicians who knew he was silent. They tried to stone him but had bad aim allowing him to quickly doge them by hiding in a pottery shop.

"Thanks," Danais said meekly to the shop owner, who had allowed him shelter from the stoning.

"You should hurt the little minions next time," the shop owner said to Danais.

"I don't hurt people smaller than me," Danais responded with a sigh.

"Just get on out of here. I've got clay to mould," the shop owner said with a smile, and Danais left.

A few shops down, he came upon a glass shop called Jovi's—the best in town—on Liath Street. Danais thought that whoever officially named the streets got out of hand with the letter L. Thankfully, as far as he knew, the other towns in Nera and the other provinces of Atorath did not fall to the same fate, either out of protest or the fact that they just changed all the original names, which equated to the same thing.

"Mr. Jovi? Are you in?" Danais asked as he walked in. Jovi wouldn't leave the shop open unattended, but it was only natural for Danais to call out.

"Is that young Danais?" Jovi asked as he came out from the back. "What brings you here?"

"I need something made. A plate infused with blue, black, and purple. And semi-transparent."

"That will be pricey," Jovi responded with a note of concern.

"I'll get the money. You know I'm good for it," Danais responded almost desperately.

"Who's it for?"

Danais wasn't about to tell him unless he swore not to repeat it. "Swear on Jantu the Goddess of Truth and Promises."

"I swear on Jantu I won't tell a soul. Or the person holding the soul either."

Danais sighed to stop from laughing. Then he said directly, "The son of a Vardon."

"Really? Now, that is impressive. For that, I'll do it for free."

"Jovi—" Danais tried to reject the offer, but Jovi held up his hand to silence him.

"I insist. Good for business when a magician family such as that is gifted something of mine. Sales will rise. I'll make back in quick time what you won't pay me."

"I will pay you." Danais was going to try to put up a stronger argument, but Jovi was forcing him out of the shop while pretending to not hear him.

"And why do you smell of expensive drink that I know you can't afford?"

That final statement was more than enough to stop Danais from fighting and to leave more quickly.

"You're not answering me, child!" Jovi shouted as Danais ran, but Danais had no intentions of trying to explain it and continued to run on.

1
LEO

Leo woke up to find himself in a very comfortable position. Across his chest lay a red-haired beauty. She was from his home province, Mironi, named after Miron the God of Good Fortune. The Mironians were known as builders. Their magical talents allowed them to be exceptional at carving stone and wood, but mostly for building purposes. When it came to magical stones of the provinces, they were by far the best at moulding them—some stones only the Mironians could mould. Leo, being a Mironian himself, wasn't really concerned with that at the moment.

He was more concerned with the woman, the feel of her nipple, and the fullness of her breast on top of his left side. He leant down and inhaled the scent of her hair. It smelled of sweet flower oil; a scent that almost matched the body oil she used, which sent his mind reminiscing about the previous night. The sun shining through the window reflected off the yellow stone walls, giving an otherworldly hue to the room. As she woke, she opened her eyes and let out a seductive chuckle at her first vision.

"It would appear that you have not had your fill. Alas, I have buildings to build," she purred.

"You toy with me. Suppose I just decide to take it," Leo said as he rolled on top of her.

"I knew you were no gentleman from the moment I laid eyes on you. It would not surprise me." Her playful tone betrayed her words.

"That cuts deep," Leo said with a sigh, feigning hurt and putting his hand across his heart for emphasis.

"Besides, I'll scream."

"After all the noise you made last night, I doubt they'll know the difference."

The girl sighed and said, "It wasn't that amazing." She emphasised *"that"* to downplay the *"amazing."*

"Is that so?" An accusatory smile formed on Leo's face.

"We didn't even commit any indecent acts."

"Since you've clearly had better, I should be allowed the opportunity to prove myself. It's only fair, after all."

"You drive a hard bargain, sir," the girl said with a slight chuckle.

"And you drive me insane with pleasure."

"Enough talk about driving; now drive yourself in me. That is a command."

And Leo willingly obeyed the command of the woman.

If there was one thing he was glad about, it was that men and women were equals on a sexual plane, so there was no fuss, like in the old days, over marrying every woman a man bedded—and the women didn't have to stress over being belittled for enjoying sexual pleasures.

"Looks like you had a good time last night. And you're almost late for morning break," Leo's sister, Adwina, announced as he entered the kitchen. She was reading a book and got right back into it after commenting.

"I saw the Atorathian you brought home last night. I wasn't the only one," Leo retorted with false venom.

"Must you walk around with no shirt on? I don't need to see the evidence of your night. Is there any part on you not marked?" his sister asked with obviously fake disdain.

"She wanted to dominate me. I let her. Besides, you know you like it, sister,"

Revelations

"I have other brothers more suitable for incest," she said as casually as if she had said something mundane like, "The sky is blue today." Leo just shrugged at that comment.

"I might head into the market." Leo thought a change of topic was in order.

"The Leanor Temple Market?"

"No. I'm going mainland. Nera."

"Ah. It is one of my favourite markets."

"Really?"

Adwina ignored the amusement in Leo's tone and continued. "Yes. We've travelled a lot, but I must admit I do like it. Very much. Especially the pastry shop. Garnter's is the best around the realm in my opinion."

Leo agreed, but he had another issue to press. "So, it has nothing to do with you soon being married to his eldest son? The soldier? And does he know you fuck other Atorathians besides him?"

"You know if anyone is free minded in the areas of intercourse, it's the Atorathians. Hell, they invented the art of fucking, some will say. Furthermore, we've even—" Adwina stopped short. Leo had an idea of what she might say. For all his sexual adventures there were some things Leo had yet to broach. Mostly just a mental block. There were hardly any real indecent acts left. It just sounded much more fun to still call them that. "You should get cleaned up. You smell of sex, and you don't want to miss the boat," she added with a sigh.

"I don't mind riding with the peasants."

"What you mean is that some are more than moderately attractive, and you, unlike some magicians, aren't opposed to bedding the ungifted," she said and continued to read the book she had without giving him a glance.

"Sometimes I think you know me just a little too well," he said as he went off to the bath.

The bathing pool was large enough to fit ten people. It was heated with the best fire stones and had running water—by far one of the better inventions made by a peasant. He added flower petals and spices and oils to the water. A special magical blend designed for a calming effect. He eased into the tub, and let the warmth and steam soothe away all anxiety, or so he thought.

"Tara's teeth. Can't I even bathe in peace, sister?" he said as his sister got into the water.

"There is room enough for three of us each. And my name is Adwina. Not 'sister.'"

"But you are my little sister…?"

Adwina scoffed. "You are adopted. And I'm older than you. So do I have to ask for a back rub?"

Leo smiled as she turned and handed him a bath sponge over her shoulder. "Why can't you just say you want to fuck? It would be so much easier."

"It's not like we haven't already. Just pay attention to the task at hand and scrub."

"Is it really incest, seeing as I'm adopted?"

"By law, but not by definition. It still feels like you're my brother in the sense of family, though."

Leo had no comment for that. He just removed himself from the bath. He didn't have time to enjoy it and had only set it up so nicely for her purposes. Even though he pretended not to want her there.

Once in his room, he thought about what she said. He was an orphan of sorts, found in the Dahli, more commonly known as The Forests of Children in Keldon. Gino, a servant and then later his tutor, discovered him. Gino gave him all the knowledge he had and was excellent in all forms of combat and strategic warfare. He was one of the best companions a wealthy magician child could have. Gino left him, or more specifically stopped tutoring, Leo when he became a man at the age of sixteen.

Magician orphans had it hard. They were usually born to peasants who couldn't afford magical schooling. Having magic and no training meant more harm to the children; they could destroy themselves from the inside out and die from lack of control. Ultimately though, their powers ended up being blocked, which was the worst thing that could happen.

Leo was one of the fortunate ones, and as he stared at himself in the mirror, he counted himself blessed by the gods. As an orphan, he always pondered who his parents might have been. He could make some assumptions based only on his appearance. He was significantly larger than six feet in height and had the build of a Keldonian from the province of Keldon, named after the Goddess of Fertility, Keld, which had the largest grouping of mountains in Salinor. The Keldonians were muscular, both male and female, in comparison to other humans. Leo escaped their normally overly muscled appearance. He attributed this to his skin tone.

Leo had golden, almost tanned, skin that was predominant in Mironi. The Mironians usually had golden or tan skin tones, sometimes as dark as cinnamon and or olive, but never darker. Based on these two things, his height and skin tone, he could hazard a guess that he was part Mironian and part Keldonian. The Keldonians were cream skinned with a tinge of blue in their pigment, and he much preferred his present skin tone. He did, however, have the white hair most Keldonian mixes had, with the fiery red highlights of the Mironians. He wasn't at all pleased with this combination, but as a mixed-race it was always a surprise how the child would come out. All in all, he was pleased aesthetically with his parentage.

Leo sometimes wondered if maybe his parents were soldiers lost in battle or just peasants who couldn't afford him. Both ideas appealed to him. One meant that his parents were noble, and he was just unfortunately lost, a casualty of war. The other kept the tradition of hoping that a child would be one of the lucky ones to get picked up in the forest.

But then there was a third thought: maybe he was just unloved. Leo mentally scolded himself for thinking this. He started off staring at himself admiring his good fortune at being adopted and ended up here, as always. Leo couldn't understand how, with all the wonderful things his life had brought him, this thought always had more power. Still pondering, he pulled on some casual slacks, a light white shirt, and sandals, then headed out the door, shoving his sudden depression to the back of his mind.

He marvelled at the beauty of the city. All the provinces had a colour of magic stone endemic to it. Although each stone was spread out through its respective sub-provinces, they varied in amount; it was in the main city that the stone was most prevalent which was how the main cities were chosen. It didn't have much to do with a central location, so some happened to be a little off from central. Here in the city of Leanor, the stone was yellow. It was the hardest of all the stones to manage.

Without the magical talents of the builders, the island city may never have existed.

Lots of Atorathians and the wealthy lined the streets. Yellow dirt roads lined buildings that were a mix of wood, glass, and yellow stone. The fact that the buildings used a variety of materials helped to break up the overwhelming power of the yellow. The city glowed. It was as if the radiance of the gods lifted from the ground and buildings like magical dust particles farther into the sky. Even the people seemed to glow. Leo was glad to call it home for the last few years of his life.

As he crossed Leanor's temple on the farthest road, on the western side of the city, called Lental, Leo had to force himself not to stop and go in. Just the gate itself was a work of art, and the builder in him couldn't help but marvel at it. The redwood doors stretched a hundred feet into the sky. They were heavy enough that ten men had to pull each door to open them. The globes the size of a man with a frieze of the realm of Salinor etched into the yellowed, tall, square, pillars encasing the door. A phoenix carved out of the blue stone of Keldon Perched on each stone.

The broccoli-shaped tree of Salinor was engraved on each door and was said to be the tree in the heart of her garden in the mountain of the Gods. This was the symbol of all the realm. Legend said Leanor was birthed under this tree. The leaves of the carving were like icicles: round and heavy at the top and smoothing out to a point, layered on top of each other to form an intricate depth. The branches and trunk were even more intricately designed, carved as single vines, with the effect of full at first glance. If done correctly, this layering made the entire tree look like it rose off the wood instead of carved into the wood.

Leo sighed, said a quick prayer, and moved on. Once he finally made it to the dock, he found his friend, Barton, waiting for him with an accusatory glare. Barton wasn't a full builder, either. He didn't have the slim physique builders had. Leo assumed Barton was probably shaped as such because he was part Dani. Purple highlights streaked through his fiery hair, and this was what Leo used as evidence for his claim. He always thought it odd that Mironians were the slimmest of all Salinor when they did the most heavy lifting, but he wasn't the master of creation, so it didn't really need to make sense, he reasoned.

"What took you so long?" Barton inquired.

"I was busy," Leo retorted.

"Ah, with the girl from last night? Well, we builders are the best," Barton said with a chuckle as they walked onto the ship.

"She was okay. I've had taller." This was more a crack on Barton than the girl.

"That is something a tall man would say. At least I'm a full-breed. Who knows what you are?"

Leo could not take this seriously when it was obviously a lie. "More of that talk and I'll throw you off the ship!" he joked.

"Sure, and crush me with your oversized hands! All just empty threats." Barton didn't bother to hide his amusement as he snickered behind his hand.

"You laugh, my friend, but one day my words may speak truth."

"I'll believe that when I splash into the sea." He paused for a moment. "My sister still writes about you, you know."

"Barton—" Leo cautioned as he leant on the edge of the ship looking out into the water.

"I know. But I promised to tell you, so I must. What do you do to these women?"

"Maybe I have the Atorathian touch?" Leo said with a coy smile.

Barton laughed hard at that. "I doubt even you are that skilled."

Leo just shrugged and stared out to sea as Barton meandered away. The other boats and the smell of the ocean contributed to one hour of uninterrupted bliss for Leo. He could stay on the sea forever.

"In a trance already? Why not marry the sea and dive in? Be done with it," Barton announced upon his return.

"Must you always interrupt my peace?"

"Serenity is for weaklings."

Leo forced himself to sigh with disapproval. He couldn't laugh at all of Barton's jokes. Too much ego-stroking might go to his head.

"And for the record, your tallness doesn't make me short," Barton explained. "I'm almost six feet. Being as tall as the tallest Keldonian doesn't mean good average height people are short."

"If you say so, small man. Ale for morning break?"

Barton ignored Leo's protest because he knew he'd drink it. Leo decided not to press the issue and took it.

"It happened again this morning, didn't it?" Barton said, knowing his friend had a depressive bout.

Leo hated and loved that Barton knew him so well. "Yes. I was thinking about my parents."

"And?"

"I don't know. I try. I try hard; I do. But—" Leo took a gulp of ale before continuing. "Don't you understand? How could you? You know who your parents are. You couldn't understand the overwhelming need to know you were wanted. To hope that you were just lost, or the family simply couldn't afford you. I just want to know."

Barton looked at his best friend and didn't know what to do—or, more accurately, he knew what he wanted to do but couldn't. He did understand Leo's insecurity of feeling unloved was what ate him up. Anything else would be acceptable. But the one thing Barton could say to help Leo was also the one thing he absolutely couldn't say. He was beginning to wonder if he was out of lies to tell. He had to do something. What could he say?

Barton sighed, resigned, knowing this could come back to haunt him. He offered the only thing he thought he could say: "There isn't much I can say. I'm not even supposed to reveal that I can't say anything, let alone actually say something. I'll tell you this though. I'm older than you think."

Leo's head snapped up from staring into his drink in silence. "I'm sorry?"

"I'm older than you think. Mug." Barton said reaching for the empty mug. "Give me your mug. I'll get us more drink."

Leo handed him the mug and Barton walked away.

Older than I think? Leo thought. *What could that mean? And why tell me now, after almost twelve years of friendship? And if he's older than I think he is, he may not even be who he says he is. What other lies could he be telling me? Or, more accurately, what is he trying not to tell me about himself? Maybe there's something about me I can't know, something I have to figure out on my own or will be revealed in its own time? Maybe I'm not crazy for thinking there's more to me. This is probably Barton's way of telling me there's more to know without actually telling me anything. I guess beating myself up over it has finally gotten to him. If there's anything I know about Barton that is true, it's that he hates to see others feel hurt.*

Leo's confused thought process halted when Barton returned.

"Don't think too hard. You might drop the mug I just shoved at you," Barton said.

"Thanks."

"For the ale?"

Leo had to laugh at the genuineness of the response. It was no wonder he was good at keeping secrets for all these years. For his part, Leo wasn't going to press for more information.

"Yes. For the ale."

"That's what friends are for."

"To get them drunk when they're depressed?" Leo said, chuckling before taking a swig.

"Um… yeah."

Leo smiled as Barton went on talking but didn't hear much. His eye and mind had drifted toward something he saw at one of the shops. It was only but a moment, seeing as what caught his eye was finishing off a drink and left shortly after Leo had spied the person. Barton's timing was right on cue. The person was leaving just as he commented on Leo's lack of attention.

"Tara's teeth. You've ignored me again. What could have been that beautiful that you ignored me so long?" Barton asked with mild frustration.

"What?" Leo was genuinely shocked by the comment.

"What were you spying on in that shop?" Barton demanded.

"Nothing that's still there…"

"Must've been spectacular. You've ignored me before, but to block me out entirely—"

"The boat will be docking soon. Let's head to plank," Leo interrupted.

"Ah, so I am right, Toma."

Leo pushed past his friend. He wasn't going to allow Barton the chance to embarrass him. Leo was often referred to as a Toma, after Toman, the God of Passing or Death. He was the one you had to go through before getting into the underworld. A minor god, but a god just the same. He wove his sexual web through the humans and gods and was the brother of Salinor, Goddess of All. Using people for their bodies wasn't an entirely terrible thing if it was consensual, Leo thought; the only problem was that once smitten, an endless pool of jokes would follow to remind him of how he used to be and still is. Leo wasn't prepared to admit he had another beauty in mind just yet. Especially since that someone was a stranger. Leo's older brothers and friends never stopped joking about how he had been tamed after he fell head over heels for his last wife. Their relationships lasted barely two years, so he really wasn't in the mood to go through all of that again.

Once back on the mainland, the lack of yellow was especially noticeable. The natural colours of earth and stone in both the roads and buildings were a drastic difference. It reminded people that there was a whole other world beyond the main city. Leo breathed in the real world and enjoyed every minute of it. Who knew, maybe he'd catch the person from the shop if the gods were kind. Maybe it was fate. If he hadn't lingered outside the temple of Leanor, he might have got on a different boat. But he felt no need to think on that; he was more inclined to think about the big meal he was going to have after strolling through the market, and he knew just the place.

"Let's eat here. They make good food," Barton announced once they made it down the street to the market a few minutes after disembarking.

The stroll to kill time in the market was complete, and Leo clearly wasn't going to be making the lunch choice today, yet again. He could only dream they'd eat somewhere other than this diner one day. They were a block away from the market, heading away from the river on Licol Street.

"Are you sure it has nothing to do with the server?" Leo asked with a slight chuckle.

"I would never pick a place purely on aesthetics. It takes more than a hot temptress to get my attention." Barton's statement was rendered worthless by how much he glowed with delight as he entered the diner.

"Well, if it isn't my favourite customers." The server beamed at them and walked straight to Leo and gave him a double cheek kiss.

"You bed me, and he's the one that gets the kiss," Barton

said with a sigh. He followed that up with a pointed stare.

"Men. It's just never enough," she said coyly.

"Remind me again why I love you," he said; it was all he could get out before she mauled him.

"Okay, break it up." Leo pulled them apart, then the two walked to a vacant table. "How did you manage to get an Atorathian *and* convince her to marry you? I'd say you put a spell on her, but I'm sure her gift is strong enough to resist anything you can concoct."

"That's something a Toma would say," Barton laughed. "Besides, what would you know of the complexities of love?" Barton chided as Leo's eye drifted toward another server.

"It's probably the red hair," Leo mused.

"Why don't you find some peasant to fuck and leave the matters of love to me? Jealousy will get you nowhere."

Leo rolled his eyes as they finally took their table.

"Seriously though, you are a good man. Why are you unattached?" the server inquired as she came back to their table. Or, more accurately, stopped as she walked by.

"I don't know. I'm sure it will happen just like last time. Love at first sight. I'll just know immediately."

"Is that why you are so glum, then?" the server, Mai'n, probed.

"He doesn't like that," Barton said with a smile. "He thinks about things, and he would prefer if his love did like ours: grow over time. But it never happens like that for him."

"Aww. Well, look on the bright side. At least you're the type of person who accepts it, whether you like it or not," the server said to Leo.

"And that means?" Leo asked.

"You know how the gods deal with the beginnings of love for you and aren't bent on trying to make it the way you'd prefer it to be. It takes some people a lifetime to let go and accept some things about themselves—and you are still a child."

"A *child*? You aren't that much older than me," Leo retorted with mock irritation.

"I'm old enough, and I've got to go now and pretend I was taking your order, so the owner doesn't get suspicious." Mai'n left and came back with two mugs of a cherry-flavoured ale and then got back to work.

"You want to ask me something," Barton said to Leo. It was a statement, not a question.

"You read me so well without reading my mind."

"You read me the same way. We are friends, after all."

"Does she know about you?" Leo had decided that if he asked about the situation on the boat, he'd be willing to drop it if Barton chose not to respond. He was, however, still hoping he would respond.

"Yes. It's been dangerous for me to have a real relationship for many years. I didn't want to have to tell so many lies and was unsure if I trusted anyone to tell my secrets. She knows as much as I felt comfortable telling—which is a lot—but I've been allowed to stay with her, or more accurately, I've been allowed to stay on my task."

"I want to ask you so many things," Leo said, a little downheartedly. It was somewhat frustrating to be on the cusp of discovery with no chance of unearthing the truth. However, he was well aware some things could be too dangerous if probed. When dealing with magic, one could never be too careful.

"There are clues everywhere," Barton said. "Now that you're alert, you might just find them. Ah, the wine is here."

"Well, don't just stare at it. Pour me a glass."

Barton poured a glass, but what should've been red wine came out orange. Before he had a chance to digest the situation, Leo was staring out the window and stringing together a line of profanities that caught Barton's attention.

"Those young magicians are attacking an ungifted Atorathian! Come on, before anyone else gets there. This could be trouble."

"Hey! What do you think you're doing!" Leo yelled as soon as he ran out. The thre magicians, two young girls and a boy tried to run away but Barton had a freeze spell on them faster than they could think to run.

Having stopped the situation they walked, angrily, to the thre youths.

"In Atorath. You decided to do harm to a local. Don't you know the consequences of what could happen to a magician with ill intents in atorath?" Barton spoke. Leo opted to stay out of it. Barton didn't always get angry. It was his last resort, but bullying was high on his low tolerance list.

"Sir he was," the boy began but immediately stopped. Looking at both of them, clearly powerful magicians, lying wasn't the best route.

"Did you provoke this?" The one being attacked didn't respond. Neither Barton nor Leo could've invaded his mind but it wasn't necessary to violate his privacy.

"He's just a stupid ungifted Athorathian." One girl said.

"How would you like to be ungifted, because clearly you are already stupid. Give me your hand."

The girl, who suddenly looked for real afraid, handed over her hand. He wrote on it and as he travelled up her forearm she realised just how much trouble she was in.

"If your parents don't see this. I'll know." Barton said as her hand glowed with the words before becoming invisible. He then said a quick spell and let the energy fall over all three of them. "If you do anything else over the next few days to harm the ungifted, especially Atorathians, I'll know, and I absolutely guarantee you your parents will allow the justice I serve. Do better. Is that understood."

"Yes Sir." The three of them responded before going on their way.

Leo assumed there was something extra in the message that made the children very afraid. Something they recognised. It had to do with whatever secret Baraton was hiding but he was very careful to make sure Leo didn't see what he wrote. Maybe a symbol? Because it couldn't be the words. That would be too easy to interpret.

It was trouble to pick on peasants, especially if they were Atorathian and in Atorath, for that matter. There was strange magic protecting outright evil in Atorath so who knew what sort of ills the children could come down with. They should have known better.

"Are you okay?" Leo asked as he talked to the victim for the first time.

1

"Yes. I'm unharmed. Thank you," the boy said. He cleared his throat. "My name is Danais, it's a pleasure to meet you."

"I'm Leo, and this is Barton. You must come eat with us," Leo said, pleased with the response. Yet again, Danais found himself faced with turning down a magician. He'd only managed to walk off half of his drinks, and now the prospect of having more was upon him. Then again, he was starving.

"Okay."

Danais followed them into an establishment he had never been able to go into. He sat at one of the best tables to drink fire orange wine out of a bottle he was sure produced red.

"Did you put a spell on the wine?" Leo asked.

"Yes," was Barton's immediate response to Leo's question.

Leo found no fault in merely changing the colour. If that was what Barton had to do to amuse himself, then it was what it was.

"Are you silent?" Leo asked the boy sitting next to him. He knew the answer, but it made for good conversation.

Danais studied his hands for a moment. "Yes, sir."

"And you love your wine," Leo said before he ordered another bottle.

All Danais' good sense screamed that his body couldn't handle the shock of so much expensive liquor, but it tasted so good. Leo, on the other hand, was enjoying watching the inner struggle. It appeared this young boy was having a problem deciding if he should refuse, or just throw all caution to the wind and ask for another glass. Rather than wait, Leo decided for him and just poured another one.

"So, Mr. Magician, sir. Do you have a name? I'd like to be able to thank you properly someday," Danais asked.

"Leo." They both seemed to realise the name thing had happened already but the reintroduction continued.

Barton gave him a look after hearing Leo say his name. To be that informal to a peasant meant a hidden agenda. Barton was quite sure he knew what it was. Danais was also taken aback; magicians shouldn't give him a first name only.

"Do you have a name, young sir?" Leo asked immediately realising he was doing the same thing. Asking for a name he already knew.

Danias chuckled. If this Leo was being informal why not him? And why not tell him his name again. "Danais."

"After the God of Moon and Water?"

"Yes, though I've never actually been on the ocean. I only look at it from the docks. I'm a farm boy; milk cows, unearth vegetables, pick fruits. Grunt work. What do you do?"

"He beds people," Barton joked before Leo could respond.

"Barton!" Leo chided, trying to control him before he got started, but Barton could not be side-tracked.

Danais just stared at Barton.

"Just this week it's been eighteen conquests." Barton chuckled.

"Fourteen," Leo corrected, falling right into Barton's trap.

"Okay, fourteen. But it's only the fourth day."

"Sounds like he's a regular Toma," Danais said with a hearty laugh. "Maybe he's secretly Atorathian."

"Only in his dreams. I think it's just because he's tall."

"Bah! Height has nothing to do with skill," Danais said as he took another swig of wine.

"See. I told you so, Barton," Leo said.

"However, I'm sure with you it does have to do with height. Specifically, the height of your manhood," Danais continued.

Barton snorted wine out of his nose at that comment and went into roars of laughter.

"Ah, I take it I am right then. You're not just tall as in from the ground," Danais said, which only increased Barton's laughing fit.

"How do you know I'm not just skilled?" Leo asked, trying to turn the discussion around.

"Your friend laughs at my jokes, therefore they must be accurate."

"You are only repeating the same jokes he throws at me. Therein lies his amusement," Leo said, and then gave Barton an evil glare.

"Well, what true friends can't make fun of each other?" Danais asked.

"I raise my glass to that," Barton agreed. He and Danais raised their glasses in a toast to friendship.

"Since we're talking height, how tall are you?" Danais asked with a coy smile.

Barton took another sip of wine and waited to hear the response. Nothing like a good double entendre to keep the mood flowing.

"I only put my manhood on display when it's about to get action," Leo said.

"Ah, so you're the modest type."

"Are you always this forward?" Leo asked with a chuckle.

"Not with Richies, but I've never had expensive drinks before today. I fear it's affecting my tongue. Then again, I am Atorathian. Sex speech is far from beyond the norm here."

"Well, in answer to your earlier question to my profession, I'm a musician."

"So, you get to travel and get paid for it." It was more of a statement than a question on Danais' part.

"Yes, he does. And I can say he is quite good," Barton added. "So maybe there is some truth to this skill and height business."

Danais and Barton laughed. Leo just rolled his eyes.

"Why are you encouraging me to drink, seeing as I was already half-drunk? You get to see me relaxed but not me you. I'm at a disadvantage." The sight of food disrupted Danais' train of thought. "Salinor's phoenix! Is this whole leg of lamb for me only?"

This made Leo smile. The genuine look of amusement on the young man's face was worth all the wealth Leo possessed. Danais' eagerness to eat it was also encouraging. Danais went straight at it with his fingers and didn't pick up a fork until he dropped a particularly hot piece of sliced carrot back into the plate. The garlic mashed potato with parsley and caramelised onions was something he didn't eat every day.

"Are you enjoying the meal?" Leo asked.

Danais managed to grunt out a "yes" between swallows of food.

"This is the last stop on our tour of Atorath. We have a few more stops to hit before we get to Nera. You can come to—"

"No," Danais interrupted as he swallowed hard. "I can't watch you play for free. I've already accepted too much. My uncle has probably heard of my day already. I could be getting in trouble as we speak for taking advantage."

"I'm glad you accepted, then. Some hot cider to wash down the meal, then. Peach." Leo didn't wait for a response and ordered a glass plus a bottle for Danais to keep. It was strong, probably even stronger than the wine. But something about the warmth and mixture of sweet and spice just made it feel harmless.

"It was a pleasure meeting you, but we've been here almost long enough to go into dinner," Danais said as he wobbled to a stand and prepared to leave.

"Can I take you home? You seem a little unsteady," Leo offered.

"I'll take him home. And no protests from either of you," Barton said, mostly to Leo.

There was something very finite in Barton's tone. It wasn't harsh, but both Leo and Danais seemed to hear it, and neither put up much fight.

Barton managed, at a very slow pace, to get Danais to the farm, reaching their destination only just before nightfall.

"What happened to my nephew?" Torak, Danais' uncle, demanded of Barton when he opened the door to see a clearly drunk Danais. "And no matter who did it, you're going to fix him."

"Sure." Barton was unphased. Nothing a good spell couldn't fix. "It will sweat out of him. He'll be fine. A little repugnant, though." Torak looked like he was about to smile but instead chose to change the conversation.

"What brings you here? Haven't seen you in almost twelve years now."

Barton made sure that Danais was out cold before working a sound spell so no one who approached from outside could hear. "Orange wine," he answered Torak finally.

"So, it has begun."

"Yes. The spell on them will slowly start to unravel. Soon we will have to act."

"I know. But he's still a child. Only a few cycles from his eighteenth name day."

"I know, Torak."

"And you shouldn't have said what you did on the ship. I understand, though."

"You know? Indeed, your eyes do stretch far."

"Yes. And you still don't have to worry about what you've told the girl, or what you've just now told Leo."

"How do you know what I told the girl?"

"I stopped the message and delivered it myself to make the news go over more smoothly."

"To think I doubted you for this task—fought against it, even."

"You were a lot younger then. And I was aware you only did it because you thought I had fought against you in this task."

"You didn't?" Barton had assumed as much but didn't feel up to the challenge of directly asking, considering how badly he handled the situation in the beginning.

"No. I'm sure a lot that went on in those secret meetings has found its way back to you. I was not part of anything said against you."

"And I took so long to forgive you or accept I was wrong, but—I feel ashamed. I don't usually let anger get the better of me, but with you—you were like my mentor, and I thought you abandoned me just like the rest..."

"It is as it is. I knew what you thought, but I couldn't fuel your hate. I knew you'd figure it out in time. Even if you were never bold enough to come right out and say it." Torak smiled before continuing. "And you have exceeded my expectations. And as you well know, have proven to others, beyond a doubt, that you are every bit as capable as the person who put your name forth said you were."

Barton really did feel ashamed. Torak was a man who was his friend and mentor, and Barton had turned against him out of retaliation. How could he even bare to stand in the same room as him?

"I'll heal him and be out of your way," Barton offered. "I'm not much of a healer, but I can do this."

Barton did his task but wasn't allowed to leave.

"You should stay," Torak insisted, "and see if he's okay. You don't have to rush somewhere, do you?"

"No, I do not..."

"Then stay. Let's talk like we used to."

Barton knew it was as much a command as it was an old friend knowing he needed to talk. How long had it been since he'd actually expressed his feelings on anything?

"It's been a while," Barton conceded.

"Yes. So what troubles you?"

2
DANAIS

Danais awoke to find himself in the tub being sponge-bathed by his cousin. There was a strange odour in the air, and he had a feeling it was his. After a lengthy and not-so-enjoyable scrub, he made his way to the kitchen and saw what he thought was Barton's back leaving the room. Danais grabbed a bottle of his uncle's home brew and sat at the table.

"I hear you took advantage of not one, but two magicians," Torak said as he entered the room. "You even sang to one of them, and I've got one of the best bottles of wine and also one of the best ciders in town." He laughed. Torak had no intention of punishing the boy, but he was still interested in his response.

"Well, I figured that if I was going to be immoral and break all known rules of etiquette, quality drink might soften you up some."

"Ah, so the bottles are for me then?" Torak smirked.

"Yes, most certainly, Uncle. However, if you feel inclined to share with me—but that's entirely up to you, of course."

Torak couldn't help but laugh at that. The advantage of being a chronic overthinker was that Danais never failed to have something interesting to say—sometimes stupid, sometimes just plain witty genius, but always entertaining at the very least.

"Be more careful next time. You almost poisoned yourself with drink. I had Barton clean you—the smell was horrible."

Danais never for a second thought he had drunk enough for alcohol poisoning. If Barton wasn't with him, he could've become violently ill.

"The magician who overheard me singing has invited me to sing at a name day event. With pay."

"Really?"

"Yes."

"You know I don't let you go to the city."

Danais sighed. "I know. But you also told me that when the time came for me to go to the city, it would just present itself. It didn't have anything to do with him knowing you. He genuinely wanted to invite me before I told him my relation to you."

"And who is this magician in question you two are talking about?" his cousin asked as she stepped into the kitchen.

"Lord Vardon," Danais responded.

"*The* Lord Vardon? The one rumoured to be related to Ameri, the greatest sorceress of all time? More powerful even than the Tyrant? She only fell due to some unknown spell she encountered during their duel. That was during the last direct attack on his forces by the Alliance. She got hit by a few multiple spells and just disappeared. Seems you've made good company," his cousin responded, somewhat impressed.

"I know. The legends say she did much for the Alliance. Now that would be a magician worth meeting," Danais mused.

"Yes. The Vardons are rumoured to be part of the War of Beginning—the assassination of the king overthrown at the time. You know the legend about how one of his brothers conspired with the first Alliance to take him out and form the new treaty?"

"But that's not true, is it, Uncle?"

"There's a level of truth in every rumour, Danais."

"Is this a 'yes, I can go?'"

His cousin and uncle laughed. No amount of talk was going to hinder his chance to finally set foot in the City of Light, the *God City*.

"Yes. I shall accompany you. Tomorrow, we go to the market. I must purchase some material that's suitable to be worn in the presence of the Vardons."

"You're coming?" Danais blurted. He was shocked.

"You're only seventeen, and I hear all his children are quite beautiful."

"Are you accusing me of some flaw of character?" Danais

Revelations

tried to ask with anger, but his smile diminished his intent.

"I'll rephrase. I've seen the way people pursue you. I can't have you marry a Vardon and forget about me due to sudden wealth."

"I see, so it's not about coming with me into foreign land?"

"Nope. It's all about me. I'm going to take you to see Lela as well. But neither of you can repeat that."

Danais had no words for this. Lela was a well-known seer, without question the best alive in all Salinor. Even the Tyrant respected her. This made him wonder; who was his uncle to know the Vardons and to see a seer of such magnitude on such short notice?

"We'll sail across on the sixth day and should arrive just before the stars hit the sky."

Danais couldn't hide his excitement at the prospect of not having to work. I won't be working again till the second day?"

"No. Four days to yourself. I'm sure you will survive." Torak responded as if working were the more appealing option. Danais scoffed.

"May I ask why it is that I'm going to see her?"

"I was told that when you were presented with a chance to go, I should take you to her." Torak shrugged, not giving much more of an explanation.

"Okay. So, this isn't so much a chance meeting as a predestined one." Torak cave a noncommittal response which only raised more questions for Danais.

Who was his uncle?

He said goodbye to his cousin as she left for Chin to drink with friends. Then he headed out for a late-night walk. He enjoyed walking through the trees in the mountains, looking up at the stars and the moon. Out here he allowed himself to let his fantasies run wild. He wasn't unlike most peasants, dreaming he was the son of a god. He just had the added advantage of being named after one. Danais, God of the Moon and Water. Now that was a god to be the son of.

Danais' favourite rock to sit on was on the edge of a cliff that looked down onto fields of trees. As the crisp air hit his face, Danais allowed his fantasy of being on the ocean to flow even further through him. Soon the thought lost its way, and the cool breeze became a chill; he was Danais the orphan again. He sighed. How could he be born into such an amazing world without the means to enjoy it?

"To the two gods whose name I share, I pray, I plead: let this not be all that's meant for me. Don't let this seventh day be the last important day of my life."

"You should be careful what you pray for," came a voice from the treeline.

Danais jumped, completely unconcerned that jumping too high would mean falling to his doom. He'd been followed. Sometimes he wished he was even a smidgen gifted. He would've sensed being followed.

"Who's there?" he asked as he edged closer to the trees. He'd rather have a fight in the cover of the forest he knew so well than be close enough to the cliff to be pushed off the edge. Just before entering the freedom of the trees, he heard the voice again.

"Over here on the rock."

Danais turned and there on the rock was something he thought he'd never see: one of the most magical creatures in all Salinor.

A Kentai.

They were as special as dragons and unicorns.

Danais, having never seen a Kentai other than in a painting, took in its appearance. The creature stood about two feet tall with a face shaped like a bear cub's and circular ears and a nose like that of a rabbit. From the side on all fours, Danais noticed it had the profile of a fox cub with a longer tail. Though the Kentai's limbs looked animal, they transferred quite seamlessly to human function when standing. It moved its arms and legs almost the same as a human. At first, Danais thought this Kentai was quite human, even though he was hard-pressed to find anything human about it physically.

It had beautiful chocolate-brown fur just long enough to move in the wind. Good omen or not, Danais wasn't ruling out the fact that it could only be talking to him to bring bad news.

"Come. Sit with me," it demanded.

Burnt-orange eyes glowed in the night and call him back to the rock, so Danais did as he was commanded.

"You like the night?" the Kentai asked.

"The stars relax me—and the water, though I know not how

Revelations

to swim." Danais looked away shyly. He'd never really considered how strange loving water but not being able to swim might sound.

"You'll learn. You are named after the god of the sea," the Kentai stated matter-of-factly.

"Are you the answer to my prayer?" Danais asked. He did just ask for something and a magical creature showed up. Stranger things had happened in the realm before.

"I just happened to be hunting in the area."

Danais didn't dare probe further.

"So what brings you running into the woods in such a mood," the Kentai asked.

"It's just I'm born into this world with magicians and magical creatures and all types of amazing things, and I wake up every day to this peasant life. I don't know who my parents are and the people who know them just don't talk about them. Almost like they're hiding something. It's like my life seems all wrong. Like it's missing something and sometimes it feels like... just one big empty void."

For a while there was silence. Danais tried not to think about it too often. That beyond the happy carefree life of a man finding his way that he genuinely felt lost.

"One cannot be great without test and trial. There is more to you. There is more to the people around you."

Of all the things to break the silence, this wasn't the type of response Danais had expected to get. That there was indeed something more to him.

As the frustration and anger of this thought built up in him, he jumped up from the rock and with rage and determination set out to get answers from the only person who would have them.

His uncle.

Visiting the seer, going to the island he was forbidden from going to, meeting a famous magician from a family with ties to the end of the war... none of this could be coincidence.

He didn't make it very far though.

"Sit," the Kentai demanded.

Danais had barely taken two steps away before being ordered to sit down.

Under normal circumstances, Danais might've protested but

there was something dangerous in the creature's tone that he felt best not to deal with.

"Don't be impatient, boy," the Kentai cautioned.

"I am a man!" Danais took great pride in the fact that he'd become of age and this being was challenging that.

"You are a child, and you will listen," the Kentai spoke in cool authoritative tones.

Again, Danais backed down. Legally, Atorathians were considered men and women at age sixteen, but he obviously hadn't matured as much as he had hoped. This was clear by the fact that he was being spoken to like he was five.

"If it was meant for you to know, you would already know. You need to learn patience. To be happy with who you are. You can't appreciate what you will become if you see no value in who you are now."

Danais thought about it for a while. A long while.

"I guess you're right," Danais offered. "I haven't travelled, don't read that much. I haven't done anything most young boys do as they grow into manhood. Maybe I'm not the man I thought I was."

"Don't doubt unless you have reason to," was the only response Danais received. To fill the void of silence that followed, Danais began to play with the Kentai's hands.

"Three fingers and a thumb. Same for feet."

"Yes. Five fingers are highly unnecessary."

Danais laughed as did the Kentai.

"I believe you'll mature much faster than you think. Your journey will begin at the drop of a stone."

Danais didn't know what to make of the stone bit, so he ignored it. "Do you have a name?"

"Kale."

"Like the green?" Danais replied sceptically.

"Yes.

Kale took Danais' hand and licked his palm, signifying they were friends; it also left a magical mark only other Kentais could see. He then took it a step further by joining himself to Danais, similarly to how Betaves joined with Magicians. Kale's eyes went from burnt orange to the same green as Danais' taking on a feature he found appealing. Peasants didn't join with a magical creature. Only Magicians. This meant something much deeper than even Danais' hyperactive mind could delve into.

"It is not safe out here," Kale stated. "There are roaming magicians and wild beasts. I will walk you back home."

Once back in his room, Kale hopped into the bed with Danais, who, on impulse, petted him the same as he would a regular household pet. Much to his surprise, Kale didn't even seem to notice. If anything, he reacted much the way a pet would react to being petted. There was much Danais didn't know, and he knew there was much he had to learn. Still, the gods finally seemed to have their eyes on him, and he was grateful—eternally grateful.

2
LEO

"Only just getting back, Barton?" Leo asked as Barton walked to the table he was sitting at.

"Yes. I was forced to stay and see my spell through. I sent a message with Kay."

"I got it. I was just asking to ask."

"Where's Xan?"

"He said his brother was in town. I would imagine he's gone to find him."

"I'm still awed that you have a Kentai as your Betave."

Leo thought on that. Betave was just a crude joining of 'better' and 'half.' When a magician was born, sometimes a creature of the forest would come to him. This creature would ultimately take on more human characteristics. It would do so in much the same as a Kentai is naturally. Its height either grew or diminished to around the same as well.

Leo was always shocked to hear Xan was there the day he was found. Kentais were one of the three spirits of the realm. They rarely became a Betave and most revered them.

Why would he, a nobody, be of interest to a creature such as this? Things like this only happened to great wizards, whether good or bad. Being a musician, it just didn't add up to him. But now he knew he was something more, it was becoming clear. He could only hope what he would do to make history wasn't going to be evil.

Leo thought about Barton's story. He didn't entirely believe his explanation for staying with Torak so long but couldn't find an alternative. He was going to have to deal with it another time.

Kay, Barton's Betave, was a rabbit. Unlike Kale's joining with Danais, a Betave's joining meant the start of that direct connection that made their thoughts and actions, though independent, as one with the magician. Kay was also attracted to the eyes. Barton's were grey. She adopted it into her fur, a lovely shimmering grey. She was previously a tan rabbit, and she loved her new form. As Betaves go, she was exceptional. She made the transition from mere rabbit to talking magical being smoothly. And as all Betaves had wings, she went for hawk-style wings for herself. It was her favourite bird before she became enlightened. The wings disappeared into a Betave's body when not flying. Xan was snowy white with blue eyes just like Leo's. He changed his entire fur colour to match Leo's hair.

"You are right, it is impressive, but even Xan has praise for Kay. She may not be a spirit of the earth, but she's exceptional. Xan trains her sometimes," Leo responded to Barton.

"I'm just happy he deems me worthy to talk to. I know it's more than special to have a Kentai talk to a human." He paused as Xan and Kay entered the room. "Xan. Kay. Where have you been?"

"We were training. Xan is an excellent teacher," Kay said.

"Learning lies in the abilities of the student. Even the best teachers can do nothing for the inept." Xan shrugged.

"Don't compliment her. It's not good for Barton's head," Leo said with a smile.

"My head…" Barton protested.

"Yes. Kay can take a compliment with dignity," Leo added, and Barton scoffed.

"Walk with me," Barton said, and the two of them headed out into the streets. Kay and Xan climbed up onto their shoulders and sat as the two walked.

Leo knew exactly where this was going, but he refused to

Revelations

broach the subject. He was going to stall as long as he could.

"Did you have a nice time today?" Barton asked.

"It was okay. Nothing to thank the gods for."

"Really?" Barton said with a sly smile.

"Yeah. I woke up to a beautiful woman, enjoyed an extended lunch had a late afternoon rest, and now I'm here with you. Typical day." Leo tried his best to downplay the day's events as average.

"So would it be safe to assume he was the person from the dock that had you so distracted this morning?"

Leo was stumped. He was prepared to be drilled about him acting out of sorts during lunch. He had his answers—denials actually—all lined up. This, however, was not a question he prepared for. He was going to have to think fast.

"Ah, so I am right." Barton chuckled triumphantly before Leo had time to come up with a defence.

"That is merely an assumption."

"Then why the informal introduction? Trying to get him to like you before knowing who you are?"

"That's insane." Leo was glad to be back to the lunch. This was an accusation he could respond to. "Why would I be pining for someone I just met?"

"Unless you hadn't just met."

"Again: only assumptions."

Barton had a very calm smile across his face. "Why so defensive?"

"Uh, because I'm being attacked," Leo stated as if it were extremely obvious.

"I'm just asking for answers, and you have neither denied nor answered anything."

"He's a child! I'm ten years his senior."

"Bah! Age is but a number. And he may be young, but he is clearly well trained and capable of serious talk. He'll mature fast enough. And don't you deny that you were evaluating him as well."

"Why can't you let me be?" That was as close to an admittance as Leo was willing to give.

"I've never seen your mind so preoccupied after a mere glimpse. For our whole walk through the market, you were in a daze. You only came out once we saw Mai'n. More than two hours of floating on air that was."

"And you wouldn't let me walk him home," If Barton was in support, then he should've let Leo walk him home. *Fair is fair*, he thought.

"No. You're going to have to work for this one. No easy bedding."

"I have a feeling it would be hard work without your interference," Leo said as they reached the dock. They walked out to one of the emptiest loading platforms and sat on the pier. The smell of salt air and wood was calming to them both. The glow of the city reflected in the water, giving the ripples a nice sparkle.

Leo thought about Danais: green eyes, skin the tone of perfectly milked chocolate, and an infectious laugh.

"It was obvious I was taken with him. I could not hide it. I doubt he noticed. I got him too drunk." Leo chuckled to himself at the thought of that. It seemed like a good plan, but it didn't end the way he'd hoped.

"He thinks of you as a Richie, so that's not a good start. And he's an ungifted Atorathian."

"The lowest of peasants. I know. I feel like a fool," Leo responded in a final tone. He's bound to have ill feelings toward magicians. Especially if he gets stoned or attacked often, like today. It can't work."

"This is true," Barton admitted and looked out over the ocean, not offering up much more as the two of them dipped into silence.

A silence that left Leo feeling uncomfortable. Barton wasn't pushing for a response worse so Leo could bow out of admitting anything. However, running from the truth wouldn't get him anywhere.

"Then why do I not care?" Leo was mostly speaking to himself.

"Well, you aren't getting any younger," Kay interrupted.

Leo tried to give her an evil glare, but it was weak. Xan laughed at his feeble attempt. "Why haven't I seen him before? Three years I've been travelling to the town. This is where I've lived with that evil ex hell wife."

"Destiny. It was time," Barton responded.

"He will be good for you. For us. Pursue him," Xan spoke in

a way that only a Kentai would.

"Do you see this, Xan?" Leo asked. He wanted to know if it was a vision or just intuition.

"I had a vision. It tells me this is the road to travel."

"Then I'll follow. Did you find your brother?" Leo inquired.

"You'll meet him on the seventh day."

"Is he also a Betave?"

"I cannot say. He did not reveal all in our mind link, as it is not time."

Leo knew Xan well enough to know this was wordplay. It was likely more accurate that it wasn't time for Leo to know.

As Leo stared into space, wondering about the discoveries of the day, Xan made eye contact with Kay. She nodded in receipt of the message. This went unnoticed by both magicians.

Finding out there was more to himself was one thing. However, finding out that Barton isn't who he seemed as well was also intriguing. And what were the odds of meeting someone and having Xan tell him it was wise to pursue his interest? He was also going to meet Xan's brother at the end of the week, and he would be coming with a human. But Leo had no idea if he was coming as a Betave or a regular companion. Humans didn't have Betaves, after all. Neither did Atorathians. He was certain there was a connection but couldn't find it; a small clue he couldn't grasp. Good things came in time though, and Leo was a patient man. Maybe the answer would come in the morning.

"What are you doing?" Barton asked.

"Removing my clothing. I'm going for a swim," Leo said, then dove into the water. Xan dove in right after. Leo breached the surface and smoothed back his hair from his eyes. "You joining us?" Without waiting for an answer, he ducked back under the water.

While Leo was underwater, Kay looked at Barton. He nodded in receipt of the message. Barton decided a swim wouldn't be so bad as he stripped and jumped into the water.

"Now don't you try anything. My betrothed would not approve," Barton jested as he swam to Leo.

"What you mean is she'd be jealous." A mischievous smile crossed Leo's face.

"Bah! She isn't the jealous type." Barton sounded more than

confident.

"Besides, you aren't my type."

"Ah, so I don't have green eyes and aren't chocolate enough."

Leo shoved him underwater in response to that comment. Xan and Kay laughed.

"I'll consider that a 'yes.'"

3
DANAIS

Danais woke up the next day not sure if the previous one had been a dream—especially the ending moments of the night. Could a Kentai really have spoken to a peasant boy? It had to have been a dream. He was thankful there was no rain after he slept, meaning a dry floor as his feet hit the stone ground. He hadn't closed the window before he slept.

After fully convincing himself last night was a dream, he went to look out the window where he saw Kale leaning against the side of it, staring out onto the farm. Seemingly unaware he had woken up.

"You are awake, young one," Kale greeted him.

"So, it wasn't a dream?"

"I'm afraid not. You've got a busy day ahead. You should be getting ready."

"Yes. Forgive my ignorance, but I'm not sure how to treat you."

"Just go with your instincts."

That was the last Kale said before flying out into the morning sky.

The sun was still making its slow climb over the hills and trees. Danais assumed he was going hunting for whatever it was Kentais eat. As he was getting a cold wash, his mind pondered all the questions he wanted to ask. The problem was that he couldn't think about the questions without thinking about

Revelations

Kale's reaction to his wanting immediate answers.

Being young was clearly a disadvantage. No matter how smart or adept, he lacked the certain life experiences that came with age. Something was going on. Would his impatience and direct need for information change the sequence of things? Would too much patience lead to missing something important? Too many thoughts; his mind couldn't seem to latch onto one, and all he could do was scream. This new life, whatever it was, was going to require a certain amount of insight and intuition to which he was not accustomed.

After getting dress, Danais looked in the mirror and sighed, thinking how much he looked like a peasant. Then he went to the kitchen. He grabbed an apple, a bottle of milk, and fresh cookies. His cousin must've made them before heading back to her post. These cookies even had chocolate chunks.

"Uncle," he managed to say through a mouth full of milk and cookies. Finally acknowledging his presence.

"Don't talk too fast. I would hate for you to lose a chocolate chunk. How was your walk?"

"It was more enlightening than normal."

"Really?" Torak said, raising an eyebrow.

"Yes. I'm going to have to lose my 'I'm a man' rebuttal when people annoy me."

"My, my. Now that *is* enlightenment." The level of sarcasm was more than palpable. "I've been trying to win that argument for almost two years. And in one night you realise what it takes to become a man? I'm in awe."

"I'm a fast learner." Danais shrugged and finished his fourth cookie.

All Torak could do was smile.

Danais, while stuffing himself with sweets, was coming to a new realisation. He needed to curb this sweet habit. If he were in a torture chamber, one piece of expensive cake would get him to tell all his secrets. But the cookies were so amazing— why not eat the seventh one? They were all for him anyway. This was his reasoning cause surely his uncle wouldn't request cookies. Assumptions were being made. He was too busy eating to question their validity.

"You should be more careful," Torak said.

Suddenly Danais was panicking. If there were something

special about him, could he now be endangered? The cookies could be poisoned... or worse. They could be magicked somehow. And he was swallowing his seventh. His cousin may not have even made them. But his uncle was letting him eat them. Could it be that he was meant to die? He wondered if someone thought that his death was essential and that's why he was being encouraged to eat the poisoned cookies. How could he be so careless?

"You've created a mess," Torak added.

Torak's words brought Danais out of his thoughts. "Huh?"

"On the floor. Crumbs. We are on farmland; no need to create more insects than we need."

Danais felt relieved. He still thought it careless to eat the cookie. But now that he was safe, why not have just one more?

Torak eyed him. "You okay?"

Danais told him his whole thought process right up to the part about Torak goading him to his death.

"You really overthink things sometimes. As it is, I know who made them for you. That doesn't mean your idea is that far of the table. But there are easier ways to take you out besides wasting delicious cookies." Torak smiled and took a swig of ale.

Danais slumped into his chair and grabbed another cookie. "How can I handle such things? I know nothing of war or the world like older men and women. I'm more worried about doing myself harm than others doing so."

"You can only learn these things through time, and I'm sorry to say I don't know how much you have."

"Time I have till what?"

"I cannot say. But you'll have to trust instincts and just be yourself."

"Be myself?" Danais thought that strategy hadn't exactly done wonders for him so far. Kale flew into the room before he continued to talk and hopped up on the table. Danais absentmindedly petted him for a few moments. "I panicked over a cookie. If destiny thinks my present self is okay destiny's credibility is questionable at best."

They laughed together, and Danais ate yet another cookie. He almost offered Kale one, but decided he was perfectly capable of grabbing his own cookie. Kale pouted while grabbing one.

Revelations

"You have a new friend?" Torak said moving his head in the direction of Kale.

Finally, after being prompted, Danais realised the strangeness of the situation: a Kentai shows up, jumps on the table, and lets Danais pet him—even willingly takes food from Danais. This was not everyday action.

"Uncle, this is Kale. Kale, Uncle,"

Torak gave a head bow to Kale, and he did the same. As the two nodded, Danais felt something new, something he would never have dreamed to do in his lifetime: mindspeak.

"He says his first words to you will be in the market," Danais stated awkwardly still a bit shaking by hearing Kales words in his head.

"I shall look forward to it," Torak said, as if it was the most natural thing in the world. Well, we should be going. We don't want to miss the fresh pastries at Garnter's. But seeing as you've had a whole tray of cookies..." Torak said with a bit of a smirk.

"No, we can still go," Danais quipped. There was always room for more sweets.

"No. That was a lot of cookies. I don't want you to overindulge." The sincerity with which Torak said it was almost believable.

"Cookies? I don't see any cookies."

"Indeed. I hope the woman of your dreams can bake. If so, you'll be putty in their hands."

"Everyone has their weaknesses. And it could be the man of my dreams. You coming, Kale?" Danais didn't want to presume Kale would just tag along. Kale left ahead of them, which drew a sigh from Danais. He did want to walk with him, but it wasn't meant to be.

As he and his uncle walked down the mountain, Danais thought about his mother. He knew very little about her and even less about his father. Maybe this new him he was becoming might shed some light on his parentage.

When they finally arrived, Garnter gave them like they were extra special customers. Since his uncle was so ordinary, Danais sometimes forgot he had status and the money to go along with it.

"I must say I'm impressed by the Kentai. That is a surprise even to me," his uncle said once they settled in to one of the best tables in the shop.

"To me as well. I think he may have changed the way I think. Just like the cookie. I've always been a mindless rambler, but my panic seemed a little bit more structured than my usual overthinking. Not that the structure matters; panic is panic."

"Well, that's good to know. I would hate for your overthinking to just go away. Making sense of your rambles will be missed if you start making sense of them on your own. But I guess you had to grow up at some point." Torak sighed in disappointment.

Danais frowned, yet somehow managed a laugh. His uncle had a way of finding the humour in a sentence, no matter how dull it might be.

"So, wine? I know how much you love to drink," Torak offered in jest.

"No. I'll have something boring and unfermented."

"So, strangers can get a show but not I?" Torak put his hand over his chest in mock hurt.

Danais laughed again. "I really wanted to talk with Kale more, even though he makes me feel small. Like Leo."

"Leo?" Torak responded, face full of confusion.

"The peach cider, uncle."

"This is the first I've heard his name. I know only of Barton, and that is because he brought you home."

"Fair enough. Well, he's tall, taller than the tallest mountain person. Rainy blue eyes, white hair with fire red highlights, perfectly golden skin. Toned-down build of the Keldonians, but the look of a Mironian."

"Mixed race?" His uncle concluded.

"Yes. He seems so accepting of what he knows and what he doesn't. If he were my age and in my situation, he'd probably handle it much better. Much like Kale. It's something about the patience and the cool of their speech that reminds me I am a child."

"And this bothers you?" Torak took a bite from a jumbo muffin and waited for a response.

"Only with the magician."

"Why?"

"It's their fault the war started. Why should I be silent and ungifted, and he so much more self-assured and gifted? It's not

Revelations

right. I'm an Atorathian. I should be better."

"You know I raised you better than to be that self-righteous. No race is better than the other. If anything, we Atorathians should be trying to keep the equality. So many of us have forgotten the point of the War of Beginning. And Atorathians especially should not forget."

Danais knew his uncle was right. But even as a peasant, he still couldn't help thinking that Atorathians were superior to Magicians.

"Uncle, can I make a confession?" Danais said not even sure if he wanted to but was committed to the task all the same.

"Speak."

"I am a peasant. I can't see the world through your eyes. I'm not equal. Even peasants from other provinces look down on me because I'm an Atorathian peasant. How then can I not see my race as better when my whole life is riddled with inadequacy? The need for more. To be more. I cannot see something I have not experienced.

"I am not the same, but believing that my race, as a whole, is better, it gives me something to hold on to. A sense of pride and worth that belongs to more than just me. I need to believe what I believe, even if I know it's wrong. Maybe one day I'll change."

Torak stretched his hands across the table and took Danais' into his own and smiled.

"I understand but no one man is better than the other. That type of thinking, that need for vengeance and power, is how the Tyrant came into power. And we don't need another one of those, okay?"

"Yes, Uncle."

Torak smiled and then got back to eating the meal, as did Danais.

"Don't we have some clothes to buy?" Danais commented a few minutes later.

"Yes. The tailor already has your measurements and slaved away all night at my request. And the glassblower said he'd have your gift ready today as well."

"He gave me a few moon cycles to pay him," Danais added in quick defence.

Torak just chuckled. "You don't have to lie to me. Let's go

by the tailor and see if we have to make any adjustments. Then we'll have lunch."

That was the last they said before finishing their meal and leaving the shop.

Danais was glad to be with his uncle. He almost felt, for just one moment, as if they were father and son on the way to make a purchase together. No one was trying to attack him, and he could enjoy himself without his mind being preoccupied with looking over his shoulder. He caught a glimpse of windows with blinds and made a mental note to ask his uncle to fix his. He looked at barbershops which made him take notice of men and women who had hair colours that only dyes or magic could've created and new styles that would hopefully die out soon.

When they reached their destination the two were jovially greeted. By the shop merchant.

"Torak! So nice to see you. I am almost finished with your order. This is going to be one of my best. And for such an attractive young man."

Danais didn't have time to say thank you because the tailor quickly put Danais where he wanted him to stand, instructed him to disrobe, and promptly disappeared in the back. When he returned with the clothes, he wasn't looking too impressed.

"And why are you still in your undergarments?" he gave Danais a glare of disapproval.

"I wasn't informed to remove them," Danais said, glancing toward his uncle, quickly shifting the blame so he would not have to deal with what came next. He did his best not to laugh as his uncle received the wrath of the tailor, and he ignored the evil stare his uncle gave him. With a sigh, he quickly removed all remaining clothing/

"Here you are." The tailor handed Danais smaller undergarments. "Nice stretchy material. It'll hide your manhood, somewhat, should you be aroused by one of the many beautiful people at this event. Not that an Atorathian would care about such things as visible manhood, but other lesser beings might."

Danais couldn't help but laugh. Undergarments were definitely an afterthought item so he got this on a personal level.

"It's expensive, but I've noticed even the peasants don't

consider it a waste of money. Especially women. It helps give them breast support. Comes in handy when spending so much time bending and lifting on the fields."

"Can it breathe if it's this—well, tight?" Danais questioned. It did feel good on his skin.

"Breathes almost as good as Mironian cotton," the tailor said with a smile.

"I wouldn't know; I've never worn the best cotton in the world before," Danais replied honestly.

"Well, you are now. Put these pants on. Mironian cotton breathes like Dani silk, but it is sturdier in a strong wind and much less sheer."

"It's blue?" Danais commented. He sounded shocked but blue was a colour like any colour. It was mostly he was expecting something more... tan. He didn't have an explanation for this but it made sense in his brain.

"Sky blue. Goes well with your skin tone. Your measurements are proving to be quite accurate. Won't have to adjust the pants too much. The shirt is the same tan as your original pants, but for this I have options. Would you like silk or more cotton?"

Danais didn't hesitate. "Cotton." He reasoned it was the start of spring, so something just a little heavy would shield the cool breezes, but it was still light enough on the chance the air was warmer than he expected.

"Your nephew has expensive taste." The tailor smiled because that meant more money for him.

"Two options. I never get two options. I should pay you this much more often," Torak joked.

"Yes, you should."

Danais found this funny because even though it was a joke, it was clearly stated as an obvious fact.

"Would you like me to make the shirt more fitted to accentuate your build?" the tailor asked Danais.

"Is that okay?"

"It's no different than what women with curves do to display them—and what women without them do to exaggerate their other qualities. If you've got it show it whatever 'it' may be."

Danais nodded in agreement. He then got another message in his head like the one from Kale at the kitchen table that morning. He gave a glance at his uncle, and Torak knew what he must do. The tailor was too busy to catch this exchange.

"Might I go out the back for a moment?" Torak asked.

"Aye, but steal anything, and I'll pull out your spleen," The tailor pointed a pair of scissors at Torak and gave him a hard stare. Which Torak dutifully ignored.

"Well, at least you'll leave me my heart."

Danais chuckled, and the tailor grunted pretending to not be amused.

Torak went out to the storeroom, and seconds later Kale appared. Being able to just appear on demand was definitely a skill Torak wished he had.

"There will be a meeting during the celebration tomorrow," Kale announced.

"Danais?"

"Do not worry about the young one. Someone will be protecting him," Kale replied.

Torak frowned. He was concerned about his nephew. "Do you know who will be there?"

"No, I do not. I didn't ask. I have ways of quickly escaping dangerous situations. But this won't be one of those."

"Thank you, Prince," Torak responded.

Kale smirked at that. "You know who I am?"

"I do, Prince Kale. And I pay my respects. Will I be able to continue talking with you, or is this message to be my last?"

"I will continue to talk with you, both by choice and necessity. Things are changing. More creatures might find it necessary to let humans back in. The boy is dressed now. You should go."

Torak did as told and went to retrieve his nephew. He thanked the tailor and left him to finish the work.

After picking up some boots and books, Torak took Danais to lunch. Danais ate more than his share. Because this was his second quality meal for the week, he saw no harm in overindulging himself. This lunch even came with an interactive play during the meal. If it was possible to best the previous day's lunch, Danais was sure this had done it.

"Hurry! Thank the tailor and let's be off. You want to see the city while the last of the sun shines don't you?"

Danais could barely contain his excitement. He'd never been on a boat before, never even been to the city—and was now going to do both in the same day. He could only imagine being able to touch the endless sea of yellow stone buildings, to walk on golden-dust streets. Leanor, the city of gold, was finally going to be within his reach. As he took his first steps on the wooden pier and heard the water gushing underneath him, fascination turned into fear.

He couldn't move, and his mind started racing in another direction. Boats were made of wood. What if something happened? Something like a fire? What if there was a storm and they sank? Or worse, what if they ended up on a deserted island after being sucked into a magical portal? He couldn't willingly walk into unknown danger. This was insane. One misplaced fire spark—no more ship and he'd drown. He couldn't swim. Maybe he'd burn to death if he was lucky, and not have to worry about drowning. But what if the ship crashed into a rock? Then he would have to wait for it to slowly sink, and he would inevitably sink with it. This boat thing was a really bad idea. There had to be another way.

Danais was vaguely aware his face was mirroring his terror, and people looking on could see it. Some were even smiling silently to themselves. But his sudden fear of boats and the ocean was fully justifiable, or so he thought. Nothing was going to make him move from his spot.

"Come on," his uncle said, holding his hand and tugging him forward.

Was this man insane? Surely he must see how nothing but doom could come out of this, Danais thought. *What was wrong with him?* Somehow, his thoughts distracted him enough for his uncle to guide him halfway down the pier, and then out on one of the planks to the boat. Once aboard, he immediately pressed his back to the first wall he could find. Torak made sure all the items were secure and came back to find Danais in the same spot he left him in. It was a long journey ahead, and Danais couldn't move. After so many years of wanting to be on the water, he was about to miss every moment of it.

"Are you okay?" Torak inquired.

"Terrified," Danais responded quickly and without hesitation.

"Then you should go indoors."

"That would require moving."

Danais had no idea how it happened, but he found himself leaning over the side of the ship and his head was a bit fuzzy. He was, however, feeling better. It would seem vomiting over the side of the ship had its benefits.

"Are you feeling better? Not projectiling over the edge of the ship anymore? That's progress."

"Feeling much better." Danais was starting to feel like he maybe could, possibly, at some point in the future. enjoy being on the ocean. From the safety of a boat, that was.

"Good, 'cause we are preparing to dock." His uncle directed Danais' eyes toward the dock.

"Already?" Danais was genuinely disappointed.

"You spent the whole voyage spewing into the ocean." Torak chuckled and patted him on the back.

Danais couldn't believe this. He went from fear of boats to motion sickness, and now that he was breathing normally, the dock was well within view. There was not enough time left to conquer his fear of water. He couldn't remember a second of the journey.

"So… am I going to have to walk you to dry land?" Torak joked.

"The water is far enough below," Danais sighed as he got his things. How was he going to learn to swim with such a fear of drowning if he barely had enough time to get over his fear of boats?

Once off the boat, his uncle hired one of the workers to cart their belongings to the inn.

The closer Danais got to the city of gold, the more awestricken he became. The godly glow was such that his eyes needed a moment to adjust before he could see clearly. The slow walk through the town took them past Leanor's temple, and Danais was dumbfounded. He managed to take in the expense of the door, get a glimpse of the inside courtyard, and say a quick prayer before his uncle shouted back to get his attention. He ran up beside his uncle, and they continued to walk to the inn.

The inn was amazing. The walls were made of yellow stone, but the columns were a mix of white stone and wood. It gave the walls another colour to reflect so the yellow wasn't overwhelming. The Atorathian stone was very reflective. This was probably why the glow was so tolerable.

"Are we—" Danais started.

"No. We are on ground level. There will be no climbing of stairs."

Danais marvelled at his uncle's perceptiveness but not for too long—not after entering the room, anyway. His eyes were drawn to the light fixtures: oil lamps with sheer patterned lampshades. There were also off-white, soft-cushioned furnishings and plush rugs, and a bed that would take up his entire room on the farm. If the gods weren't smiling on him before, they certainly were now.

"I'll come for you after sundown. We will head to the seer in the dark of night. No lamps. It takes only a little light to reflect here, and we do not want to be seen—not of our own means at least."

"Yes, Uncle."

Danais yawned. Was he that tired, or just overwhelmed? He couldn't tell. His Uncle left the room and Danais got into the bed to test if it was as comfortable as it looked and immediately fell asleep. When he awoke, he somehow knew the sun had been down for hours. He hurried out of bed. Rushing out of the bedroom knowing his uncle would be waiting in the next room but, as he turned to leave, he found his uncle already there, sitting on the couch with a visitor. The two stood upon hearing him enter, and one of them walked over towards Danais.

"So nice to see you again."

"And you, Lord Vardon." Danais bowed.

"Give me your hand."

Danais did as told, and then heard something he'd never heard up-close before: *word weave* or *word song* but he wasn't sure. It was the language serious spells were spoken in; smooth, intoxicating, just above a whisper at a perfect rhythm. The speech was so layered with natural tongue and a touch of magic so he could not tell, almost as if more than one word was being spoken at the same time.

Then he panicked again.

This could be it.

This could be the spell to take his life.

How could he have let his guard down again?

Before he had time to really panic, it was over. He looked to his left and nearly jumped out of his skin at what he saw.

"It's me." Danais commented not really having much else to say.

Beside him stood the perfect copy of his image. Danais almost reached out to touch it but thought better of it. Who knows what might happen from touching a magic-made doppelganger?

"And a very good one. This would fool even the best magicians. Nice work," Torak said, and he patted his friend on the shoulder.

"Thanks, Torak. He can't talk much, though. Only so much you can do with a few minutes. But no one will doubt it's real should they come in." Lord Vardon nodded, impressed with his own work.

"This next spell was harder, but I did what I could with the time." He held up a long, white piece of fabric. "This sheet is now an invisibility cloak. It will work for you and only you." He gave it to Danais. "It's more of a reflective spell than a full invisibility cloak, so it blends you in with the surroundings, as opposed to making you completely see-through, like a real one would. Shadows can still show. You'll have to be a little careful if full light hits you, but most people won't notice a shadow if they can't see what's casting it. You'll get more than enough time out of it for the night before the spell wears off. Good night, Danais." That was the last Lord Vardon said to him before leaving.

Danais put on the sheet, and they made the tedious journey to the seer's residence.

Following his uncle was interesting. He sometimes forgot his uncle was a full Atorathian. In his younger years, he'd trained in Mironi; they were known for their tracking skills much like Atorathians but leaned more into covert and assassination

Revelations

areas. Watching the way his uncle guided them through the night, he doubted they would be seen, cloak or not.

"This is it," Torak announced as they stopped to face a stone wall which enclosed some sort of courtyard and the residence of the seer.

Torak rapped the knocker on the entrance three times. Moments later the door opened. Another surprise awaited Danais inside the stone walls. Instead of the expected massive villa that would be behind such a wall, there was a medium-sized house of grey stone at the end of a traditional courtyard.

The garden was of the size Danais would assume, but not with such an unassuming residence. It was small in comparison to what he thought someone of her stature would live in. He expected something either extremely grand, or more whimsical. Eery even. But this was your typical home with a beautifully maintained garden. She was old enough. Maybe she went through phases of eccentricities. He didn't have enough knowledge about seers to draw real conclusions. Only that, he expected… different.

Inside, he was again pleasantly surprised.

"Black wood!" The exclamation escaped him in a mere whisper. The black wood was some of the most expensive wood. Danais couldn't recall the name of the tree, otherwise, his exclamation would've reflected that. Being a farm boy, he knew a think or two about trees. Even if he had never seen a particular tree before he knew of it. Just one of those things that came from living in a wooded area.

Among their magical qualities was a resistance to all of nature's elements, very hard to kill without uprooting them. The wood took on whatever light shone on it, and it had a red tinge. Danais noticed there was incense burning with a red smoke, so this accounted for the colour of the wood.

"I see you like it," a voice spoke behind them.

Danais was so deep in thought about the wood and incense he hadn't noticed just how far he had walked into the home. Danais turned to see a woman entering the room. She had the curvature of the sea people, by far the most voluptuous of Salinor's people: solid people, both men and women, with a purplish tint to their skin.

"You're from—?" It was on the tip of his tongue but Danais

couldn't' quite say it.

"Danais. Yes."

"The only province to be named directly after a God, and one that associates with the ocean. Like the God it's named after."

Danais had never seen someone from the province he was named after more than just in passing. He stood in awe, but the seer only smiled.

"Your uncle has taught you your history." She glanced over at Torak. Danais sensed something was there based on how she looked at him but didn't press the issue.

"Some, Seer. Yes."

"It wasn't a question. I have waited long years to lay my eyes upon you. Come out of the entrance way and into my living space. Dine with me."

Set on the small table by the couch was lobster for Danais. Some of the best seafood in Salinor came from the sea province so it was no surprise to him that lobster was on the menu. This, however, was a very special blue kind only found in their waters. He felt, as he continued walking towards the table, that he shouldn't be so impressed that a Dani had lobster from her own province no matter how far away they were from their homeland of Danais.

"The vegetables and spices are from our valleys. Not nearly as good as your uncle's or those in Keldon, but they are passable."

"How'd you know I'd be hungry?" Danais asked. He was essentially always hungry, but this was their first meet, so he considered it a legitimate question.

"I was informed you slept for hours after arriving."

"Oh. I didn't think you'd waste your talent to feed me." Maybe it was custom for Danis to feed guests on the first visit? He'd find out later. For now, he was going to enjoy the lobster.

"I see you didn't start with the legs." The seer commented.

Danais face turned into that of horror. How could he have forgotten this? Unless a Dani, it was always best to eat the legs first. The Dani people had a natural resistance to its poison. The blue lobster was notorious for making people ill and even killing them if not eaten in the correct order. Danais was finding so many things to panic over lately; he was beginning to wonder if he was going to survive much longer in life.

"Don't worry. You'll live." Torak laughed as he encouraged him to enjoy his meal.

"That doesn't mean I won't get ill." Danais eyed the offending lobster sceptically.

"You're a smart one." The seer chuckled slightly. "You won't get ill either."

The implications, Danais thought, were endless—not because there were a lot of options but because of what the few options said about him. Still, the only conclusions he could come to, though few, were still too big for him to tackle immediately.

Mere minutes later, Danais was finally satiated, and the seer had a servant take the food away. She poured them some orange tea which immediately developed a white mist floating over the top of the glass. The smell was much sweeter than that of the incense. Danais would not have thought that possible.

"Lira berry," the seer explained. "Grows through all of Salinor, but the best for burning is in the Atorathian mountains." She nodded her head towards the incense burning behind her on the mantal.

"Our mountains?"

"Yes. Most of the best herbs and plants do grow in Keldon, but not all. Do you know why their mountains are the most special? Besides the stone?"

"No, seer." Danais, for once, was eager to learn something new instead of rushing things along.

"It is because out of all the realms, their secrets are the hardest to penetrate. No magician has been able to penetrate the secrets of the halls of their mountains. And the Keldonians aren't telling. Even dwarves have struggled with it, and even though the dwarves have long been friends with the Keldonians, they never shared its secrets."

"I thought they were like the elves. I heard they fled from the race of men." It was here that he finally began to drink the mist covered tea.

"Yes. But even still, they have a love for humans that can't be entirely destroyed even if they find us self-destructive. The orange berry that made the tea, Tele, is native to Mironi. However, when grown by a special stream in Keldon, its magical qualities are enhanced. It calms the spirit, is a relaxer of the mind, and an… enabler."

"Enabler?"

"Yes. Whether you are extremely or even mildly injured, the aroma alone will significantly help healing. However, if the sickness or wound has been partially healed by magic, it acts as an enabler to enhance the spell."

Danais listened attentively. He didn't know the next time he'd be in the presence of someone so important. He couldn't afford to not pay attention.

"Just like with most magical herbs, there are things they do on their own, and things they can be used to do with something else." The seer paused, then looked directly at Danais. "Today is not a normal prediction. I will not be telling you what I see. I will tell only your uncle."

"Why? I came all the way over here for nothing? I came to you by stealth and risked death by sea, only to be told that I'll still learn nothing of who I am? Why can I not know!" Apparently, his usual self hadn't been completely subdued as his combative need to know nature overtook him.

The seer and Torak merely stared at Danais, neither making any hint of commenting nor showing signs of anger. Danais grunted. He was going to have to get his outbursts under control. It would've been so much better if they just shouted back at him.

Obviously, there was a bigger picture, but yet again he was letting his personal needs cloud the issue. He was meant to figure this out, and wild outbursts wouldn't help him any. Before he could run away with his thoughts, Danais started to feel calm.

This tea must be starting to work, he mused.

"There are some things you can know and some that will be revealed in time. The things I will find out today you cannot know. I'm not sure what it will be, but I am sure of that. Give me your hand."

Danais immediately put forth his right hand even though he was left-handed.

"Interesting," she said, as he rested it palm up in her right hand. She placed her left-hand palm down on his, sandwiching Danais' hand. At first, there was nothing; then suddenly his

Revelations

breathing became heavy. A chilling wind rose in the room as if they were outside.

Then there was darkness. There came the sound of thunder, and then a crack of lightning illuminated the darkness of the room, followed by another.

As visibility returned to the room it went from an enchanting red mist to heavy red clouds. The red storm clouds reflected so well on the black floors and walls that Danais felt like he was floating in the windy centre of a thunder cloud. The mix of total darkness, wind, and sudden bursts of lightning overhead was maddening. Danais' heart pounded at a pace so fast that it seemed ready to burst or shoot right out of him.

The seer's orange locks flew wildly in the wind. Black pools of emptiness filled her eye sockets. Her body streamed within an intricate vein work of lightning. It was scary, frightening, intriguing— so many things. There was too much for Danais to understand. Was this storm natural? Is this how all readings were? Was he supposed to be terrified? Because he was definitely terrified.

Something was taking hold of him. He was reaching the breaking point and finally exploded with a scream of sheer terror.

The room went dark again.

Danais wasn't entirely sure whether this was a good thing or not.

The wind died, and things returned to normal.

Danais gasped for air. Tears streamed down his face. Lela, the seer, did not let him go until his breathing returned to normal. Danais found that quite comforting.

"Lela—" Torak said but was cut of. This was the first her name was mentioned and Danais' uncle using it so informally spoke volumes.

"I shall tell you when we next meet, Torak."

"Surely you must—"

The wind suddenly rose again.

"Enough!"

Then the wind was gone.

"Drink, both of you," she demanded while still looking at Torak.

Danais did as told, and so did his uncle. Danais knew she was a feared and revered seer, but also knew that she was well respected. Until now, he was having serious trouble understanding why people would fear her. She seemed so kind. Clearly, there was more to her, especially if his uncle didn't even dare question her.

"So how are the four children of yours?"

And just like that, she'd become pleasant again.

Danais was beginning to like her more and more. Especially her hair. He'd never seen anyone with hair so neat yet so tightly knitted together. Locks, they were called. He wondered if his straight hair could adapt to the style.

"They do as kids do. My youngest is about to get married. The oldest is engaged," Torak explained.

"He only just left the farm?" the seer responded as if he couldn't have possibly fallen in love that fast.

"I know. Says he fell for one of his Mironian trainers."

"Ah, so he went to Mironi for his training instead of staying with the armies in Atorath."

"He's more interested in becoming an assassin. He says the Mironians are the best at the intricacies of killing." Torak rolled his eyes.

"I see. So, you approve, then?" There was a bit of challenge in her tone that did not go unnoticed by Danais.

"Yes. He was almost wed to a Mironian peasant. Thankfully, he avoided that mistake."

Danais' jaw dropped at hearing his uncle talk like this. Was his uncle only pretending to like peasants all these years?

The seer didn't seem to be moved. She looked amused. "Now, now, your own nephew is silent. Surely you can't mean that the way it sounds." She gave a sly smile and looked up over her cup at him as she sipped her tea.

"Ungifted Atorathians are the lowest of peasants," Danais mumbled.

Torak smiled. "All right. I only meant he was dim-witted. Even the ungifted in Salinor can at least acquire some level of intelligence. And you shouldn't be feeding his temper. You knew I was only jesting."

"Point taken. And you shouldn't attempt to order information out of me."

"Bah. A minor lapse in judgment. And this is more than tea."

Revelations

Torak said seriously but then took another sip so he was, to Danais, obviously not serious.

"I like a drink now and then; it makes my inner eye see better." The seer said it with a bit too much conviction.

Torak looked at Danais and pretend whispered, "That's why only one drink before the storm. Just a little nip is required for inner-eye site."

Danais nodded and took another sip of his tea, wondering what the liquor she added to it was.

"Bah. That was a mere breeze." Lela waved off the comment and grabbed a biscuit from the tray beside the teapot.

"Sure," Danais said, also grabbing a biscuit. Oatmeal raisin? He wasn't sure. It was delicious but he wasn't sure what the currant was. "And the storm clouds were just puffs of fog. Maybe the lightning was even a trick of the eyes. The thunder was only the growling of my stomach, right?"

Torak laughed, and Lela glared at him but looked more amused than annoyed.

"I would expect nothing less from a relative of yours." Lela took another sip of tea, glaring at Torak as she drank.

"I will take that as a compliment," Torak said, which procured a sigh out of Lela.

Friendly conversation went on, and Danais thoroughly enjoyed it. Especially the bits that hinted Torak and Lela had a much deeper history than his uncle let on. They were just too friendly.

Unfortunately, all good things must end and soon Danais and his uncle were heading back to the inn.

Torak was already outside when the seer spoke again to Danais alone. "Let your instincts guide you, and the answers will find you." She took a ring infused with the purple stone of the Danais province and silver from the dwarf caves to Danais. It fit perfectly on the fourth finger of his right hand.

"I had this made for you. The moment I had my first vision of you."

"You knew I would live?" Danais questioned.

"I knew you would be born, and I knew what could happen if you survived to this day. But no, I was unsure if you would make it. Things can change. You could drown or burn in a building. The smallest accident or change can alter the future.

What I did see is you wearing this ring. But I haven't had any glimpses of this future since that one, so I've been praying to the gods that it held true. And here you stand; and here is my gift to you."

"Thank you. I wish there was something I—well, you already told me what I can do for you."

"Yes. I have."

"I will try."

"Try is not an option."

Danais sensed her doublespeak. It wasn't a command; it seemed more desperate. It was as if she wished he did have the option to merely try but knew it was not so. Danais left with that thought and still was unsure if he could just do, instead of try.

"Was the storm natural?" Danais inquired once they were seated in his room back at the inn.

"No. A reaction like that means things are dangerous or complicated or both."

"She seemed to be made of lightning. It was like she was there, but I could see right through her."

"She has the power of the elements."

"She's an elemental?" Danais was shocked. Out of all the rare gifts of the people of Salinor, this was one he never dreamed he'd encounter.

"Yes. And a great seer and sorceress. Sometimes what she sees manifests itself in her own abilities. A show of such magnitude…" his uncle sighed as he trailed off. "Maybe all the years of planning and waiting—"

His uncle stared into the distance, clearly distraught, and then he continued, "I just hope it's not disastrous." He fell silent for a moment, then added: "Do you care to tell me what she told you? I understand if you don't. I have many secrets I must keep from you. I am willing to let you keep yours."

"She instructed me to let the answers find me. It sounded more like a plea than a demand. It was said with too much… I can't explain it."

Danais didn't want to talk about it. He wanted to keep his opinions his, and Torak seemed to be thinking the same as he nodded and didn't prod further.

Soon they arrived back at the inn and Torak left him in the

room to sleep. Danais couldn't sleep, though. He thought about the many unanswered questions hidden in the words of the seer this night; how he didn't get sick from the lobster. Why she implored him to do his best not to look so hard for answers. He couldn't make sense of anything, though he could see they were connected. How could he see the connection yet still have no answers?

He closed his eyes and tried to stop thinking. It wouldn't do to stay awake all night and risk being too tired to perform his best at the ceremony. Maybe answers would come to him as he slept and visit him in his dreams.

4
DANAIS

Danais couldn't believe the morning he was having. After hours in the bathhouse, he had been massaged, oiled and scrubbed, and he smelled like freshly coined money. If this was what being rich felt like, he could surely get used to it. Getting his hands groomed was understandable, but other than keeping his toes neat for toe sucking, he'd never gotten a full treatment. After a soak, a scrub, and an oil massage, he was sold. His feet felt brand new. And now he was standing outside the destination for the day.

Danais looked up in awe. He couldn't imagine anything short of spectacular hiding behind this wall. "The palace is behind this wall?"

"Villa, not palace—and yes," his uncle responded.

The perimeter of this building was even larger than that of the seers. That made sense, however, Danais doubted that he would be dealing with the same modest living space once inside. And he was not to be disappointed. The courtyard was massive. Too much for him to ever explore in one day. The gardens he could take in during the quick walk were beautiful. Better than anything he had seen.

"Good day, Master Tomal," a servant greeted them. "There has been a small change in seating. You will be at the head table."

Torak rolled his eyes at Danais as they followed their greeter. "Your master is full of surprises."

"It would appear so," the servant replied. "You will be beside him and the seer and the singer, by the guest of honour." The last part seemed aimed at Danais.

"Will I be required to stay with the entertainers?" Danais asked. His uncle chuckled.

"You were just told you are at the head table. Beside the guest of honour. Are you too lost in the beauty of this villa to hear correctly?"

Danais decided a glare was the only logical response to this. Especially since his uncle was still smiling.

"You are at the head table, young sir. You would be ill-advised to leave your seat empty for so long." He threw open the massive oak door entrance and ushered them inside. Danais was so lost he had no idea how far into the villa they had gone or even which building they were in. His uncle was correct in his assessment of being mesmerised. He groaned at that realisation but luckily no one seemed to have noticed.

As they entered, Danais was again taken in by great architecture. The floor was redwood and polished to a beautiful shine. The entrance hall itself had a glass-dome ceiling—the most glass Danais had ever seen for just one wall in a home. Temples did have glass domed ceilings, but he'd never seen something that opulent in a home. Much as he wanted to take in the scene, they were now late due to the last-minute change. The head table had already been walked in and introduced. The only person left to be introduced was the guest of honour. Lucky for them Lord Vardon had already made the apologies for their tardiness.

"This corridor will take you right onto the stage. Do you know Barton?"

"Yes," Danais replied.

"Leave the seat beside him empty and take the next one." He turned to Danais' uncle. "I trust you'll have no problem finding your seat, Torak."

"Certainly not. And I'll see to it that Danais gets to his in the

Revelations

event he can't follow your detailed instructions," Torak joked.

"Good. I shall hold you personally accountable if he doesn't find it."

"And what will happen to me if I fail?"

"I'll turn you into my sex slave."

"And that's supposed to be punishment?" Torak raised an eyebrow, and Danais shook his head. His uncle was a character at the best of times.

"That depends entirely on what entices me." The servant replied. Danais could only assume they had history if this was the type of conversation the two of them were having.

"Torture? Now that's just bad. Does Lord Vardon know you proposition his guests?" The look of horror on Torak's face was too good to be believed.

"I am sure he wouldn't mind my torturing you—especially after your last meeting." A wicked grin formed across the man's face.

"That was an accident!" Torak protested "I tripped and just happened to pull down his pants. Do you think I would intentionally unclothe him in public?"

"Only an idiot would think that fall wasn't a fake."

"I'm not going to entertain that with a response," Torak said as the other man laughed and walked off to other duties.

Torak and Danais finally made their way down the hall. Once on the stage, Danais was mesmerised again. Blue Keldonian stone shined on the floors, and several glass French doors lined the hall, all separated by the yellow wall. Blue stained glass shaped like swans covered what might have been ordinary looking lamps between all the French doors. Danais thought it must take gallons of oil to keep the place lit at night. Then again, the yellow walls were quite reflective, so maybe it didn't.

He looked up and saw three enormous crystal chandeliers hanging from the ceiling. Then he noticed Barton and the serving girl from his dinner the other day were there. What were the odds they all knew whoever the guest of honour was? Why was the seer sitting beside his uncle? Was this the blue wine of the magician province that he was sipping on? Or was it the hallucinogenic type from the realm of Danais? He didn't have time to scold himself for shifting his train of thought so easily because the guest of honour was finally coming down the aisle.

2

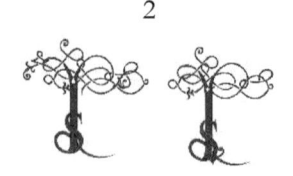

Leo walked in late for his own celebration. He thought for a moment that his father would be mad at him for being late. Then he realised that had his father expected him to be on time, he wouldn't have had the musicians ready to play a processional as he entered. And the abysmal burial music they were playing was clearly a sign that his father had predicted that Leo would be late. Some of his musician friends were trying to stifle their laughter in the crowd. Leo decided to look straight ahead and not at his father. He wasn't going to give him the satisfaction of knowing he won this round. There would be payback another day.

For a twenty-eighth name day, this was a pretty extravagant affair. Leo was still unsure why he would ask for such a celebration and even more why his father would so readily agree to give him one. But here he was. He was so intent on looking professional that he didn't take notice of anyone on the stage until he was finally ready to take his seat. Leo recovered fast at the sight of Danais. Danais, however, wasn't nearly as quick.

What were the odds Danais would be the special guest seated next to the guest of honour? Furthermore, why had no one bothered to tell either of them what was going on? Could this mean that what was going on between them was somehow connected?

So many questions. Too few answers.

Danais was so deep in thought he realised too late that he was holding up progress. Since he was next to the guest of honour, he had to sit with Leo to start the celebrations. He should've stood up the moment Leo hit the platform. Danais got out of his seat. He took Leo's hand, and the two of them sat together.

As they sat, Xan made his appearance. He took his place sitting on Leo's shoulders. Most of the guests were magicians, so there were Betaves everywhere on top of shoulders, some just roaming the hall, others resting on laps and even more lounging on the tables. Still, having another Kentai would be unusual. When Leo saw Kale walking toward them, he was shocked, but he was even more interested in seeing who he was going to. Having never seen Xan's brother, Leo was curious as to what he was doing walking behind the head table.

Danais absentmindedly lowered his hand and rubbed behind Kale's ear. Barton exchanged a glance with Leo, but neither had time to consider their thoughts. The celebration was about to begin. There were acrobats and storytellers, interpretive dance, sword displays, and even a short play. The storytellers were Danais' favourites. They usually told the tales of the land: whether true tales of the gods or fabricated legends. The skill was in the mastery of language and song together. One didn't have to be a great singer, but those adept at singing usually wrote the most entertaining stories. Some were so good they became part of regular touring musicians' portfolios. That was the greatest honour for a storyteller.

One such was the story of Atora. Naturally, many storytellers had versions of this tale. But one that had been deemed the definitive version was called *"Ronilas' Poison."* It was stylised as a love song, which made it extremely easy on the ears and passionate enough to command the attention of the listener. It was only twenty years old and the writer of this particular verse—Langi Main de Zar Mironi— was at the celebration. Zar was the sub-province in Mironi where Leo was raised. Langi introduced the song by revealing his inspiration for writing it.

Danais was panicking; he was going to sing this song. How could he do it after the original composer? He had to think fast and come up with an alternative. He hadn't even had time to rehearse with a musician. This was going to go bad quickly. And that was when he heard his name. Langi was introducing him.

Much to Danais' surprise, Leo stood with him and led him to the floor. This was making him really nervous. Leo was a professional musician. Danais was simply a naturally gifted singer and by no means a professional. He hoped Leo wouldn't be attempting to play for him, but that was a wasted hope. Leo picked up his guitar and took a seat not too far from Danais.

"Don't let him intimidate you," he heard Kale's voice mind-speak with him.

"Are you saying he's not a good musician?"

"No. He's excellent. But so are you. Besides, he's obviously trying to intimidate or impress you."

Danais heard Kale chuckle but didn't have time to sort his last comment out. Leo was already playing a lead-in, in the style of what would be called Spanish guitar in a world amongst the worlds.

Danais finished his song and received enthusiastic applause. He never sang for an audience, so applause he expected—but not applause like this. Some were even crying. He even managed not to mess it up while singing unrehearsed with a musician by trade. Maybe he was better than he thought he was if he could evoke this much praise from such an upper-class audience.

Leo led him back to the head table before he could have a chance to be too overwhelmed. The main meal finally made it to the table after his selection. Danais lost count of the number of courses, but he wouldn't dream of passing up food. Before long, Danais had drunk as many drinks as most in the hall and was on the dance floor. Leo somehow managed to work his way toward Danais so they could talk.

"Let's get out of here," Leo whispered.

"You can't leave?" Danais protested. The evening was all about Leo. He couldn't just up and leave. Then again at this point, the party was no longer about him.

"With all the ale and spirits tonight, I strongly doubt anyone will miss me. This party has officially reached the 'all about fun stage'."

Danais realised he didn't have much of a choice and let Leo drag him out under the stars. The city looked so much different under the light of the moon. The glow seemed much warmer and inviting than bright and grand. Leo wasn't hurrying their walk through the city. It was too quiet, with most of the people in this part of Leanor either asleep or at the celebration he just left.

"You have an amazing voice," Leo complimented.

"You play very well. Don't you sing also?"

"A little. My voice isn't that spectacular." Leo sighed and

looked out. "So, you've never been across the lake before?"

"No. And now I'm getting a whole week's end, and I'm on first-name basis with a Vardon."

"I did not know that Torak had another child; that is, if a nephew counts as a child. He's been a family friend for years, and I've never known of you. Guess he's had his reasons. Do you know about your parents?"

"I don't know much about my parents."

"Nor I mine. Guess we are both the same in that."

Danais was shocked. Leo looked like he belonged in the world where people who had parties as big as the one he just left, lived in. "You're adopted?"

"Yes. Why so shocked?"

"I dunno. Since you don't favour your mother, I just assumed you were a bastard son." Danais shrugged. It wasn't a bad thing.

"Of my father?" Leo knew the answer but didn't see the harm in asking.

"No, of your mother. I assumed you looked like your real father."

By now they were far enough away to hear none of the noise left at the celebration. The yellow sand felt cool under their feet as they walked along the beach. Leo decided a change of topic was in order. Even then, knowing that there was more to him than meets the eye, he still couldn't shake the feeling of abandonment when it came to his parents.

"I want to see you again," Leo announced as they walked in the sand.

"Me? Now I know you must be drunk," Danais said, and the two laughed together.

"Seriously. Stay with me–tonight even."

"Me? Why would you want to see me?"

From their position on the shore, the roofs of Leanor's temple could be seen. The ocean itself seemed to be struggling with whether it wanted to shine with the yellow or shimmer in the moonlight. The moon seemed to be winning, causing the yellow of the city to sparkle above the surface which mimicked the look of floating sawdust.

"Isn't it obvious?" Leo asked with a hint of frustration before he headed towards the ocean while ripping his shirt from his body. At least that's the way Danais would tell it. Leo was merely hurriedly pulling his shirt overhead then diving into the sea over the first small wave. But that wasn't nearly as interesting.

Danais scolded himself. Why else would Leo refuse to tell him his title? Why get him drunk so as to have the advantage of soberness over him? Leo's father had made Danais sit next to him. People in attendance could already be speculating. And then there was Leo's insistence they leave the party together. Kale had even said Leo may be trying to impress him on purpose.

"Why did he have to go in the water?" Danais said softly to himself before walking further down to sit on some rocks heading out close to where Leo was swimming.

Barton entered the room. Inside was Lord Vardon and his Betave, along with Torak, Kale, Xan and now Barton and his Betave. He took a seat and waited a little while before speaking. The party was also the setting of a private meeting. Danais and Leo were not the only ones to slip away.

"Is this all?"

"No. There is more," Kale said.

"And you are—?"

"Kale."

"Two Kentais that deem me worth speaking to. My luck must finally be changing," Barton said with a smile.

"It would take more than Miron himself to change your luck," Lord Vardon said.

"Bah. Have you seen my future wife? I don't need good fortune. Clearly, the gods are already smiling down on me."

"You know you poisoned her," Xan commented.

"A mere poison spell wouldn't work on an Atorathian," Barton protested in his defence.

"That only means you used powerful blood magic to do it. To have something like her, you must've had to sacrifice a whole leg to do this. And clearly, you did it with enough passion because I haven't noticed any scars on either leg," Torak said.

"I'd reckon he done it so well that it grew back even better than before the sacrifice," Lord Vardon added.

Revelations

Everyone was having a good laugh at Barton's expense, but he was used to it. One had to be quick to avoid being the topic of taunting.

"Why am I always on the receiving end of this?" Barton complained, trying to conceal his amusement. Funny was funny, after all, even if it was at his expense.

"It would appear you are an easy target. Or... that you're an easy target," Kale said, which brought more laughter.

"And you're the new addition, and already you're making fun." Barton crossed his arms in frustration.

"Clearly, I missed a good joke," the seer said as she walked in. "I'll have to come early next time."

"Sit. Have a glass of wine.," Lord Vardon said as he refilled all the glasses. They raised a toast to Ronilas, Goddess of War and Wisdom and mother of Atora and a toast to Atora, God of Strength and Courage.

"May the gods watch over us and grant us wisdom during this meeting," Lela said, and they all finished their drinks. Lord Vardon refilled.

"Things have begun. Soon, the magic keeping them hidden will die, we need to already be on the move before then," Lela announced.

"Yes, Seer. I was told that I would start this. I knew it had begun once he told me his name. But I didn't think it would be so—"

"Simple," Lela finished for Lord Vardon.

"Yes. He sang; I invited him and knew things had changed because I was told I would invite him into my home without knowing who he was. He told me his name after the invite. I knew Torak had a messenger watching, so I found her and let him know immediately."

"And how was your first meeting with the boy?" Lela addressed Barton.

"Leo had caught sight of him probably only moments after this invitation. I didn't think much of it until after we saved his life and Leo insisted we feed him. I was told that blood would bleed orange at the touch of glass. I had assumed it meant that someone would be cut by glass, but the red wine came out orange. That was when I knew who he was."

"And I was told to avoid allowing him more than a glimpse

of the city," Torak added, "and that the moment we needed to go to the city would present itself in time and that would be the start. I told him there was more to him and let him go into the woods without being followed, as was instructed. I was not sure why, but I know now it was because Kale would be walking through the forest. Had I not given him the incentive to leave, they would not have met."

"My apologies for the last-minute change in seating, Torak. Kay sent a message to my Betave, Darla, only this morning to tell me that if I did not get them together before the ceremony, they would not leave together," Lord Vardon said.

"I am not entirely sure how I knew that, Lord Vardon. It was more intuition than vision, and I could've been wrong. I did not think I could risk the chance of not acting even if it was just a feeling and not an actual premonition," Kay explained.

"And you were smart to do so," the seer spoke "I did not see the importance of that until much too late. It is good you trusted your instincts. You were right; I had seen Danais going home and Leo retiring with some woman. Had you not acted, they would not be together now. I cannot see everything, and their being together was more important than the future given to me. It would seem that my predictions so far have come true. However, I'm interested in the things I didn't know. I would finally ask for the story I did not know to be told to you as it was me. Xan will now tell you his part of the tale.

"I had a vision. A dream about an abandoned child in the sacred wood. A child put there to be found yet also purposely hidden. This made it all the more curious: how I would know where to find the child if it was hidden by spells? Still, I flew to the spot, and there was the child with its name embroidered in the cloth he was wrapped in. The other part of who would be guided to the child by me I did not know. I knew only that I had to fly until I saw the child or the boy would not be found.

"The vision was also clear that I must help raise the boy. I came to the seer for clarification after finding the child. She did not know of my part in this and was helpful in piecing together my vision. I feared it might be too difficult and need the help of a dream-reader. My job, and that of his teacher, was to teach him wisdom and patience because those were the things he would need most through his journey. Still, I know only my part and not why we are here today."

"And you, Kale, what is your story, which I have only just learned?" Lela prompted

"The same day of my brother's flight, I was in line to be the next king of our people. Our other brother was better suited, but in any case, I had a vision that I should roam the forest of the land and live the wildlife of our spirit people—basically to do my job as a Kentai, but just not in the kingdom. The vision said that one day I would come upon a young man, and I was to stop him from doing whatever it was that he was going to do. It turns out that he wanted to storm back to his uncle and demand answers. I calmed him. Judging by his character, I'm confident that that was the thing I was meant to do."

There was a pause after this new piece of information. Neither Kentai knew what it was that they were helping to move along. It was not meant for them to know but maybe today would be that day. It seemed while the seer was doing her part, the magic in the realm was doing its own as well.

"Salinor itself apparently agrees with our cause and is helping us. The land wants to heal its people." Lela spoke. It was always nice to see how everything was part of the bigger plan even the things one didn't know.

"I would like to know everything, as would my brother. I believe that this is why I and my brother are here," Xan said.

"So do I," replied the seer.

Danais sat on the edge of the rocks and let his feet rest in the water. Leo swam over and looked up at him. Danais smiled. His uncle was right: he was easy game for a cute face.

"So will you stay, and how's your second day?" Leo asked.

"I will stay, and I'm working on the second day. Uncle's only giving me the weekend."

"That's okay. I will still be here."

Danais jumped up at that moment with an accusing look on his face. "You've put a spell on me."

"I haven't—"

"It's raining, and I'm still dry."

Leo held up his hands. "Don't run!"

Danais was making good time, considering the rocks weren't

too smooth. Still, he managed to stop just before getting wet.

"It's just a small protective barrier..." Leo explained.

"Protection?"

"Yes."

Danais slowly made his way back to the edge.

"I have reason to believe we need protection, even against sound," Leo explained. It keeps people who mean harm away and is soundproof to all but the best magicians, and it can sense if harm persists in coming towards us."

Danais should've thought of that. After all that was going on, he had to be under protection he didn't know of. All the people who knew were left behind at the villa. How was he being protected if he was now important? He was a peasant with no power and was easy prey for anyone. However, Leo had casually thought of this like it was second nature. Danais realised he had a lot of scolding himself to come in the future if this conclusion jumping kept up.

"That's no small piece of magic," was the conclusion Danais came to.

"It is for me."

"Why do I need protection anyway? All this secrecy? Why can't I know?"

"Life doesn't work that way. We will know when we are meant to know."

Danais got a sudden urge to vault something at him. Unfortunately, there were no loose rocks, so Danais was forced to glare at him until his temper ebbed.

"Come in the water with me," Leo insisted.

"These are expensive clothes."

"Take them off."

Danais thought about this. He could be stubborn and protest, but Leo wasn't stupid. He'd figure out that he just couldn't swim.

"I cannot swim."

"I'll hold you. Come."

It was something in the way Leo said *"come"* that seemed to tear away at Danais' resistance. He started to strip. "How deep is it right here?"

"Too deep to stand."

"Should I walk in?"

Revelations

"Just jump. I'll grab you."

"Suddenly I'm starting to question your sanity," Danais said, almost flirtatiously.

"Trust me."

Danais thought about this. If holding up this barrier was minor, Leo should be strong enough to save him—in theory, that is. He decided to throw all caution to the wind and jump in. The worst that could happen was death.

That thought came as he hit the water. Immediately, he panicked, regretting his decision. His mind was about to go through its usual thinking process when he felt something wrap around him and pull him to the surface. Then he was again breathing the air—and not even gasping.

"You sank faster than I expected."

"You said you'd grab me, so I figured flailing for my life would kill me faster."

"Really?" Leo wasn't buying this explanation, and his smile was evidence of this.

"Maybe you saved me before I had time to panic. It's possible," Danais conceded.

"Ah. Now that's a story I can believe. You're tensing up. Afraid of something?"

"The water. Apparently, I have a fear of boats and drowning. I spent years dreaming of going out to sea, and I turn into a jellyfish as soon as my feet hit the dock."

Leo chuckled. "I see."

"Yes. My uncle had to pull me along, and then I spent most of the time hanging over the ship."

"Sounds ideal. Relax. I won't drop you."

Danais didn't hear this and tightened his grip. Leo just smiled. He could get used to this.

"You could crush me with your hands. They're huge."

"Well, I am half Keldonian after all."

"Yes, but I'm sure you wouldn't need magic to kill someone."

"That's a fair assumption."

"So why me?"

"Why is the sky blue? I don't know why. It just is. Why not you?"

"I'm an Atorathian peasant. Bedding me is one thing, but a

genuine interest? You are like the sea, and I'm just a stream. You are the lake, and I'm a pond. Out of all the eligible magicians and true Atorathians, why would a Vardon, of all the magicians, choose me? I got more. The list is endless."

Leo smiled and nodded before speaking. "Logically that makes sense. But you've never been in love before, have you?"

Danais ignored the question and the implication. How could Leo make him seem so small, young, naive, and inexperienced in one phrase? Leo seemed to be nonplussed whether Danais answered or not. This sense of calm annoyed Danais. Danais stressed over everything, and it seemed that everything would be okay with Leo even if he cursed him. On the other hand, if Danais admitted the truth, Leo would probably be okay with that too. Danais was irritated by this—and impressed at the same time.

"No. I haven't."

"That's okay. We all start somewhere. However, love isn't logical and knows no boundaries. If it did, mixed breeds like me wouldn't exist." Leo watched Danais mentally work through that point. It was interesting to watch him think. He wondered what it would sound like if Danais mused verbally.

"So how deep is it here?"

"Plenty deep. At least twenty of you."

"Really? And you just let me jump in?"

"You are named after the God of the Moon and Sea. You shouldn't fear water."

"I don't. I fear drowning. It's different."

"You have a good sense of humour," Leo said through a laugh. "I'm going to let you go." Danais opened his mouth, but Leo continued before he could speak. "Don't panic. This will be hard to do if you are not calm."

Danais took a deep breath and nodded, not realising that Leo had already let him go.

"Watch."

Leo squeezed his right hand into a fist hard enough to draw blood. He then put his left palm out over the water and started to mumble. The *wordsong* was very appealing even though he couldn't hear what the magician was saying. As he spoke, a pillar of water rose toward his hand. He cupped it at the bottom with his bleeding hand and separated the column from the water's surface. He moved his hands slowly together in a way that he would roll a large ball, forming the column into a small sphere that he could hold in one hand. Then the whispering stopped, and he looked at Danais.

"Take it." It was said as a demand, but it felt as if he were saying, "This is for you, Danais."

Danais hesitated at first, and Leo was unsure if he'd made a mistake. Maybe he shouldn't have done so much magic around someone who was opposed to magic. He released an internal sigh when Danais finally reached forward and took it into his hand.

In his hand was a small globe. It was the perfect size for Leo's hand but just big enough for Danais to feel the need to use two. Inside was a replica of the temple of Leanor floating beneath the water and under a red moon.

"This is amazing."

"Thank you."

Danais was impressed with the modesty of it all. "Why is the moon red?"

"Drop of blood. It seemed the logical thing to do."

"Your hand is already healed." It was a question and a statement.

"Yes."

Danais didn't want to work out the implications of this, at least not at that moment. He was just going to enjoy the gift for now.

"I left my gift for you at the inn."

Leo smiled. By all rights, he shouldn't have been interested in someone so boy-like. But somehow, through his innocence, Leo could sense a maturity in Danais. He was almost certain that it wasn't just because he was attracted to him. Almost.

"Let's go get it, then."

It was at this moment that Danais realised how far they had drifted from the shore. How had he let himself get this comfortable? Was there more magic at work here than Leo was telling him? There had to be something at work here. If Leo could get him this relaxed without magic, that meant his uncle was more right than Danais cared to believe. He was prey for an attractive face. Throw in the deep voice, and he was more than prey, he was an easy target.

Leo was enjoying every mental struggle Danais had. If he were an indecent man, he'd pry into his thoughts, but he wasn't. And there was a certain pleasure to be had in not knowing and guesstimating from the reaction. Besides, if he had assumed right there was only one course of action.

"Get behind me," Leo said suddenly.

"Huh?"

"Behind me. I'm going to swim us back to shore. We are a long way out."

Danais did as told and was well aware that they could move much faster if assisted by magic. Leo, however, wasn't using any. Once they were on the shore, Danais allowed him to cast a slight warming spell to dry their clothes. They weren't under the protective rain barrier once they went further out to sea.

"Are you ready to head to the inn now?" Leo asked. The rain had stopped by now.

"Yes."

"I know a fast way from here. Come."

Leo clearly knew his way around the city. They did get back to the inn considerably faster than Danais thought that they would. Once Danais handed the gifts to Leo, he could tell that the glass blower must've done an excellent job to impress someone of such wealth just by Leo's reaction.

Danais had handed him a plate and a drinking glass of blue and grey. It was in a swirling pattern, much as if it were a smooth storm, if such a thing were possible. But what made it pop was the very subtle bits of orange, almost like red lighting trying to break through the swirl of clouds. It was beautiful.

Leo wasn't quite sure what to make of this. But this was an obvious sign that something of epic proportions was about to happen. This gift was the perfect gift in ways that Leo would never admit.

"So can I see you on Mal, the second day, or Tanda, the third day?"

"Wait!" The seer had just finished explaining all the details the two Kentais did not know, and Kay was quieting the room. Someone was at the door. Moments later, Mai'n the assassin came in. She had three bodies—alive but immobilised—with

Revelations

her.

"I couldn't effectively follow the conversation and hide three bodies."

"They followed us?" Barton asked.

"Only out of curiosity, Barton."

Mai'n was trained by the builders. She was as good an assassin as any, by Mironian standards. Being a waiter just happened to be her present job. There was much more to her than Barton had told Leo.

"I sent her a message three days' past," the seer stated, "I knew she needed to be here but was unable to ascertain why. Since I didn't see her in the meeting, I told her to follow Barton to the meeting. As with most things when I'm unsure, I have to trust my instincts. If I assumed the future had changed, she would be in here, and they would be running off with information."

"So, what do you think about what's going on?" Lord Vardon asked Mai'n.

"I agree with Kale. Plans change and we must adapt. My need to be here when the week before I was not, proves the seer's point: any decisions they make seem to have more drastic changes than they normally would. Still, I feel the course should stay the same, even though the route needs to be adjusted. I'll do away with these three when you are done with them. I doubt anything will come of probing them though. Even if they were still alive."

"You are an amazing woman," Torak said to Mai'n. A bit off-topic, but he had his reasons.

Mai'n raised an eyebrow. "Only amazing, Torak?

"My eldest son is unattached. How's your cousin?"

"Still not interested. I hear your youngest is finally marrying."

"And who told you that piece of information, Mai'n?" Torak looked at the seer as he spoke.

"I might have let it slip over wine at the celebration," Lela replied with too much innocence.

"Slip?" Torak did not sound convinced.

"She was talking about how our oldest still pines for her cousin. I merely replied by saying the youngest was getting married. Women talk," Lela said as if this justified the fake slip.

"Why did I marry you?" Torak shook his head not bothering

almost as if the very thought of him and the seer was perplexing.

"Because I'm a force of nature to be admired."

Everyone in the room groaned at the obvious nod to her elemental powers. Lela continued as if the joke was well received. "Before I take my leave, thanks to you, Lord Vardon, for a wonderful night. I'm leaving the province and may be gone for a time. I want to deliver an account of this meeting directly. And yes, I'll talk to our son and meet this love who you approve of so much more than the last." Lela looked at Torak as he seemed to be about to say something. "I'll make sure one of your messengers sends full details back after my report to the Alliance, Torak. Good night, all. May Salinor the Great Mother watch over you." And with that, the meeting was terminated.

"So, this is what a room bigger than a chocolate box looks like," Danais said as he entered the room. The bed probably wouldn't even fit in his room back home. It was a dark brown bed with blue satin sheets and sheer blue curtains on the canopy. In the corner close to a window was a small study area and a bookshelf, and a deep brown table with papers strewn across. By the fireplace was a multi-shades- of-blue area rug with a small centre table, also chocolate brown.

"Why such dark furnishings?"

"I like how it neutralises the yellow walls. And the blue is because I like blue."

"It gives the walls a tinge of green, like the ocean. You could've gone for red and gotten a more orangey, fiery feel."

"Opposites. Interesting."

"I've been told I run hot and cold."

"Really? That sounds dangerous. Maybe I should put a stronger force field around myself," Leo joked. Danais smiled back at him.

"Like I could really take you out. You're twice the size of me. Your back's a little tracked there."

Leo had just taken off his top. "Well, I *was* late today and she, he, they were biters. And not at the same time. I was bout to be ready when a Dani guy I'd been with before showed up and…"

Revelations

Danais shook his head but couldn't help but laugh. No judgement on his end. Well, maybe a little, Leo was late for his own celebration.

"Let's not judge me until you know me better."

"I'm an Atorathian. I would never judge the sexual adventures of another human. I'm slightly offended by the accusation."

Leo was not moved by the comment as he continued to strip for bed.

"Even more reason why you would judge me. Aren't you getting into bed? Come," Leo said as he climbed into the bed.

Danais stripped as well and got into bed. Stared up at the curtains and was a little envious that he would never get to see this life again, and more so now that he had been introduced to it by a magician. He was an Atorathian, so he wondered why he should not be shown this by a noble of Atorath.

"You comfortable?" Leo inquired.

"Yes," Danais replied.

Leo propped himself onto his side and put his hand on Danais' chest. He moved his hand down over his stomach and back up, then down again.

"Do it, and I'll chop off your hand," Danais said with his eyes closed. He opened his eyes and stared into Leo's. They were the blue of the clearest ocean. Leo's hands seemed like magic as they moved over his body.

A sigh escaped Danais as he spoke. "You're good at this."

"I studied massage."

Silence dropped between them. Danais closed his eyes and sighed. "What is it that you see in me?" He had been wondering all night and now was as good a time as any to ask. Leo turned him over before answering so he could work on his back.

"I don't know, really. From my first sight of you, you were too far away to see clearly."

"Love at first sight then."

Leo didn't answer; he just continued on Danais' back, then turned him over and crawled on top of him. "Is it okay that I'm on top of you?"

"Well, you're holding your body up."

"That's not what I meant."

Danais looked down then back up again. "You like me. It is

only natural that I excite you. I see my jest about your manhood was a little off."

"Really?" Leo asked, smiling and raising an accusing eyebrow.

"It would seem that I underestimated."

Leo let out a hearty laugh. "If it is too much, I can stop pursuing you."

"Is that what this is? Are you sure it isn't kidnapping by force?"

"You can leave if you want."

Danais flared at Leo's statement. He was tempted to go, but Leo had left him in the bed to consider this and didn't give him any time to get angry. Danais didn't even remember him leaving the bed. Did he leave the bed or just materialise on the balcony? In any event, Danais realised he didn't want to leave and went through the French doors and out onto the balcony. Leo put his arm around him and pulled Danais beside him.

"I wasn't serious," Danais said.

"No?" Leo sounded doubtful.

"Really." Danais tried to sound as sincere as he could.

"No. You were. It was in your tone, the insinuation that I must've used magic to force you here. You don't trust magicians. I respect that. I don't like it. But I understand."

"So, you're a mind reader now?" Danais was immediately upset with himself. That's two times he'd taken what could have been sarcasm and said it with too much anger. Leo, though, hearing the second accusation, decided that he was going to ignore it.

"The view is good from here," Danais said.

"Yes. I find the moon calming. I can tell you do as well. Can I spend the day with you?"

"I must work early on Mal."

"I'll be sure to have you back to work on time. I will ask your uncle at morning. Will you say yes?"

"I'm going back to bed."

Leo let out a sigh, but he didn't take his gaze from the moon. "Should I come with you?"

"Yes."

Danais was shocked at how fast he said yes. Leo was just happy to be following him back to the bed. Danais had planned to turn so that his back would be towards Leo but before he could, Leo had grabbed him, pulling him closer to steal. Then to his surprise, Danais initiated a second one, much more intimate than the first—the kind that lingered in the body long after the kiss was done. Then Danais turned around and let Leo pull him back against his chest. He loved the feel of having Leo's arms wrapped around him. And Leo was more than happy to feel the warmth of Danais' body within his embrace.

This was a nameday that Leo was sure to never forget.

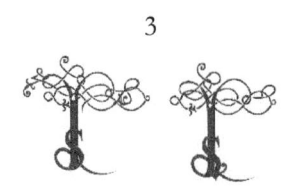

3

Leo woke pleased to find himself still with Danais. Danais had a light snore that Leo thought was cute. He was about to get out of bed, but Xan jumped into the bed to give him a message.

"He suggests you take the boy across in the morning rather than spend the day in the city. He also says that Danais likes the large pastries." Xan seemed to find the second bit of information quite amusing. "It seems he wants to help you but has informed me to ensure you tell no one he's interfering."

Leo also found this amusing. It was clear that something was going on and others were supposed to let it run its course. But he had no doubt that there would be meddling.

"I have that effect on people. What do you think about Danais?"

"I think he's trouble."

"And that means."

"What does it matter? He's no trouble to me. He's your problem."

Leo chuckled before responding. "Would it have been so hard to just say you like him?"

"I have no idea what you mean," Xan replied defiantly, but he couldn't conceal his smile.

"What does your brother think about it?"

"I think you're too good for the child." Kale was already in the bed on the other side of Danais. Leo was too distracted by Xan on his side of the bed to notice.

"Did you sleep with us all night?"

"I had an itch behind my ear, and the boy was happy to relieve it."

"For a race so sensitive about talking to humans, you certainly aren't shy on the sarcasm." Leo let out an awkward scoff-chuckle combination.

"We have to talk amongst ourselves. Why should we lose our wit when we talk to humans?" Kale responded.

"There is some truth in your logic. I'm going to stay in bed for a while and enjoy the moment."

"If you want to miss the boat that is an excellent idea," Xan said.

Leo grudgingly tried to wake up Danais. Danais' response was to glare at him, roll over and rest his head on his chest. Danais mumbled to himself, "the gods must be toying with me." Leo laughed, and Danais mumbled, "If you value your life, you will stop laughing. It's moving your chest and I'm trying to sleep."

Leo chuckled some more. He was enjoying the vibrations the groggy mumblings were making against his chest. "Come on, we have to go. We may miss the boat."

"But the sun isn't up yet," Danais protested while absentmindedly playing with the hair just below Leo's navel. Now it was Leo's turn to say the gods must be toying with him. Danais was lying on his chest while playing with the trail of hair on his stomach. How could he get up from this? But he knew that he must.

"We must get up, Danais. Come."

Danais finally managed to get out of bed, but his eyes were struggling to stay open. Leo had to guide him to the bath. Danais found the bath so relaxing that he almost fell back asleep in the water. But Leo had him out, dressed, and on the dock in double quick time. Danais was in his regular clothes and looked like the peasant that he was. He didn't remember picking up clothes at the inn the previous night so how did he get back in his own clothes? Leo—well, he was Leo. The man everyone was eyeing up.

"I see your second boat ride is going much better," Leo joked as they looked over the boat's edge.

"Just drink your beer," Danais said with a smile.

"If you insist."

"You're tall. Really tall. I don't even make it to your shoulders. Even by Keldonian standards, you're tall."

"You have a problem with that?" Leo asked amusedly.

"No. It's just an observation. I'm climbing on the edge. Just hold me."

Leo did as told and held Danais so he wouldn't plummet to his doom over the side.

"You do realise if I drop you, you'll die." Leo gave Danais a coy smile.

"You won't. Besides, Xan and Kay will destroy you if you let harm come to me."

Leo smiled. "I enjoyed our night."

"I did as well."

"So, you agree we should do it more often then?"

"Persistent." Danais shook his head while smiling. There might have even been a slight eyeroll.

"Yes. And I'm aware that once you are seen with me, people will become interested. And I'm in Atorath, which means the competition will be tough." Leo stared at him seductively. It was always a challenge for a magician to win over Atorathians entirely. Bedding them was one thing but making them yours— they usually finally settled down with their own or a peasant from any province. It was just one of those things. To win Danais and have him stay with him would be impressive.

"I guess I can take you seriously, then. What do I tell people if they ask?"

"That you belong to me. Don't let that stop you from having fun, though," Leo said with laughter in his voice. He was not the jealous type by far. "The ship has stopped. Come." Leo said this and took note of something that he saw. Danais didn't seem to notice. Leo was going to have to remember to ask Barton what it meant.

Danais, though he enjoyed the gold city very much, was glad to be in his own town, where the otherworldliness of the yellow city was gone. He was back to the natural colours of the earth.

The sun had finally risen, and it was just the right time for some delicious pastries. He wanted to watch the boats come and go. As he walked beside Leo from the pier and onto Londar Road, he realised that he may have exaggerated, even if only slightly, the height of Leo.

The mountain people, Danais mused, were the tallest in all Salinor, save the dragons when in human form. At their shortest, they were usually six-feet-five. Leo, Danais thought, was definitely in the middle range—seven, seven foot one, maybe. In any event, he still dwarfed Danais, but at least amongst his own people he'd fit and wouldn't be the tallest amongst them.

"You're practically a giant."

"Not so. In T'nagig, I actually get to feel short."

"You've been to the giant island." Danais could barely contain his excitement. "Is it true they are relatives of the elves? Do the elves exist?"

"Yes. They are immortal as well. They used to roam freely amongst us, debating whether or not they should retreat to their own lands. As I'm sure you know, humans are quite self-destructive even without all our small wars. It was the Tyrant that finally did it. The elves, dwarves and giants finally decided to leave men to their own devices. His quest for burning down cities, stealing magical artifacts for his own means and recreating the divide between magical creatures and humans, they wanted no part of that.

"They each allowed their spirits to roam amongst the lands: the sea sprits, Spartas, which had their homes off the shores of the Giant island; the Kentais, spirits of the earth, whose homeland was in the mountains of the dwarfs in Keldon; and the dragons, spirits of the sky and watchers over all magical creatures, whose homeland is in the realm of the elves.

"Each of the three was created in their homeland in conjunction with a god which is why Danais is lord of the sea spirits. He, in turn, entrusted the Giants, who helped him create them, to guard over their homeland. The same goes for the Kentais. They are creatures for Nuri, Goddess of the Earth, in the care of the dwarves and then the dragons, created for Leos, Goddess of Sun and Sky."

Conversation stopped for a while because they had just

entered the shop and Garnter had some new beans on display Danais had to inquire about.

"Those are Waikin beans. They have a strong scent like cocoa," Garnter explained. "They seem to give you an extra boost and keep you awake, so they call them Waikin. These ones are chocolate-covered so you can just eat them. I can brew you a cup if you like. Give it a try."

"Yes and—"

"Master Vardon. Happy belated name day."

"Thank you, Garnter."

"Are you two—?" Garnter hinted at them maybe a couple.

Leo laughed. "I'm hoping. But the little guy's hard work."

Danais side-eyed Leo.

"That he is," Garnter replied. "But with a heart of gold. Just twelve days ago—"

"Garnter!" Danais protested.

"All right, Danais. I won't tell him what a catch you are." The smile on Garnter's face was annoyingly big, and his tone wasn't making things better.

"Must you glow about me every time I come in?" Danais asked, not giving it the attention the statement required. He was too focused on the displays. "I'll take one of those, oh and three of these too. One of that. Have you anything fresh?" Danais asked. Maybe he'd take something still warm instead. So many choices but only one belly to fill.

"I have a small-pie-sized apple cinnamon, chocolate muffin."

"Great." Danais replied.

Leo thought why not just call it a jumbo muffin but kept that comment to himself.

"I'm sure Leo wants something, too. How about one of the Waikin cups as well?" Danais offered.

"It's best with vanilla liquor. And some like it with milk, though some prefer sugar. I'll make it black, and you can taste it and then add to it to decide your preference."

"Okay." Danais was expecting a fight after ordering so much food. Leo just paid and shared a laugh with Garnter. He didn't order much because Danais had indeed over-ordered. It was more than enough for the two of them.

He led Danais out to a table. It wasn't long before the Waikin arrived. Danais decided that he did like it better with liquor. Leo was not shocked by this. He chose to drink his black. He wondered if they could even be made stronger much like tea had different levels.

"I didn't know what you told me earlier. It was interesting. Maybe it's no coincidence that a Kentai chose to be your Betave. Aren't the dwarf mines hidden within the province of Keldon?"

"Yes. Just like Gornala, one of the cities of the elves. The giant city, you can't find it unless taken by its inhabitants, or you are allowed to remember the secrets of how to find them. Many have tried and failed. The magic hiding them is beyond what most humans can accomplish. The Tyrant fears them. Even though they can all be killed just like humans, he fears they may join the Alliance, making it much harder for him to destroy them."

"This is much more complex than just good and evil."

"Yes. So have you ever been in a relationship before?" Leo already knew the answer from their swim but decided to broach the topic again.

"No. You're the first to pursue me, and I've never tried myself. Or the first I know of. My uncle may have been receiving many requests since I became a man and not told me. I wouldn't put it past him."

"Clearly you've done your share of bedding."

"I'm an Atorathian. We fuck. It's not uncommon for us to start much earlier than others."

"Fair enough. I only just started using the word fuck. Peasants always come up with the most useful words."

Danais had to laugh at that. If it was efficient but unorthodox chances were a peasant came up with it.

"Have you been in a serious pairing?" Danais enquired. He thought mention of a wife had occurred but couldn't remember.

"Twice. Andad and Felat."

"Boy then girl."

"Yes. Been a free man for three years now. Andad was okay. I really loved him. But Felat…"

Danais took note that Leo's entire body language seemed to react to the mere mention of her name negatively.

"I'm still trying to erase that marriage from my mind," Leo

added clearly annoyed he had to even say her name.

"You going to eat that?" Danais asked, gesturing toward Leo's muffin.

"Yes."

Danais pouted, and Leo ignored it. "When is your eighteenth name day?"

"As yours starts spring, mine begins summer, twelve moon cycles from now."

"Ah. Three months. The month of Atora." The irony of falling in love with an Atorathian born in the month of Atora was not lost on Leo.

"And you the month of Salinor. The beginning of spring and the new year."

"Yes. No one knows for sure the precise day of my birth, so they chose the day Atora started his journey up the mountain to save his mother and ultimately falling in love with the goddess, as most men do. With the difference being her falling in love with him back."

"You believe the story?"

"It is one of Salinor's best. He knew that Salinor was rumoured to make a journey up the mountain on the first day of spring. So, he made his way to the island to find that the rumour was true. Then he followed her trail using the tracking skills taught to him by his mother, Ronilas. The start of the trail can only be seen on the first of spring, but once on it, even if you lose sight of the goddess, the trail is still there. To this day, Atora is the only one to follow the right trail after losing sight of her.

"By the time he had made it to the top of the mountain, he was so bruised and broken that he shouldn't have been able to move. But the sight of the gate of the gods, which was the size of a small mountain, gave him strength to move on. That surge of strength was in vain because he stumbled and broke his good leg. He cursed the gods, condemning them to death, and with his one good arm dug his dagger into the ground and slowly pulled himself toward the edge of the mountain to sacrifice himself.

"He threw himself over but was saved. He cried out in anger, defeated. Even after saying a prayer of sacrifice, he was denied and found himself back atop the edge he had thrown himself from. That was when Leanor appeared and asked why he had followed her. Her mother and a few other gods were present, as well…"

"Because I thought you were your mother, I came to ask a favour of the Mother of All."

"And what would you ask of her, Atora?" Leanor asked, an amused look on her face.

"My mother was poisoned. A magician used blood magic to poison another, but the barman put the poison in the wrong glass. My mother is now ill with no chance of survival. We tried many other avenues to save her, but all the magicians told us that we had to go to the original magician. The blood magic used was very strong. We went and asked him to undo his mistake, but he refused. Laughed at us. Knowing that you walk up the mount in spring each year, I made the journey through winter to come to the Island of the Gods in hopes of catching you."

"So here I am," Atora continued. "After days of climbing and broken limbs, after throwing myself to my death to ask you this one favour: will you save my mother?" Atora had no idea if he could just ask a god for a favour without offering something in return—especially the mother of all. But the damage was already done; he'd asked.

"Was it you who decided to journey up?"

"No. I am the youngest of three. Normally, the eldest would be set such a serious task, but it was my mother's idea, and she insisted that if anyone were to survive the journey, it would be me. There were other tasks my brother and sister were better suited for should I fail."

"Do you even know if your mother is still alive? If she was so poisoned, she may not have survived the winter." Leanor was still speaking while the rest listened.

"My mother is a strong woman. And we did manage to slow the result of the poison but not the effects; the pain grows still, even though she is taking much longer to die."

Finally, Salinor spoke. "No."

Revelations

"Then I have failed. But before my life is taken and I join Tara's halls, I would like to say that I am in love with your daughter. I fell in love with her from the moment I saw her, thinking that she was you. She is as beautiful as all the beauty in every world not known to man and this one. Even if I were the greatest god in all the realm, I would still be unworthy of her love. I will be happy to die knowing that I can look upon such beauty."

"You can see me?"

"Yes. Am I not to look upon you? Forgive my ignorance."

"You are the first to make it up the mountain and the only human to be able to look upon me without me dimming my aura. Furthermore, you don't seem to be entranced by the spell I hold on men. You are unique."

"I am my mother's son." Atora thought very highly of his mother.

"This must be some woman," Leanor spoke to her mother words that Atora could not hear.

After a few moments, Salinor addressed him saying, "Tell me, why should I, Salinor, Goddess of All, grant you this request? Who are you to deem yourself worthy of the favour of the gods?"

"And that was when the Atorathian oath—and the oath for the realm of Salinor—was created." Leo finished. "In strength when we are broken, in faith when doubt was certain, in hope against hope we believe."

"We believe," everyone seated outside said. They had all gone quiet to listen to Leo's version of the legend. He said it with such conviction. And it was not uncommon to reply, especially in Atorath, when the oath was spoken.

Leo continued with the oath, "the blessings of Salinor through all the realm," to which the people responded, "the blessings of Salinor." Then he stood, raised his glass, and said "Unity!" Everyone stood up, raised their glasses, and said, "Ronilas, bring us unity forever!" Leo shouted with them. Then they all finished their drinks before sitting back down.

Danais didn't know what to say. He could've said the story

without the oath. But Leo told it in a way that made one want to quiet down and listen. Then he said, "The blessings of Salinor throughout all the realm," instead of "Salinor smile down upon us." Such a proclamation would've typically gotten a "Hail Salinor" in response, and that would've been the end of the oath. But the way he continued was the Atorathian way which led to the different response. Danais was nothing short of amazed by this. It was said that Ronilas was the first human to become a God, so leading to the 'unity' ending of the oath was very Atorathian and other provinces didn't always do it.

It was well known that people believed this story was somewhat of a hoax and that Ronilas was already a God, as were her children. The other version was that they were sent down in human form to save the land. It was more of a legend of sacrifice than that of a wise mother and her children's devotion to save her. Luckily, there were enough people from other provinces that did believe, so the truth never died.

"I'm impressed. You believe our version of the story," Danais commented.

"I feel compelled to. It is said that the Vardon family is one of the lines that came out of Salinor's affairs with humans. She is now one of the gods that doesn't mate with mortals anymore. I've always believed there was a chance I was from her line. I've been doing research for years but found nothing to prove whether or not it is true. Rumour has it her brother, Danais, also favoured the Vardons. I'm not really a Vardon, but still, it would be exciting to find out that my ancestors were related to Salinor herself.

"And I can't want to be a part of her family without believing in this story. Ronilas was behind the War of the Beginning. The only human to be so loved by a god, not only was she made one but sits at her right hand. It's a story worth believing in. And I seem to have a habit of fantasising my birth was the start of something great."

Danais laughed at that last sentence. "I dream the opposite: that my birth was already a part of something great."

"Must be an orphan quality," Leo said with a smile.

"I suspect you are knowledgeable in many areas." Danais mused mostly to himself as he dug into another pastry.

"One could say so. My teacher and Xan were very good. And

apparently, I'm an eager student."

"I've never been told the particulars of the curse. I guess because I am Atorathian I just take it for granted."

"That is to be expected. You don't know much of the father, mother, or the other siblings, do you?"

"I don't. Should I?" Danais was genuinely concerned. How much didn't he know?

"Yes. They all played a very important role in shaping each province. Their father has the distinction of being the only person raised from the grave to be a god. This is the most important family in all of Salinor's history and they were Atorathian."

Danais didn't respond, just finished off the last pastry in silence sensing the mood had changed. After which the two of them left the shop and walked with the dampened mood hanging over them threatening to ruin what could've been a great day.

"It shames me that so many people have forgotten or just take for granted what they did for us. But even if we have grown so accustomed in our ways that we've forgotten where we came from, you should know. Your people should remember. You are Atorathians."

Barton often warned him that sometimes he looked past basic human flaws and expected too much from people. "Humans are flawed. You can't expect them to have such a deep desire in faith and history as you," Leo recalled Barton saying. And Danais was young. It was unfair for Leo to make Danais feel guilty for his shortcomings or for his peoples.' This was one of Leo's flaws, but he wasn't going to stew over it. He'd made Danais feel this way, and he was just going to have to deal with it.

"I am sorry to take my frustrations out on you."

"You are right. I should be ashamed. If not you, someone would've pointed out the fact that there are major gaps in what I know of my own history. I would take it you encounter this in your travels often: people who have misconstrued versions of the beginnings of their provinces, serving gods blindly, and even some things have been lost."

"I do. But as Barton would say, everyone can't be like me."

"True, but we are partly to blame. We just tell our own

versions of the stories when we should seek out the truth. If truths have been lost, it is in part because of us." Danais felt the truth of the sentence as he spoke it and felt a little bit more shame. His uncle and cousin had readily offered many times to teach him more history. He stubbornly refused it for what he thought were better things. He even once had a reading habit. Where did his thirst for understanding desert the action to obtain it? When did he start asking for answers that he could get on his own and start becoming frustrated when he didn't receive them?

"Can I hold your hand?" Leo asked.

Danais obliged, and they walked together in a much more comfortable silence than at the start of their walk. Danais sang to himself when he was relaxed. Leo loved it. The lack of training gave his voice a real quality that set it apart from those of the professionals Leo dealt with. A texture that was hard to come by. Raw and real.

"You have a beautiful voice," Kale said, suddenly walking beside them.

"I do okay. How old are you, Kale?"

"One hundred and fifty of your years. Many years your senior, young one."

"I guess I am still just a child."

"But you have potential."

"Potential?" Danais responded not expecting an answer.

"Yes. That means the promise of something more," Leo spoke like this were a teaching moment.

"I know what it means." Danais nudged him. Leo smiled in response.

"Come," Leo said, directing Danais to climb on his back.

"It hasn't been a week, and already he's taking my spot," Xan said to his brother, exaggerating fake jealousy. Kale just laughed.

"You know you don't mind," Leo said.

"You can still climb up here. I'm not that big. There's plenty of room," Danais added. Kale let out a hearty laugh. Xan rolled his eyes, sticking his chin up clearly stating he did not share. This only brought more laughter from everyone.

They walked on in this way a bit longer. Talking about nothing and everything. Enough time passed that it made sense

Revelations

to have more food. At least this was how Leo felt.

"You hungry yet?" Leo asked, already knowing the answer.

"Hungry? Can a fish breathe underwater?"

"I'll get us something from a shop up ahead. They make decent sandwiches."

Danais hadn't been this far down through Londar for a while. He mostly stayed on the side of town close to the farm.

"Now that's a word I don't understand. Where did that come from? 'Sandwich' refers to food in-between bread? Why not a word that incorporates bread? What does 'sand' or the word 'which' have to do with food?" Danais asked, seemingly at random.

"You ask an interesting question," Leo responded to Danais' statement. "Sadly, no book I've ever read seems to hold the origins of that word. But then, that's like asking where the word "steak" came from. The only other form of steak sounds like something you use to hold up tents. They are known as pegs as well. Or you can say to stake your claim, which makes a certain sense, seeing as in its literal form that's exactly what a stake does: it holds fast to something or holds something steady. So why is cow, or beef, known as steak? And even more, why is it spelt differently?"

"I'm sorry I asked about the sandwich. I'll have to be more careful with my words. Next, you'll be trying to explain to me how water isn't really blue and it's just the reflection of the sky. You could've stopped at the beginning when it was still interesting."

"Don't make me drop you, small fry." Leo moved like he actually would drop him.

"You would do that? I knew you were no gentleman."

Leo laughed and entered the shop. Once to the front of the line, he ordered two of the same sandwiches. Steak, of course, which was listed as beef on the menu. Leo almost decided to add that to his steak breakdown but decided not to. He also ordered loads of some sauce that he wished he could get the ingredients for, but the chef was still refusing to sell their secrets. After paying, they headed a little way out of the town and sat under a large oak tree. Danais broke off a piece of his sandwich before starting and handed it to Kale. He knew if he didn't, he'd just eat the whole thing.

They mostly ate quietly and looked out at the people walking about. Danais loved his sandwich which Leo was very pleased by.

"You look tired," Leo noted as he set aside the paper his sandwich had been in.

Danais swallowed the last bite of his sandwich before glaring at Leo. "You didn't let me sleep."

Leo ignored the accusation and persisted by asking Danais if he was tired again.

"I am."

"Let me take you home, then."

"It's still a ways to sundown." Danais had a much longer protest, but a massive yawn slowed his momentum. He was extremely annoyed by this. How dare his body betray his emotions.

"Let's go. Come."

Danais did as told and followed.

It was a fairly long walk across the whole city to Chibal Way, but soon they were approaching the farm. As soon as they reached the farm, Danais went straight to bed and was snoring in seconds. Leo, not seeing Torak, decided to go. Danais hadn't really invited him in, and he didn't think it was appropriate to impose himself. Besides, there was always tomorrow.

3
LEO

Having planned to spend a lot more time with Danais, Leo got back to the inn on the mainland much earlier than intended. He had found out Danais' regular route included Licol Street, so he had purchased a room there on the way to the farm. Leo spent the time reading and was in the middle of a very tragic love scene when an annoying sound interrupted him.

"Well, you look amazingly happy," Barton said as he took his seat at the table. One of the servers was already heading over with large mugs of ale, an extra-large one for Leo.

"I had a good day. Short, but good. A walk through the market, lunch under the oak tree. Last night we swam. Well, I swam and held him up. He's of the 'since he's Atorathian he's much better than the rest' mentality. And he doesn't know his history."

"Ah, not this again," Barton said, feeling the need to gulp down his beer and call the server to fill him up. "Not everyone is a serious historian." Barton gave an unnecessarily pleasant thank you to the serving girl. She gave him that beer for free and told him where she stayed. Leo gave him a glare and a smile. "Okay. They are his people, so if he doesn't know any history, he should know a little bit of his own," Barton said.

Leo was glad to see that Barton was faking strain in admitting the truth just to make him feel better that this time he was right.

"Exactly. But it isn't just him. I guess I shouldn't be put out about it," Leo said, thinking that two could play that game. Leo wasn't beyond putting a sigh in that sentence to make it seem like he was forced into seeing Barton's point. Barton laughed. Leo drank his beer to stop himself from laughing.

"You still are interested?" Barton pressed.

"Yes. He's a good listener, though—unlike someone I know who would rather flirt with the staff than listen to me."

"Maybe I'm just tired of talking history all the time. I like it better when you talk about men and women... fuckin'. Now that's a topic worth entertaining."

Leo had to laugh at that. Barton was clearly in high spirits, or at least he was happy for him, and that was why Barton was so cheerful. However, he was about to change the tone.

"What did you get up to after we left?"

"Nothing."

"I know there was a *thing* happening."

"I know how you know, and so you know why I can't tell you. Or who else was there, for that matter."

"I guess I could deal with that," Leo said. He was patient enough; he'd get answers in his own time. "He has issues with magic. He nearly ran out of my field before I could tell him what it was."

Leo noticed the quick smile Barton gave at that statement. "But does he want you in return?"

"Yes. I'm still trying to figure out if this is a good thing."

Barton slammed his drink down on the table, which put a dent in the wood. "You know that even if the warning signs were strewn across the heavens, you'd still pursue him."

Leo really didn't want to admit that his statement was true. That would validate Barton's response. Somehow, he knew he didn't have to. Barton knew him as well as the back of his hand sometimes.

"So, when's the wedding?" Leo asked, trying to take the topic in another direction.

"End of summer. Month of Tomian."

"Sounds good. The weather will be perfect here then."

"Just the way we want it."

"I have questions." Leo felt it was time to reel the conversation back to the point.

Barton took a sip and calmly placed the mug back on the table, contemplating his response. "I can't guarantee you answers."

Leo nodded, accepting this. "Is my father involved?"

"Yes."

Leo's next question was about Torak. He was fairly certain he wouldn't get an answer to that one, so he asked one he was more sure about.

"Is Danais involved in mine, or is his something different?"

"The same."

"We are going to have to leave," Leo sighed, taking another swig of ale. It was more of a statement than a question.

"Yes."

"But I can't tell him."

"No. He has to figure things out for himself—just like you. Help him? I'm sure you can, but you can't outright tell him anything or make it too easy. He must find himself; same as you, even if it's at a slower pace. I take it you haven't bedded him yet?"

"It's not always about that," Leo grunted and took a long swig from a stupidly large mug that looked perfect in his hands.

"So he told you no."

Leo just growled, but he was perfectly sure Barton took that as confirmation. "Don't you have people your own age to harass, Barton?"

Revelations

Barton laughed, but Leo was serious.

"How old do you think I am?" Barton was still chuckling when he responded.

"I don't know. Three hundred and ten?"

"So young," Barton said, keeping up his laughter. Leo just smiled and had his mug refilled.

"Tell me then. Can I at least know that?" Leo realised there was too much seriousness in his voice. He'd intended to fake exasperation at what he didn't know, but it just came off too real. He desperately did want to know, and it showed.

"Are you sure you want to know this?"

Barton had noticed, and Leo didn't feel the need to lie. "Yes."

"Only two hundred and seventy-three. Still got a good three hundred years left in me."

"I was close. Should I indulge his need for more knowledge, or should I just get to know him and let him be?"

"Your teacher and Xan spent the first sixteen years of your life instilling patience and knowledge—even wisdom—into you. Maybe this is why."

"So, you don't know?" Leo was genuinely surprised. He expected Barton to know and refuse to answer.

"Some pieces I must also put together. And I've never met the boy before that day."

"But you knew of him."

"Yes."

"And you knew his uncle, though you haven't spoken to him in the three years we've been here."

"I could've just known of him, same as Danais."

"I doubt it. You've known him maybe even longer than I've been alive. It was in the speech patterns. That leads me to believe this plan was in effect since before I was born, which means that you and Torak know more about our origins than you let on. And Danais." Leo said the last phrase as both a question and a statement, peering into his mug of ale as if deep in thought.

"What about the boy?"

"I noticed something today." When he saw the entire aura of Barton change at that statement, Leo knew the friend he usually talked to was gone and had been replaced by someone much more serious. Leo now considered maybe he shouldn't have brought this up, but it was too late to back out now.

"Explain."

5
DANAIS

Danais woke up in the kitchen. The smell of beef stew engulfed him as he took his waking breaths. He remembered falling asleep in his room, so he had no explanation for why he was waking up in the kitchen. The only explanation might have been that he woke up to relieve himself and was just too tired to go back to his room—or even refasten his pants, apparently. He quickly adjusted his belt and sat up straighter in the chair.

"It wakes," Torak announced, as if Danais were rising from the dead.

Danais groaned. "It would seem so, Uncle."

"So, you had a good week's end?"

"I did. Leo is—interesting."

"Really?"

"Yes. There's something about him. He says he'll stop by tomorrow."

"You're harvesting potatoes tomorrow."

"I know. I told him he would have to talk to you."

"You did, did you?" Torak chuckled and raised an eyebrow, but it was lost on Danais; he was deep in thought.

"Yes," Danais said after a minute. "You made stew? It smells different."

"Lady Vardon made that. It's authentic Mironi stew, made with goat meat. It's just thick enough to have substance and not be too heavy. The perfect viscosity."

"Why are they being so nice to me?" Danais wondered out loud. They didn't even know him before a few days ago.

"She told me you were an exceptional dancer—even better than Lord Vardon. Don't tell him I have said that. After all, he thinks his dance skills are superior."

Danais had no doubt she had said that, but that wasn't the answer he was going for. He did share a few dances with her before he and Leo made their exit.

"It's because of who you are?" Torak responded.

"And the town's people—do they know who I am?"

"Only Garnter would remember back that far. The locals are nice, mostly because of who they know you to be now. You have that effect on people."

"Kale thinks I'm an impatient adolescent."

"He said that?"

Danais could see his uncle was holding back a laugh, but nothing could conceal the amusement on his face. Danais just pouted while saying, "Not in so many words. He said I 'have potential.'" He poured some of his uncle's home brew into a glass and sat back at the table. "Tell Lady Vardon I said thank you."

"She said 'you're welcome' in advance."

"Leo knows a lot. He knows our legends probably better than the scholars here. He even believes it's not a coincidence that he was found by the Vardons on the very day that Atora went up the mountain. The first day of spring."

"And why is that?" Torak was genuinely intrigued it seemed.

"Not sure. Something to do with the Vardon line being one of the human races directly linked to Salinor."

"Sounds like he is an interesting man."

"Very. He speaks to me much like Kale. They both have this way of making me feel ashamed of what I don't know, yet not making me feel so bad as to let it get me down. Did I show you what he made me?"

Danais ran to his room and back before giving his uncle time to process the question or even formulate a response. Then he handed him the orb upon his return.

Torak turned it over in his hands, his face a mix of surprise and appreciation. "Wow. Now this is exceptional. Someone's really trying to impress you. Why the red moon?"

"It's a blood moon, he said."

"Blood?"

"Yes." Danais served them both some stew that was so good they ate in silence. If it were possible, it tasted better than it smelled. Once he was finally done and sipping on the homebrew, Danais decided to ask a question. He wasn't sure if he should, but he needed to know.

"Was this blood magic? Creating this gift" Danais noticed his uncle was taking time to respond. Maybe he had asked the wrong question.

Torak paused, studying his near empty glass before he answered softly, "It is."

"Isn't blood magic supposed to be bad?"

"It's... complicated."

"I need to know, Uncle. Should I keep a gift made with dark magic? Is it a bad omen? Should I be concerned? And if I'm going to spend my time with him, isn't it necessary for me to know what type of magic he uses?" Danais was sure the last sentence was accurate. And if he got the answer to that one, he wouldn't necessarily need an answer to the rest.

"It's easy enough to explain. Blood magic is sacrifice magic. You have to give part of yourself for it to work."

"Part of yourself?"

"Yes. A finger, a nose. Just blood for something small. The problem with it is that you must tap into the dark part of your soul to do it. You must rip it apart and put it back together. Even if you don't fully succeed, the darkness in the person gets stronger each time blood magic is done."

"Don't succeed?" Danais repeated quietly. He wasn't quite sure what his uncle meant by not succeeding.

"Depending on the conviction and skill of the magician, the success of the spell may vary. If you don't do it well at all, whatever you give will not grow back. The more serious the sacrifice, the more powerful the spell and split of soul."

"So, giving an eye would be more sacrifice than an ear?"

"Exactly. That is why there are some magicians missing an eye or a finger. It's not always a casualty of combat. Sometimes they cut off a hand and one finger doesn't grow back. Sometimes the whole hand doesn't grow back. It takes a certain amount of inner conviction and natural ability to pull off blood magic. And to pull it off repeatedly takes even more skill."

"It's called dark magic because it deals with your inner darkness."

"Yes, and also what it does to the person. Their general aura becomes darker. I'm sure you sense it in Leo."

"He does seem to be more than just serious when things get serious." Danais frowned. "But generally, he seems so light-hearted."

"Yes. Some still hold on a little to themselves. Does it mean the wizard is bad? No more than those who don't practice it are good. You are either good or bad. Practicing darker magic may enhance that but it's easier to hide ill intentions by avoiding it all together. Most of the most vial magicians don't use blood magic and help to promote that it's evil to hide their true intentions. Nothing is ever as simple as it appears but the seed of all blood magic being evil instead of simply dark has been set and it would take centuries to undo that."

Danais considered his uncles words. It definitely gave him much to think about. He continued on with his questions and decided to really dive into it at a later time.

"You know Leo. I can assume you are a close family friend after that whole 'pulling down Lord Vardon's pants' conversation at the Villa."

Torak laughed which was what Danais was going for. He smiled before continuing. "How much of a user is he?"

"He's a heavy user, one of those you should sense from a thousand leagues away. However, he's one of the few that can appear normal. He didn't lose his original personality. But no matter how much a magician holds onto, you can still sense it there underneath the longer you talk to them. It's not something they hide; it just happens to not be so obvious. There is no way you can't get a little darker when you do blood magic, unless you only do it when you're desperate. Leo isn't one of those. It also says a lot about him as a magician that he is the way he is and uses it as casually as regular magic. He definitely didn't need to use it to make this globe, but he did."

"That makes a certain sense. Sometimes while I'm around him, I do feel like I should be on my guard. On the other hand, I still feel like he couldn't harm me. It's a mixed feeling—not quite like my natural hate toward magicians. Different and only after one full day with him."

Torak nodded. "Understandable."

Danais thought about this. He found multitudes of reasons why this Leo thing was an overwhelmingly bad idea. But even though it seemed that way on the surface, there was one thing his mind refused to let go of: he was interested in Leo.

"So how do you feel about him?" Torak asked, trying to change the topic if not the subject a bit.

"He's everything I'm not. Smart, patient, fair, educated. Tall."

"Tall?"

"Yes. He has more than two feet on me."

Torak laughed. It was true enough.

"Come to think of it," Danais continued, "he made this globe while holding me afloat and putting up a protective field. Wouldn't it take a certain amount of mind talent to do more than one spell at a time? Even if they were small?"

"Well, that would depend on the reach of the field and what it was capable of doing."

It was a reasonable answer.

After what Leo had told him about magic, Danais was sure that at the very least this was a medium—power shield, barrier, field. Which word was more acceptable? He would have to ask Leo. At the time, however, he had thought it was more, though. To accurately perform magic while holding the field up and keeping him above water, Leo had to be a pretty exceptional sorcerer. Wizard? Magician? What did he prefer to be called? Were there rules to the titles?

He would respect them whatever a magician chose. Why was he even thinking about chosen indentifiers anyway. He'd have to real his overactive mind before hi got so lost he couldn't stay in the conversation. Still, what did Leo prefer to be called. Sorcerer Leo had a nice ring to it. A certain flair that matched they whole blood magic conversation. He thought it one more time. Maybe sorcerer Vardon.

"One day I'm going to teach you how to let your mind breathe." Torak shook his head amused.

"Is it that obvious?" Danais asked with an exasperated sigh.

"It always has been. Your mother was the same way, except she was more intuitive, not so much prone to panic. Wise, even. I remember one time we—"

Danais was all big-eyed and open ears. His uncle was about to tell him something about his mother. It was very rare he heard anything about her. Why had he stopped? What was he about to say that was so important he just trailed off?

"Why can't you just tell me who she is?" Danais shouted then stormed out of the house.

He ran through the woods past his usual spot and down a trail that led to a river. He walked over the cool sand and smooth rocks and waded into the water. That was when he noticed something overhead.

Kale flew down and landed in the water with a soft splash.

"How do you know where I am? You aren't a Betave. Do we still have that same type of connection?"

"Yes, but it's not as easy. It doesn't usually happen with a human and one of the spirits of the earth and is even more uncommon when that human is not a magician. Magicians are the only ones with Betaves after all. There's something more when it is with the spirits of the earth too because they were already magical to begin with, unlike a normal Betave.

"You and I have something similar, but the connection isn't quite the same as with a magician so it's new territory still. I'll have to look into it to see if another spirt-nonmagician bond has been recorded before. You are troubled?"

"You sensed that?" Danais knew the answer, but it was the only response he had.

"Only because I've put myself on alert for such things."

Danais nodded. There might be times that a natural detection might happen but under the circumstance opening Kale specifically opening himself up to certain emotions made sense.

"My uncle almost let something about my mom escape him. I can only assume by the abruptness of his stop that it must've been something important. It might've changed what little I do know about her."

"And I take it you stormed out and ran from the farm in a fit of anger," Kale stated matter-of-factly.

Danais laughed. Hearing it said like that made his own behaviour sound immature. But Kale's tone was like the tone of a much older brother scolding him—and the humour was obvious.

"I did. Why can't everyone be like Leo?"

"Leo?" Kale raised an eyebrow.

"Yes. I thought he was like you, but at least he has the decency to blatantly ignore my ignorance and continue talking.

He's always neutral."

"From what I understand he's always had a cool demeanour, probably because of the blood magic."

"Can Kentais naturally disappear and reappear like Betaves learn to do?"

"We can."

"What's it like to fly?" Danais looked to the sky. There were Atorathians who could fly. Even the peasants. They were direct descendants of a particular line of Atorathians that had been granted the gift. It wasn't guaranteed otherwise there would be a lot more flying humans. But Danais had always dreamed he'd be one of them.

"You'll know one day."

"I will?" Danais was taken aback by this response. What were the odds he'd think this, and Kale would speak it? He had a feeling a lot of stranger coincidences were in his future. Hopefully, they all proved to be good.

"Yes. One day you'll soar like the eagle." Kale waved his hand towards the sky as they both looked up to the stars.

Soon after, the two of them walked back towards the land. Danais laid on his back across the smooth stones lining the river while Kale sat beside him, just close enough for Danais to absentmindedly pet him.

"You have any children?" Danais made a mental note that if this flying thing were true and not a metaphor it meant big things about who he was. Monumental even.

"Five sons. Six daughters."

"Any Betaves?"

"Xan is the only Betave in the family at present."

"Your brother?"

"Yes, it isn't that often one of the spirits becomes a Betave. Even less for the dragons. They are particularly touchy about it as in the beginning of the Tyrant's reign he sought to use their power. Their homeland, which he could find easily before he went so far evil, was closest to where he was raised. Closer than where our homeland is hidden. Also, in Keldon."

"Dragons? Like huge flying beasts, or shapeshifters?" Danais talked his way into the answer, realising neither of those could be true, but he couldn't pull the question back inside his mouth.

"Small. Not much bigger than us. They were here before our

time. The first of the three spirits to be created. Trying to steal power from a magical creature, even humans depending on what you're trying to steal, is a painful torturous process. Worse than simple interrogation. But it's all a part of where the Tyrant's power comes from."

"I'll have to ask Leo about the dragons. I don't know much about them. Or the water spirits. Or Kentais, really." Danais walked out of the lake onto the smooth grey stones that lined it, stripped, and then looked up at the stars. It was a warm night. "I need to learn to swim. I wonder if Leo will teach me."

"You could ask him."

"I guess, but I'll be busy all week. Maybe I'll—" That was the last he said before falling asleep. Kale said a prayer to the gods, Danais and Atora, to watch over the boy. Moments later, the water spirits arrived. Four of them came and lifted Danais into the water as Kale flew away.

In the distance, a man looked out from amongst the forest trees. He couldn't believe his luck. A stroll of solitude in the forest and he stumbled upon this. Who could this boy be that a Kentai and the children of the giants and Danais, would watch him? He walked a few paces and heard something. He threw a stone and was rewarded with a thump in the trees. He walked a few paces and found a dead badger, not a Betave.

"You won't be reporting to your master tonight. But I will be reporting to mine. In time."

"Are you sure?" Barton asked after hearing Leo's story. He'd just told him the thing he noticed on the boat ride with Danais.

"Yes, I'm sure."

"This could be bad."

"How so, Barton?"

"Well, it's fast. Faster than predicted. Something's changed."

"Should I be on alert?"

"Yes."

"And don't tell Danais."

"No. He won't become more alert without an explanation— an explanation that you can't give him. If he figures it out on his own, then that's okay."

"I will hire an Atorathian guard, one who's discreet, so no one knows we're being followed."

"Do you want one or two?" Barton agreed with this choice.

"One. If they have the killing skills of a Mironian, even better."

"You think it means someone's after you already?" Barton thought it could be a possibility.

"Not sure," Leo said with a shrug. "But if you're concerned, I should cover all angles; if it's important we stay alive, then alive we shall be. Kale?" Leo was surprised to see him appear before them.

"Yes. I just left the young one."

"Alone?"

"The sea spirits are guarding him."

"The sea spirits. And why would they guard him? Who exactly is he?" Leo wasn't expecting an answer, but he was intrigued.

"They did it because I requested it," Kale stated.

"It is possible that a spirit can make a request of another spirit. Yet, somehow, I think there's something more here." Leo looked at Barton who sipped his drink feigning cluelessness. Leo could only smile at the obvious fake innocence. He wasn't going to get a response but that was fine.

Kale shrugged. "If you say so. Four came. They took him into the ocean."

Leo made an instant connection, but without enough proof, he was just going to have to wait to verbalise this discovery. "I made him an orb with a blood moon."

"You used blood magic?" Barton was shocked. He knew his friend was a user, but something more seemed to be going on in his mind.

"Yes." Leo had the sudden feeling he'd made a big mistake.

"Why? Suppose you scared him away?"

Leo shrugged. "Clearly, he didn't understand. If I am correct, he asked his uncle, and now he understands quite well. It won't bother him."

"And you're sure of this?" Barton didn't look convinced. More worried.

"I think I know enough of him to be sure."

Revelations

Leo was full of confidence. Enough so it killed Barton's worry instantly. "You spent a day with the boy." Barton laughed.

As Barton laughed Leo thought maybe it wasn't such a bad mistake after all.

"What could you have possibly learned in that time?" Barton added.

"It was an informative day."

Both Kale and Xan rolled their eyes at that response.

"It wasn't that informative. Leo just happens to be very intuitive," Xan said.

"Xan—" Leo cautioned.

"What? It was a compliment?"

Leo could see that no one was convinced.

"Compliments don't count when they are disguised as insults."

"Well, that explains why you miss so many of them. To think I thought you were genuinely accusing me of being hard on you when it was just you stubbornly ignoring praise." Xan's acting was so genuine he almost fooled himself.

"Praise. So that's what chipping away at my self-confidence is called." Leo accused.

"Yes. Clearly, all my hard work teaching you was wasted."

"How so?" Leo had the distinct feeling he didn't want the answer, but this conversation was so fun he risked it.

"You should know how to accept a compliment, no matter its form, with grace and dignity."

"Bah." Leo dismissed him with a wave of his hand. "Was he always like this, Kale?"

"I don't know what you are implying. He seems alright to me," Kale said, confused.

Leo let out a defeatist sigh as the three of them laughed. *Why have enemies when you have friends who are evil?* A subject change was needed.

"The boy can't swim. He wants you to teach him," Kale said, and that was when Kay arrived and hopped onto Barton's lap.

"Peach liquor?" she asked as Barton rubbed behind her ear.

"Yes. Peach for a peach. Hop onto the table, and I'll pour you a glass," Xan said smoothly.

"Thanks, Xan. At least someone knows how to treat a lady."

She directed that comment to all the others. No one took her up on it though.

"Thanks. I do what I can."

"Stop gushing over her. Besides, a rabbit is way beyond your dating scale," Leo said.

"Jealousy will get you nowhere." Xan didn't bother to look in Leo's direction.

"Jealousy of what?"

"The fact that I'm bedding, and you—well, you are being strung along by a child," Xan spoke coolly, which made it all the more funny to everyone else.

"I've known him only four days," Leo responded, knowing it was a mistake the moment it escaped his lips.

"Usually it only takes you moments."

Leo sighed and laughed with them. He decided on an 'if you can't beat 'em join 'em' approach. After the laughter died down, Leo spoke again.

"So how do we all feel about me getting a guard?"

"Wise. Something seems to be changing. And not at the pace it should be," Kay said.

"Should I return to the seer?" Leo asked.

"No. Readings so close together, especially storm-inducing ones are not wise. You have to let the magic around it settle. Besides, she has many other readings to do. Premonitions that she has to follow. It isn't just about you and Danais with her. It's about everyone. Even the Tyrant," Barton offered.

"I take it that being a seer is much more intricate than I believed it to be."

"It is. But the seers with mediocre powers always break the rules, and that's why some things seem the norm when they're really not."

After that statement, the innkeeper came over with a letter and handed it to Leo. Leo opened it and inside was a small seed. The letter read:

"For your 28th name day. It is only just arriving because it took me a while to perfect it. But I got it right and flew it here personally. Follow the instructions carefully and choose wisely. Your friend, Lor."

"Lor? Who is Lor?" Barton asked.

"Now that is a secret I can't tell you," Leo said. He delighted

Revelations

in the fact that Barton wasn't the only one with secrets.

4
LEO

Leo woke up the next day ready to go. The weekend seemed too short, but here he was on the second day, washed and walking to the farm, even though the sun was still trying to creep its way over the trees.

The first day was part of the weekend which he found odd. Why not have the end be the end, but what did he know? He wasn't there when the moon cycles, weeks and hours and other such things were set in stone, so it was a conundrum for another day.

"Already working?" Leo had just arrived at the farm.

He didn't know why he was so shocked to hear Torak say Danais was already in the field. He knew Danais took his job seriously, but still, the sun was only just managing to shed some light on the fields and his only experience with Danais in the morning involved him trying not to get out of bed.

"Yes. I suggest you go out and get to work unless builders are afraid to get their hands dirty."

Leo didn't even dignify Torak with a glare. If any of Salinor's people were accustomed to getting dirty, it was the builders. It was a running joke that one could only tell what a Mironian looked like after he washed off the dirt.

As he walked out across the fields, for the first time he realised just how large the farm was. It was no wonder it could supply the town and the closest parts of the city of Leanor. It was even harder to believe that all this land was halfway up the side of a small mountain.

It took him a while to find Danais, and when he did, Danais wasted no time in showing him the most efficient way to get a potato out of the ground. By the time the sun was in full bloom, Leo realised that he couldn't survive the sun with his shirt on.

It wasn't so much that it was that hot; it was much hotter in Mironi, but the work made the shirt a burden. His pants were okay, but the shirt he wore just wasn't equipped for the gruelling work, and he was bound to rip it to shreds.

"I'm glad that you came," Danais said.

"You mean I have large arms, big hands, and hanging sacks over my shoulders makes for quick work."

Danais let out a good laugh. "True. However, you're good company, even if we haven't said much so far."

"So how does lunch work on the farm?"

"A cart travels around with bread, and there are carts of water around the fields. Bread serves as energy. Too much real food tends to make us satisfied, and we don't feel like working. Usually there's a very light meat broth, also. We eat real good during breaks, though. Uncle treats us well. Considering the pay of a peasant, it helps to not have to bring your own food. I hear most farmers aren't so generous."

"They aren't. That would explain why the workers here are so happy." Leo looked around and indeed the atmosphere felt good.

"So, tell me about Ronilas." Danais inquired.

"Ronilas?"

"Yes." Leo was impressed. Danais seemed to have an interest in learning more about his own people and Leo was always happy to dish out some learning.

"Ronilas was an exceptional woman. She was good in everything that each province is known for." They off-loaded some potatoes then headed back to their spot before Leo continued. The potato carts followed the workers in each row and left when full, only to be replaced by other empty carts. "She taught her children these skills and each excelled in a different one. She was also an excellent seamstress, which gave her good standing in a magician-ruled world."

"Good standing?"

"There wasn't equality through the land during that time. There were magicians and peasants. Everyone not a magician was lower class, and Atorath was the only province without any native magicians. Occasionally, there were a few people so good at what they did that the magicians gave them a certain amount of status in the realm."

Revelations

"How did she teach her children such skills? I thought it was unlawful for non-magicians to learn combat and writing back then."

"It was. But one of her great-great uncles on her mother's side—her mom, although Atorathian had a great-aunt who was a second wife to a magician who had many wives—was born a magician. In those days, magicians were immediately sent to schools in the area and cut off from their less worthy families so much that they didn't even recognise them in later years. Ronilas' uncle, however, never forgot his poorer side of the family. He kept in touch with all his non-magician relatives, and a few generations down Ronilas was born. There was something about her that made him go beyond just keeping in touch and secretly providing things for his less than fortunate family. He taught her."

Danais took this all in. Magicians didn't marry peasants, so the fact that one was a second wife meant it was just a ruse. If it was legal, she probably would've been his first wife. Lastly, what are the odds that only one child of this mixed relationship was a magician and that this child kept interest in all his mom's peasant offspring and their offspring as well? And what was it about Ronilas that made him go above and beyond for her?

"It wasn't easy work; he had to do it in secret. But she was amazingly adept at all he knew, so he encouraged friends he trusted to also teach her what he could not. Ronilas then taught these skills to her children. The eldest, Stran, was the sculptor. He was very good with his hands, and he would wield them as weapons. The second, Nera the daughter, was the assassin. She had a keen eye for detail. She was exceptionally good at stealth, unarmed combat, and all forms of weaponry. And the last, Atora, was the hunter. He could track anything. Ronilas kept her talents well-hidden but enforced them through the guise of a seamstress. Wisdom was by far her greatest talent."

"How so?"

"When she would get invited into the homes of the rich, they would naturally hold important conversations while she measured and consulted with them on colours and material. She would manipulate them into doing things that would benefit the less fortunate in such a way that they wouldn't dare hold her accountable, because it would admit they were not smarter than a peasant. And an Atorathian at that."

"But they would've figured it out. Why keep using her?"

"Simple vanity. They wanted her work so badly that they were willing to sacrifice the chance of being used. You dropped a potato. Sometimes she also helped them with political endeavours as well, so the meetings also worked to their benefit. She's the only peasant in that time recorded to have gained the trust of the magicians in such a way; they used the guise of seamstress much the same way she did."

"So, they valued her but were too ashamed to admit it. It's too bad no one could help get rid of the poison spell and the one who did wouldn't. If they knew what that one decision would lead to, I doubt any magician would've let him refuse her."

"You're probably right. But then the Atorathians of today and even Salinor itself would not be what we know it to be now. It was meant to happen this way."

"So magicians and Atorathians, though they can be enemies, have found a way to work together. Magic has its uses, and our gifts seem to blend well with that."

"Exactly." Leo may have sounded a bit too excited.

"What is different now than when she did it?"

Leo decided not to answer. He was willing to give the boy all the answers, but Danais had to learn how to figure things out on his own if he was ever going to get through his impatience. Leo remained calm and impassive through Danais' tantrum and then dug in silence for a few moments after.

"The Tyrant."

"Things are different now. The lines aren't clear anymore. All humans will work for whatever serves their best interest whereas in the first war it was a fight for freedom, now it's all about power."

"There are Atorathians working for the Tyrant?"

Danais' whole mood changed. He wasn't surprised it was just that verbalising it made it real. Leo looked like he was about to formulate a response. Possibly to make Danais feel better, but he spoke before Leo could.

"Don't do it. Don't lie to me."

Leo could see the anger that had risen on Danais' face and decided to move on.

Revelations

"So... I told you Atora's story yesterday. And now you've asked for Ronilas'. After they reached the top of the mountain. . ."

"Would you allow my mother the chance to save herself?" Atora asked.

Salinor considered this. She decided there was only one answer. "Yes. I commission her to weave my daughter a dress. And she is to use the material of the gods."

Atora knew that only the gods could work the material. Setting this task was just a more elaborate 'no' like the one he had previously been given. Still, he journeyed home and relayed the message. Salinor had only given her three days to do this task. On the night before the first day, Salinor's Phoenix arrived with the material to be used. All three children were present at the time. She sent a message through the phoenix asking for the whole week. Salinor, thinking it an impossible task, granted the extra days, speaking through the Phoenix.

As the bird left, Atora and Nera fled the house. Ronilas took the fabric and slept with it for three days then toiled over it for the last four days. On the last day, a big ceremony was being held on the island which had not yet been named after Leanor. The Gods were sure this would be a death celebration. The humans were just intrigued by the idea that a human was commissioned to do a work for the gods and that they had come down from their mountain to celebrate. No one knew if she had succeeded, but everyone doubted she could do it. No mortal could work with the material of the gods.

"I see you have come bearing gifts."

"Yes. My apologies for capturing your Phoenix."

The Phoenix was a hard creature to catch for humans. They always seem to disappear right before one can entrap them. "But I needed it for your gift. My son is an excellent hunter, and my daughter has eyes better than any mortal. He tracked him, and she took it down. With my youngest son's memory of your horse from atop the mountain, I commissioned my eldest son to carve a life-size likeness of you atop the horse with the phoenix perched behind you. I assure you no permanent damage was done to the Phoenix."

All this was well and good and Salinor seemed intrigued, however, nothing was mentioned specifically about the main gift yet.

"How did you handle the yellow stone? It has never been done before. None of the buildings here are built with it."

"I assumed that some of the power of the gods would be imprinted on a Phoenix that spent so much time beyond the gate. It was a very hard spell to work, but a magician friend of mine managed to give my children power just long enough, under my eldest's guidance, to complete the statue. I doubt it will ever happen again unless another creature that has spent more than a lifetime beyond the gate should happen upon us."

Salinor could not hide her amazement. She was thoroughly pleased—not pleased enough to spare the woman, but enough to give her the praise due for such a godly gift.

"Am I to believe that is the dress you have in that bag? Or are you stalling because you have failed?"

Salinor seemed too confident. Ronilas looked at Leanor and could see that she looked broken at the fact that Ronilas might soon be gone. Indeed, it would be a loss for a woman on her last days to be given renewed strength for a week, only to be killed.

But there was more.

Ronilas was prepared to stake the life that was already on the line, that Leanor was as smitten with her son as he was her. And he could stare directly at her: a feat Ronilas was finding more difficult with each second. Her glow did not bother Atora at all, and he was not overwhelmed with unnerving lust or the need to kill to see more of her beauty.

That was the effect she had on men and women who looked at her for too long.

"What is your name, mortal?" Salinor inquired.

"Ronilas."

This Salinor also found interesting. It was, of course, her name in reverse. Maybe that had something to do with why she was so intrigued by this person.

"My mother, though unable to read, was fascinated with any verbal wordplay, puzzle, or game. If she could have written, she would have spelt it backwards. As it was, she could only play with the sound of the name."

"Ronilas took the dress and handed it to her son," Leo continued. "There were gasps from everyone and a look of complete shock on the face of Salinor. Leanor smiled as Atora brought the dress toward her. She stripped, put on the dress, and only then decided to let down her glow so all could see the gown. The bottom half of the gown seemed to be made of different layers of sheer blue. As it flowed in the wind, it gave the effect of a rippling ocean. The middle section of the dress was embroidered with the Phoenix: red, blue, and purple in more than one shade of each.

"There was a laced rope design zagging across the chest. The back of the dress was also made of the same solid material as the front, and in the same shade of blue with an extremely detailed depiction of Salinor's tree, said to be the birthplace of Leanor. The sleeves were solid as well, with the sheer fabric flowing on top of it. The sleeves were loose and widened down the arm but stopped halfway down Leanor's thumb. The way the dress sparkled and the way it mimicked flowing water was breath-taking. Salinor then and there decreed that anything of indescribable beauty would be described as 'beautiful as Ronilas' gift to Leanor.'"

"That would explain why she has the largest temple in the middle of Leanor," Danais mused. "So Ronilas was the mastermind behind the operation?"

"Exactly."

It was now about an hour after lunch, and the harvesting still didn't seem to see an end. Leo continued with his story.

"She started the Alliance, which was crucial to the change in the land. With the new powers gifted to the people of Atorath—it was called something different back then—she destroyed the magician who poisoned her in hand-to-hand combat. The resistance to magic was the gift of Salinor, and the hunting abilities were the gift of Leanor because those were the talents Atora used to follow her.

"Ronilas sent her three children to help recruit for her army while she secretly trained soldiers in Atorath. It was through her children that she found out special qualities like Keldonians adeptness to healing and herbs and Mironis to building, and Danis close connection to the sea. And was about the time the Alliance really began recruiting."

"What about the peasants?"

"Sadly, peasants aren't good at fighting with other powerful humans. They died too easy, and it was risky in war. They could, however, help with things for the Alliance, so they were recruited for such things. Once they had been to all the provinces and scouted all the land, Nera, the daughter, sent word to her mother of the perfect place for the secret location of the Alliance."

"Nera stayed for a time in Mironi. This is why they are the best assassins. Those were her skills. She trained the magicians there in that area, as they were the most adept in all the provinces. Atora stayed in Keldon. That is where the best magical herbs are; Keldonians' natural skill was healing. He was good at helping the magicians there with understanding how the body works and making good use of the herbs after the magicians explained to him what they were. Domal stayed in Danais. They were exceptionally good at making weapons with magical qualities. And he could help them refine their art.

"Ultimately, once they felt they had trained at least one person well enough to continue training others, they each took a group with them to the secret location to continue training and grow the Alliance. Nera became second-in-command, working from the Alliance headquarters while her mom began to restructure what is now Atorath."

"So even right from the beginning, it was in secret. I guess it only makes sense. If the ruling magicians knew, they might have tried to stop her plans." *That's the obvious conclusion,* Danais thought.

"Yes. So that is most of the story of Ronilas. Equality began with Atorath, and it was fought hard for. That's why it's so sad that we have people in each province thinking they're better than the rest, looking down on peasants. We've strayed so far, especially in Atorath. Here," Leo moved his hands in a way to emphasise the *here* without having to say Atorath, "the example, the standard, should be being set instead of falling prey to the same prejudices the rest of the land has succumbed to." Leo could see that Danais was upset at that last statement, but he meant it.

"Thank you for coming today," Danais told him.

"I'm not afraid to get my hands dirty."

Danais looked up at him and smiled.

"Everyone's looking at you like you're a slab of beef."

"Bah. Let them look. Hopefully, they're thinking what you think when you look at me."

"You're reading my mind?" Danais was instantly on the defence.

"No. But you just confirmed your unclean thoughts of me." Leo chuckled.

"That's unfair," Danais said with a pout, getting back to work.

"Unfair?" Leo feigned confusion.

"You baited me. You knew I'd assume you'd read my mind."

"A man has to have some fun. And you look good when you pout."

"Ah, so it wasn't about getting me angry; it was more about the pout after."

"And the smile after the pout."

"Just stop talking and fill the sacks," Danais demanded with a smile.

Leo did as he was told. He was glad to see Danais was eager to learn and was growing to like him. He was increasingly sinking into his feelings for the boy—so much so that he wanted to tell him of the chance of danger.

But he wouldn't. He had promised Barton that he wouldn't.

6
DANAIS

Danais decided to just think for a while. It was so much information to take in: his own people working for evil; his obvious lack of knowledge; the intricacies of the story that made Atorath and the realm what it is today. It angered him to think that Atorathians could do such things. How could it have gone so wrong? When did the lines of good and evil become so blurred?

"The sun looks like it's finally starting to go down and we're finished. I'm sure the other workers appreciate your strength and the view," Danais said, looking down. "Not even magical undergarments could hide that."

Leo shrugged. "You excite me."

Danais loved how easy Leo was: not quick to anger, not easily embarrassed, unassuming and almost lethally handsome. Everything he wasn't. Yet here Leo was—a Richie, a Vardon—and genuinely interested in him. Something had to be wrong with the world. But why complain? As long as the gods were smiling down on him, he was going to enjoy it. And why was Leo looking at one of the other workers?

"I'm heading back to the house. Clearly, all the stories I've heard about you are true."

"Bah!" Leo said with a smile before he headed over to the girl. Danais started toward the house. He grabbed a small bottle of wine and sat at the kitchen table once he entered. He didn't feel tired, but he was clearly mentally exhausted.

That was what he concluded after waking up hours later, having never poured his first glass.

"How long have I been asleep?"

"A few hours," his uncle replied.

"Leo?"

"Out back, playing with the dogs."

"Our crazy dogs?" Danais knew those dogs saw everyone as

the enemy except for family.

"Yes. They seem to like him. Shocking, I know. But no harm has come to him."

"He stayed?" Danais was mad at himself for the obvious amusement in his voice.

"In a manner of speaking. He only just came back an hour or so ago. So how did it go?"

"Great. I learned about Ronilas today. He's different."

"How?"

"He encourages my over-thinking at times when most would stop me. And when I get mad, he refuses to talk to me. I can't stay mad, 'cause he won't teach me."

Torak lifted an eyebrow. "What you're saying is he lets you dictate the flow of conversation."

Danais could see his uncle was doing his best to hide his amusement. He doubted his uncle believed a word of that sentence.

"No. It only appears that way. He'd be letting me control the flow if he fought when I was mad or answered me all the time when I asked questions. But he's controlling me in a way that I'm...I don't know, really. I guess I'm just afraid."

"Magically?"

"No. Of what he's doing to me. But not in a bad way. It just makes me—"

"Uncomfortable," Kale said as he suddenly appeared and hopped onto the table, taking notice of the wine. "Torak, you always seem to have the best wine."

"It's a recent thing," Torak replied. Danais decided to avoid the insinuating stare.

"He scolds me in a way that I've never experienced. It angers me more because I know I'd be wrong to retaliate. He angers me a lot, actually." His uncle laughed. Danais wasn't surprised he would find this interesting—but he didn't expect him to find it *that* interesting.

"But still, you are fond of him."

"I'm young. He's older and mature. I'm at a disadvantage. And he's taller than me." Danais had no idea where that last statement came from. He was however aware that it always came back to that, and his uncle would notice this too.

"Ah. So it's the height after all. Interesting."

Danais smiled. He couldn't ignore the insinuation this time. His uncle knew him well enough. That was when Leo walked in, confirming this fact. Danais did like the height. Leo's shirt was back on, and there was only a hint of the smell of sex still on him. He must've had a quick bath.

"You're awake."

"It would seem so."

"Good. I feel like a walk down to the water. And you could use a swim. You're still dirty from work."

Danais ignored the obvious, which was that he couldn't swim. "Do you know your way?"

"No."

"Then how will you find the way?"

"You're going to show me. Come."

Danais followed Leo. He could've been difficult but a night under the stars, by the water and with Leo was much more appealing. He led him to the spot he was at with Kale the previous night.

"The waterfall is around that rock face there. Not too far," Danais said after they had been walking for a while.

"We should go that way sometime. I'll teach you how to swim now."

Now it made sense. Leo could've just told Danais he had intentions of teaching him how to swim but that would've been too easy.

As soon as they got to the water, Leo started to strip. Danais did the same and then followed him in. Leo picked him up when he could no longer stand and carried him farther into the water. Danais started panicking.

Could Leo be about to try the sink or swim technique?

Was Danais really about to drown to death?

Again, he'd allowed himself into the hands of a magician, only to be carried into dangerous territory. This was even worse than before. This time, he had allowed himself to be taken into dangerous depths of water by the very hands that might try to kill him.

"Relax," Leo said in almost a hum. Danais wasn't sure he could accomplish that, but Leo didn't give him much time to make a decision. He had Danais turned over already, holding him with one arm under his chest and the other below his waist.

Revelations

"And get your head out of the water."

"My head's not—" Danais started but couldn't finish. He pouted, and Leo smiled. He was going to have to stop pouting so much, seeing as Leo derived so much pleasure from it. He didn't see how he could do this when Leo seemed to know just how to press his buttons.

Leo instructed him in the movement of the basic breaststroke. Danais wasn't expecting such a hard first training. He wasn't sure how much time had passed but it seemed like he'd been moving his arms and legs forever. He was certain that if Leo weren't holding him, he would've drowned a long time ago, however long he'd been at it. Finally, he heard the words he'd been dying to hear. Danais thanked the gods because he was quite sure he couldn't perform another stroke.

Since he didn't have to swim anymore, Danais did what came naturally to him: he climbed onto Leo's back. Before he had a chance to thoroughly enjoy the starry sky, Leo was putting him back to work. He strongly considered not letting Leo go and putting up a fight. He weighed the options of being strong enough to defeat Leo and decided that Leo would surely still put him to work after he wasted all his energy trying to hold on. It didn't make sense, so he grunted instead and got back to swimming.

"Okay, I'm going to let you go now. I'll hold you up with magic and slowly release it until you can swim alone. Hopefully, you can accomplish that before night's end."

Leo couldn't be serious. "It won't be night's end until daybreak," Danais protested.

"Then we have plenty of time," Leo said.

Danais groaned. If he wasn't so determined to learn, he would've protested the moment Leo mentioned using magic on him. Danais also didn't want to appear weak. He kept telling himself he was a man so today he was going to keep his mouth shut and his anger in check and do as instructed. His journey toward being the man he wanted to be was going to start with learning to swim.

Danais was swimming with Leo walking beside him, going a certain distance away and then coming back, with short rest periods every few laps. Danais was shocked at his own insistence on continuing though with every stroke he felt he couldn't do another. When did his position change? How did he get so far away from the shore? When did Leo stop using magic? And how did he not notice Leo wasn't beside him this time? He swam back unassisted, realising he was only tired because he had been swimming for so long but not necessarily over-training.

"When did we get out so far? I thought you were walking beside me."

"I started pacing with you by swimming a while ago. You were so focused you didn't notice."

"When did you finally take the magic away?"

"Only just."

"Only just?"

"Yes. I admit I tricked you. I stopped swimming with you and used a little magic to assist you as you went away. I assumed you would think you swam away from me unassisted and come back on your own."

Danais sighed. "Why do you manipulate me so?"

"I don't understand."

"I think you do," Danais said; he wanted a serious answer. It wasn't so much that he had an issue with it. He had learned a lot today. He could finally swim when hours before he couldn't, but then Leo also manipulated Danais to make him pout or intentionally get him angry even though it was for good reasons. Leo seemed like the guy to give him direct, honest, answers. The kind he always craved. Danais felt that he was ready for at least one person to give him unfiltered truth, whether he liked it or not.

"You are too stubborn and strong headed," Leo explained. "I find that direct attacks or the obvious routes don't work—at least not for the tasks you ask of me, so I must manipulate your personality to get the tasks done. Maybe one day I won't have to anymore."

"I think I like you better indirect. Well, at least after that statement," Danais said with a smile. He wanted Leo to be perfectly sure he appreciated his bluntness.

"You're staying afloat quite well."

"You're a good teacher. It's not easy. You don't just become an expert swimmer after someone tortures your muscles for hours. But not sinking does feel good. That being said, swim me back to shore."

"Sure. Would you stay on the shore with me? I brought a few blossoms from the Guiya tree so we can bathe."

Danais had never seen a Guiya blossom so fresh before. He looked at it and took it in entirely. The blossom was the shape and size of an apple, with the segmented appearance of a raspberry. From what he knew of the plant it grew on the extensions of the tree. Its branches would fall to the ground and take root and form mini trunks around the tree. They usually formed appealing columns and rows sprouting beautiful green and red leaves shaped like spiders' webs and a purplish-brown wood.

The blossoms grew in the tree and on the extensions circling up and around like strawberries on a vine. Having never seen the tree Danais made a mental picture of what that might look like. He decided it was beyond beautiful. The blossoms, he heard, formed suds in water and they lasted a long time before they could no longer be used. The trees were hard to find unless one knew where to look. The special thing about the blossom was that it smelled different for each person. It had a way of taking the natural scent of the user and perfuming it much like using scented oils, except that it was a person's own scent. This was the most intriguing part to Danais. He was interested to know just how it would scent for him and Leo. Would it be similar? Drastically different? What if it was the same? Would that mean anything special? Would it just be coincidence?

Danais decided none of that was important at present. He was sure Leo knew just that one item, the blossom, would decide whether he would stay or not. Would Leo ever stop manipulating him, he wondered. After all that thinking about the blossom, Leo had brought them to shore. He didn't even bother to take Danais off his back. Danais had a love-hate relationship with how much he enjoyed being carried this way.

"You enjoy bending me to your will."

"Ah, so the answer is yes." Leo chuckled and finally put Danais down.

Just then a flock of birds flew overhead; somehow this event made Leo check the edge of the forest. Something wasn't right. Danais was about to panic but took a deep breath to calm himself before talking.

"What is it?"

"Nothing."

Danais sighed. Leo was deliberately holding something from him. However, as he looked at him, he could see that Leo was struggling with whether or not he wanted to answer. His life was so simple when he was just a peasant.

"I have reason to believe we might be being watched."

"Aren't we always being watched in secret?" Danais said. It seemed logical considering the past day's events.

"Yes. However, I'm not sure they're always here when I'm with you. They give us room. This, though, is different."

"Not our usual watchers. Should we be concerned? Has anyone told you anything?"

"No…it's more of a feeling, but we are running with it. No harm will come to us. That part I've taken care of. They didn't even want me to tell you, but I don't know it feels right so I'm going with it."

Danais didn't know how he felt about this. He didn't probe 'cause he assumed Leo probably didn't know the same way it was obvious his uncle knew things he couldn't say. Still, he was beginning to trust Leo. He had put his life in Leo's hands three times now: two times in water and once on the side of the ship. He could trust him to take measures to keep them safe, even if Leo didn't want to tell him how.

Unbeknownst to Leo and Danais, two onlookers began to talk in the distance. "It seems we may have stumbled onto something."

"Yes. We have to keep a close eye on things."

"It's too dangerous for you to get too close, but I believe the position you are already in is more than ideal. I'll do the following."

"Do that. We must keep all information secret until we can prove something. If this has links to the Alliance, they have ways of tracking things. We cannot afford to be caught."

"Don't worry. We'll get it."

Revelations

7
DANAIS

Danais woke up on the shore with Leo. He had no recollection of how he got there. One minute they were talking about danger and the next he was awake. He couldn't have passed out in the middle of such a serious conversation. Could he have been that tired? How was he supposed to get up with Leo holding him, and more importantly why was the Guiya fruit so close? Had Leo known he would be first to awake?

Danais decided to break free and head to the river to bathe. It took more effort than learning to swim, but once he was free, Danais started toward the river. That was when he noticed it was raining though again, he was dry. There had to be a spell on the soap because he remained dry as he walked towards the river. He was concerned that Leo felt he needed to be protected even when he, himself, was asleep.

As he bathed in the water, a calm seemed to come over him that he couldn't explain. He was even having trouble overthinking the spell on the blossom. Something was happening now that his fear of water was gone. Maybe there was some connection between him and the water. His mother did name him after the God of Moon and Water, after all. That was when he felt Leo behind him.

"What happened last night?" Danais asked as he turned around.

"You passed out mid-thought."

"I just fell asleep in the water?"

Leo chuckled. "You must've been very tired. You fell asleep after I got you on shore. It was an easy swim. You're a small guy."

Danais turned so Leo wouldn't see him pout this time and handed him the blossom. Leo obliged and rubbed his back. Then they left the river and got dressed. It had stopped raining by then.

When they got back to the farm, Danais was on milk delivery duty. He and Leo loaded up their cart while Danais explained his route. There was an order to things. The town needed theirs first because they started preparing for the morning meal before sunrise. Then they went to the homes on the outskirts of town to deliver the residential orders. Most of his cart today was for the residents and the cheese farm, so they didn't spend much time in the city. That was someone else's job for the day. The cheese farm had its own cows, but on occasion would need extra milk and would purchase it from Danais' uncle. By the time they made it back into the city, the sun was just beginning to dry the morning dew off the grass. Somehow, Danais subconsciously led Leo to Garnter's.

Garnter smiled wide when he spotted Danais. He reached under the counter and produce a tray. "Danais!" he exclaimed. "I was hoping you'd be in today. I saved a jumbo muffin just for you."

"It's the size of a pie!" Danais exclaimed as Garnter handed him the muffin.

"You can handle it," Garnter responded with an even bigger smile.

Danais didn't hear any of that; he was walking away with his mouth full of the regular-sized muffin. Surprisingly, once he was done, he found he wasn't hungry, so he continued the cart ride home while feeding the larger muffin to the birds. While stealing a few bites for himself. Maybe he was still hungry after all. He couldn't waste such good food on the birds.

"So, what are we doing today?" Leo asked as they got back to the farm and packed away the cart.

"Potatoes."

Leo grimaced, but Danais laughed. The look on Leo's face was priceless.

"I'm not serious. We're really doing potatoes," Danais said.

"Somehow I don't see a difference between the joke and the reality?"

"And to think I thought you had a good sense of humour."

"That was a mistake," Leo said, and Danais found himself looking at Leo's back after Leo threw him over his shoulder. Danais did what any boy at a disadvantage would've done: he took a bite out of Leo's other shoulder. Leo dropped him, and

Revelations

Danais instantly ran into his back, taking them rolling down a small embankment toward the edge of the tomato fields. Danais ultimately managed to wrestle his way on top by the time they stopped rolling.

"Looks like I pinned you mountain boy," Danais said, basking in his victory.

"I think I can deal with that, though."

"This is about me beating you, not about me on top of you."

Leo shrugged off the comment, smiling, and Danais tried to hide his amusement unsuccessfully. Danais was inclined to kiss him, but he didn't want to give Leo the satisfaction of knowing just how much he was enjoying it. Leo, however, kissed him on the forehead— something no one had ever done to him before. Danais found that significantly more pleasant than he thought it would be.

"Are you going to get off me?" Leo questioned.

"It took me all morning to pry myself out of your arms while you were asleep. I'm not about to try it with you awake."

Danais knew Leo didn't believe a word of that, but he wasn't going to admit the truth even if he knew Leo knew it already. He stubbornly waited for Leo to let him go, even though he could tell that Leo was only doing it to see if he'd crack and admit he'd rather stay there all day and not work. Leo never broke his smile, but he let him go.

"Thanks. Now let's get to the carrot fields."

As Danais stood up, a rock hit him. He turned, only to see who it was before doing what he usually did: running. He could escape easily since he was only moments away from the fields. Leo stood up before he could run. Danais was unsure why they left without a fight and was even more concerned with why they threw one rock. They had to have seen him and Leo tumble down the hill, knowing Leo was a more powerful magician than they were. But still, these two girls threw a rock at him. Just one rock.

"Why did they just walk away? Usually, they stay to torment me." Danais was surprised he was more concerned about the oddity than the attack itself.

"This wasn't the same as when we met."

"How?"

"They threw a magicked rock at you."

Danais was very unsure of the significance of that. He was silent. The rock would hit him, magic or not. What was happening around him? What was changing?

"Tell your uncle what just happened."

"What did just happen?"

"And don't harass him for a response."

"Leo—"

"Just do it!"

Danais was upset at the demand and lack of information, but he said nothing. He wasn't entirely sure that was a good idea, but he reasoned he might be able to figure it out if he was quiet. This was what Leo kept trying to make him do: use his over-thinking as an advantage. Still, try as he might, he just couldn't make sense out of any of it.

After lunch, Leo began to describe the four provinces in detail. The one that interested him the most was Danais, the one after which Danais was named. It was said to be the most beautiful of all the land.

"Is it true that they are partly underwater?" Danais asked.

"Yes. There are ways to get to their homes and towns from the land as well, though. There are many caves through their partially submerged mountains, and their main city seems to just appear as you approach it. No matter how many times I've been, it always catches me by surprise. It's just beautiful to see small mountains surrounded by water instead of land."

"It does sound amazing. I've never been beyond the forest," Danais admitted.

"Why not?"

"I'm not sure. I'm assuming it's for the same reasons I was not allowed in the city. My uncle was very stern about making friends outside the farm. I always thought it was a bit extreme. He even put me in the worst room on the farm and insisted I not accept gifts from people."

"Well, that last part I know you've failed at."

Danais laughed. This was more than true, especially when it came to Garnter. How could he turn down free treats? "Why do you think he did it?"

"You tell me, Danais." After wracking his brain for solutions, Danais really didn't think that his brain was up to the challenge. The problem was that Leo, as usual, was perfectly willing to wait until sundown for him to figure it out. It took almost a full half-hour of considering the idea for him to come up with the answer.

"I would have to say that it's because of who I am. We are both somebody and you were allowed to stay in the open, and I wasn't. Why? That I don't have an answer to. But I believe it's changing."

"Why?"

"You're preparing for something. My life is changing already, from being just a farm boy to moving about more now that I've met you. How else do you explain your interest in me? How do you explain me wanting to learn more, and you having a love of teaching and being equipped with the right attitude to force me to learn with ease? It can't just be coincidence the attitude that was instilled in you by your teachers. It was designed so you could teach me. I thought I was just resistant to learning before but now—"

"But now?"

"I think I was subtly influenced to not care about history. I strongly doubt my uncle knew why he helped nurture my aptitude for impatience and stubbornness, but now that you're here, it makes sense."

"I believe you are right. And it helps that you're a good listener."

Danais smiled at the compliment. "Still, I wonder why for you?"

"For me?" Leo inquired.

"Hiding someone in the dark makes sense. But hiding someone in the open? Why would someone want to do that?"

5
LEO

The moment he said it, Leo remembered that they were going to be leaving at some point. It was all preparation. He was going to have to help Danais travel across Salinor. This he couldn't tell Danais, but he was still just as stumped when it came to himself being hidden in sight.

"The people of Danais are concealers. Becoming invisible is hard. They, however, can do something more. They can enforce that into their weapons. The best of the Dani weapons, and most costly, are the ones that can conceal whoever uses them during extreme situations or with the right spells. I have a Dani sword. It's helped me out in situations when I've needed to escape."

"I didn't know they were more than expert smiths."

"Well, now you know."

"It took just over a year for the Alliance to finally be ready to attack, and still the war was slow to ensure they had time to gain the trust of each sub-province they helped."

Leo was pleasantly surprised at finding out that yesterday's talk wasn't just a chance discussion. Danais had a genuine desire for knowledge and enjoyed serious conversation, no matter the topic.

"Do you have a second name?" Danais enquired.

"Leo is my second name." Leo absolutely hated his given name. It was a name he associated with pure evil, the name of the brother of the Tyrant himself. "I do not usually speak the name."

"Okay." Danais wasn't going to pry apparently.

"But I will. For you. My full name is Lynton Leo Vardon."

"After the Tyrant's brother?"

"Yes. The brother of Cortell the Tyrant." Leo knew it was rare that anyone said the Tyrant's name. But there was no harm in it, or any weird spells attached to it. "We are almost done. Let's not talk about my name."

Danais appeared to be struggling with a thought. And Leo found himself doing something he would never normally do.

"*I like Lynton,*" Danais said. "*It's not a bad name at all. A name is only a name, much like Cortell. Besides, the brother has been dead for a few centuries. So what if he was the Tyrant's right-hand man? I think I like Leo as a Lynton better.*"

Leo grunted, and his face grew more stern. Leo realised that Danais knew something had happened. How was he going to tell him what he had just done? How, when he looked at

Danais' face. A face that said it so wanted to be wrong but knew Leo had done something. He had to hide it, but he didn't know how. Then Danais' face changed. Leo could only ascertain that Danais could see the guilt in him. There was no way he could hide it now.

"What did you do?" Danais was uncharacteristically calm. This made it so much harder for Leo. He turned away, not being able to hold Danais' gaze. He was usually so careful not to impinge upon someone else's personal space. How could he not have realised this until he was deep into Danais' thoughts?

"I listened to your thoughts."

Danais started at that. "You did what?"

"Listened to your thoughts."

Danais didn't say anything for a while. Leo took this as a cue that he was waiting for him to turn back around.

"How could you do that?" Danais exploded. "Why? You magicians are all the same. Just prey on the weak. I trusted you not to use magic on me. Just go."

Leo looked at him but couldn't find the right words.

"Go," Danais repeated.

It was deep into the night, more specifically, it was the next day when Barton finally made it to the inn. Leo had slipped into his dark mode when hearing Danais say he liked the name Lynton better, and he had not yet come out of it. He knew that Barton didn't like him in this state, but this was the price of dark magic. He was lucky to have as much control as he did.

"What's wrong?" Barton asked.

"I lost control of my powers today."

"In what way?"

"I went into Danais' thoughts. I didn't even know I had done it. I realised it too late. Even still, I could've pulled out before hearing the part that allowed Danais to sense my presence."

"Sense?"

"Not in the way an Atorathian would. Just basic human instincts. He told me to leave."

"And you left?" Barton's tone let Leo know this was not the best choice of action.

"I was angry and ashamed," Leo admitted. "He liked me

better as Lynton, a name I've spent years making people forget. All the evil he did in the name of Salinor. Both he and the Tyrant claiming they do her will. All the shame they have brought upon us. How could he like me with that name? How?"

"It is only a name. Neither he nor you are the only ones with it."

"So you agree with him?" Leo's temper began to rise.

"Don't make me harm you. You don't know who I am. Calm down. Now!"

Leo had never heard Barton speak to him this way. He wanted to throw a spell at him, but even in his darkened state, he found that he was not physically capable of doing it. There was a certain type of magic happening here that he didn't understand, something he couldn't sense. Something strange was at work here.

"A name is but a name. And for someone who's always looking for signs, you should see something here."

"Something? Something…" It didn't take Leo long to figure it out. "He likes the name, and for years no one has even asked or questioned about my full name. That can only mean there's something in the name. Am I a descendant from one of the evil families, the traitors to the land? Am I just a lost, would-be villain? Could the gods have been that good to me? It doesn't make sense. If only I knew my title: that would solve this."

"It would, but as you know, that information was not left with your body when found. At least you know you aren't from the Tyrant's family. They don't leave any of their family around; all pregnancies must be reported to the Tyrant—and he has ways of finding out."

"Danais may not want to see me again. I have a feeling this is very bad."

Barton didn't look like he wanted to respond to that.

"He's changing as well," Leo continued. "Should I tell him? And I don't know how to assist in that area."

"It will sort itself out, and you definitely can't tell him."

Leo could sense the disapproval in Barton's voice about the situation. This made him feel even more ashamed. It was almost as if Barton was a disappointed parent—and it wasn't a feeling that he was accustomed to feeling from his friend. He was going to have to be more careful. More was expected of him here

Revelations

since Danais was the child.

"This is bad, but I understand. You're not generally so careless. I shouldn't be so upset, but if you knew what went into this. The pressure just has me a little stressed. We know you're being followed for sure, but nothing solid."

"I want to ask you a question." A change of topic was in order, and Leo had been waiting to ask this ever since Danais posed the question earlier.

"What is it?"

"Why was I allowed to be free and Danais wasn't?"

"I will answer this only if we make the dying vow."

Leo was a little taken back. There were two unbreakable vows: the indestructible and dying. Indestructible meant the person who made the vow died, but the dying vow meant the other person died; it put more trust on the vow-maker because if they broke the vow, they would have to live out the shame of dishonesty. The spell could be reversed by the one who initiated the vow, but that somewhat defeated the point of making it and was rarely done.

"I will make the vow."

The two of them connected their right palms and interlocked their fingers.

"Do you swear never to ask this question again or any indirect form associated with this question?"

"I do."

"To only talk about it with Danais and no other?"

"I do."

"To never repeat my answer under any circumstances until you are sure it is safe to do so, beyond doubt?"

"I do."

"Breaking this vow will result in my immediate death. Do you make the vow, accepting these conditions?"

"I do. I make the dying vow."

Their hands glowed for a moment and then it was over. Barton increased their shield to ensure that no one could hear them.

"The Tyrant would look for you. Even having your band perform at his court was part of pushing you right out into the open. We had to ensure he would not look for you. It is much harder to hide the gifted than the ungifted. You'd need much more training than a peasant. Danais was different. Since we knew no one would look for him, we kept him hidden. There was more of a chance of him being accidentally recognised for who he is, considering he was raised to be nothing. You've only known him for a few days and you see it. And if he was found out many people would die. If you were found, you would die. We are hiding you to save you and hiding him to save others."

Leo was full of questions after this statement. He had, however, promised not to ask any more about it. Things were getting too complicated. If he had been Danais, he'd have stormed out, screaming, *Who am I?* That thought made him laugh.

"So how went the day otherwise?" Barton changed the subject. He seemed to be in better spirits now, so Leo went along with the topic change.

"Good. Except the rock thing."

"Rock?"

"Yes. Someone threw a magicked rock at Danais today when we made it back to the farm. After the milk deliveries. Don't worry; it hit him. But it is more confirmation we are being watched. It could've been a lot worse if the rock didn't hit him."

"Worse? How much worse can it get?" Barton asked, genuinely concerned.

"Well, he pinned me." Leo smiled knowing that this response was not what Barton was expecting

"You? How'd he manage that?" Barton chuckled. The thought of an Atorathian pinning him when they were a short race and Leo was so tall was just hilarious.

"Not sure, really. But he felt good on top of me." Leo was glad to see that Barton found that funny as his laughter intensified.

"I bet he just loved to hear you say that." Barton responded.

"Not really. He forced me to let him go and got off me. That's when the rock hit him."

"What about the seed you got last night?"

"Haven't decided yet," Leo replied. He had been thinking about it, though.

"Well, hurry. I want to know what it grows into."

"Yes, father," Leo said, knowing that Barton would force himself not to laugh and end up laughing harder.

Revelations

"He is on his way," Barton announced and the two of them let down the shield. Moments later, Danais arrived at their table.

"Can I join you?"

"Yes," Leo told him as he scooted over to allow room for another chair. Once Danais sat down, Leo turned to him. "I know it's late, but I am sorry. It was an accident. I would never pry into your thoughts or use magic on you without permission. I don't know how it happened. That's the truth."

"I know. But that doesn't mean I have to like it."

"I don't know what else to say."

"Nothing. Especially when I start calling you Lynton."

Leo was shocked. He couldn't be serious. Why did Danais like this name so much? What had he done to deserve having his name reborn? "I understand," he replied, thinking there were things much bigger at stake than a name.

"Kale? Where have you been all day?" Danais asked as he hopped onto the table.

"I do have a life of my own," Kale responded, "but I've been watching you mostly from a distance. Leo is a good teacher."

"Hear that, Barton? At least someone appreciates my talents."

Barton rolled his eyes but offered no response.

"Okay. Guess I just missed you," Danais admitted.

"I won't always be here," Kale replied.

"No one will. But I've been alone for so long. All of you are my first real friends. And recently Mai'n."

Leo glanced at Barton. The look on his face said he must've been thinking the same thing. That meant that he didn't know about this friendship. But more, something was in his eyes. Leo was sure this friendship shouldn't exist.

"Does anyone know about this?" Leo asked.

"No." Danais responded.

"How long have you been friends?" Barton inquired.

"Not too long. Only since my seventeenth name day," Danais said, offering Kale a bite of a breadstick, and then finishing it himself. "She's pretty good in other ways."

Leo laughed so hard wine came squirting out of his nose.

"What's so funny?"

"That's my future wife you're bedding there. And why didn't you mention that you knew her at that first lunch?" Barton replied.

Danais shrugged at that.

"You're a lucky man," Danais said to Barton.

"Really?"

"From what she did to me, you're more than lucky. Makes me wonder how you are."

"You're stroking the wrong manhood, boy," Barton said with a smile, before gulping more wine.

"Come on—a builder like you? You should broaden your range."

"Are all Atorathians sexual animals?" Baton shook his head with a smile.

"Yes. So, is that a no?"

"I don't do men. And you shouldn't flirt or proposition me."

"Why?"

"Leo is still a conservative."

It was obvious Leo wasn't a one-man or woman kind of guy after his run-in with the girl on the farm. That didn't numb the humour one bit, though.

"Really? After all the naughty tales I've heard about him?"

"I'm right here!" Leo protested and glared at both of them, then broke into laughter. It was only a matter of time before he became the brunt of the banter. He would have to move faster next time to make sure it was directed at Barton. He couldn't have them attack him every time the three of them were together, even if he did find it entertaining.

"Lots of sex doesn't equate with the really exciting, dangerous stuff. I'm sure you know you can be exceptional without it. Leo, apparently, is one of those." Barton added.

"Really? Such a shame. If it's that good, just imagine what a few indecent acts might do. I'd be happy to show you a few, Barton."

Barton chuckled. "I've been alive for many years. No man has convinced me yet."

"Can't blame a man for trying. Besides, there's good money to be made in the used-to-be-unclean acts."

"Money?" Leo inquired.

"Yes, Leo. Why else do you think I am still in town at this hour?"

Leo shouldn't have been surprised. Danais was Atorathian.

Revelations

They were by far the most gifted in all forms of the art of love. Being a prostitute was the equivalent in status of being a hunter or guard, and they never serviced peasants. Rather, they commanded the highest pay. They even taught the arts as much as they could, considering there were some skills that only they possessed: much like how only builders could work with the yellow stone. Still, in Leo's mind, a prostitute was a prostitute. He resolved that he was trying to teach Danais to be non-judgmental, so, therefore, he could not be. This was becoming much more complicated than it should have been.

Leo stopped his train of thought to watch Danais absentmindedly playing with his fingers. He seemed fascinated by the size of his hands. Leo smiled. It reminded him of a small child, spending hours playing with a toy: a remarkably unspectacular behaviour. However, Danais was enthralled by it. It reminded him that Danais was younger than he was—just over ten years younger. He was pleased to find out he still didn't care.

"I didn't think you would be the jealous type." Though the question was direct, Danais didn't seem to have lost interest in Leo's hand.

Leo chuckled. "I'm not."

"I'm definitely not. I'm Atorathian. We've never been traditional in that sense. And I'm sure you thought about this when you decided to pursue me. And here you are, still showing interest. Maybe you aren't quite the way you think you are."

"You may be right," Leo admitted.

It was about this time Danais started to play with a mole on Leo's right hand. Leo let out a chuckle; watching Danais was adorable.

"If you press hard enough, I'll turn into a butterfly," Leo joked. Danais grunted, but Barton, Kay and Kale laughed. Leo just smiled and enjoyed Danais' feigned irritation. He still hadn't stopped playing with his hand.

"Where's your room?" Danais inquired.

"You're staying?"

"Why would I come here and give you a chance to apologise if I had no intention of staying? I could've just let you do it tomorrow. For someone so intuitive, you really missed the obvious this time." This time, everyone was laughing at him. At least Leo got in the one good joke. He pressed on through the hysterics.

"And that would be—?" Leo asked.

"That I'm interested as well. Why else would I, someone so opposed to magic, come back to you when you broke my trust? I'll even go so far as to say that I'm even surprised at this. I'm still not entirely happy about it, though."

"Okay. Well, one can't get it right all the time." Leo was going to add, "Next time I read your mind by accident I just won't tell you." But he was fairly sure the joke wouldn't go over well.

"No. But here I am. So you must be doing something right."

Leo decided it was time to head up to his room. Even though Danais said it as a one-off, still clearly focusing on the mole, it made him feel good that he had to be doing something right. He got up and proceeded to leave the dining area. Danais apparently felt that talking and drinking with the others was more important. Once Leo realised Danais wasn't following him, he turned to call him.

"Danais!"

Danais looked away from the table. "I thought you wanted to leave," Leo said. Danais just nodded. "Come," Leo urged gently.

Danais smiled this time; he didn't always. Leo had no idea why sometimes he said it. He didn't end any phrases with his other friends with the word 'come'. But on some level, he knew that Danais liked hearing it as much as he enjoyed saying it.

Danais was out of his clothes and in bed before Leo could close the door behind him, but Leo took his time getting into the bed. Once in, he stared at Danais for a while, then stretched out on his back, clasping his hands behind his head. He was content to fall asleep in this position, but Danais stirred in his sleep and ended up with his head on Leo's chest. This was an infinitely better position to fall asleep in.

Hours later, Leo woke to find Danais mumbling agitatedly to himself. Leo reasoned he must've been in the throes of a bad dream. The only word he could positively make out was Lynton. He sighed and reasoned that at the very least, he could calm him. That was a bit of magic he knew Danais would not protest, much like the warming spell for the clothes on their first night together. Leo kissed him on the forehead and wrapped his arm around Danais' shoulder. He decided to let him have his dream.

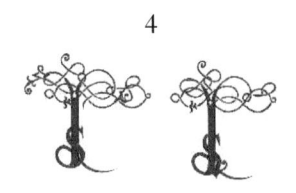

4

Time moved on, and more lessons were taught. Danais was warming up to the fact of belonging to someone, especially a magician. Leo was happier than he could imagine being. There was something to be said about being a magician and being able to earn the love of an Atorathian. Being able to do it stroked one's ego.

The townsfolk were already spreading rumours about the magician and the peasant. Since Danais had kept mainly to himself all his life, no one knew much about him, so being left to their own devices, they told stories of him being an undercover noble to a spy sent by the Tyrant.

"So how's my Tyrant spy doing?" Leo joked.

"I'm not a spy anymore Now I'm a deceiver, trying to manipulate my way into your heart for your wealth." This Danais said before running up a trail, over a cliff face and diving at least a hundred feet down into the ocean. Leo loved to watch him swim. He looked amazing in the water under the stars. And as Danais walked back from the shore, water dripping from his body, a vision in chocolate, glistening in the moonlight, Leo found it hard not to think unclean thoughts of him.

Danais crawled on top of him and ran his fingers through Leo's hair. Leo loved when he did this.

Danais thought Leo couldn't hide his lust even if he wanted to. He looked Leo in the eyes then got up and ran back into the water.

"You enjoy teasing me, don't you?" Leo shouted after him

"I do what I can!" Danais said before diving into the river.

"Okay. It's been just over a month. Anything to report that

I don't know?" The seer inquired.

Torak answered, "A magic stone was thrown at Danais." There was a collective silence that felt like a groan of stress. "They threw the stone to see if his body would repel it. As I told Lord Vardon and Barton, this confirms the child is being watched."

"Yes. The situation is becoming dangerous. What about Leo, Barton?" The seer kept the conversation going.

"He's more worried than us. He thinks they should move before Danais' name day. And we've stumbled upon something I've kept secret until now. It seems that Mai'n has been a friend to Danais for almost a year. Maybe she's the one watching him." It was a direct accusation. Mai'n was in the room.

"I assure you; she is not," Lord Vardon confirmed.

"Then what is going on?" Torak asked. "I knew nothing of this, either. Apparently, no one knew."

"I can explain. Torak, you remember your daughter telling you she had an important task to do." Before Torak could answer Mai'n's question, she did something.

Twice.

She shifted into another form, that of Torak's Daughter, then back to her own form. "Your daughter has been playing another role that isn't the one you thought—a role worthy of her shape-shifting skills. She is the only person not present in this room."

"My wife, Lady Vardon?" Lord Vardon was shocked.

"Yes. Her job was to watch the Leo task force and mine was to watch Danais. None but the orchestrator of this mission and the seer knew. They are the only two to know all parts of the plan and who will be what. And of course, the Commander of the Alliance."

"What was the task your daughter said to you?" Lord Vardon inquired of Torak.

"She told me that it was her job to pretend to grow up with her youngest brothers, that it was essential to lose her position in the Alliance and that I could tell no one. It was an illusion. No one outside the walls of our house would see her. My sons and I have worked very hard to hide the fact that only we can

Revelations

see her from Danais. Now I find out it was you, the serving girl, all along."

"Your daughter was better suited for the other task, especially considering she married Lord Vardon."

"So, if Lady Vardon is his daughter, then you must be—" Barton couldn't finish the sentence.

"I am she. I am the Mai'n, second in command of the Alliance. I made friends with the boy to have a convenient excuse to be around him when the image of his cousin was off at war. Barton was convenient in the sense that when he knew my skills, he hired me to be the secret guard of the two. I am not a magician, so spelling myself to be only seen by the family was difficult. But that is a story for another time."

"You must've also worked a spell to make us forget your true form. As I remember now, this is your true form and yet none of us recognised you."

"This is true. As you know, we both exiled ourselves from the Alliance many years before the plan began. This was to ensure that we could keep our true forms and still be unrecognisable."

This was when Lady Vardon entered the room. She was a mix of Atorathian and Dani. She stood beside Mai'n while everyone else stood and bowed to their two commanders before taking their seats. Lady Vardon was a general, third in command.

"Now we have serious things to attend to." Mai'n began.

"Was—" Lord Vardon was cut off by Mai'n.

"No. She was quite smitten with you. In truth, it wasn't until she fell in love with you that we decided to choose you. We had someone else in line, and the seer did not foresee a union. Something changed, and you became part of the plan. Just as you were originally part of it to begin with long before my time, then removed. Clearly, it was always destined to be. Besides, you have many kids before and after you married her."

"Okay, let's not talk about all the amazing love we made," Lord Vardon joked.

Both Mai'n and Lady Vardon rolled their eyes.

"I'm a grandfather and didn't know. But you did," Torak said looking at the seer. Lela just shrugged.

After the lightness of the mood dimmed, Mai'n instructed

Kay to speak.

"The other day, while in the presence of the two, I noticed the presence of a Betave," Kay explained. "Nothing was too out of the ordinary, but there was something different: a magic I didn't understand or recognise. I took my information to the seer, and she said that this meeting would be the time to mention it."

"I think I know what it may be," Mai'n began. "With our other sources, we've discovered a trail. Kay's discovery confirms our findings. There is another shapeshifter in Atorath. There is a special hint of magic that most shapeshifters hide. It gives them an advantage over other magicians. It's taken us weeks, but we think we've gotten all the stories together. There is only one conclusion: the Betave is a shapeshifter as well.

"Rumour has it that throughout the provinces, people have been disappearing and been found much later. Not all of them were killed because the killer needed some of them alive for information. The rest were killed."

"There is only one magician I can think of whose Betave inherited the shape-shifting skill," Xan mentioned with a hint of disgust.

"I am certain you are right, Xan. Inform Kale when you can. He is the only one not present," Mai'n responded.

"What is it that we are looking for?" Lord Vardon asked.

"Form a circle," Mai'n said. They did as told and joined hands. "We will hide everything but the aura that is a shapeshifter, so you'll know exactly what to look for. What you feel is much more than what you will ever run into, but you should be able to sense it if you're looking for it. The situation is much worse than we thought it would be. The Tyrant's son is in our midst."

"You should just stay on top of me," Leo tried to encourage Danais not to move.

"Really? And why is that?"

"Do I really need to answer that?" He laughed. "And what are you doing?"

"Kissing your chest. Is that a problem?"

Leo thought it best not to answer. Maybe his luck was about

to change. Before he could dwell on his good fortune, he felt something he thought he'd never feel. His mind stopped working, and he could only focus on the pulses running through his body, and then he just... exploded.

"That was, um, fast." Danais didn't have any other words for it.

Leo was still breathing heavily, so it took him a while to respond. "You just—"

"Yes. You've never had anyone do that to you before?"

"No. It's an indecent act, performed only by the lowest of peasants and cheap whores. Why would I?" As soon as he saw the look on Danais' face, Leo wished he could've sucked that comment back in.

"So that is what you think of me then?" Danais stood and ran toward the water just as it started to rain. Leo tried to run after him, but the sea spirits blocked his way. This was very strange.

And what would the spy think of this?

"Kale. Why are you here?"

"I apologise, seer. I know I was told to stay with them, but something has happened. I believe it will take both Lady Vardon and Barton to settle him."

"Tell us what happened," Kay demanded, and Barton was first to show his stress.

"We will go to the inn and see what we can do. At the very least, we may convince him to want to be friends with Danais still," Barton said.

"You do that," Mai'n said. "And I will see what I can do with Danais."

6
LEO

Barton was sat at a table drinking alone when Leo barged in with his demands. He'd probably just destroyed something special over a minor act of oral pleasure. Why not demand answers?

"Why would the sea spirits protect him?" Leo demanded as he stood across from Barton. "Why does he not notice these things and why does it always rain, even if only for a moment, when we are together? What connection does he have to the God Danais?"

"Perceptive, aren't you?" a voice popped up behind him.

"Mother?" Leo sputtered in reply to his mother's voice. What was she doing here? She couldn't be part of this as well. Were both of his parents leading double lives?

"I won't ask you to calm down, but you will sit. Drink."

Leo did as he was told. He was starting to think that this secret network was treading carefully with him. He should be scolded for his demands, but he knew there was a better way to get answers than by rage. Danais was handling his stubbornness and naivety a lot better than Leo was doing in trying to control his darkness.

"The truthful answer is that we don't know. We are fully confident of who his father is, and it is not the God Danais. We are just as shocked and intrigued as you are," Barton responded.

Leo did what he could to calm his anger. Sadly, his anger and darkness did not go hand in hand, and the darkness he could not at this time control.

"So you know what happened?" Leo enquired, not really interested in the response.

"You told him he was less than a peasant," his mother responded.

"That sounds about right. I'm sure he will never speak to me again."

"You seem really upset. I guess you do like him. At least from all the stories I've been told."

Leo glanced at Barton, who was conveniently eyeing one of the servant girls. He was the only one he'd blame for divulging information to her.

"It is true," Leo said slowly. "I might possibly even…love him."

"Then don't give up. Fight. Fight until your hands bleed

from battle."

His mother was getting way too passionate about this. As if Leo's love life were the stuff of romance novels and not an actual real-life problem.

"But the battle is already lost?" Leo sounded defeated.

"Not if your heart hasn't given up," Lady Vardon responded.

"So you approve?"

"Obviously. We all do. Why else would I be here trying to save you from yourself? Besides, love is difficult. Deal with it."

"Spoken like a mother," Leo said, and he gave her a weak smile.

"So, what are you going to do about it?" Lady Bardon questioned.

"I can't tell you that," Leo quickly responded. "Not yet anyway."

"Tsk. It's your lack of openness that got you into this mess. It's time to spread your wings and grow into new love-making adventures." The way she used her arms to animate flying and then flowing into new places, especially with the added sigh, pulling her hands towards her chest, was enough to make everyone at the table cringe. She was really overdoing it.

"It's no wonder your daughter came out the way she did. Must you always be so direct in this area?" Leo shook his head.

"Must you always be so sensitive about it? Your dad doesn't have such issues. Just this morning—"

"I really don't want to know." Leo made that face that clearly stated, 'too much information.'

"Well, I've got business to attend to, so I'd best be off," Lady Vardon announced.

"Father would be one broke noble without you, you know," Leo added.

"He'd be a lot of things without my prudent guidance." As if her words weren't enough, the way she sat up straighter in her chair and proudly stuck up her chin spoke of just how much she believed this.

"I'm sure—like stress-free and in control of his business." Leo chuckled.

"Details. Love is compromise." She waved her hand not allowing Leo's comment to breathe.

"Spoken like a woman," Leo responded, only to annoy her.

"Like a supreme sorceress, young man," she chided him. Leo just rolled his eyes.

"This is too much pressure." Leo decided to bring the topic back on course and away from his ridiculously over-theatrical mother.

Lady Vardon raised an eyebrow at her son. "How?"

"There's just so much more at stake than just us. He's decided to call me Lynton."

"Aww. I'm certain that warms your heart with joy," she added a lost-in-love, misty-eyed look to her words which Barton chuckled at while almost choking on his ale.

Leo remained silent.

"You aren't going to tell her, are you?"," Barton said, but Leo had no intention of responding to his mother.

"He does like it. A lot. He hasn't actually said it yet but it's hard not to see."

"This can't be true." She gasped and put a hand over her chest in mock shock. "Not my son. Who are you, and what have you done with the real Leo?"

Leo couldn't continue not to laugh at her. She always seemed to have this effect on him.

"I do. It's because he loves it so much. When he says it, I can hear how good the name is. It is a nice name. I just never gave the name itself that much consideration."

"Ah, so the boy shows up and you suddenly warm up to a name I've loved for years. It never worked for me."

"You're half Dani. You'd have to be a full Atorathian. Short and male," Barton said, which got a good laugh from Lady Vardon.

Leo was sensing more jokes at his expense were coming. "Didn't you say you were leaving?" Leo said hoping she would get up and go.

"There's still more wine," she said as she quickly finished of her first one, and Barton poured her another.

Leo gave Barton a withering look. "You're helping her?"

Barton raised his hands in defence. "She forced me to do it."

"She said one sentence and didn't even push her glass toward you."

"Didn't you hear the threat in her tone? I was genuinely scared for my life."

Revelations

Barton was almost believable. Almost.

Nevertheless, Leo was happy they were here. He needed a serious pick-me-up after what had just happened.

"Tell me about the boy," his mother offered. "I'm always doing business and I don't get to hear much. Besides, you know I'm better at these things than your father."

"Really?" Leo raised an eyebrow.

"Yes. He knew nothing of love before me. I am half Atorathian after all."

"That doesn't *really* mean anything. You're also half Dani, but you can't breathe underwater."

"Just answer the question before I turn you into a shrimp."

"Now that would be some piece of magic, considering his size," Kay said she had not yet moved from Barton's lap. No sain creature would move away from free back of ear rubs.

"I know, but even someone as amazing as I may not be able to accomplish that." The fake self-importance had everyone impressed besides Leo.

"Well, that depends. You could turn him into a jumbo or tiger shrimp. That might be doable," Xan said, bringing much laughter from the others, including Leo.

"Do what you will, but I'd be the tastiest shrimp in the bowl," Leo quipped.

"I thought you had a problem with people putting you in their mouth?" Barton teased. Leo wasn't too shocked. He deserved that on some level.

"Answer the question," his mother demanded again.

"I don't know what it is—but it's something. How did you guys know this plan would work anyway? That I'd just see him, and it would be love at first sight?"

"We didn't. But at the very least, you had to be friends. In all truth, we were expecting a girl after you were born, but another boy child was born. Then again, the seer never specified; it was just assumed that it would be boy-girl or girl-boy." She finished off the glass, and Barton refilled it swiftly.

"You mean love was on the table then?" Leo asked.

"Yes, but by no means definite, and we had all but ruled it out until you lost your innocence to both."

"So, it was about me?"

"He was Atorathian; it was a given Danais would have no

trouble in that area but the rest of us—well, we either are or aren't. Only one of my brothers is. He, apparently, doesn't find women attractive at all." She was referring to the youngest brother the seer and Torak were always joking about. Leo didn't know this, however. Just like he didn't know the seer and Torak were married or that his mother was Danais' real cousin and Torak's Daughter. Torak didn't even know until this very day's recent meeting with Mai'n and Lady Vardon present.

"Really?"

"Yes. Which is such a shame because he's the only brother I've not bedded."

Kay, Barton, and Xan laughed at that statement. Leo just took another gulp of wine.

"How did I know this would get back to you and fucking?" Leo was not amused as always. Incest wasn't weird by far. The only real taboo was marrying them and procreating.

"Seriously?" Lady Vardon laughed. "Look at me. How could he not find me tantalising? Stimulating, even? Why, Leanor herself would fall madly in lust with me!"

If Leo didn't know his mother so well, he might give her a snappy comment, but he knew she didn't mean a single bit of it.

"I'm sorry, but my incest only goes as far as brothers and sisters. No parents. That's just wrong. And you're not my type."

"Me? Not your type? Well, shoot me right through the heart."

"I don't like purple. I prefer blue."

"That's something a Keldonian would say." She side-eyed him then took another sip of her wine.

"Besides, if I were going to go Dani, you'd have to have more of a purple hue to your skin. Right now, you just look like you're trying to be a Dani, but not quite making it. Actually, you look almost pure Atorathian. And you can't even breathe underwater."

"I can breathe underwater!" she exclaimed exasperatedly.

This time Lady Vardon was the one being laughed at. This was the one topic Leo knew that if he pushed long enough, she would get agitated.

Leo smirked at his mother and crossed his arms, leaning back in his chair. "I was wondering when you'd finally protest that one. I only had to say it twice this time."

"Bah. I've had too much to drink." She murmured one more word around her cup, "Bitch."

"Did you just swear at me?"

"You mean 'Bah'?"

Leo rolled his eyes. To her credit, bah was by far the most common curse word in Atorath, just like "fucking" was for bedding or sex. But if she wanted to pretend she didn't call him a bitch, he would let her have it—this time. Bitch was one of the words to come out of Mironi peasant culture.

Just then the door opened with a bang, and all three of them looked up.

Leo, however, only gave cursory glance toward the door. Walking in was an absolutely beautiful black jaguar. Betaves with such predatory natural forms usually turned into their Betave form before entering an establishment, so as not to be mistaken for the real animal. This inn, however, had a doorman who could sense the different signals in a Betave, so it wasn't necessary.

"Sole! I'm so glad to see you," Lady Vardon said as her Betave changed back into his Betave form and hopped onto the table. She hugged him and started to sniffle.

"Oh, my dear lady. What has the child done to you now?" Sole consoled her.

"Trying to downplay my Dani bloodline again," she cried.

The fake weeping was just too much. How everyone Leo knew were undercover people trying to save the world or whatever it may be they were doing, was so far beyond Leo. When they could be this moronic and immature how could they also be qualified to save mankind?

"Well, if he didn't make a complete fool of himself by saying something he doesn't even believe anymore, he wouldn't be here making you weep," Sole responded.

"Not you, too," Leo said, wondering how everyone could know so fast.

Sole let go of the weeping woman to glance at Leo. She sobered up almost instantly. "So you're saying you do still believe in that?" Sole stated.

"No, it was a reflex," Leo tried to explain. "Call it instincts. I just said what I've gotten so used to saying over the years. And

I didn't even believe it when I said it. It wasn't until after the sea spirits that I flared up and realised what I'd actually said and the implications behind it. I would've taken it back right then and there. But that just stalled me, so I came here."

"You're a very powerful blood magician. You could've very well survived them," Sole stated simply.

"I couldn't use that much magic and at the same time expect him to take me back," Leo protested. "Besides, I wasn't entirely sure I could take on the sea spirits. That, and they deserve respect. I didn't want to attack them. Would you have taken on, say, four Spartas or more, Sole?"

"I don't think I would have. You were right not to chance attacking the powers of the land. I just wanted to hear you say it. What are you going to do?"

It didn't take Leo long to think about that. "Whatever it takes."

8
DANAIS

It had stopped raining, and Danais was feeling quite dry. He didn't stay in the water long or notice he was being guarded by the sea spirits. He was happily throwing rocks into the river when Mai'n arrived.

"Did Kale bring you here?" he inquired.

"In a manner of speaking, but I actually walked of my own accord."

Danais smiled. Maybe tackling this conversation wouldn't be so bad after all.

"So how are you feeling?" Mai'n inquired.

"How would you feel if your partner said you were lower than a peasant whore?"

"Ah…so that's what happened."

"Yes. Sometimes I wonder why I'm so involved with a magician."

Revelations

Mai'n sat down beside Danais. "You haven't figured it out yet, then?"

He sighed. "I have. I just don't know what to do with the information. After this, I just don't know if it's worth it. There are so many issues I have, but his—it's just so wrong to have me learn such equality and help me deal with my faults when he so easily slips into his and expects me to just accept it."

"I see. Sounds like love to me." Mai'n calmly stated and looked out over the river.

Danais pouted then grunted when he saw the smile it pulled from Mai'n. "I don't remember saying that."

"I am much older than you are, Danais. I know love when I see it."

"I've never been in love before. Leo has had practice. He handles it better even when he gets mad. I'm almost positive he would've apologised instantly if I didn't run away. But I'm still considering not accepting it. Why can't I just move on from this space?"

"Do you want to?"

"I do."

"Then—?"

"I don't know. I just don't know. I'll accept it, but I just need more time this time. He's so sure of his feelings for me. I need to be sure about mine." Danais could see that this was not the answer Mai'n wanted. Why was it so important they remain close? Did it even matter if they loved each other? Were they just supposed to be friends? Was it the love that was complicating things?

Maybe he should've just ignored Leo's offer and given friendship. Maybe then whatever it was they had to do would be easier to do. Unfortunately, he couldn't backtrack and change things. He also wondered if the storm created by his reading would even exist had he and Leo not had feelings for each other. Love really did muddle things up.

"You aren't who I think you are." Danais meant it as a statement, not a question.

"I'm not?" Mai'n sounded surprised by the question.

"Don't act innocent. I caught a glance between Barton and Leo when I mentioned you. They thought I didn't see it because I was rambling about something. You're part of this."

Mai'n smiled. "That I am."

"So, you've been watching me, then?"

"Yes."

"Can—can you explain the rock thing to me?" Danais figured that if she was a part of this, there was no reason she wouldn't know.

"It was a test to see if you were more than a peasant. The fact that the rock hit you works in our favour, at least somewhat. They may be convinced you're a peasant, but not that you aren't important. Just that you're less of a threat."

"Okay. That's so obvious. I don't know why I didn't think of that. I hear you are to marry, Barton."

"Yes."

"You're a lucky woman. And he is a lucky man. I told him as much but he refused to let me test the theory."

Mai'n laughed. "I believe that. I have tried to get him to try men but the most I can get out of him is dual penetration. He just isn't into them sexually."

Both she and Danais laughed at that. Being Atorathian they would always try cause all genders were fair game to them.

"When is the date?" Danais inquired.

"The beginning of fall."

"How will you be able to marry if you're both living a secret life?" Danais inquired. It didn't seem like something that would be easy.

"That is all on him. He hasn't talked to either of our parents yet."

"And why is that?"

"Something about not being worthy of an Atorathian. I'm afraid he has even more reason to feel unworthy after tonight," she said, thinking about him now knowing who she really is.

"We are going to have to leave at some point, aren't we?" Danais looked off into the distance

"You will. I am not sure when or who will get that task."

"Do you think that I'm being unreasonable?"

"You are doing what you think you must."

"Will you stay? I sometimes have bad dreams."

"Why don't you have Leo give you dreamless sleep?"

"I didn't know he could do that."

"He tries his best not to use magic on you, even when it will help. He does this for you."

"Is that unusual?"

"A good magician's first instinct is to help those he loves. I have no doubt that the first time you had a bad sleep, he considered calming your dreams. The fact that he did not is saying something."

"Magicians just perform magic on each other subconsciously?"

"Mostly if they fall in love with peasants. It's easy to calm someone or heal a wound. To give them a peaceful rest. Most are happy for some comfort."

"He always asks me. Even from the first night. I thought that was just how it's done."

"With a peasant? Certainly not. Leo is just a better magician than most. And I'm sure he sensed you would not approve."

"Maybe I won't make him wait so long then," Danais said before finally stretching out on the smooth stones and falling asleep.

7
LEO

"He doesn't want to talk to you, Leo," Torak said as he stood in the kitchen talking to Leo a few months later.

"It's been almost two months now. Summer will be here in a week. It will be his eighteenth name day soon." Leo said exasperatedly. He'd been trying for so long he was more annoyed than anything else.

"I know, Leo," Torak replied.

Leo plopped down at the kitchen table. "How long must I be tortured?"

"He's just trying to sort things out. I promise you it's not a bad thing. Just be patient."

"I can't stand not being with him. How could I be affected so after only one month with him?" Leo was himself impressed with his patience. Every morning he'd come to the farm, hoping Danais had forgiven him.

Today was different, however. Today he had his band outside waiting on him. They were travelling to the next town in Nera to perform. There was a festival to bring in the start of summer and the end of spring. They were to perform during the celebrations. He couldn't stay long but would have if Danais would talk to him. He would've forced the band to cancel the journey. More accurately, he would've attempted to force them to cancel if it meant just one word with Danais.

"Well, I have to go."

"So, you only came to have a mug of my home brew and leave? Danais will find that highly entertaining. For what it's worth, he misses you... more than I think even he knows."

Leo smiled and headed out to the cart. One of the servants was running towards the farm, sweating and wide eyed. Clearly, she was ordered to come take Leo back by force. Peasants hated being told to force a magician to do anything. This one, however, seemed more impatient. She must've just been on edge to go and was probably more than happy to come and get him.

"They didn't have to send you to fetch me."

"Yes, well they feared the worst."

"The worst?"

"That the boy might actually want to talk to you."

Leo rolled his eyes at that comment. Was there any one of his friends that didn't feel the need to tease him about his situation?

"Back so fast? We sent the girl for nothing." Dom, another musician said.

Leo mounted his horse and ignored the jest.

"Leave him alone, Dom. The man's in love, albeit with someone who doesn't want to talk to him," Nolem, the soloist and occasional fiddler, offered.

Leo hadn't talked to them much about Danais. Actually, he'd done his best not to. He spent a lot of time on the road with these guys, and the last thing he needed was to give them material for the journey to tease him with.

He glared at Nolem, but it didn't come off as well as expected. She just laughed at him. Dom was the percussionist, and they also had a harp player, flautist, and full-time fiddler.

"It's going to take us until nightfall if we go at a steady pace. We won't have to race ourselves," Leo said, hoping it might change the topic.

"Yes. While we're moving, can you tell us something about this, Danais? Anything? You spend more time with us than anyone, so why no letters or any talk about this relationship? We had to wait for news to travel about like some secret spy of the Tyrant trying to take you down. Or some peasant trying to steal your wealth." Dom almost looked genuinely hurt.

"Well, he is a peasant, with skin the shade of perfect milk chocolate. He's more than two feet shorter than me—around five foot three, the low range for an Atorathian. He has a smile that stretches from here to eternity and a pouting habit that he tries desperately to break because he knows I think he's attractive when he pouts. He overthinks a lot. A lot." Everyone laughed at that statement. "I guess he just makes me feel whole. I know he's the one. His eighteenth name day is on this seventh day—the first day of summer.

"Eighteen? He's that young?" Dom responded.

"Yes. He's mature enough, though. And he needs me. He needs me like I need him. We need each other. And he sings. He has a voice like an angel. And I have other news. Mai'n is pregnant. Almost ready to have the baby."

"Really?"

"Yes. She doesn't look it, though. But they say that can happen sometimes, and we shouldn't be worried. Barton was excited. He says he hasn't had a real relationship in years and now he's been in one for two, is getting married, and is having a child all in one go."

"Sounds ideal. Glad to hear that. If anyone would be a good father, it would be him. Such a shame he isn't here. All the things I could do with that man," Nolem said, and Leo laughed.

"I'm not sure he'd appreciate being locked in your home and treated as a slave to love," Leo said. Nolem was undeterred.

"You have not seen me in action. Any man would be honoured to be my slave."

"I've been told you're pretty good at potion-making," Dom added.

"If you two keep at this, I'll come down with some strange

illness, and you'll have no vocalist." Nolem threatened.

"Dom is pretty good. And we have a full band. I'm sure we can manage without you," Leo commented.

"What? You guys would be nothing without my vocal genius."

Leo knew where this was going. And sure enough, Nolem started to show off her perfect pitch and amazing range. Then she made an obviously intentional mistake.

"Well, it was almost perfect."

Leo remained calm, as did Dom. Nolem was clearly hoping one of them would mention she intentionally ruined the song, but neither of them was going to give her the satisfaction.

"So how is the Atorathian? Or should I say, do you live up to his standards?" Dom asked.

"Well, we haven't gotten that far yet…"

"Really?" Everyone was listening in, even if not talking. Dom and Nolem weren't the only ones to respond. Leo wondered if things could really be so bad that everyone finds the news shocking. It couldn't be that out of the norm for him to not bed someone.

"You must really love this guy. I haven't seen you this worked up since the demon you married," Nolem mused, which received a few nods of agreement from the rest of the band.

"She wasn't that bad."

"You could see her horns from another world. But you thought she was a *goddess*," Nolem said in a singsong voice.

"Okay, she was evil. But she spelled me."

"How many times are you going to tell that lie? Is it really so bad that you can't admit you fell for the woman? It could've happened to any man," Dom said. This time Leo's evil glare did work. "Okay, maybe not."

Nolem choked, trying to stifle a laugh, and Leo just sighed; this was going to be a long half-day—a very long half-day.

The rest of the day went by without problems and Leo was more than happy about that. They arrived in town at sundown and Leo decided to go straight to his room and read a book. As he had requested there were some books there—the innkeeper's private books that Leo was interested in reading. It was part of why they decided to be at this inn.

Revelations

They arrived in town just in time to miss the mad rush of travellers, which was part of why Leo went straight to his room: to take advantage of the quiet. His first task was to write a letter to Danais to let him know he was here. He knew Danais would've wanted to come, so he was going to give him a full account of what went on each day. It was the least he could do. Maybe this would finally count as a good-enough apology.

It was the third day, and the band had given their last performance. They'd had three days of multiple performances, and now they could get drunk, enjoy the festivities and go to some of the competitions.

Torak was coming up on the fourth day with some melons and vegetables. The festival usually had competitions that were zoned around the province they were in. There'd be hunting games and things of that sort, and of course home brew and wine competitions. It was one of the biggest events of the year.

Leo, however, wasn't going to be drinking on his first free night; he had other things to do. In his room waiting were a man and a woman. He was going to take his first step down the road of sexual exploration. He could just imagine the look on Danais' face when he read this letter.

The next night, Leo was sipping his way through more than a few drinks; he was getting used to this indecent act thing in only one day.

"Torak! It's been a long time. Grab a chair." Dom said noticing him before Leo did.

"Thanks, Dom."

Leo looked between Torak and his band member. "You two know each other?"

"Yes, we do, Leo."

It didn't take a genius to know how. More of this secrecy. Were all his friends infinitely older than he presumed? "So how are the twins—Log and Leg?" Torak asked, with a straight face and took a swig of beer.

Leo and everyone at the table had a good laugh at that comment. "That would be Dim and Dan. And they just went three years of age," Dom responded.

"Oh." Torak looked genuinely confused. Leo knew he

wasn't. "I always get them confused." Dom glared at him but Torak sipped on a drink that had just arrived ignoring the look. "Gods. What is this Dom. How can you drink this."

"That's what happens when you insult my children and steal drinks that don't belong to you." Dom responded as Torak mad a scene pretending to be quite ill from the offending beverage. It got the desired laughs from everyone accept Dom.

"Leo's looking a little dazed there." Torak said to Dom as if Leo couldn't hear him.

"He's probably thinking about Danais again," Dom commented before taking a sip of his drink. "He writes him a hundred letters a day. Especially now that he's overcome the indecent act thing."

"Really? That's what's been in those letters? No wonder Danais is smiling so much these days."

Leo lifted his head sharply at that. "He reads my letters?" Leo's entire spirit lifted knowing Danais was reading his letters the past two months.

"Great. See what you've done?" Nolem teased. "Now he'll never stop talking about him."

Leo let out a long sigh and stared down into his empty cup. "Am I really that bad?" The silence was answer enough. "Okay. I swear I won't mention his name again."

"Sure, and the sky is pink," Dom scoffed. "You've had him on your mind more out here than you did when you were closest to him."

"How does your wife put up with you, Dom?" Leo offered with a smirk.

"She doesn't. She sends me off to be with you humans. And when I'm home, she practically refuses to let me talk unless she's given me the order to do so. Something about not being able to form sentences of any intelligence, and she wants my children to have some. She claims to have saved all our children from idiocy."

"What you mean is she's smarter than you," Leo said with a laugh.

"Nah, she's just scary," Torak added, garnering more laughter from the table. "I've met his wife Leo. She could force anyone to bend to her will without magic. It's in the eyes."

"So, she has a little rage." Dom shrugged.

Revelations

"A little?" Torak chuckled. "I'm Atorathian, and that last fireball she threw at me knocked me off my feet and gave me a small burn," Torak said, glaring at Dom.

"You deserved that."

"All I said was her stew was okay. That meant I liked it. How was I supposed to know in her world it's a nice way of saying the food was awful?"

Everyone was in hysterics now. Leo was glad for Torak's arrival. It was distracting him from thinking about Danais, and it made for good entertainment. Between Dom and Barton, Leo doubted he'd ever have a dull moment.

Dom decided to take the conversation away from him and his wife. "So how are your children? You've got a few yourself."

"My daughter is doing her part for the cause. One of my sons, the youngest, is getting married, and my second youngest is still in his long-term partnership. My other four boys are still unattached. The oldest still pining for the love of his life who doesn't want him."

"Are any of your children, Dani?" Nolem asked. She was aware that his wife, whoever she was, was a Dani.

"The daughter's half, in appearance. She's a magician, so she doesn't have any of our gifts. It's extremely rare to have an Atorathian magician. And only two boys are Atorathian, both of whom are unattached. The rest, like my daughter, are clearly mixed but magicians all the same."

"Ah. And how's that nephew of yours? All I know is what Leo has to offer. But I doubt I can trust his opinion." Dom wasn't really concerned, but he thought it might be funny to ask.

"What is that supposed to mean?" Leo asked accusingly.

"You are insanely in love with him. Your opinion is questionable," Dom responded.

"I don't remember saying anything about love," Leo quipped.

"Are you or are you not writing a song for him?"

Leo hated how well-informed Dom seemed to be about this. He had no doubt that Nolem, who was looking incredibly innocent, told him about the song. She always caught him when he wrote a song for someone he liked enough.

"Don't look at me. I merely told him I heard you working on

a new song. What he does with that information is out of my hands. I'm just the messenger."

"I have no doubts you explained the details of the tune." Leo glared at her.

"And what would that matter? Unless of course, it was a tune that would lend itself to being written for a loved one."

Leo was clearly losing this battle. He honestly didn't know why he was trying to act like it wasn't true

"He's all right. A handful. I haven't told Leo this before, but I've had a few propositions for the boy before he came, even though he is a peasant. He has hardly any friends, so I don't know why anyone would want to marry their children to him."

"It could just be because you raised him. And from what I know of your boys, they aren't marrying anytime soon. It's a prize to get one of your children," Dom offered.

"True. I've had a few offers after Leo as well."

"Really? Why haven't I been told of this?" Leo wasn't too happy with this news. Could this be the real reason Danais wouldn't talk to him? Could Torak just be saying Danais was still interested in hopes he'd speak to him again? And who were these other offers coming from?

Leo ran out of thinking steam. He wasn't designed for this over-thinking like Danais was. That, and he didn't care enough to keep going.

"Yes," Torak drawled, "but Danais doesn't want any of that. He's been firm in asserting that he belongs to you. And if he asks, I was so drunk that last statement just fell out of me. I'm not supposed to be telling Leo anything that might strengthen his hopes."

Leo smiled. "Why is it that you like me so much? You go out of your way to shed light on an apparently hopeless situation and told me about his sweet habit."

"I like helping others win over my children. They're notoriously hard to catch. And besides, they know I'm doing it. They vent and drop subtle hints at my interference; I feign innocence. Did Leo tell you about his voice?"

"He did," Dom responded.

"As beautiful as his mother's."

"Wow." Dom gave a low whistle. "Now that's saying something."

Revelations

"You mentioned his parents?" Leo was a little taken aback. He thought all topics of Danais' lineage were off-limits.

"His mother was my sister," Torak explained. "It's not uncommon for people to talk about their family. However, she was not blessed with a long life. Many alive today were not alive when she was living. Which of course is why it's so easy to not talk about her."

"Ah. I was just grasping for something that might get you to talk about my parents."

Leo was glad Barton wasn't there; he absolutely hated when Leo did this. Leo surmised it was more because he wanted to say things to make him feel better than actually being about Leo's depression. In Barton's case, the secret-keeping was equally burdensome as it was to Leo wanting answers.

"Well, this conversation has been fun, but there's an Atorathian over there giving me the eye. Who knows? I might be able to make him want to marry me," Nolem announced before leaving the three men at the table.

"Seriously, with all the drinks and food, I'm surprised anyone is still walking around with their clothes on. This is Atorath, after all." Dom stated.

"True enough. It used to be that dangerous to have this festival in Atorath, Leo. Things have gotten more civilised. They just act indecently with their clothes on now." Torak responded.

Leo had a good laugh.

"You are old enough to remember those days?" Torak asked, already knowing it to be true.

"Remember I met my wife on one of those drunken days."

Leo glanced toward Dom. "Sounds like there is a lot about you that I don't know," Leo said.

"Well, you can't expect me to tell you everything." Dom said.

"I suppose not. So how many children do you have?"

"More than Torak. And yes, they are for my wife."

"Are you going to do anything special on this seventh day?" Torak asked.

Leo considered Torak's question. It was Danais' eighteenth name day. There had to be something that he could do. It didn't take him long to figure it out. It was a gamble. But it would answer some questions for him. Both secrets he would have to keep. One would tell him about Danais' parents, which would also simultaneously answer a question no one seemed to know. Still, all these answers depended on whether or not his idea worked. But he was going to try.

"I think I do have something worked out."

9
DANAIS

Danais had just finished a long day of work and was sitting with his thoughts and drink in the kitchen. It was the sixth day, and he knew his uncle would be back any moment to tell him how well he'd done at the festival. Why his uncle refused to stay until the end was beyond him.

The festival in Atorath ended on the day of the first month of Atora. This meant that it would extend one more day to the first day of the week, Mal. He assumed his uncle had more important tasks to do. He also assumed that as long as his uncle had been alive, missing one festival wouldn't be that drastic. Or it could be because his eighteenth name day was the following day. So many options to choose from.

"Atora," he thought to himself. Wouldn't it be amazing if he was the son of Atora? His earthly children notoriously died at age eighteen. If he were the son of Atora, he wouldn't live past the following day. As wonderful as it sounded, Danais wasn't too sure he wanted that. Fantasising about being the son of his own name was much more rewarding. The god Danais' children at least lived.

No letter had come for him that day, much to his disappointment. He was still a little mad at his uncle for not letting him talk to Leo the day he left. He was ready to beg him to take him along, but work had to be done. If Leo said it was too late to join the journey, he didn't want to have wasted valuable work time. His uncle, unfortunately, had made a point by saying that if he had changed his mind, Danais should've informed him. He couldn't be held accountable for lack of information. And if he wanted to go that bad, what's an hour or so of no work? It wouldn't have been the end of everything. Danais pouted, which only served to make him think of Leo more.

"Uncle?"

"Were you just waiting in here for me to arrive?"

"No. I only just came into the kitchen." Danais could see his uncle wasn't believing him. Lying wasn't going to serve him at this point, so Danais decided to just say what he was there for.

"Did Leo send anything for me?"

"He did."

Danais wasted no time opening the letter after his uncle handed it to him; however, he didn't know what to make of it. He gave his uncle an inquiring look.

Torak lifted an eyebrow. "Well, what does it say?"

"'Be at our spot at midnight. Love, Leo,'" Danais read out loud.

"That's it?" Torak sounded disappointed.

"Clearly, you're as shocked as I am."

"Considering all the previous letters, yes. No details or descriptions? I guess I assumed this one being before your name day would be more—"

"Impressive. Maybe he's going to surprise me and show up like betaves do. It's usually not done over long-range 'cause it saps energy with long distances. Apparently in combat, it doesn't take much at all, so it's much more effective."

"That is an option. But why not just come back now and save himself the magical effort? Like I did."

"Maybe he's going to bring something with him that he doesn't want anyone to see but me?"

"I doubt even you believe that," Torak responded.

Danais didn't bother confirming what Torak already knew was true. Instead, he decided on a change of topic. "So how was the fair?"

"Okay."

"I take it that means you didn't win first place in anything." Danais smirked.

Torak *harrumphed*. "The judges wouldn't know good food if food could talk."

"So?"

"Second in everything! If I knew that was going to happen, I could've fed my first-class food to people who would appreciate it."

Despite the protest, Danais knew his uncle well enough to know he was pleased. It's one thing to not win, but another to have so many top spots. That showed quality in all areas. Still, Danais thought it his duty to pretend to be outraged at this. His apparent disapproval must have made an impression.

His uncle saw fit to pour Danais some of his expensive wine. Danais had the idea to up his performance even more, but there was no point in overdoing it. His uncle knew he was faking so overdoing it might result in no more wine.

"So how is Leo?" Danais asked casually, trying not to look his uncle in the eye.

"He is doing well. Looking much better than he was when he left. I guess he's feeling better, even though you don't write him back."

"Did he ask about me?"

"He's dangerously in love with you; why wouldn't he ask about you?" Torak admitted. "And I told him that you're like a puppy here, just pining for his return."

Danais gasped. "Uncle!"

"Okay… maybe I didn't say it exactly like that. But it amounts to the same thing."

"You meddle for your own enjoyment."

"I do not," Torak took offense.

"You do. You did much the same with all your children. When you think someone is worthy, you go out of your way to help them win your child's love." Danais smiled and crossed his arms. "It doesn't seem to work very well for you."

"I care about my children's well-being as any parent should," Torak protested again. "Besides, I've always liked Leo. Having him like my favourite nephew is brilliant in many ways."

Danais raised an eyebrow. "Ah, so it's more about him than it is about me."

"I don't remember saying any of that," Torak said with a frown.

"I heard it though."

Torak sighed. "It's a parent thing. You can't blame me for

trying to exert my influence when I think my children aren't making the right choice."

Danais gave his most serious and disapproving look to his uncle. "How can you expect them to make the right choice if you're *helping* the choice? They'll be falling for the person you create!"

"Bah. You sound like my wife."

"Who is this busy wife of yours? I notice your children are either Dani, Atorathian or an obvious mix."

"You may already know who she is."

"I've met her?" After all that had happened recently Danais wasn't entirely surprised by this information. "I'm not going to hurt my head over that. I'm too busy over-thinking this short letter."

Torak couldn't help but laugh at that.

"So what did you really find out about him, Uncle?" Danais asked after a moment.

"He daydreams about you all the time. Has all his letters proofread before he sends them. He agonises over them."

"I doubt that." Danais chuckled.

"I cannot tell a lie. They say they have to force him to stop thinking about you to entertain serious or even unserious conversation. I will say he expected you'd take him back."

"He knows me too well. And I'm sure all your hinting helped."

"Alright. You've made your point about my meddling," Torak said and they both chuckled. "Also, I think he just decided he'd done all he could and accepted it had worked." He paused. "He could still be wrong."

"But he isn't wrong. Why wouldn't he be waiting patiently for a known outcome?"

"You look a little pleased with yourself," Torak noted.

"I am. Have you seen Leo?" Danais couldn't help but smile. It was more than obvious Leo was someone to be proud of having.

"Indeed, I have. So, it's a physical thing then?"

"We haven't done anything like that... yet."

"And when he comes back, have the decency to sleep with him at the inn. You know he's too large to fit in your bed."

"He said he doesn't mind sleeping on the stone floor. It is

quite warm now, after all. And there's much more floor than any bed can provide."

Danais did his best to avoid the glare his uncle gave him. He was quite sure Leo didn't mind sleeping on the floor. They'd spent many nights sleeping outside by the river, after all. Still, it was wrong to a degree. If they were going to come inside, what was a few extra minutes' walk down the mountain to the town?

"It's rude to ignore someone when they're glaring at you," Kale said. Danais glared at him in response. This appearing out of nowhere was very inconvenient sometimes. Of all the moments to arrive during this part of the conversation is when he did.

"Uncle, were you married more than once?"

"No. And I have no children outside of my marriage, but only by luck—not from lack of fucking."

"How did you know she was the one?"

"How do you know Leo is?"

Danais sighed; he thought he was going to be thinking about it for a while, but found he was answering almost immediately. "I don't know that he is. I just—it just is. I can't explain it. It just feels right without me actually having to know. Guess the two don't go hand in hand."

"Not all the time." Torak sighed. "Look. Here's my take on love. In my experience, love isn't in the knowing. When you get that unexplainable feeling that pulls, connects you to someone, then you know. It's not knowing in the regular sense. Love doesn't conform to human rules of knowing. And even then, it could turn out that that thing fades away. Leo himself has been married twice and we both know how well the second one didn't go." Torak chuckled. He, much like everyone else, teased him about that mistake. "How he didn't see that from a mile away is still baffling."

Danais thought about it for a few seconds. "So, it's a combination of feelings, then. No one way to know. It just is. That's... complicated."

"Yes and no. Clearly, you're there. Knowing is in the unexplainable: the absence of pinpointing any one thing that defines why they are the one. Love—well, it just exists."

"It just is." Danais thought about that. It had been repeated quite a lot during their talk. It was something so complex and simple; it amazed him. He had never thought that something could be easy to understand based on its complexity. But now, for him, that thing— was love.

Danais wasn't quite sure if he would have to wait until midnight, but his name day wasn't until then, so it was the most logical option. Maybe he should've asked for a clock for his 18th name day. He wasn't even sure what a clock looked like, though he was sure a few people had them in the town. Who was the first person to split the days up into twenty-four hours anyway? Why twelve months? Why seven days a week, thirty days a month when twenty-eight would've been an even split? That was something he was going to have to ask Leo.

The time of day was invented long before the clock, so who invented the first sundial? Were they peasant or magician? It wouldn't be the first thing to come out of a peasant that stuck. Like the different styling of hair, and colouring. Even tattooing was invented by the ungifted. Some things just required a skill that one either had or didn't. Magic helped, but if a person had no skill for it to start magic would have to do all the work which, naturally, required more powerful spells. Better spells, especially for the non-magician, cost more money.

Why wasn't it midnight yet? How long was he going to have to stand here? Why didn't his uncle, who had an impeccable sense of time, not tell him he came down too early? He was going to have to complain as soon as they next spoke.

Furthermore, why was he so nervous? Maybe it was because this was the first time he'd be awake on the first hour of his nameday; the first time he'd get a gift that meant something; the first time he was in a relationship with someone on his nameday. Not that that was a great feat. He'd never paired with anyone before after all. And why not birthday instead of nameday. It was the day of his birth after all. Maybe he should start calling it that. See if it caught on. Could this be how all the new words got created? Someone just connected dots or simply said 'I'm going to call it this,' and it landed?

Danais felt a cool breeze sweep past him. It smelled of— Danais was about to assess the situation when he saw something he never thought would be possible in his lifetime:

a sea spirit was walking towards him. It was the same height as a Kentai, with smooth blue skin with a purple transparent sheen, a face shaped like a kangaroo, and ears shaped like pear drops. It had perfectly round eyes of grey that shun in the way that opal was black, with locks much like the seer's and the same grey as its eyes. It had webbed feet and a long tail with a ridged triangle at the point.

"Hello, Danais."

Danais was so shocked he couldn't reply. The spirit continued to look at him and smiled warmly. Eventually, Danais came to his senses.

"Hello…" Danais paused since he didn't have a name to complete the sentence with.

"Karn."

"Karn. You're a sea spirit."

"That I am. Much like Kale is an earth spirit."

"Are you a prince as well?"

"I am. I roam the seas and help creatures of the ocean and the odd human here and there. I prefer to wander, much like Kale does."

"Why are you here?"

"I am here because you have a very special friend."

"I do?"

"Leo. He has asked something of the God, and the God is pleased. He sends you a gift." The sea spirit handed him a bracelet. Danais was so shaky he almost dropped it.

"This… this is a god stone." He looked at the object in his hand with awe. "Many god stones."

Danais stared in awe and shock. God stones were smooth, transparent, and always shifting in appearance; they never looked the same. It was a subtle effect of movement that couldn't be matched by most magicians. And they were touched with a trace of the God so that only the people gifted them could identify the God who created the stone if they saw another stone from that God on someone.

Danais' bracelet was a sea-green with purple flecks that seemed to move in a revolving swirl. They were linked together by a nearly indestructible, rare, reddish-brown seaweed. The strongest ropes and bindings were built from this sea grass. The stones had the smooth feel and transparency of glass, so he could see the chocolate of his skin through the stone.

The sea spirit then handed him another, larger stone set: an anklet. This one was purple and solid. Not linked like the other one was. Which was... strange.

"How will I get this one on?" Danais eyed it sceptically, finding no way to open it.

"Try."

Danais took the stone and attempted to slide it over his foot. To his amazement, it slid right on, even though it was too small to go over his foot and heal. It was, however, the perfect size for his ankle.

"Are they both from the God Danais?"

"The bracelet is. But the anklet, no. It will take the shape of wherever you choose to wear it. Somehow the God felt you'd wear it more on your ankle. In any event, you are not to talk about who these are from to anyone unless, of course, they recognise it. Then it is acceptable." The sea spirit smiled, a cool, cold, unfeeling smile. "The anklet, however, is special. I cannot tell you aloud for fear of who might hear, but there are some who will know intuitively, not because they can actually recognise it. Should someone look at it and recognise it, they must be apprehended immediately. This you must tell the others. But it is on the God's orders that you cannot speak any more of what you know to anyone who doesn't already know. Is that understood?"

Danais nodded slowly. "Yes." Danais reasoned it was likely that only those considered to be the enemy owned a stone from that particular god.

"After all that, I can say that all things are subject to change. You will know without question if it is okay to reveal who the bracelet is from. Otherwise, they both came from Leo. That is enough." She pulled out another stone set. "This one is for Leo. There are no rules attached to this stone necklace. It's from the Goddess of the Sun. Leo's. A late name day gift."

"Is this—?" there was very vibrant and busy flame within the stone.

"Yes. She chose to make it with actual flames from the sun."

"Was there anything else?"

"Anything else?"

"I know Leo. He wouldn't ask of the God to deliver me gifts.

He would ask that they deliver me a gift of his own first. And to gift me if they so choose."

"Leo is a wise man. He instructed me not to give you his gift unless you asked for it. He seemed quite sure that you would ask, though. We decided to humour him and follow orders."

Danais smiled. It was just like Leo to anticipate his actions without magic. He knew Danais would find that impressive.

Apparently, the sea spirit thought it was impressive as well. "It would seem he has a lot of faith in his perception of you."

"I have no doubt he knows me much better than I think I know me."

"Here is the letter." Karn handed over a plain, white envelope stamped with Vardon family seal. "Do not open it until I have gone."

"Will you stay?" Danais asked as he took the envelop and tucked it close to this heart. "I seem to do most of my talking to things most humans never talk to. Kale, Xan, and now you. I wish I knew why there was so much, ah, supernatural interest in me."

"Your friends are a product closer to who you are than you think."

"How so?"

"In Leo's short life, he has helped many. It's easy for us to be partial to you because he is one of the few magicians, and a dark one, who are genuinely respectful of all the creatures of Salinor. Your uncle isn't the only one who likes him."

"And I treat him so…" Danais couldn't find the words to finish.

"You treat him as you should. You have done the one thing no one else has ever been able to do."

"And what is that?"

"Break through the last of his prejudices," she responded simply. "No one is perfect. You make him rethink his opinion on things, and he does the same for you. You are good for each other."

"Can I swim with you?"

"Why?"

"I would like to know what it's like to breathe underwater."

"You mean you would like to remember?"

Danais, confused by the response, gave Karn a questioning

look. "I don't understand?"

"And you won't. Not for a long time."

It was daybreak, and Danais woke up alone on the beach with no memory of the swim with a sea spirit.

He pulled himself to a sitting position. It was now time to open the letter. He made sure the sea spirit was gone before proceeding. The last thing he wanted to do was ruin its contents by opening it too soon.

He opened the envelope pulled out the letter and gasped. He knew what this was. This was magic anyone could identify: blue parchment with golden words that lifted off the page.

He read it, but the spelled letter didn't take effect on him until he reached the end:

Danais,

If I knew the only way to see you happy, to hold you in my arms, was to draw my last breath… I would gladly give up my life. I would be content to die knowing that my last wish brought you extreme pleasure. Compared to your happiness, my life is as useless as lost thought. I hold my breath in anticipation of when you will allow me to breathe my love again for you.

Love

Leo.

Danais started to weep. As his tears hit the letter, a mist arose from the parchment. It swirled up as high as his chin, making a thick fog. Then it started to thin out, and Danais saw in front of him a gift that even he knew was special: a black rose with a red stem. Leo had gifted him an immortal rose, a gift that would never die or fade.

A gift activated by his tears.

He folded the letter up and slid it back in the envelope, then grabbed the rose out of the sky and walked back up to the farm. For the first time in a while, he didn't feel the urge to work. Danais loved his job, so such days were few and far between.

His uncle was downing a mug of ale when he arrived. "What is that?"

"Leo's gift." Danais handed his uncle the letter, and if his uncle was shocked or impressed, his face didn't betray his thoughts.

"It's an immortal rose," was all Torak said.

"Yes. I'm not even sure how the spell works. I've heard of the immortal rose, but I'd have expected him to torture me like an evil magician before performing this type of magic."

His uncle let out a slight chuckle at that statement. Danais continued. "Not even someone who despised magicians as much as I once did would deny this type of gift. I hear that even the best of magicians can't get it right."

"When he tells you how it is done, you'll know why. My wife gifted me much the same. Maybe I'll show it to you one day."

"You have an immortal rose?"

"In a manner of speaking."

"Do you know when he'll be coming back?"

"No. It's a long journey. He will be here today if that helps."

"I know that, Uncle. I meant the time of day." Danais sighed. He was going to be forced to be in high anticipation all day.

"Of all the things Leo could've taught you, the least you could've picked up on was patience."

"Bah. He should've left early to be here. Why send me such a gift and not be here to see my reaction?" That was when he felt the presence of something much too large to be a cat and not one of the dogs on his lap. Kale.

"And you're going to tell him that?"

"More or less." Danais wasn't entirely sure, but it made sense in the moment.

"I have to admit this is something worth sending you to the river for."

"You have no idea when he's going to be back?"

"Not really. But his band is having a good time. If he comes back today, it's only because he managed to force them to leave a day early."

"Oh well. If he must, he must." Danais took a bite out of a cookie as he watched his uncle leave. Kale seemed to have settled in enough on Danais' lap to fall asleep, so Danais stroked his fur while finishing the cookie with the other hand. Leo just had to show up any minute, he thought, so why bother to leave? He decided to just wait in the kitchen until Leo arrived.

Danais woke up much later with a half-eaten cookie in one hand, and his head on the kitchen table. How long had he been asleep? Did he miss Leo? Had he already come and gone? Was he still here? How could his uncle let him sleep almost an entire day?

At least he still smelled clean, so if Leo did magically appear, it wouldn't be too bad. And since he slept all day, he was spared having to live the anxiety of waiting for him. That is if he still didn't have more than an hour to wait.

He went outside and the dogs attacked him. Danais ended up rolling around on the ground with three energised and playful beasts who didn't understand he had things to do. It took him a minute to escape from them and then convince them not to follow him. He enjoyed the love, but he had an important meeting to be ready for. He picked a nice spot on the hill overlooking the fields and it wasn't long before one of the dogs came to him. At least now it wasn't trying to suffocate him with joy, and he was alone.

Judging by the setting sun, it had to be close to the end of the working day with no more than an hour or two to go. Danais realised that this was the hill where the rock was thrown at him. He stopped suddenly.

Where is my rose? he thought and went into a panic. He knew for sure it wasn't in the kitchen before he left. He'd grabbed some more cookies and some milk, so he'd circled the kitchen well before leaving. So where was the rose? He went into the kitchen with it. His uncle saw it. Would his uncle steal it? Could someone who the gift didn't belong to even touch it?

"Panicking is definitely one of your strong points," Kale's voice came out of nowhere. He was standing beside the dog, petting its side.

"You have a better idea, Kale?" Danais demanded, his voice shrill and quick. "I'd rather panic and think of where I left it than start running around looking for it when it could be somewhere close!"

"It is close enough."

Danais instantly knew what that meant; at least, he had an

idea.

"Do you have it?"

"No."

"Then you know where it is?"

"Yes."

"Are you going to tell me?"

"I'll trade you the information for that chocolate brownie you have in your hand."

Now Danais was struggling. He knew the gift was obviously safe, but he did need to get it back before Leo returned, and this really nice, gooey, sweet treat was the key to this mystery. He had no doubt Kale would tell him after Leo came, but after not talking to him for weeks. How then could he expect Leo to respond well to knowing he lost such a gift?

"I'm waiting," Kale mentioned with a smile.

Danais sighed. The gods were so cruel. He reluctantly handed over the last square without taking a bite. Kale took a bite before answering.

"It's on your arm. Tattooed. It transferred during the conversation with your uncle."

Danais looked at his left arm, and sure enough, there it was: a tattoo of the rose, almost glistening as if with morning dew. Annoyed, he realized he gave up his chocolate for nothing. On his arm? Leo would've known it was there.

"You tricked me! Leo would've known to look for it somewhere on me."

"Yes…But you see, this was a particularly tasty-looking treat."

"Just eat it," Danais commanded with an eye roll.

"You can at least give him half of it back, you know."

Danais turned around, and even as small as he was, practically knocked Leo over jumping into his arms.

Leo chuckled. "I guess you are happy to see me."

Danais smiled widely. "Yes. I am."

Leo returned his smile. "I am as well. A lot can change in one week."

"Yes, so your letters tell me. I guess you won't be calling anyone a common whore anymore."

"Must you remind me?" Leo said with a smaller smile and put Danais down.

Revelations

"Yes. I must." He playfully punched Leo's arm. "I enjoyed all the gifts. I even have one for you." Danais handed him a black leather necklace with a God stone on the end of it. Inside this stone appeared to be a mountain with a storm of fire circling it.

"It's from Leos--Goddess of the Sun."

"For me?" Leo turned it in his hand and examined it. "But why?"

"I wasn't told. The sea spirit just said to give it to you. You know who both of these gifts are from, then?"

"Yes, though I don't recognise any of them."

"I was told I could tell you everything, but only one thing to everyone else."

"What is it?"

Danais explained everything that had transpired. Leo smiled. He had confirmation of one thing he was sure everyone already knew, and of another that he was still unsure if anyone knew. That would raise a lot of questions he didn't have time to delve into presently. He knew he couldn't tell Danais for now, but he was okay with that.

They walked hand in hand down to the river just as the sun had gone down. Leo thought this was the perfect time to let Danais read the letter he had gotten for his own nameday. The one with the seed from the dragon that Barton had brought up many months ago. He hadn't told anyone what it was specifically for but now, Danais knew.

"Are you sure that you want to do this with me?" Danais had finished reading the letter. It explained the seed that came with it would allow them to create a child. Leo wanted to have a child with him. Danais was stunned. Leo couldn't be serious—could he?

"Yes."

"I don't know what to say. Does anyone know about this?"

"Yes. But only you know that it is from a dragon and what it will grow into. We can do it right now... if you don't mind me performing magic."

"No, I don't mind," Danais said slowly, "but this seems complicated. I don't know anything about magic, and I can see that."

"It is a complicated spell," Leo offered. "He's been working on it for months, so it doesn't have anything to do with us. But I've thought about it." Before Danais could interrupt, Leo held up a hand to stop him. "Even if we don't last, you've probably made me grow the most anyone will for the rest of my life. Actually, I'm sure a lot of my issues would never have sorted themselves out quite so well if you weren't so moody and stubborn. If I'm going to do this, I'd rather do it with someone who made me a better man. It's probably the only chance I'll have at a child if I never fuck a woman again."

Danais was both glad and shocked to hear such a thing, especially from Leo. "Never?"

"Anything is possible." Leo shrugged.

"Not even with me? I hear you've done a few of those without me—up to five in one bed," Danais playfully chided. "Especially the one about the girl who refused to let you put it in her," Danais said, getting the laugh he wanted.

"You've made your point. I do like women still. And you've seen it. It's big, but not the biggest. She was clearly overreacting."

"Apparently *she* thought otherwise. Still, it is exceptional. You could hurt someone with that. Considering how big you are outside of that particular appendage, it makes sense. It'd be weird if it was smaller, you being so big and tall otherwise."

Danais laughed as Leo rolled his eyes and thumbed the seed which was red and blue melding together "And when are you going to let me try it out on you?"

"Honestly, I don't know. Does that bother you?"

"No." Leo kissed him, and Danais practically fell into his arms. If this was what love felt like, he could drown in Leo's kisses—and in his arms—forever.

"I have a question. How does the gift you gave me work?" His uncle thought it was an impressive gift as did he, so might as well find out while it was fresh on his mind.

"Well, the letter is spelled, as you know. For it to work, the reader must be moved to cry. They have to feel that emotion they get when they're so happy or so sad that they want to cry. The magic of the letter will take over from there, producing tears and then the rose, as in your case."

Revelations

"It's not always a rose?"

"No. It usually takes the shape of the emotion the reader feels— usually it is some kind of plant, though. It wasn't just that you expected it to be a rose, but to your heart, that would be the one thing that would most definitely remind you of me."

"Then why is it black and red?"

"That's complicated. I use a lot of dark magic, so it could be that. Then it could also be because of the pain from what I did to you. Mix that with the emotion of whether you should've already taken me back. I guess the love would be in the red of the stem, and the storm of emotions would be the black."

"So, a storm of emotions would always be black?"

"It depends. The spell works purely on the connection between you and me. For someone else, if their situation were similar, different colours could represent the same thing on a rose. That's what makes this spell so special. With the array of emotions colours and plant life it could be anything."

"Blood and dark magic are involved. I didn't realise it was that complicated of a spell," Danais admitted.

"It's circumstantial magic, so it's hard to make, but once it's done, it depends solely on the situation. If you get it wrong, chances are that even if the crying part of the spell works, there may be no gift. It took me until moments before midnight to get it right. I said my prayer and chucked it into the ocean on faith and you received it. The God could've ignored me."

"But he didn't." Danais kissed him again. "Thank you. Two gifts from the gods and a night spent with a sea spirit. It was the best gift ever. What more could a guy ask for?"

"Guy?" Leo questioned with a raise eyebrow.

"New word the peasants are using for 'man.' Boy, girl, guy, gal. It's informal."

"Most of the good informal language comes from the peasants."

"This is true," Danais admitted. He looked up the sinking sun. "It will be dark soon."

"We should head back up. I want to talk to your uncle."

8
LEO

Leo was perfectly happy to have Danais in his rightful place: on his back. After weeks of being without him, Leo was back to explaining magic: telling Danais who made the first clock, explaining how the months are named after gods and humans, and how the days of the week have names chosen at random. Leo wished he could've taken Danais with him. Danais was overloading him with questions about the festival.

"I see I must relinquish my spot again," Xan said.

"Must you always complain? I don't carry him that often," Leo responded, somewhat exasperated.

"Really? Then why do you think I'm always complaining? There must be some reason why. You think I do it too much?"

"I didn't say you do it too much—only all the time," Leo said. Danais stifled a laugh.

"Uh huh. I'm hearing the difference. No, really, I am. Always complaining is very much different from all the time," Xan responded this time Danais did laugh.

"Must you be so difficult? And why do you always laugh at him?" Leo asked Danais.

"I don't know what you mean. Are you saying I am always laughing or that I'm laughing all the time?"

Leo would've glared at Danais, but it would've been lost on him, seeing as Danais couldn't see his face. Leo growled instead; that he could do. It had no effect other than to send the other two further into an uncontrollable episode of laughter. Danais' laugh was infectious. Leo was finding it increasingly hard to maintain his mock annoyance.

It took longer than it should've to get to the house. Leo had walked slowly just to enjoy the clever banter and to get in some hits of his own. They couldn't all be jests at him, after all.

Revelations

"So the man has returned."

"That I have, Torak, that I have." Leo replied.

"You know you've got something unsightly growing out of your back there?"

"I've been trying to get rid of it, but it refuses to go away," Leo said as he put Danais down. Danais ran straight for the fresh bread. Leo laughed. Danais would consider food to be more important than a wisecrack.

"I have a question," Leo inquired. "Would it be possible for us to do a spell here? I have all the ingredients." Leo handed the spell over to Torak. "These are the instructions."

Leo waited patiently for an answer. It was the thing to do. One never performed serious magic without permission on private grounds. Things could go wrong if a person invaded someone's space knowingly and without asking if it was okay. If Torak said no, he would have to go outside the borders of the property, which meant edging the forest. Leo much preferred to brew the spell in open air, so the mists could have free range to shape as they needed, without the restriction of trees.

He didn't know how the spell would react. Most could just be done in random spots, hiding amongst the trees but if he needed a glade or open area, he didn't know the woods well enough to find one quickly.

"Sure," Torak said as he perused the piece of paper. He looked up at Leo and frowned. "This is a serious potion. Danais has agreed?"

"He has."

"And you did not think to ask me if that was okay?"

"Did any of your children ask if they could have a child? He is a man capable of making his own decisions. For good or bad."

"True." Torak nodded in agreement. "Well, if this is to be, then I'll make sure all the servants and workers are gone. Then you can start the spell."

A few hours later:

Leo scried his sister to grab some ingredients from their

home and went down the mountain to meet her at the docks. After he returned Danais helped Leo build a stone fire pit, and they rested the cauldron on top of it. It was large, but not too large, and red: just big enough for the two of them to stand in. Next to the cauldron, a small table held a variety of ingredients: eye of newt, Phoenix feathers, a scorpion, a Kraken Tentacle, unicorn horn shavings, dragons' blood, soil, and many other seemingly unidentifiable—to Danais—substances.

"Most of these are extremely hard to get," Danais mused. "You've got legs of the golden tarantula? This assortment must've cost a fortune, even to a Vardon!"

"Yes. Over the years, a magician slowly grows their storeroom of ingredients and potions. Some potions must be made to use as a drop or two in another potion. Being part Keldonian, I've taken a bit of interest in making potions."

"So some smaller potions are more or less just ingredients? Can they be used on their own?"

"Some can. A drop of the drought of death can destroy on its own, but it's more subtle when mixed in another potion. It can even be used in a strength or love potion but seeing as it's so strong, you have to be careful how you use it. And some potions, as you said, are useless but extremely potent in the right spells. It's good to make your own potions because some magicians charge high prices."

"Why?"

"Some of the potions are quite complex, but even the simple ones are hard to make perfect. If they aren't perfect—the right colour or smell or thickness—things can go horribly wrong. Or just wrong enough to be missed which is sometimes, if not most times, worse. That's why schooling is a must for magicians. I grew into potion-making. It wasn't one of my stronger skills but like I said being part Keldonian I was always interested, and I am sure that's why I became so adept at it.

"Also, some spells work better with a potion than just using natural magics. Barton is an excellent potion-maker. Which is interesting as he is Mironian. He might be part Dani, but he hasn't ever admitted to me what his other side is and I suspect he dims it a bit. But that's irrelevant to what we are doing now."

"What are we waiting for now?"

"The water to get to a boil. Then the first potion I put in

already should release a green vapour. Then we begin. Are you okay with your part?"

"I'm not sure."

"Would you like me to do it for you?"

"Yes. I'm scared. What if something happens?"

"You don't have to."

"No. Take it all. I want to give as much as you give. Maybe more."

"You're okay with me putting a spell on you so you can understand me?"

"You've already done it. No need to ask."

Leo was more comfortable speaking in Mironi even if Danais couldn't understand the language. He also wanted to be absolutely sure Danais was in agreeance with this. What Danais was about to do wasn't something to take lightly. He knew Danais had a longer personal journey than he: a peasant overcoming his hate of magic and magicians, yet he seemed to embrace it so well. He would've never guessed that a whole season, three full months ago, Danais would be so willing to do this.

This made Leo fall in love with him all over again.

He looked up and saw the moon. It rained for a moment, as it always did around Danais. Leo took that as a sign that the gods were watching. Or at least one God was. Even if a god wanted to get directly involved, the window for meddling was over for what they were doing unless something drastic happened. Still, the presence of a god before calling on one was always welcome.

"Should I remove my shirt?" Danais asked in a small voice. "Yours is off."

"Yes. With the summer heat and vapours we'll be inhaling, we will soak them through, even though it didn't rain long enough to do so."

Danais smiled as he took off his shirt. Leo could stare at that smile forever. But the vapours were rising, and the smell was potent.

It was time.

Leo stood on one side of the cauldron and Danais on the other. The heat was smouldering. He started the incantation, and he and Danais began to circle the cauldron counterclockwise. He threw the first potion in as instructed. The cauldron sizzled, the mist turned blue, and the contents turned black.

Leo spoke in the low whisper singsong of magician speech. He gave cues to Danais, and he would grab ingredients from the table as instructed. Sometimes they would stand still and sometimes they would walk clockwise. Leo had given Danais specific instructions on how each ingredient and potion should be added to the mix. Numbers and timing were the keys to a perfect mixture. It was never as simple as simply adding this and adding that. Leo, with what little part of him hadn't given entirely over to the magic at hand, could tell that Danais was accurate.

The final ingredients had to be added while stirring, so Leo didn't have to be as magically enthralled and could simply ask Danais to get the ingredients. After more counting of turns, seconds in between turns, dropping in ingredients at precisely the right moments, mixtures of clockwise and counterclockwise movement, the potion was finally almost complete. Leo and Danais stripped, and Leo spoke to the cauldron's milky-coloured mixture before they entered.

"After I add this, the water will cool instantly, and we will get in," Leo announced.

Danais nodded, and as Leo said when he dropped in the golden tarantula leg, it bubbled and went completely cool. An orange mist escaped. The two of them got into the cauldron. The water came up to Danais' waist, but Leo had to kneel, bringing him down a little lower than Danais.

Danais chuckled. "Ah, so this is what it's like to be taller than you—if only by a little."

Leo laughed. "Okay, now this is the difficult part."

"Lynton—"

Leo hadn't expected to hear his true name, but after so long away from Danais, it was welcome. "You must completely give yourself over to this, or it won't work. Are you sure you're okay with it?"

"Yes. Just scared."

"Fright is okay, just so long as it doesn't diminish your commitment and conviction."

"If this fails, will I lose my sacrifice?"

"No. It only affects people with magical powers that way and the person performing the spell. And I'm wielding the magic."

"So even if I had magic, if I didn't lend it to the spell, it wouldn't affect me?"

"Correct."

"What will it do to you?"

"Double spell, double split of soul. Same as if I gave two arms. Then it pieces back darker but stronger than before, so for me it's the same. Nonmagicians won't ever have to worry about much with these spells." Leo looked at Danais as he contemplated this. He could give as little or as much as he wanted, but the spell would be that much stronger and better if the sacrifice were equal. Keeping the energy of the spell going wasn't using up too much of his energy, so he was willing not to do it until Danais was sure.

"It's okay. Do it," Danais said finally.

Leo nodded. He took Danais' hand into his own, pulling it away from Danais' body just enough to put his other hand with the blade beneath the arm at the shoulder. He felt something, though, some sort of resistance. He couldn't do it like this. He waited a moment or two. He stared into Danais' eyes.

More time passed, and then Leo felt it.

He knew Danais was ready.

In one swift stroke, he sliced Danais' arm clean off at the joint and then did the same to his arm and started the magician-speak.

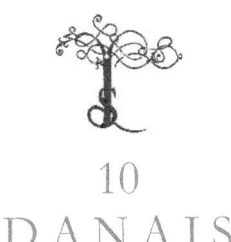

10

DANAIS

Leo's soul was going to be sliced open multiple times. The

larger the sacrifice the bigger the split. An arm, in his mind, could be an easy double split of a soul so two arms four? Leo said double, but he could be downplaying it. Could Danais really deal with that? Danais thought about it for a moment and decided that he could.

"It's okay. Do it."

Danais felt the blade against his body. Leo was preparing to slice, to take the arm from the shoulder. Then something peculiar happened. There was an absence of everything. The power of the spell, the emotion behind it, anxiety—everything was just gone.

Something wasn't right.

Danais couldn't feel the potion he was standing in, couldn't smell the vapours, couldn't feel the air. Sense the heat rising from the burning cauldron. How could there just be—nothing?

He looked into Leo's eyes, wondering what could've gone wrong. His eyes were cold like blue ice, yet still, there was something there, an emotion that could only be detected and then seen. Then he heard Leo's voice as clear as the starry night sky.

"Trust me. Believe in me. Believe in us. Let go."

Leo was speaking to him, though his lips weren't moving.

Danais was blocking.

Resisting.

He wasn't letting his all flow into the spell. He wasn't willingly sacrificing.

He took a deep breath and attempted to let go. He wanted this, and even more, he wanted to do this for Leo. Leo chose him. Whether they remained together or not wasn't important; he wanted this child with him. That was enough; it was more than enough.

The feeling came back, along with the pain of losing an arm. Danais knew the spell wasn't over, so he let himself continue to release until he was so lost in the spell that he didn't realise what was going on. Leo had cut off his arm; the water was bubbling again, and the vapours were an orange haze that was consuming them like a fog.

Leo had closed his eyes and was deep in the wordsong. His

Revelations

voice seemed to carry far: appearing more powerful without actually getting louder. Then the orange mist seemed to float away in the wind. The bubbles settled, though the water was still boiling hot. Leo instructed Danais to get out of the cauldron.

"What will happen now?" Danais asked.

"Wait."

Danais did as he was told, and soon he saw the black rose floating above the cauldron. He had given the arm with the immortal rose. Leo had assured him that even if the sacrifice was incomplete, the rose would return. Danais then felt a warming sensation in his left shoulder. He watched as slowly, but gradually his arm re-grew. It was the most intriguing magical feat he had seen.

He realized that he'd been a part of blood magic. He grabbed the rose and then pulled his pants back on, as did Leo. The moon was beautiful in the sky above them, but Danais wasn't going to be allowed to stare at it for long.

"I want to plant it in the forest. Do you know a place?" Leo asked.

"There's a small glade we could go to. What will grow?"

"What would you like to grow?"

Danais knew exactly what type of tree he wanted. Leo was different: too calm, too smooth, too cool. This was what blood magic did. This was what extensive blood magic did. How had Leo managed to keep so much of his former self when this was the essence of who he was now? Danais was afraid, but somehow his sense of safety overwhelmed his fear. His fear of what would be called a dark wizard. This was that thing about Leo that always seemed off. What he couldn't describe. It was always there but now just in full view.

"Show me. Come."

Danais for the first time felt complete trust in the real Leo, resulting from just one word. This was something Danais recognised to be the same. Amongst everything from the changed speech patterns to Leo's aura and the lack of obvious physical emotions, that one word sounded exactly the same. This was the Leo he could identify with, and it belonged more to what he saw now than what Danais usually saw. This was the man he loved.

"Come."

Danais did as he was told, and when he reached Leo, he grabbed his hand and led him into the forest. The glade seemed much larger than Danais remembered and was far enough away from the farm to be easily missed. If one knew the way through the woods, chances were one would never come across here unless they were looking for it or lost.

"Plant it. In the middle, here," Leo said as he handed Danais the seed. "The tree you want to grow will grow."

Danais did as instructed. Leo handed him a phial of the potion from the cauldron, and Danais poured it onto the patted soil and waited, though both knew nothing spectacular was going to happen on the first day.

The two of them walked down the mountain and to the inn. It was nearing midnight. Danais was figuring that the spell must've taken at least two hours to complete. He was sitting alone while Leo was at the bar. Kale and Xan were with him.

"I know I've asked this before, but should I be worried?"

"No," Xan replied. "I'd suggest you just be yourself. Chances are the more time you spend with him, the more you'll notice that he's like this most of the time. It's just not obvious unless—"

"You really know him," Danais finished.

"Yes. I'm sure your uncle explained it well enough."

"He did. Still, it's hard to immediately get rid of evil and replace it with dark. Though they're different, they are also similar."

"No. They are drastically different. It's something you'll have to learn about magicians. No matter their choice of magic," Xan replied.

"It doesn't determine who they are. Magicians that never touch blood magic can be evil," Kale added as confirmation. Danais already knew this. He was just opening up conversation for reassurance that he was indeed safe to not worry.

"What do you think?" Xan asked, but Danais didn't have time to answer. Leo was back at the table with two large beer mugs. It was going to take some getting used to, but what he was looking at was Leo. Lynton. Lynton Leo Vardon. The man he'd just created a child with. "Thank you," Leo said.

"Thank you?"

Revelations

"For staying. Heavy users find it hard to connect with people. Strange things can happen around those deeply steeped in blood magic. Friends are easy. But someone who's more than a friend is very hard to come by. Once people find out about me, they tend to just want to be friends. I'm shocked I was married twice."

"I didn't realise that."

"You don't mind."

"No. This is you. My Lynton."

"Your Lynton." Leo smiled, and Danais saw that as a good sign.

"Ah, so you can show some sort of emotion." Danais was glad that brought another smile.

"Yes. Rarely, but yes. I'm sorry, but that took a lot out of me. I can't seem to get back to the me that I usually am."

"For how long?"

"Don't know. I never know."

"Did you speak to me? In the cauldron?"

"No."

"I heard you say something at the end." Danais told him what he heard. Leo seemed to be unmoved. Danais was sure he was thinking, though.

"I believe that you must've read my mind. Sometimes magic works in ways we don't expect. You could see what you needed in me and somehow were allowed to hear my thoughts."

"Okay."

"I don't want you to go back to work,"

"But—" Danais stopped himself. He had to be careful. With Leo's full self on the surface, there was no telling what Danais' usual stubborn self could provoke. He had no idea how much control or lack thereof Leo had.

"Why? You know I like to work. What do you have in mind?" This was a response Danais felt acceptable, under any circumstances. Maybe there was something to this thinking before you speak nonsense.

"Tour the main city with me. I want to spend real time with you that doesn't involve work," Leo said.

"Okay. Your low voice is rather interesting in this even tone. Calm, yet scary."

"I scare you?"

Danais was ready to say no, but he was sure that Leo was perfectly capable of detecting a lie. He probably always was but allowed Danais freedom by not using that skill. Danais began to wonder about Leo and lies and how many other non-invasive magical things magicians naturally did that Leo consciously avoided when dealing with him.

"Can you detect lies?"

"I can."

"You can detect lies, read minds, influence actions. Sometimes I think I'm wrong in the way I treat you. You don't do so much around me."

"Well, those are things most magicians try not to do unless absolutely necessary or for a specific purpose. The lying, I will admit, is natural. Some people can hide a lie well. Most can't, and then there's the people who specifically block the truth. Those are people I really don't trust because they want you to know they're hiding something. Occasionally, it can also be used to tell the truth. Sometimes you magically block something in hopes the other magician will figure out what you aren't saying. So, for you, I just read you the way a normal human would. The same way you read me. I'm just more practised than you.

"It's just natural to not want people to pry into your mind so magicians are taught young about how to put up natural barriers around their secrets and as we get older… stronger ones, and learning how to defend against intruders. This is even a type of magic Atorathians can do. No one wants a foreigner prying into their mind. It gets much more intricate depending on the occupation you have and so on but that's too much for a quick conversation."

Danais thought that made sense. With peasants it wasn't a big deal. They couldn't read minds. If you could though and were surrounded by people who could then a natural defence would be needed. That would explain why Leo was upset by his accidental breach of Danais' mind. Danais reasoned reading thoughts without permission was just wrong. That was a good point to know.

"You're not bothered by my speech?" Leo took a drink from his mug as he waited for a response.

"It's different, and I already told you that I like the way your deep voice sounds in somewhat unvarying tones. Erie as it may be the loss of variation in your demeanour is equally as enchanting."

"You surprise me... I surprise myself."

"Love does that to you."

"I don't remember saying I love you."

Danais could see the sly smile in the words even though it wasn't as obvious on Leo's face.

"Nice to know you still have your sense of humour. So, are we going to get some rest? It has been a long day for both of us."

"You don't want to talk with me." Leo responded.

Danais could tell it was a statement and not a question.

"I just did serious magic for the first time. And I'm now experiencing an even calmer version of you than usual. It's been a long day. It's mostly about being tired."

"That's a perfectly reasonable reason to want to go to bed. Barton told me to be a bit careful about it all."

"Really?"

"A non-magician and an Atorathian at that, doing blood magic. This could've gone south quickly. That and…"

Leo stopped for a moment. Not sure if he should continue but decided he should.

"I have depressed thoughts. Have tried to end it all a few times. I'm better these days, but if it wasn't for Barton, I'd have been gone from this world long ago. He just seemed to appear when I was at my lowest and hasn't left since. Sometimes I still think that way. He was afraid if I didn't handle your reaction well things might be bad but everything's fine."

"Does anyone know this about you?"

"That he saved my life or that I'm suicidal?"

"Both."

"No. He and my personal teacher are the only ones who know all my secrets, save the one about the dragon in the letter. That's something only you know. And Xan, of course, because he was there when I helped the dragon."

"Are you still suicidal?" Danais queried.

"Sometimes. I haven't handled my lack of parentage nearly as well as you have. And I'm downplaying just how bad a shape I was in when Barton literally saved me. He changed me or made me see who I really was. And it doesn't hurt that he's attractive?" Leo smiled.

"Have you two ever—?"

"No. He only likes women, and he wouldn't entertain me in any event. Something about playing with my emotions. You'd have to hear him explain it."

"I see. I'll have to thank him the next time I see him."

"Why?"

"If it wasn't for him, you may not be here. Whatever he did that day kept you alive. We are supposed to be doing something spectacular. Without Barton, there would be no we. There would just be me."

"There is some logic to that. My teacher played a major role too. I would've been in no state mentally to even be saved without him."

"It's the only logic. Now that you know him, do you think anyone could've stopped you from doing what you were about to do the day you met? Anyone at all?"

"No. He always has an uncanny habit of showing up when I'm about to do something stupid. Like when I called you a common whore and lower than a peasant. He was here moments after I got here. With my mom as backup."

Danais could sense the amusement in Leo's voice. Maybe having to rely on intuition instead of normal cognition was a good thing. He wondered if it was easy to do and if he was just lucky. He was getting more comfortable talking to this new Leo.

"No, I didn't magic your apprehension away. You're getting comfortable."

"Is it that easy to read me? My uncle has this habit of answering questions I don't ask."

"Sometimes yes. Sometimes no. And I'm a good detector, as we have already discussed. You seem to be more truthful than usual— careful with your answers."

"Okay, let's not get into a repeat of the whole conversation about reading people."

"Okay. We'll go to bed. Come."

5

Revelations

Barton found himself the last to walk in on a surprise meeting. He assumed they had intended for him to be there last. Even his older sister, Adwina, was there. She was posing as the closest sibling to Leo in age.

Torak took a glance at him as he entered and gave him a look that could only mean trouble. Mai'n was standing to greet him in the usual way. For someone higher ranking than him—and probably able to destroy him in combat—she willingly fell into the role of loving spouse. It was interesting. She never once evidenced the person she was in the years they'd been courting: a commander of armies, his commander and soon-to-be wife.

"I know you're wondering why you're here. Dom called an emergency meeting, but I think it's *a* just meeting," Mai'n said.

Barton nodded and sat in the only empty seat, the one beside Mai'n. Then he looked around the table. Dom was looking at Barton with hidden shock. Not only did he just find out that both the commander and her second were alive, but she was also in love with and betrothed to Barton. Barton, of all people, was sitting beside the second and third in charge of the Alliance. How? Dom was almost about to retract his reason for calling this meeting. But what was right was right, and he had to move on. Besides, he'd already told them all the purpose of this meeting. Accept for Barton of course but that was intentional for all the wrong reasons.

"I know the topic for the meeting doesn't have much to do with the ongoing task, but I thought it was long overdue. As we know, there was strong opposition to Barton having any position on this mission. Not all of the people present during that time are here, however. Some of us are. I think we owe it to Barton to explain."

"Some of you? Torak didn't tell me I actually knew the people involved." Barton responded.

"You didn't ask," Torak responded, and he continued before Barton could glare at him. "I trust that means you will tell the whole truth, and this isn't just some cover-up apology." Torak didn't usually get aggressive, but the air in the room grew thick at his words. And he gave an exceptionally withering look at Dom. It would appear they were only being friendly for keeping up appearances during the festival. The seer rested a hand on his shoulder, and that seemed to calm him down. The next to speak would be Mai'n.

"It is true that I, Dom, and the seer were part of a group that worked against you. It was a grave mistake on our part. We made many enemies and caused a rift amongst the ranks. My ranks. My soldiers. This was during my beginning years. I have only been first commander for just over a century."

Lady Vardon spoke up. "I protested as well. Who would get the tasks done was something I couldn't entirely see. But somehow, I was certain it could not be you. I was one of the leaders against you. You were younger than most and much less experienced. It just didn't seem right."

"We didn't like your tactics," Dom protested. "You were slow when we thought you should be fast, soft when you should be hard. And emotional. We thought this task should be full of people like us. More direct. Tactical. Willing to do whatever it takes at any cost to get the job done. When I heard your name suggested, I started to talk to all those I knew I could trust with just enough information to not reveal the plan and brought them together. It got ugly; we did have more support, but the leader of the Alliance overruled us." Dom said all this with a bitter edge on his tongue.

"She believed in me?" Barton responded. He knew things were bad, but as Torak had mentioned, he went on assumptions and never asked.

"No. She just had faith." Dom replied. "She wanted to be wrong. She wanted to believe. She trusts her instincts, and they're usually right—but not always—so you can imagine how furious we were that she did this. She and her advisor plus your mother were for you, Torak, well that's without question. You could probably stab him in the back, and he'd still support you. Before she overruled us though, once word leaked that you were being turned down for a task of some kind that was when things got ugly.

"That softness of yours had spread through many of the lower soldiers and helped a handful of the higher-ranking ones.

Revelations

There was a short internal war that you did not know about. We were told it would interfere with your progress, so we sent you on a small mission and blocked your ears to the turmoil in the Alliance.

"It was three years before order returned. But the anger was still there. Friends lost; new alliances made. But it turns out we were wrong. As the commander says, we were gravely wrong. You watched him for sixteen years and never once were deterred from your duty. You then did something that even his teacher refuses to give full details on. Leo was, to us, a lost cause. The mission was a failure, and you did something when Xan and his teacher had given up. The mission exists still because of you."

Barton knew if anyone thought he wasn't strong enough to be in the Alliance, it was Dom. When it came to matters of war, Dom had always thought him weak. He had despised and opposed Barton's every rise in ranks. And now to find out that it was he who organized everything. He who fueled his anger all these years. He who made him a slave to the cause and determined at all costs to prove to whoever his detractors were that they were wrong—well, if he knew that, he might not have even cared enough to prove them wrong. Whoever decided to keep him in the dark about the whole thing was a genius because it worked.

"If we are going to admit how wrong we are, I'll speak for myself." The seer began. "You reminded me of something that I forgot. You didn't lack the ability to make hardcore decisions. You just refused to accept that it was always the answer. After so many years of life, I had forgotten that. My heart thrived in my personal life, but there was nothing for it when it came to the Alliance. That is one thing that led the general to overrule us. She never stopped trusting beyond what she could see. She thought the same as us and yet still sided against us.

"Over the years watching everything that you've done, I can no longer justly say that you aren't fit for any task—which is more than I can say for any of us, and which is why people hide behind your character. They don't want to admit you're perfectly capable of doing what they can do, and sometimes better than they can. For so long, I've been staring into the future and dealing with the present that I didn't leave room for the unexpected. War hardens you, yet you've survived. You remind me so much of your mother's first love, so you've reminded me of why I do this, why I joined the Alliance. And it helped me become the leader I once was before I got lost." The seer spoke with much conviction and a hint of gratitude.

"I concur. You've changed a lot of people, including me. You've put us back on a path we believe in rather than a path we just fight for, so when Dom said it was time to formally apologise, we agreed," Mai'n added.

Dom wasn't about to admit all of that; he figured he'd said enough. Besides, there was business to attend to. "There's also the matter of your connection with Leo. You've formed the type of bond that can be useful. I fully believe that Leo will do anything you tell him. Anything."

"I don't—" Barton began but Dom persisted in talking.

"It's true. In the same way you would die for Leo, he trusts your judgment, your opinion, your friendship."

"I don't like where this is going," Barton said, and he glanced at Torak, who seemed to be struggling to compose himself. Torak had mentored him until he thought Torak was behind what he now knew Dom was behind. Could Leo really see him how Dom said he did? It was possible, and if so, he wasn't going to abuse that kind of trust.

"So… what is it that you haven't asked me yet?" Barton asked, and when Dom told him, Barton stood up in mild rage and said very firmly, "I will do no such thing. I will not be a part of this just to prove your point. We're leaving, Kay." She jumped up onto his shoulders to leave with him. "Are you coming with me, Mai'n?"

This was an official meeting, so by all rights Mai'n or the person who called it—Dom—should end it. Mai'n, however, decided this to be a moment to prove that she meant that he had changed her for the better. She'd been madly in love with him for years and was going to marry this man in a few weeks. She looked down and was amazed at how after months of not showing, she had suddenly become extremely visible. She stood up and glared at Dom, which was very uncharacteristic of her usual cool demeanour, but she felt a need to let him know she disapproved—as a commander, a human, and his friend.

Torak wasn't very happy either. He thought of Barton as his

son. He accepted his role as the target for Barton's aggression, knowing that one day things would be normal again. He didn't approve of this at all. How could Dom even consider it? Why didn't Mai'n just rip his head off? His wife was right. Barton had affected them all somehow, he just hadn't noticed. The Mai'n who fought against Barton would have dismissed this plan with a quick beheading, cold and efficient.

"I can't believe you would use him like that," Torak said. Then he paused. "Actually, I can. If only your mother were here."

"Uncle—" Dom began.

"I'm not interested in your explanation. I don't even want to know, so I can claim I had no knowledge of how you made this happen if you *do* do something stupid. And I swear upon Nuru, the God of Vengeance, that if I find out any of you helped him in whatever he has planned, I will kill you. And don't be fooled by Mai'n's lack of response. Trust and believe that if she finds out you helped, she will do worse to you than what I will."

He looked at Lord Vardon and his wife Lady Vardon who he now knew was his daughter, even at the seer, Lela, his wife. Then he glanced at all of their Betaves. Dom seemed unmoved, but the rest were deep in thought. In their own ways, they were all equals, but Torak was one of the most respected in the Alliance, even though not ranked higher than any of them. And he was first to train Mai'n. If he made a threat, you listened.

"Where are we going?" Mai'n asked.

"To see my father," Barton said. "It's long overdue. I've never officially introduced you to him, and I haven't talked to him in a while. I want you here when I do this. I'm going to ask him to come to the wedding, and I'm going to talk about what just happened. I want to talk to you, and I want to talk to him, so I'm going to talk to you both."

"Okay. Matters of the heart is your area. Where you lead, I shall follow."

"You really think you wouldn't have been the commander you are now without me?"

"Yes. When I first became commander, I kept my ethics and increased my no-tolerance policy. That gets complicated. I'd kill someone for being unjust just as easily as I'd kill a betrayer or an enemy. Some things need a little more tact."

"You mean heart," Barton said and wrapped his arm around her. Mai'n was the height an Atorathian usually was, about five foot five. Short but deadly.

"Yes. I destroyed many a good human, some who I didn't realise I would miss or even cared for until it was much too late. Once I started to care more for my soldiers, they started to trust me more. Still, I think the seer overdid her speech just a touch."

"Meaning what?"

"Sometimes you do just have to cut someone's head off."

Barton let out a hearty laugh. "You know I'm perfectly capable of making cutthroat decisions. My problem is desire. I'd want to be like you but not in your position. I know what it takes, and I know I'm capable of doing it. I don't want to be that type of person, and I know I would be maybe even worse if I had to be."

"And that is why I love you. You're one of the few people I know who doesn't let your skills dictate who you are."

"You can thank Torak for making me into mush. He always told me there was no point in doing anything if my heart wasn't in it. That was merely a summary of what my earthly father would say. I miss him. I miss him a lot. They'd say you have to believe it and enjoy it; otherwise, you're just doing it to do it. Like walking in circles: no point in it."

"Unless you're going somewhere or running away from something. I'm right in assuming you were walking towards me?"

"Father!" Barton exclaimed.

Barton's father had appeared and injected his opinion before they even knew he was there.

That was the one thing Mai'n loved about Barton: he never once actually called the God that she could think of, but somehow, he always appeared, just as if he knew Barton was looking for him. It was so much more impressive than having to call him out by name.

"It's nice to know you remember who I am," Barton's father said with a smirk. He nodded at Mai'n. "Always a pleasure to see you, Mai'n. You look ready to give birth any day now."

"I am. And it's always a pleasure to see you."

Revelations

"I came to tell you that we're getting married," Barton told his father. "I know I've never actually said we were together, but she's pregnant, and I'm marrying her, so it's beyond avoidance now."

"Why didn't you just tell me?"

"I thought you wouldn't approve, or I was afraid you would think she was too good for me. Then you said you liked her, and I just forgot to tell you officially after that because I knew you knew."

"Understandable. Why haven't you been to speak with me? Your sister chats endlessly to me whenever she gets the chance. Even the rest of my children talk to me but you, my favourite, the one I look forward to talking to, hasn't talked to me in months."

"I've been busy stressing over Leo."

"Sit." Barton's father commanded. Mai'n found that they were in the God's home. She never even noticed when they stepped into it.

"Then there was the meeting today," Barton started.

"What happened?" Barton told the story and Mai'n and the God listened. Mai'n found it hard to believe that this man could lack passion for anything. Conviction was in every word he breathed, as was a strength that could match her own.

"I didn't think it was possible for you to not like someone," the God told Barton.

"Nor did I. How long have you hated Dom?" Mai'n asked.

"Hate is such a strong word, Mai'n," Barton tried to diminish his emotion.

"It is a truth. And a truth you have hidden. I don't think you like that you despise him."

"It's not right. It's okay to not like someone maybe, but to totally hate someone is wrong. No, I don't like it. Yes, I'm having trouble accepting that about myself. And he knows. He presses me. Pushes me. Tries to break me. He looks at me like I'm less than anything just because I react differently. He thinks me weak."

"Lots of people think that about you,"

"Yes, Mai'n. But they don't look at me the way that he does. He loathed me long before I grew to hate him."

"He's jealous of the relationship you have with me and the

one he's working to rebuild with his father, my son," the God said. "I doubt my son will have anything to do with Dom at this point. He's also jealous that people just gravitate towards you, and that you get things done in a way that he's always thought inferior with superior success."

"But he's a user. He bends people to serve his purposes. I understand why we need him, but I don't have to like it. He's like the Tyrant except he's on our side." Barton didn't like how he was feeling. The negative energy was getting uncomfortable, so he changed the subject. "Will you come? To the wedding. I know my earth mother can't, but can you? And my Goddess mother as well? Mai'n's real parents will be there."

"You know I would do anything for you. You're my favourite. Out of all my children. Not just the ones for your mother."

"You're not supposed to have favourites."

"Your siblings don't care that I like you more; why should you?"

"Because it's wrong. You should love us equally."

The God laughed. "Never one to squirm away from lecturing those who can annihilate you," he said.

"Well, when they continue to be wrong, I must."

"You are definitely your mother's child. And still my favourite. And I am only in love with your mother's children because I am in love with her still. And yes, Mai'n is too good for you, but here she is: ten long years and still madly in love with you. That's saying something. It says a lot about you."

"How long will you stay?" Barton wasn't in much of a hurry to go anywhere else. He didn't want to be transported back to the woods.

"As long as you need me."

Danais woke up the next day in what should have been a suffocating hold. Leo seemed to be holding him with much more— well, "conviction" was the only word he could come up with at the time. Still, he felt safe. He had work to do, though. Work didn't stop because it was the first day. He had to get up. This hold, however, wasn't breakable, unlike the many holds Leo had him in before. Leo had no intention of letting him leave.

Leo was swimming in the dark of his dreams. He knew he should be unnerved by dreams of so much blood and the screaming of his torn soul, but this was where he was. He had put himself in this fix by an extensive overuse of blood magic that no one had seen for centuries. But he had failed at destroying himself. He had survived. He swam through the darkness, breathed in the stench of every self-sacrifice, joined the chorus of his soul, and screamed with burning desire. Until he saw something. It was an unexpected addition to his dreams: a presence that was also now a part of him. Danais was awake, so now Leo must be.

Leo could feel Danais trying to escape even though it was impossible. "You are trying to leave," he announced.

"I must work," Danais replied.

"I told you that I am taking you with me today."

"You feel different." Danais was perfectly sure that he said the wrong thing when Leo loosened his grip, but he hadn't meant to. "Lynton…"

"You are uncomfortable."

"I don't know. But you can't keep taking things so literally. Emotions are complicated. I am okay with the new feeling. I like it more. But I'll probably randomly comment on things different that I notice. That doesn't make it a bad thing."

Leo responded by holding Danais tighter. Danais was playing with his hand again—something so simple, yet it brought back pleasant memories.

"You've changed. But you haven't."

"But I haven't," Leo restated. The dark was slowly leaving him, or more accurately he was becoming whole again as the dark never really left.

"You still feel the same. Why didn't I notice it before?"

"I was trying too hard to appear normal, I guess. Didn't want to scare you off. But I'm definitely feeling better." Leo kissed the back of Danais' shoulder. "The next time you get mad at me, at least stay and fight."

"Why? Ignoring you seems to work so well. I have the tattoo to prove it."

"Let's just get to your uncle." Leo chuckled as he spoke. Danais never ceased to find the humour in a situation. It amused him much.

"You still haven't let me go." Danais was wondering how this trip to his uncle would work if he couldn't get out of the bed.

"It's been a long time since I've had you naked beside me. Can't I enjoy the moment?"

"No. Now let me go." Danais attempted to move again but it was futile.

"You know I could force you to stay?"

"You wouldn't dare."

"Wouldn't I? Try to move then," Leo challenged Danais—and Danais knew before he moved that he couldn't, but he tried anyway if only to see how much more his movement had been restricted. He could tell there was some magic involved.

"Hmm. Well, I guess I'll just have to find me someone else, then," Danais said in response to his helplessness. "Besides, I hear that bad things happen to a magician who rapes an Atorathian, gifted or not."

"Hmm, you drive a hard bargain, Shorty."

Danais attempted to shove Leo playfully but hadn't gotten his movement back. No one had ever called him "shorty" before. He sort of liked it but wouldn't dare admit it.

"And you need me. I doubt anyone feels as good in bed for you as me. And we have some unknown tasks to do. I dare not think of what Barton would do to you should he find out you used magic on me, raped me, and then faked my disposal to cover it up."

"How would he know if I fake your demise as an accident?" Leo asked.

"I'm sure he has ways, and he knows you well enough to know without using them."

Leo laughed. There was a lot of truth in that statement. "Fair enough. Besides, what would be the fun in forcing you? Especially after it was so hard to win you."

"Hard? Bah. The only thing hard is your manhood. I'm inclined to think that woman who ran from it might be right."

"Don't think you'll get off nearly as easy as she did."

"Is that a threat?" Danais asked with a smirk.

"It's a promise on Miron, God of Good Fortune."

"I see. Are we going to bathe?" Danais asked as he got up to go to the bath. Leo smiled. Danais never thought for even a second that the spell was still on.

"I guess seeing as it's my duty to wash your back."

"I like a man who knows his place in life."

Leo had no intention of accepting a "no." In fact, he told Danais not to even bother coming to the farm, mostly because he didn't want to lose him to the fields. He also didn't want to chance Danais being persuaded to side with the uncle.

"You want to take my nephew away? And you expect me to water your seed with this potion?" Leo tried not to laugh but Torak looked more upset about having to water the plant.

"Yes," Leo answered truthfully.

"And you left Danais?"

"He has never travelled. And I know how hard it is to let go of a child. My parents are still struggling with letting go of all of us. I didn't want him influencing your decision."

"You don't trust my judgment?"

"I don't trust it around him. You would stuff his face with pastries and fall for the adorableness of it all and decide that he'd be better off on this side of the river."

"Bah. I would not have been that easily taken. You can have him—not that you needed my approval. He became a man at sixteen. He can do as he pleases."

"I strongly doubt you would've said that if he were here."

Torak laughed, and Leo joined him. "I will take care of the watering and let you know if it hatches before you get back."

"Don't worry, Torak. It won't."

11

DANAIS

It had taken them a whole week to get from one side of Leanor to the other. Danais had apologised many times for slowing the progress, but Leo didn't seem to care.

"You know we can just go back home. The temple of Ronilas will always be here," Danais mentioned for the third time that day. They were just leaving Salinor's temple, which was more than a day trip with Danais.

"Are you going to stop asking me to speed along this journey?" Leo responded.

"Are you going to insist on pretending my nagging you with questions isn't annoying you?"

Leo laughed, and Danais didn't look at him. He was trying to be serious and laughing with Leo wasn't going to help his cause.

"You know you enjoy it too. You're only getting mad so you can hear me say how much I enjoy answering them."

Danais grunted. Leo knew him entirely too well. He could only hope one day that he could read Leo just as easily. Still, he really wasn't feeling a pull to go to the only other temple left on their weeklong journey. He wanted to go, but somehow, he felt that right now wasn't the time.

"Take me home, Lynton."

"Okay."

Leo got the servants to load the waggon so they could head home. Danais felt a little awkward having workers, seeing as he too was at servant status, but Leo wasn't one of those evil masters he heard so much about. After spending much time on this side of the fence, Danais was beginning to realise that those tales about evil masters were exaggerated. As far as he could tell, most magicians treated servants decently. It got better work out of them. They didn't even consider them slaves just humans they employed.

"So back through the towns or the back roads?" Leo asked as the two of them got on their horses.

"I've seen enough city. I'm a farm boy; there's only so much lack of foliage I can deal with. I need some plant life."

"I can understand that. I am half-Keldonian. I have an affinity for plants as much as buildings."

"So why are elementals so rare?"

"Not sure. It's probably because of the amount of power needed to have control over all the elements. Having extreme power over all five elements is extremely rare; an elemental usually has an affinity for one in particular. Sometimes you will get two strong powers and the rest will be passable. Equal power over all five is exceptional. The seer is that exception."

"That would explain the storms."

"Yes."

"Do you have to be an elemental to have a specific power?"

"No. I am good with fire."

Danais heard a few chuckles when Leo said that. He sensed that Leo wasn't telling the entire truth but said nothing.

"Others can control the weather. It's just that being an elemental means you can work with all five effortlessly and one with even more ease. To have a natural element ability isn't that uncommon, but to be good at the level of an elemental, it could take years."

"What is an earth magician?"

"Ah, I see you've been reading that book I gave you. It's the only reason you could be overflowing with these questions. What took you so long?"

"I don't know. The book seemed an odd gift after the rose and the child. But I'm guessing you knew I'd enjoy it, even though I didn't know," Danais pouted. Again, Leo had figured him out. Danais was going to use the book as kindling, but just the other night something urged him to read it instead. It turns out it was a small book on the different types of magicians, about their power classes and how they were born. There was nothing too in-depth, but it was worth reading. Leo was smiling. Danais realised it was because he was pouting. How could he be mad at someone who thought his pout was attractive?

"Just answer me. I don't understand the whole importance of the birth."

"When a magician child is born, sometimes he may get sick. It's not obvious that a child is an earth child, so some tests are done to be sure the baby isn't just naturally sick. If they are an earth child, they must be buried or put to sea, or the nearest natural water source. There is no set time as to how long the child will take to float to the surface or come out of the ground. Usually though, it happens within two months. The child can live for a while without dying, so the choices become difficult if you can't tell if they are an earth child."

"What if they don't bury or submerge the child?"

"Well, the child will ultimately die. On the other hand, if the child isn't an earth baby, they will die in the earth or water. As far as I know, no child who got in the water or underground in time has died. It's usually because it was too late and not because of a mistake.

"The difference in these children from a regular magician is that the child is directly connected to the land. Magic is just floating around in abundance, and that is where magicians draw their energy. For earth children, it isn't so. They need the plants and ocean: all the living things of the world to survive. It's possible to trap an earth child in a bubble that only allows them to breathe but disconnects them from the world. A normal magician can thrive off of only air, but an earth magician will slowly die; it's the worst kind of torture."

"So they don't breathe the way I do, then? The land and sea are their life sources. So how do they die?"

"Well, the same as all humans. However, if they just merely suffocate, there's a long period in which they can draw off of the world to revive themselves. On the other hand, if they die because of disconnection—"

"They die. Is it painful?"

"It's been described as more pain than pain itself."

"Okay." Danais paused and took a deep breath. "I didn't just want to get away from the city," Danais said. "I feel—uncomfortable sometimes."

"Why?"

"The way people look at us. Me. I feel like I don't belong. I'm a peasant, and you're a Vardon. I should be in the back with our stuff. A slave. Those are my people back there, but here I am riding up front with my own horse."

Leo sighed. Danais wished he hadn't said it, but it was the truth. Maybe Leo wouldn't take it too seriously.

"I love you," Leo said reassuringly. "I don't care that you're a peasant. The question is, do you love me? Should I walk away? I don't want to, but I don't like this conversation. I don't like having it, and if you feel this way, maybe I should just take you home."

"No. I was just stating the facts. Why does it always have to be an ultimatum? Why can't it just be thinking out loud?"

"I do what makes you happy."

"Even leaving me?"

"If I must."

It was the matter-of-fact tone in Leo's response that made it so believable. Danais had no doubt in his mind that Leo would do anything for him. The thought was as scary as it was comforting. "Can I—?" Danais stopped. He had the sudden urge to change his question. "Is this horse mine?" Danais had never owned anything other than dogs, so a horse was more than just a step up. Still, he felt that he was right.

"Apparently you know me well also. Yes. It was a stray. It's young, not quite an adult, though sizable. Took her in and trained her."

"Really?"

"To a degree. We found her before I left, so we did as much as could be done with a wild horse in seven days. But I was right. She is perfect for you: which says a lot since she lets only two other people ride her. And I'm not one of them."

"You have to have that special touch."

"Evidently."

Danais ignored Leo's mocking tone and enjoyed the scenery. It was definitely more pleasant for him heading home through the country than through the main parts of the city. Granted, it was still nothing compared to real country; it was still more earthy than building upon building. Danais didn't even know it was possible to build stone buildings that almost reached the sky. He was glad for the increase in trees and for any decrease in busy streets.

"Always a farm boy at heart."

"Yes. I like the trees and earth."

"You have a worker's hands."

Danais had no idea what to make of that comment. Was it a jibe against their roughness or was it a testament to their manliness? Why was he even getting so worked up over this? Hands. Who cares what Leo thinks about his hands? Unless it has some sort of weight in this pairing they had commenced. Maybe Leo found his hands attractive. Why did Leo suddenly make a statement about hands? Maybe there was something to it. All these months and he never knew Leo had issues with his hands.

"That is by far one of the most adorable things about you."

"Huh?" was the only response that Danais could muster as he was forcibly brought out of his internal assessment.

"Your over-thinking again. You make this face that's worth a thousand coins of silver. And what I really like about it is that I never know what might trigger it. Hands?"

"Well…" Danais shrugged as if to say it made sense to him but held out his hands for Leo anyway.

"I like your hands. I like that they've seen work. Man hands. In case you haven't noticed, they are builder's hands. I did more than my share of physical work in my homeland, so I'm better than a novice, though I'm not quite an artisan. And you are more than fascinated by my hands. I distinctly remember you playing with a mole one night at the inn." Leo smiled.

"Okay. You seem to find all of my worst qualities intriguing: from my pouts and frowns to my excessive thinking. Do you like any of my good qualities?"

"You have good qualities?"

"The urge to throw something," Danais said, but Leo only laughed. Danais enjoyed that he could make Leo laugh. There was something about his smile, something about his laugh that warmed Danais' heart. It was pure like the innocence of a child.

Leo was greatly depressed over not knowing who he was. Much more so than Danais was about not knowing his parents. As confident and self-assured as Leo seemed, Danais saw it as a wall that Leo just couldn't break through.

All the research, all the knowledge, all the pride in humanity, the belief in all the provinces' stories of their gods, Leo's love of everything whole and true and even his ability to self-asses himself when he felt he did things against his morals—all of this was to somehow define who he was.

Did knowing where he came from define who he was? Or did he create himself from scratch? If his parents were evil, he knew he could still be good. If they were stupid, he could still be intelligent. Why was it so hard for him to see that the man he became didn't depend on his parents? As Danais thought, even more questions came to him. He found himself travelling down a road that consumed his attention. Only to be brought out by a question.

"What are you thinking?" Leo asked.

"Nothing. Nothing out of the ordinary, anyway."

It was at times like this that Danais hoped that Leo was reading his mind. The times when he wanted to talk about something. He wanted to know exactly what Leo meant when he said that Barton had saved him. How had he saved Leo's life?

"Tell me what went so wrong that you needed saving."

9
LEO

Leo had no idea if he was ready to broach this topic. Did he want to give more details? Did he want to admit that he still hadn't broken free, and that he occasionally thought about doing blood magic to such extremes that it would consume him? Did he want Danais to know that he was in this perpetual world of discovery because he felt he was a nobody, an unloved castaway? At least Danais had his uncle. He had family and people who knew his mother, even if they couldn't talk about her. But what did he have? Nothing but the blanket he was wrapped in when they found him and a small glass bottle containing the soil he was buried in.

"I told you most of what there is to tell."

"But how can you use blood magic to the extent that it consumes you? Wouldn't it just make you darker?"

"I was destroying other things as well."

"Like what?"

"Animals. People. While my arms or whatever it was I had used grew back, I would just hack people. I snapped and had the power to bend people's minds to my will. I picked a secluded spot and was just performing magic for a whole day. My teacher left to find Barton, whom I had only just recently met. He persuaded me back to the real world somehow. I had slipped into the other."

"The other?" This was something new to Danais.

"The world within the world. It's the best and most

dangerous place to train magicians. But you can get trapped there. So even though my physical body was acting out, my actual essence was doing it on the other side. That was a feat in itself because usually when you fully go, your physical body stays immobile. Somehow, I managed to make my physical body move, though I had left it. I hoped to do so much blood magic that I'd mutilate my soul; it would fall apart on that side and hence be gone forever. If you die intact, your soul can be released to the heavens."

"Has it happened before? A soul destroyed while the body remains?"

"I have not seen it, but I've heard many stories. A living body without its essence, especially when the person does it to himself, is the worst thing—worse than death. It's the worst kind of suicide and the worst kind of torture because a slight bit of awareness is still there, but it only acts to remind you of what's not."

"You murdered innocent people?" Danais asked.

Leo didn't look at Danais. He hated to face the awful truth of it all. He had murdered many—so many faces haunted him in his dreams, and so many animals. Because of the conviction of the blood magic used no one officially died but they were gone long enough to remember leaving the world. And after all that Leo still felt the same, depressed.

"I'm sure my teacher could've saved me. But he went and got Barton. And Barton—well, he's just amazing. I owe my life to him. He brought out all the things that my teacher and Xan instilled in me. He was sent by the gods, and he understood me. There are very few people that would've let me live. I should be dead. I should be punished. But Barton refuses to let me feel down about anything. He even sorted everything out with all the families ruined by a stupid child's actions. So many people treat me well but I'm not sure that I deserve it."

"How do you feel now?"

"Much the same. I'm not as together as I seem. But I think you realise that."

"Yes. I just wanted the details. That's all. Have you, um—?"

"Have I tried again? No. I think about it, but I just can't bring myself to do that to Barton. And then there's you."

"Me?"

Revelations

"I haven't even considered ending my life since I've met you. This is why I had to have you. No one has ever made me think that living is really an option. But I want to live for you. I feel needed. You might make me whole."

Danais sighed. Leo didn't take this as a good sign. Why did he feel compelled to reveal so much truth? To reveal—what?

"This is why I work so hard to instil hope in others. To make them believe there's so much to live for, because I know how that feels. I can't come to terms with who I am or who I'm not. And if I am nobody, why should I live?"

"But Lynton—"

"Don't argue. I've been through this many times with Barton." There was silence, and Leo was filled with the sudden dread that this was the one thing that Danais could not accept. "I understand if you don't want to be with me, a cold-hearted murder."

"Don't decide for me," Danais responded, annoyed. "I understand. I am an orphan as well. Though I know my family, I can understand what you feel. How many people was it?"

"Not too many. I only moved on to people after I ran out of animals. But to me, one was enough to make me beg Barton to kill me once he brought me back. I cried for hours."

"I could imagine."

"You're taking this well," Leo said with a hint of disbelief.

"I'm trying. I'm disturbed by this—very disturbed—yet I have to understand it. I need to know what I'm dealing with. You're dangerous. I need to know what that entails."

"I would never harm you." Leo didn't know why but he suddenly felt defensive. What was Danais implying by calling him dangerous?

"Others? What about them."

"If they deserved it. But that goes without saying."

"Well in that case there's this guy from back home..." Danais chuckled, and Leo rolled his eyes.

Danais surprised him. Leo was sure that this would turn him away. Though Danais was not okay with it, he was still riding beside him, showing no indications of leaving. Well, he did take his horse farther ahead of the pack, but Leo was sure that that was just to think.

Then Leo realised he wasn't alone.

"Xan. Have you been here through all of that?"

"I was. I didn't think you would tell him. Only you and two other people know about that day."

"And you."

"And me. Why? Why did you reveal that when Barton gave you explicit instructions not to? He told you only bad could come out of revealing that part of your past."

"He would understand."

"Why did you tell him anything? He could've gone through life never knowing. Just like your family."

"They aren't my family."

"They are the only family you know."

Leo didn't have a rebuttal for that. "I don't want to keep anything from him. If he found that out later, I'm sure he'd be angry; much more so for not telling him."

"But he wouldn't have found out."

"So, you don't think I should have told him? You think it was a mistake?" Leo sighed, and Xan moved from in front of him to sit on his shoulders. "Maybe you are right. Maybe I should've taken Barton at his word that only bad could come out of it. But I feel this is right. I didn't do it because I wanted to. I didn't want to tell him, but when I opened my mouth, it came out."

"You love him more than I think even you realise."

This statement put Leo off. He was sure Xan was questioning him because he didn't agree with the decision. He thought he was being questioned because of his actions. But the voice he was hearing didn't sound like the voice of someone opposed to what he had done.

"You don't have a problem with it, then?" Leo wasn't too sure, but it was the only other option.

"I am not sure. However, whether I trust your instincts or not is irrelevant. It doesn't matter what I think about your decision."

"What does matter then?" This was getting more confusing by the second.

"What I think about the object of the decision. Even if I explicitly trusted you, what does that matter if I have issues with the other person. The one you shared with."

"So even if you do trust me, that's not enough. Is that what you're saying?" Leo groaned. Dealing with Danais' overthinking was task enough; he didn't need Xan being so intentionally obtuse.

"With some things, it's more than enough. But with the way things are changing, I'm just going to have to be more vocal."

"So how do you feel about him?" No harm in asking now that Xan had opened the door.

"I trust him, but Barton did say that nothing but bad will come of this."

"No. He said something bad would come of it, not that bad things will result from it."

"I think what he actually said was that something bad will follow if you tell anyone. He didn't tell you not to reveal it at all."

"You know I think you're right, Xan. It's been so long since we've thought about it."

"Yeah. I wonder what event will happen."

They were finally back at the Vardon villa. At the end of just over a week of travel across a large city, Danais was already naked on the bed and falling asleep. Leo got in beside him and almost struck up the conversation about bedding him: knowing the answer but anticipating the playful amusement it would entail.

"Not today," Danais protested sleepily. "Just let me enjoy a night's sleep."

"Are you sure? Because I can make this much more entertaining than mere sleep."

Danais chuckled, and Leo smiled, even though he knew Danais couldn't see him. He got down behind him on the bed, but as usual, Danais stopped him from doing anything beyond heavy petting. This didn't bother him at all. There was something about the sensuality; the way they moved together and how they came to such heights in each other's arms without penetration. Leo didn't know what it was, but he was sure it had to do with Danais being Atorathian.

As they lay there after another few hours of passion, he ran his fingers through Danais' two inches of hair as Danais laid on his chest. Danais' hair was perfectly straight; a feat his loose curls could never accomplish. When wet they got pretty close to being straight but still didn't make it.

"I like the way you smell," Danais commented.

"Even after sweat and exchange of fluids?"

"Yes. You always seem to smell fresh. Well, on the farm not so much, but you have a strong scent. It just comes through all the time."

"You know real Atorathians have an acute sense of smell. Helps with tracking."

"Ah, so just one skill equates with suddenly being gifted. I knew it was only a matter of time before I reached my inner levels of awesome on the outside."

"You did get one other gift—one I've yet to experience."

"What we do isn't enough." Leo heard the playful tone in Danais' voice and smiled.

"I can feel you."

This took Leo by surprise. "Feel what?"

"I can feel when you smile. I don't know how to explain it, but I can."

Leo couldn't attribute that to a skill from any of Salinor's people. This had to be something unique. All couples shared certain intricacies that were theirs alone, especially when magicians were involved; some things just happened.

"Even when you're not visibly smiling, I can feel it. Makes it easier to talk to you; to know what to say when you're in your expressionless moments."

Leo found this as much intriguing as he did amusing. "You have surprised me more than I thought."

"Really?"

"I'll tell you someday. But for now, just sleep. Sleep."

It was the next day, and Leo woke up knowing something was wrong. Danais wasn't there. It wasn't just that he wasn't there: Leo knew when Danais was close because he was in the habit of putting up a field around them. If Danais woke first and left the room Leo could sense where he was and follow him. He could feel nothing.

Leo did the only thing he could do: he sent a mental message out to Barton. Barton appeared instantly. Leo didn't even know

Revelations

he could do it so easily.

"What is it?"

"He's gone!" Leo was in a panic.

"Danais? Are you sure?"

"I know it. I can tell by the spells I put up. There is no trace of anything. Someone had to work hard to erase not only their traces, but mine, too."

Leo was frantic—crazy even. He didn't know what to do or what to think. How could he have let this happen? He told Danais he would protect him. Now he felt he'd let everyone down. He'd broken his promise. This was bad. The one thing that couldn't happen, the worst thing that could happen had happened. And under his watch. They trusted him. They didn't keep as tight a watch when Danais was with him. They had full faith in his abilities to protect him, and he had allowed Danais to be kidnapped. It had to be. Danais couldn't be dead. Could he?

Barton took a breath. Calmly, he stated, "If I told you that he's safe but it's just not meant for you to be together for things have changed, what would you do?"

"No. I don't believe it. I won't believe it." Leo stopped talking, breathed, realised he was still naked and started to dress. Once he donned pants, he sat on the edge of the bed, facing away from Barton. He stared out a window and asked, "Is that what you are telling me—that he is safe and well?"

"Yes."

"Then I will find him."

"No. You will not."

Leo sighed.

This was Barton. The only man besides his teacher that he trusted his everything to. Would Barton lie to him? Would he do this unless it was absolutely necessary? He did not think that Barton would—or that he could.

"So, you're asking me what would I do if you told me that we had to be separated? That if the future of the land depended on my not pursuing him, what would I do?"

"Yes. I am asking you that."

"I would do what you would have me do."

Leo saw something in Barton he couldn't quite register. It was something that set him on edge. He was getting more of these looks from Barton, but this one was extremely different. He was worried, frightened even. He had the same intensity Leo himself had when driven to the darker portion of his power, yet Barton withheld it in an eerily calming, unintimidating way which had the opposite intent of how it looked. The calm with the intensity made it that much more terrifying.

"I would have you stay here. Don't leave this room until I tell you. You'll find out why it was so easy for Danais to be taken."

"How long will it be?"

"As long as it takes."

"Tell Danais when you see him that—" Leo couldn't finish the sentence, but Barton nodded in agreement and then turned to Xan.

"Ensure no one comes in here," Barton instructed. "I don't want any word of what happens to make it to Leo's ears—not until I allow it to."

And then Barton was gone.

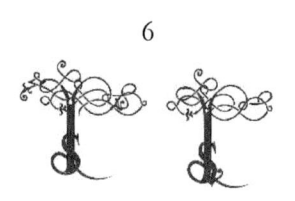

6

Two days later:

Leo was sitting outside a room with Danais. He had no idea what Barton had done, but Barton was in a rage, and he didn't know what the man was capable of. Barton oozed a certain amount of power that made Leo question whether he could wield it to save him, back when he was sixteen: trying to destroy his soul. Could Barton use it without him knowing? Maybe it wasn't so easy to save him after all, Leo thought. Danais was tight-lipped. He had said enough for Leo to know that Barton forced him not to say where he'd been the past two days.

"I know you want to know, but Barton said you'd find out in his time."

"And he also said to meet here?"

"Yes. We are going to find out who some of the people that

are watching us are."

"They decided we should know?" Leo wanted to be clear exactly who's idea this meeting was.

"No. From what I guessed, he came to this decision after rescuing me last night. He's going to make this happen with or without them, I would assume. I can say one thing: I'm glad he's our friend after what I saw."

Danais just stared into space. He'd heard many stories about magicians at war, but he had never thought to see it first-hand. There was something there that he didn't quite understand; something more to what he was seeing. Danais would've tried to figure it out, but just then Barton came toward them.

He led them outside to the Luman gardens, one of the beauties of the city of Leanor. It was a maze and was large enough to get lost in, yet with secret openings that led to spaces perfect for private conversations. In the gardens, it was easy to put up barriers to shield from prying ears.

Leo noticed Barton's dark mood didn't seem to have ebbed. He was furious about something. He glanced toward Danais, who must have realized it, too. Both had decided that quiet obedience was the route to take. Besides, if Barton was capable of such things, then who knows what the other people they were about to come in contact with were capable of.

As they finally entered an open space, there were several people seated in a circle. Mai'n was at the head, but Danais' eye was drawn to one man only.

"You?" he growled in their direction.

Leo followed his gaze and couldn't believe who he was staring at. "You?" Leo also stated and was ready to attack, but Barton wouldn't allow it.

"No."

It was only one word, but it was enough. Leo took his seat beside his father and Danais beside him. Then Barton took his seat.

"How can you expect me to not do anything?" Leo angrily stated.

"Look at him, Leo. Enough has been done." Barton said as he forced Leo to take a second look at Dom. It was a true statement on Barton's part. Dom did look like he had been in battle recently. His face had a few small blemishes, and his right hand was bandaged. The look Barton was giving him was a stare of loathing that Leo would've never envisioned on Barton's face. Indeed, everyone seemed to be looking at him.

"I demand to know what has happened," Mai'n spoke, but no one answered. She rephrased the question. "Does anyone know what has happened?" Only Barton and Dom seemed to react to that. She then ordered them as first commander to tell her. It was only then that Barton stood to speak. He paced the circle to ensure he spoke to everyone as he told the story.

"Leo mindspoke to me just after sunrise three days past. He told me that Danais was missing. I knew immediately what had happened. Dom, even with our instructions not to act, disobeyed a direct order simply to prove a point. I insisted Leo stay in his room and did all I could to make my search secret. I found Dom, fought and defeated him and took Danais back to Leo last night. For two days, I had to search. Then he still tried to convince me of how the power I had over Leo could be better used to serve the Alliance."

Dom jumped to his feet. "I still stand by that decision. We—"

"You will speak when I let you speak!" Barton shouted at him with a force that could only be described as the essence of evil. Dom sat back down.

"He used me. He thought I would just let it slide; that I would just come to you and explain it, and he would hand over Danais-winning his point: thinking he'd be in a better position to press his advantage. But I do not take it lightly when people play with the emotions of those I love. It was no easy feat to cover up the fight we had, but I managed it somehow."

"Even after finding him, why did you not inform any of us?" Mai'n inquired.

"First commander, I intended to keep it between me and Dom, but I realise now that this was not a good decision. A cover-up, yes— but not from all of you."

"And what do you have to say for yourself?" She looked at Dom, who got up and stood beside Barton, who still glared at him. Barton glanced at both Leo and Danais, who looked like they would attack Dom together. Lord Vardon was holding his son's hand, and Danais wouldn't move if Leo didn't.

"That I was right. Leo did stay in his room as ordered." Dom spoke.

"Did it not occur to you that what you were doing was breaking the rules?" Mai'n demanded. "And it was unfair to both Leo and Barton for you to test the limits of their bond so you could wield it for your purposes, no matter how justified they may be?"

"No. It did not," Dom answered plainly.

"And now?"

"Maybe. There were other things I did not account for. I made grave misjudgements about Barton. I did not think he was even close to overpowering me, but he did and much more. He's ten thousand times the warrior I thought he was. Now that I know, there are probably better ways we can utilise this power. If maybe—"

"Why aren't you ashamed? Regretful? Sorry for doubting him?" Mai'n couldn't bear to watch this fake apology for another second. "Sorry for egging him on, knowing how much he hated himself for hating you. Sorry for exploiting his weaknesses only to find out that he is indeed better than you. You know what? You should be sorry! But I know you well enough to know even with your last trick thoroughly embarrassing you, just based on how you started your non-apology, that somehow you see something new to exploit from all of this."

Dom was about to speak, but Mai'n was too furious to allow him to continue.

"How could you disobey a direct order?" she demanded. "I should have you killed. I should send you to trial. I should take you off this team immediately. Sometimes, I wish the seer could see everything. Then we could've stopped you from doing something that even I couldn't think you were so self-righteous and self-serving enough to commit. People like you make me sick. Maybe now that Barton has taught you a lesson, you won't be so smug."

"Maybe." Dom was clearly embarrassed. To know that he could not defeat Barton was a serious blow. In his mind, all men and women like Barton were weak, and he'd not only been beaten, but beaten in a way such that magic couldn't fully remove his scars. This was indeed shameful.

Not able to control himself anymore, Leo slipped into his

dark side, and the only thing stopping him from killing Dom was the fact Danais. He had jumped up the moment he sensed a change in Leo and ran towards Dom. Dom, in the state Barton had left him, was defenceless as Danais knocked him down easily. Once on the ground he kicked him continuously. Full of a screaming rage that no one bothered to stop. It seemed, to Leo, a better option to let Danais do the real work. He simply held Dom to the ground to make it easier. Danais had never met Dom, but he knew that they were supposed to be friends, he and Leo. How could he have done this to him?

"Enough! Both of you back to your chairs now!" Mai'n demanded. Danais went back almost immediately, but Leo still had Dom pinned to the ground. He'd somehow gone into the *other* and was trying to drag Dom's soul over by force so he could destroy it on the other side. Barton yanked him up with a force that nearly broke Leo's arm. Using a type of mind control on him that was extremely rare, he said forcefully, "Come back. Come back now!"

Leo found himself almost immediately coming back. He did not know Barton had such mind control powers, yet he got things done so effortlessly without using them. Leo still refused to move back to his seat.

"Don't make me force you to go back to your seat," Barton growled. "Go. I'm asking you to leave him be."

Leo looked at Barton and decided to walk back to his seat without another glance at Dom. Danais was right. It was a good thing that Barton was on their side.

Barton looked directly at Dom, as if no one else was in the room. "As long as I am alive, after this meeting, you will never come within a million leagues of these two unless ordered to, and then I will be there. If you find a way to do so without me knowing, I will kill you. That I promise on the mother, Salinor, Goddess of all. Is that understood?"

"It is," Dom responded, and he and Barton returned to their seats.

"I heard Dom call you first commander?" Danais directed his question toward Mai'n.

"It is true. I am second in command of the Alliance. Since the commander is called 'commander', they call me 'first commander.' I am also a shapeshifter. I've been pretending to be your actual cousin and then appeared as your friend as the serving girl. It is Lady Vardon, former head of one of the specialized divisions of the Alliance, who is in actuality your cousin and my second in command. Torak is an advisor on the consul, as was Dom. Adwina is not your younger sister, Leo, but a member of the Alliance. She is our lead trainer. She's trained almost everyone here, myself included.

"She was not part of the next stage of the plan, but things have changed which is why she is here. Barton has been watching Leo. And when he was not doing it, Dom was. He also was not originally given that task. But during a war in one of the provinces, the woman for the job was lost in battle. The man Adwina is replacing has become gravely ill. Barton is just a regular member of the Alliance often used for assination, and the seer is also on the board of advisers. Lord Vardon is one of the generals.

"Torak keeps up communications. He can talk to animals, so he has spies everywhere. It keeps us in more covert contact than mind links and messages can. Barton said it was time you knew who we were: at least in our jobs if not our full identities and what it is that we do."

"What is it that we should know?" Danais asked, hoping they would offer more information.

"The person we are looking for is a shapeshifter. Evidence would have us believe it is the son of the Tyrant. He has no evidence of who either of you are, but as you well know, Leo, you are being followed. The rock was the biggest decider in that truth. Lucky for us it hit Danais. If it had not, things could be very bad. Still, that has not discouraged his interest. We must find him."

"How?" Leo asked.

"We believe that he must be much closer to us than we think which is why we are having trouble locating him."

"You mean he may have befriended us? Gotten so close that we do not know?" Danais asked.

"Yes. He has been killing some of the people he's been impersonating from province to province. Chances are, purely by accident, he assumed the identity of one of our friends. He got lucky and is probably keeping them alive, as is often done, to use for information to better impersonate the person. I'm asking all of us to rethink every conversation we've had for at least six months. I know that's difficult, but something—anything, no matter how small—may be just wrong enough to show who he is."

"So, we have to work backwards." Leo asked.

"Yes, Leo. Lady Vardon will show you what to sense magically. It's probably going to be minuscule, but something is far better than nothing."

"I have something to show you all," Danais said, and he brought out the God stones. He noticed that Dom, Mai'n, Barton and Adwina seemed to recognise the stone bracelet, though they seemed to not be bothered by it. No one reacted to the second stone: allowing him a sigh of relief.

"May I examine it?" Mai'n asked.

Danais thought it was okay to let the first commander see it. She studied it carefully then handed it to Lady Vardon. She seemed to test it magically. That must be her job in some sense, Danais figured. She then handed it back to him.

"Why is this important?" Mai'n asked.

Danais felt it safe to wrap it around his ankle now. "I was told that if anybody recognised this particular stone, I was to have them captured immediately. What if I'm alone?"

"I'll be with you," Leo said.

"What good that will do him?" Dom asked Leo. To Leo's surprise, it was Adwina who came to his defence.

"It was not Leo's lack of skills that allowed you to capture Danais. There was no way Leo could've predicted the type of magic you exploited. A magic you were specifically told by the commander herself you could not use. You would do well to remember it. Barton is not the only one with Leo's interest at heart."

Dom was again forced to retract his venom and shy back into his seat. This got Leo thinking. If he was right, he had to adjust his spells. He was going to have to ask Barton and hopefully he'd get an answer.

"You said it was a good thing the rock did hit me. Is that an implication that it might not have?"

"It is."

"I am changing." Danais wasn't sure he was excited by this news.

Revelations

"Yes. The magic on you is wearing off. We have time but there are two tasks we must complete before anyone can sense who you really are. You becoming more Atorathian is still safe as long as the spell on your identity holds. Soon we will have no choice but to move. Trust me, though, it will be hard work. I have not been forcing you to train all these years, knowing you could not do it; unless I knew one day you would."

"How will it happen?"

"It just will. And when it does, you should have all the skills you need learned, no matter how bad you are at them." Mai'n said. She had walked to him and took his hand into hers, and Danais almost thought he felt a certain energy. Then Dom came over and touched him as well. Again, he felt a small surge of energy travel into him.

"This was my only task before I was asked to follow Leo," Dom continued. "I won't ask for your forgiveness. It had to be done. But I am sorry. Maybe when we meet again I'll feel different and want to be forgiven. I will go now, before I am commanded, as I know I will be. May the good fortune of Miron protect and guide your way." That was the last thing Dom said before leaving.

"Now that you know who and what we all are, anything is open for discussion, to a degree. But we will, now that Barton has expressed the importance of more communication, be much more giving than we were."

"Barton?"

"Yes, Lord Vardon?"

"I would like to thank you for rescuing Danais, but you should've let them kill Dom."

"He will be judged by the laws of the Alliance."

"I know you've saved my son before. I know my children. He was going through something. It reached a point that you've covered up quite well whatever it was. I've always meant to ask you: would he have died then?"

"No. It would've been much, much worse."

"Is this meeting over?" Leo asked.

"It is."

"Then we can leave... first commander?"

"Yes. And you can call me Mai'n again, Leo."

Leo smiled at that, as did Danais. "I need to breathe," Leo

said.

"One of my closest friends attacked my partner. He's now going to be on trial with the Alliance, and Barton has fought on my behalf. This is a lot for one meeting. It was a short meeting but a full one just the same."

"Take as much time as you need. However, Adwina is coming with you. Now that you spend more time together it's easier for us to focus your guard. We will be watching you from afar. If you want a closer watch, you should hire your own guards. Mind you, we've already selected them, but for it to look random, you'd still have to do it yourself."

"What do you want, Danais?" Leo asked.

Danais said nothing. Leo didn't like to see Danais this scared, but he said he would protect him and was determined to do so.

"There's a small lake nearby. Would you like to go for a swim?" Leo asked Danais.

"Yes. I'd like that."

"Well, I guess I'll be seeing all of you around sometime."

"No more than usual," Barton responded.

This statement brought another smile out of Leo as he started to walk away. "Danais, come."

Danais smiled, and the two of them navigated their way out of the maze with Adwina far enough behind to be unnoticed. They walked until they came to a small open area in the garden. Leo almost put up a field, but he was aware that Adwina would more than likely have brought people along to help. He would have to trust that they would put up a larger shield.

"Adwina?" Leo called. She appeared almost instantly. "How many are with you?"

"Five more."

"Is Barton—?"

"No one is sure where he is. He said he needed to think. I've learned to let him have his moments when he disappears. Generally, in such serious times, no one would be allowed off duty but Barton…"

"He's different."

"Yes. You aren't the only person's life he's changed. He'll show up when he's ready. And we have a field up if anything happens; if anyone comes by, you won't be heard or seen. You can put up a smaller one if you don't want me to hear, but—"

"Just touch the field, sister. I'll know it's you."

Adwina picked a spot by a tree and leant back and watched. Leo did much the same, except he sat down and pulled Danais back against him. There wasn't going to be any swimming.

"What did Dom do to you?"

"Are you going to attack him?"

"Answer the question."

"Answer mine." Danais had no intention of answering until Leo did.

Leo could see this as he looked into his eyes. Leo let his guard completely down without knowing it and slipped into his relaxed state.

"Lynton—"

"I want to, but Barton wouldn't want me to."

"He told you not to, then?"

"No. But I know."

That was as good as a no to Danais, so he answered the question. "Nothing really, beyond starve me and keep me in a cave so dark I couldn't see my hands. I think there was a spell on the room. I felt I had been there for weeks; there was no way I could lose my mind that fast, not in two days, but I was going crazy."

"My friend put mind spells on you? I can't believe he did that to you just to test the bond between me and Barton. I was willing to let you go; Barton told me I had to and ordered me to stay in the room. I had no idea he planned to deliver you to me. I thought I'd never see you again. I told him to tell you…"

Danais felt something wave over him as if he felt washed in Leo's essence. It was almost as if he could feel his sigh of relief or completion at the final admittance of returned affection. "I know. I love you too, Lynton."

"I'm not just your Lynton. You're my Danais, my Moon and Water God Prince."

"There was something else. I don't know what it was, but during the fight, something strange happened. Dom looked drained, or like he was being drained. It was happening during the fight, but somehow, he didn't notice until he was defeated, and it started happening faster. The air seemed to swirl around him.

"I don't know what came over me, but I screamed out to stop whatever it was that Barton was doing. It just didn't feel right."

"You said he was doing it while fighting?"

"Yes. I noticed something, but it was clear once the fight had ended."

"I haven't heard of anyone being able to do it during magical combat for centuries, but it is possible to enhance one's own magic by draining someone else's. It's extremely hard and even harder to mask; most magicians see it coming, even in a small dose. It's best to just throw your all into it and hope you catch them off guard."

"He was stealing Dom's magic?"

"Yes. Very complex. Most don't even bother with it because of the intense concentration it takes to keep an opponent from discovering it."

"Can you do it?"

"No. That's far beyond my skills. It's far beyond a lot of magicians' skillsets."

"You seem upset."

"You're good at sensing my moods." Danais could hear the smile in Leo's voice when he responded. "I am," Leo said in amusement. "Barton is my best friend. He's like my brother, my conscience, my everything. He took over after my teacher left. I don't know who he is. I don't know anything about him."

"Does it matter? He loves you. Everything he's done recently has been because of you. Everything he's hidden and done has been done because he believed in the plan, whatever it is. Isn't that enough? All these people around us gave up everything they had known before we were born to ensure we made it to our chance meeting. It could've been ten more years, and they still would've done it. Isn't their love, isn't their faith, their belief in us, enough?"

Leo didn't know what to say. Was it enough? He was about to be angry for all the lies, but they had given up their lives. Some of them had important positions while some were just regular soldiers, but all had trailed him for twenty-eight years and Danais for eighteen. Did they have friends and family? Were the others merely lower soldiers just following orders?

Leo thought about it and could only come to one conclusion.

Revelations

"It is enough. It has to be." Leo was aware he hadn't put up the field. It was possible that everyone could hear, depending on how close they were. He didn't care. It was something he hoped they'd tell everyone involved: that the sacrifice mattered.

"I'd tell you more if I could."

"Barton!" Danais was the first to speak. "How long have you—?"

"Not too long, Danais."

"How did you get here without me or anyone knowing?" Leo inquired.

"There are very few people who know the extent of what I can do. It's what makes me effective."

"You were going to kill Dom." Danais had this question burning in him since he'd been rescued.

"I was going to suck out all his power. As it stands, he is weakened, but with good practice it shouldn't be more than a few months before he regains what I took. I am glad you called out to me, Leo. Especially so quickly."

"Why do you hide your strengths from everyone?" Danais asked.

"It's the mark of a good wizard," Leo answered for Barton. "The best of them don't gloat in their power. Even the Tyrant doesn't reveal all of what he is."

"I'd rather not have to use that type of power but the powerful always find themselves forced to do things they would rather not do. The greatest sorceress of all time, Ameri, used the full extent of her power many times more than she wanted to. It's all in how you handle it. The trick is not to become a Tyrant just because you have the ability to bend the realm to your will. My mother was powerful, but she did not become a Tyrant. Burning land and reinforcing slavery were not good uses of her power. She died in war, as did my earthly father."

"Earthly?"

"Yes, Danais."

"You're the son of a God?" Danais had dreamed about being a God child for most his life, and now he was sitting next to one that had fought for him.

"Yes," Barton replied earnestly. "I feel I owe you that much. I owe you enough to say that I am indeed one of those strong enough to rule the realm. However, as you know, I don't even have high ranking in the Alliance. I've struggled with the fact that one day my name will go down in history, but that's not related to our present situation."

"I have a question. Did you force me back to life that day? You have the mind power to do it, obviously," Leo asked.

"No. I had to let you come back of your own will. Mind powers don't destroy desire. If you didn't choose, I'd have to constantly force you to live."

"There are some things. You could force me to not feel depressed again."

"Leo—"

"You could!"

"I will not!" Barton's voice wasn't a shout, but instead a firm tone that Leo was beginning to think came more with the authority of age than power. Barton knew better and spoke to him as a senior when he deemed it necessary.

"It is a part of you," Barton explained. "I have not, nor will I ever, force a change of character on a person. You must deal with your inner demons. Do not ask me again. I understand you wish to just be free, but making it disappear is not the answer."

"Why?"

"Out of all the things I find distasteful, one of the most distasteful is people who refuse to face their problems which is why I let you deal with yours. I am not perfect. I have my own issues to face too."

"You have flaws? I highly doubt that," Danais spoke.

Barton laughed at Danais. It was an innocent enough statement. "I've always hated Dom, and I generally don't hate anyone. This is why I almost destroyed him. He knows this about me: I don't like the fact that I'm capable of such loathing. I try hard to find ways to force myself to find something I like about him, and he goes out of his way to make me hate him more. I don't think I'll ever stop hating him. If I don't accept that, there will be people I hate in life who I might just end up almost destroying unjustly, by accident. I realise that I have issues with having bad feelings toward anyone. It's a part of me I struggle with. Most people are okay with hating someone. I always force myself to find redeeming qualities in the worst of people. I can honestly say that ship has sailed. We can't love everyone."

There was a moment of silence before Barton spoke again. "Well, enough talk. I've got a lady commander to get to. Just between you and me, I'd like to have an Atorathian and not a magician. Don't tell Mai'n. She wants the child to be a magician, just like their father."

"Does she?" Danais asked, intrigued by the change of topic.

"Yes. We've been arguing over it for months, but she believes her will as a woman and as a mother will somehow bring what she wants. No magic required."

"And you believe?"

"She's second in charge of the Alliance. Who knows? Maybe her will can bend nature to her demands."

Danais and Leo laughed at that. Knowing Mai'n, it didn't seem too far a stretch that she would be capable of such a feat.

"But you have the power to bend her to your will."

"If you say so, Leo." Barton quickly changed the topic. "What do you two plan on having?"

"Whatever we get, we get," was Danais' response. Barton wasn't buying it, though.

"So, you want a boy then."

"Did you read my mind? How'd—?" Danais stopped, but the damage was already done. If he would've stuck to his point, neither Leo nor Barton would know what he wanted.

"No I didn't, but now I know."

Both Barton and Leo laughed at the same time

"Aren't you supposed to be leaving?" Danais stated.

"Yes. I am."

"Well, leave before I'm tempted to attack you," Danais said flirtatiously.

"Now that wouldn't be fair, seeing as you haven't attacked Leo yet," Barton joked. Leo failed to hide a grimace.

"Obviously, I'm not his type. He wants a real Mironian," Leo said.

"Lean muscle has its advantages, Leo," Barton responded.

"Ah, so that's what you call it. I was thinking more 'bean pole.'"

Danais found Leo's comment hilarious. Bean Pole Barton wasn't even close to, at least by Mironian standards. Maybe he wasn't quite so slim because of the god he was birthed to. Then again if the God was Miron that would mean his shape was due to his earthly mother. He didn't even know if it was a male or female god. There were way too many variables here.

"Well, I'll leave you two to it." And instantly Barton was gone.

There were only a few magicians that could disappear without any loss of strength. Still, even to Leo, it was something worth seeing when it could be done so frequently. And it also explained how Barton always seemed to just show up when Leo was looking for him.

"I thought you said dissapearing like that takes away some of your energy if used over long distances?" Danais quipped, as if he had read Leo's mind.

"Not for all," Leo told him. "More than a handful are skilled enough to do it without any loss to magic. However, like with most magics, it doesn't mean they're good at anything else. And it's really precise, like potion-making."

"How so?"

"You have to know specifically the point to which you want to go. Otherwise, you can end up anywhere. And if where you're going is blocked by magic, you can be forced anywhere. Only those who are extremely comfortable with it do it often over far distances. But enough about him; how about me?"

"You?"

"Yes. Me. I've been meaning to ask you." Leo was about to start walking when he saw Adwina approaching them.

"Can you be more 'out of sight, out of mind'?" Leo said with a sigh. It didn't come off as irritating as he wanted it.

"I can. Is this going to be a continued private conversation?"

"Most of our conversations are. I've gotten into the habit of blocking and unblocking during our conversations."

"Don't we all? If I have to talk to you—"

"I'll know."

Adwina disappeared, and Danais wondered about the people she had working with her. Would they take shifts? Would someone else be the face they see at different times of the day? What was his life turning into? Or was his life always like this and he just didn't know? The latter seemed to make more sense. As he and Leo walked on in silence, Danais found himself in familiar territory. They were heading to the beach where he first found out Leo's feelings for him. It was different by day but no less splendid. Leo wasted no time stripping and diving in. Danais did the same.

"Remember the first time you jumped off those rocks?"

"You mean when you almost killed me?" Danais glared at Leo playfully.

"I had you on the surface before you had time to think I wouldn't get you."

"That's not how I remember it. I remember sinking and then gasping for air as I surfaced."

Leo chuckled. "That reminds me. I've got a question. You've been different since we planted the seed. Why?"

"I realised I feel the same way for you."

"I'm sure you've always known that; you just didn't want to admit it. I want to know what changed."

"Nothing, really."

Danais' response seemed genuine. "I guess I'm asking the wrong question. When you saw and felt the real me, you changed. I know it all happened in the same day, but the way you were before and after is still different. What made you decide you'd still want to be with me, even after learning what I am and what I try even harder to hide when I'm around you?"

"On some level, I realised that *that* you is always there. Like everyone kept telling me. It's the real you, so it can never fully be hidden. But it was something you said that did it."

"Something I said?" Danais could see the intrigue on Leo's face and decided to stall for a moment, to swim away and have Leo chase him. It was a good chase too, as Danais was an excellent swimmer now. That did not deter Leo. Danais found that Leo out manoeuvred him and forced him to the sand. It was only a matter of time before Leo had him pinned to the beach. Danais, as usual, managed to find a way to reverse positions. Sometimes he had a feeling Leo let him do this. There was no way it could always be so easy.

"You let me pin you," Danais complained.

"Me? Why would I do that? You beat me fairly, as always."

"Don't lie. You're a trained fighter and a magician. There's no way I can always pin you—and especially not after that swim."

"Okay." Leo smiled in defeat. "I like when you're on top of

me. Is that a crime?"

"I guess it's okay." Danais sighed and rolled his eyes as he got comfortable on Leo's side and turned his head to stare up at the clouds.

"You didn't answer my question."

"Come."

"'Come?'"

"Yes. It was the only word you said that sounded exactly the same. Nothing in the way you said it had changed. I realised that, although I didn't know it, I must've somehow already accepted this part of you. There wasn't anything new; it was more the knowledge of something I already accepted."

"'Come.' Huh. I had no idea. Of all the words that held my true essence…"

"Yes. It is the one I like the most."

"I didn't even know I did it till you told me. It's just habit—with you around."

"Yeah, it's much like how you like my frown." Danais chuckled.

"Pout. Not frown. Pout," Leo corrected him. Danais pouted in disapproval, and Leo smiled. Danais realised that he pouted much more in Leo's presence. That and he was sure his pout had many frown and evil glare combos. Leo was not particular on any variation, but a genuine pout seemed to be his favourite.

Danais was pretty sure that Leo didn't say "come" the way he said it to him with anyone else. Maybe it was destiny.

"You surprise me. In so many ways, you're better than me. I would've definitely left after hearing how I tried to destroy myself."

"So what if you had a dark part in your life? It could've ended a lot worse. Then we wouldn't be here together."

"This is true."

"I'm good for you."

"That you are." Leo rolled slightly to his side and kissed Danais on the forehead. He stared at Danais for a while after taking in his beauty before rolling back onto the sand.

"I still have nightmares," Leo said after a moment's silence.

Danais had the sense that if there was one thing Leo could change about himself, it would be his depression.

"Barton approved of you telling me all this?" Danais

inquired.

"He didn't bring it up. I can assume that's code for acceptance, or he wants to talk to me alone. You kicked Dom hard when he was down."

"He kidnapped me and took advantage of your friendship. He earned that."

Leo couldn't help but laugh at that. He was playing with Danais' arm, the one with the rose on it. Danais loved the way it felt. He knew something more of how it worked now. It was looking rough, but for the two days he was captured, the border remained intact. He knew internal conflict would dissolve the image, but the rose remained intact in Leo's presence.

"Will the rose always react to your emotions?"

"Only in extreme moments. Otherwise, you can will it to react, but then I'll know."

"If I were in need of you or wanted you to find me secretly, can I leave anything behind?"

"You ask smart questions. And yes, you can. I'll show you sometime."

"You relax more now. I'm glad."

"Relax?" Leo asked.

"You let down more of your guard. I suspect where you are now is how you are around everyone else. A lot less trying to appear normal and just being normal."

They laid in silence for a while before Danais spoke. "Will you play for me?"

"I don't have my guitar."

"I am sure we are within range for a summoning spell. Your villa is only a few moments away."

Leo smiled at how casually Danais said this. He wanted music, and nothing was going to get in his way. "I should turn you into something," Leo said in a mock threatening tone. He walked down to the water to rinse the sand off. Danais followed.

"Like an eagle?" Danais teased.

"I was thinking of something more proportionate, like a tadpole or mouse."

"You make another short jest, and I will leave you alone on the beach."

"You'll take away half our guard over a minor jest?" Leo

laughed. "It was only a teeny, small bit of humour."

True to his word, Danais returned to his clothes and headed toward the villa without even thinking about it. Leo got dressed, caught up with him, and laughed the whole walk back. And try as he might, Danais couldn't stop pouting. If only his legs had taken him to the boats, Leo wouldn't find his storming off so amusing. But he had to storm off to the place they were sharing.

The servant at the door let him in with Leo smiling and trailing behind him. If only he could wipe the grin off Leo's face.

"Why so glum?" piped up a familiar voice.

"Kale. Where have you been?"

"It's only just after midday. I was hunting. Then I came back for an after-lunch snack."

Danais did have some partially melted chocolate in his pocket. It was wrapped, so it didn't matter that it was soft on the surface. It was still mostly intact.

"At least we share an affinity for desserts and sweets. Or did I cause it?"

"It was always there, but I never indulged the habit, so it's only partly your fault."

"Where's your brother?"

"Some task or other to do with you two. Dom was out of order for what he did to you. The head of the Alliance will not be pleased, but I fear more what his mother will do to him."

"Mother?"

"Yes. One day you will know the extent of wrong he has done. I pray you do not forgive him. Let Leo destroy him. It's a shame Barton let him live."

This was the first time in the short time Danais had known Kale that he had ever shown such strong negative feelings towards anything. There was definitely something more going on with this whole Dom situation. "You don't like him either?"

"He's brilliant but too ambitious. I've heard your uncle has pushed to have him removed for over a century. But the bastard has done many a good thing for the Alliance, even if with ill intentions." Kale paused as he saw Danais stepping away. "You're getting in bed? It's only two hours past mid-day."

"I'm tired, and Lynton's all too happy to make me pout again. I have a mind to lock him out."

Revelations

"Now, now. That's a little extreme." Kale chuckled, and Danais forced himself not to join him.

"If I had magic, I'd shrink him down to my height."

"Now that is extreme," Leo commented. "Why don't you just turn me into a frog? I didn't know you could be so cruel."

Danais managed a glare instead of a pout at that comment. He noticed it seemed to have the same effect which only made him glare more.

"You're getting into bed?" Leo inquired.

"I am."

"So, I don't get the pleasure of enjoying your bad mood?"

Finally, Danais relented and smiled. He could go only so far before he admitted he found it amusing.

"Do you need me to stay?" Leo asked. "I'm not ready for bed.

"We have a guard now."

"I know, but you've just been kidnapped. A guard won't comfort you."

"You've done well enough already."

"Okay." Leo nodded.

"But if you must stay, stay outside the room."

Danais turned away fast so as not to see Leo's face. He knew quite well Leo thought he'd won this round. But why deny the fact that he did want him there? He could at least lessen the stroke to Leo's ego by being as nonchalant about it as he could. He wanted a good rest even if he slept the whole afternoon away. He didn't see himself getting a peaceful rest with Leo nearby, smiling about how Danais had stormed off the beach.

"Did you know where I was, Kale?" Danais asked when Leo left the room.

"I did."

"Why did you not save me?"

"Instincts told me that this was something for Barton to solve. After his and Dom's exchange before the situation happened, I didn't want to involve myself. I was, for lack of another word, afraid. The way he threatened Dom, I just saw fit not to involve myself."

"In the interest of self-preservation," Danais said with a coy smile.

"Naturally. Lucky for me and Xan, he only made us guard

Leo and make sure no one got in."

"That would explain the scar on Lord Vardon's face."

"He tried to force his way in. That was Xan, though." Danais raised an eyebrow.

"Okay. I did it. But Xan did fracture his wrist. I don't know why he healed that immediately and left the scar."

"Maybe it was how he got the scar."

"I choose not to respond to that."

That answer was enough for Danais to chuckle a bit. He got into the bed and for the first time realised just how drained he was. He was asleep before he had time to convince himself of doing anything other than sleep.

10
LEO

"Is Lynton on guard today?"

Leo grunted. Barton had arrived and the first thing that he did was tease Leo. Was there ever a time to not be teasing him? he wondered.

"Leo is on guard."

"Really? I was under the impression that when you did anything for him, you were the real you—the whole you. The you I only see when he is with us. The you I see now. That you, surprising as it is, never attacked when he heard his given name."

"I didn't?" This was a bit shocking to Leo. Even as a little child he hated his name. How could he not remember being called "Lynton" without getting angry? Then again, he didn't get all bent out of shape this time. Or any time since the incident with Danais. He'd pretty much been more himself since which.

"How do you think I gained your attention when you were suicidal? I used your real name. Your teacher did it much more often than anyone I knew, and you never got angry when he did it."

"I don't remember."

"No one bothered to tell you. But I'm telling you now."

"Why do you do this when no one else will?"

"Why do I do what?" Leo could see that Barton wasn't playing innocent this time.

"You let me know things without actually telling me. Ever since the day I met Danais; when you hinted at my parentage."

"Don't say it out loud. Even with a shield up, some things you shouldn't say even if we are protected."

"Okay. But why?"

"That is one secret that I cannot tell; the one I dare not reveal. It is the same secret that drives my protection for Danais. If you figure it out, you mustn't let me—or anyone—know. It is definitely a spell breaker, and we can't afford for the magic on you two to fail before the task is done."

"Is it only because you are bound not to tell me?"

"Yes. It is the hardest secret I've ever kept—the one secret they all thought would undo me in this task whether I revealed it or not. But I've survived. You, I and Danais survived what I can only surmise, though even Dom did not know it, our first test. What did you notice about the situation?"

"Me?"

"You will be dealing with trained soldiers, with better training than you have received. I want to know how you assessed the situation. Everything from here on out treat as a learning experience no matter how trivial."

"You threatened Dom, but—" Leo thought about how everything had transpired. He thought very hard so he could be clear. He was the one with more training than Danais, so it was his duty to understand these things much better than Danais. "Well," he said to Barton, "you effectively calmed me down without mind powers. You stationed guards outside my door and rescued Danais, and you did it all without anyone knowing what had happened or why I was locked in my room. You took control of the situation and solved it without making a spectacle out of it."

"That is correct. Even though I let my anger get the best of me, I still managed to keep the situation contained. I even managed not to kill Dom. And that was hard." Both he and Leo laughed at that.

"But Dom—"

"I know. He was your friend. But you had to have seen him for the self-absorbed man that he is. Power hungry, borderline evil. Much like his father was at one point."

"On some level. But he was always good to me."

"He saw this task as further advancement as much as we all did, but he never saw it for its importance. You were—a task, a means to an ambitious end. He wants to be head of the Alliance. However, I think even before these events, no one would've let that happen. You cleverly left out the part about my letting my anger get the best of me."

"I don't believe it did. You told him what would happen and acted upon your threat. I know you; if you lost control, you wouldn't have been able to keep me and the rest in the dark about what happened until the meeting. You would've stormed off in a less careful search, found Dom in hours, and destroyed him in an instant. Your rage may have fuelled you, but you kept your wits. That's much more than I can say about me in such a situation."

"Still, I let it overcome me too much. Mai'n supported me only because of how cleanly I handled it. She was still not impressed with how my anger took over. But…" Barton paused as if he was thinking about something else not related to the topic. Then he continued. "…I'm an emotional creature."

"Or as Dom would say, weak."

Barton laughed. "True. Knowing when and when not to kill isn't the easiest thing to sort out. Sometimes you just get it wrong, but I've done pretty good. Apparently too good, which is why Dom hates me so much."

"Will you teach me?"

"Adwina will be training you in this. She is an excellent teacher, an expert."

"Who helped you?"

"My older sister. An excellent teacher, also an expert."

Leo did not need to be told what that meant. It was hidden in the tone and a slightly hidden smile. The wording was the biggest giveaway. He simply chuckled and Barton's smile back showed that this was a secret okay for him to know. There were too many pieces to figure out. His sister wasn't his sister at all but, assumptions presently being correct, was Barton's. What about his other siblings?

"What rank does she have?"

"One that is not necessarily thought of as high," Barton replied evasively. "She is head of training. Anyone who trains a soldier whether beginner or advanced was chosen by her. She had been assistant for a while and watched others take the lead—even some she had trained—but a real teacher never begrudges students' success. Every soldier in the Alliance has, on some level, been personally evaluated by her and that's thousands of men and women. Some specifically were trained by her.

"Even with overseeing training an entire army, she still finds time to train an elite force. And it's her duty to train any higher-ranking soldiers in specific tasks that they may not know but would need for new positions. She tests them when it seems they're lacking and gives advice on who should or should not be allowed to do things as she must know her soldiers in and out. Especially the high-ranking ones."

"It must be hard, if she was second for so long before finally getting the position."

"The head of the Alliance said it just wasn't her time. And she waited and turned down many other positions. This was what she was sure she was meant to be. If you don't believe me, ask Mai'n."

"Mai'n?"

"Yes. Adwina was a low-ranked Soldier when Mai'n was just a girl. She taught Mai'n everything she knows. She mentored her."

"She must be quite old, then."

"Very. The first of us all and I am the youngest out of twenty-three."

"Twenty-three?"

"Yes. Only she and I are part of the Alliance, though. Some thought that because of our parents, we'd immediately get in. But the Alliance doesn't play favourites. We were the only ones to get in. And I was born centuries after she."

"So why have you really come?"

"You broke your promise to never reveal the details of your incident."

"Oh."

"Why did you not mind-link me first? Were you absolutely sure your wall was up? If you let your guard down, sometimes the shield goes with it."

"I did not think about that."

"You should have. Do you know what could happen to you if it was found out? You're lucky the people involved are willing to hold onto that secret. It could be used against you. The only good thing is I know the thing with Dom was the specific bad event that would come once you revealed it. You never know with predictions. I thought it would be much worse. It's still pretty bad but at least I finally got to almost destroy him."

Leo almost laughed but the conversation felt to serious for that. "You are angry with me?"

"I am angry that you did not think first or ensure that no one would hear. Were you not conscious of the fact that others may be listening? How else do you think I know?"

"You were following me that day."

"My shift was almost over. And yes, the wall broke. The shield fell. I put a larger one around us. And a tighter separate one around the two of you before your own one resurfaced."

Leo didn't know what to say. That was indeed a grave error on his part. His concentration broke with his emotional turmoil.

"Should I not have told him?"

"You should have. But I'm upset that you could not hold a minor shield spell when your emotions were unsettled. It did come back but it only takes moments. Just like you overreacted when Danais went missing. To your credit, you did reign it in. However, I would've told you that I knew who had done it, but I could not trust you to follow my orders with more information. You surely would've killed Dom after I rescued him or disobeyed my order to stay in the room if you knew."

Leo felt like a failure. Though both the failure of the shield and his overreaction seemed minor, in a much larger situation, they could be much, much worse.

"I wouldn't be allowed in the Alliance, would I?"

"You have potential. Mai'n wanted to tell you herself, but I thought the first time you were scolded, a lighter approach would be better. Her approach is to kill first and ask questions later. The fact that she allowed this shows her growth as commander. I said that to say that if she corrects you in any way, be careful how you react—very careful. What you say may very well be the last thing you say. Make sure Danais is aware of that, too."

"I feel a lot is being placed on our shoulders and I have to hold most of the weight. He sees me as the calm one, but why do I feel like I'm not?"

"If he sees you as stable, then stable you are even if only for him. Are the nightmares gone?"

"Not entirely. I hear him singing when I sleep."

"Really?"

"In my dreams. I think sometimes he wakes up and sings. To me. For me. It helps."

Barton found this interesting. Magic sometimes came from those who couldn't produce it naturally, by chance. Either this was chance that Danais had calming effects on him, or it was directly related to Danais' changing.

"We leave on the day of the wedding. Both you and I should have our children by then, and no one will miss the bride and groom and their friends after the ceremony. The tattoo on his arm, a God-stone from Danais, and another from someone I don't recognise: very precious gifts."

"Yes. I am glad you do not recognise it. He was told that anyone who does should be killed on the spot. I'm assuming this god has never gifted anyone good besides Danais."

"Don't let him out of your sight. He isn't capable yet of killing anyone on the spot."

"We are naming the child after you."

"And mine's to be named after you as well. I'll go now."

Leo watched him disappear and was still impressed. That was a skill he wished he had more control over. He sent a mental link to Xan to get his guitar. If he was going to be sitting out there for hours, he was going to entertain himself by playing the guitar, and Xan was going to listen to him play.

"Here you are," Xan said as he handed him the guitar.

"Thanks. The skills both inward and outward we will both need— do you think we can learn them in time?"

"Out of necessity, you must not allow yourself to think you cannot. It is destiny. If you two fail, then Salinor is lost. There are so many magical secrets and old cities gone to ruin by the Tyrant's thirst for power. For revenge. He won't stop till he controls everywhere, especially Keldon."

Leo knew this to be true. He'd been through one of the older cities. So much history burned to the ground. Even years after it still smelled of ash and flesh. He even thought he could hear the sound of magical power and history the Tyrant had stolen to increase his power.

"Do you believe we can do it?" Danais asked.

"I don't believe. I know that you will do it. Play the one about the centaur who falls in love with the Nymph."

"But it has a tragic ending."

"Tragedy doesn't diminish beauty. The truth will always ring through at some point or the other."

The truth will come through, and if he and Danais would save the realm, they must think they will; not just that they could, not just that it is possible, but that it will happen. Even if they lost, that way they could go on to the under-realm knowing they had wholeheartedly believed in their destiny.

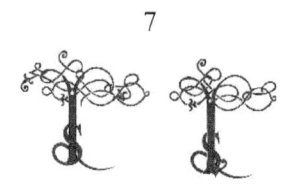

7

"Argh!" Mai'n screamed as her final push yielded her a son.

They were in the glade. Danais and Leo's child had already hatched out of an oversized Guiya berry. That was the tree Danais wanted to grow. They named the child Lynton Barton Vardon. Mai'n and Barton had decided on Danais Leo. They left out the title intentionally, so as not to reveal who either of them was. Their boy was the very picture of an Atorathian, except for the fact that a fox cub had run up beside them minutes after birth, indicating he was a magician. Barton grimaced playfully, and Mai'n smiled in victory.

Danais and Leo's boy was a mix. He was the colour of an Atorathian but had Leo's blue eyes and white and red hair. He had a bluish tint to his skin but more reminiscent of the dragon variety than the Keldonian people. Not too strange seeing as he

Revelations

was a gift from a Dragon.

"Is he a magician?"

"Yes, Danais," Leo answered. "No Betave though, so he will have to pick one on his fifth nameday. Sometimes, dragon and human mixes grow wings. They can hide them, of course."

Danais let out a little gasp at that statement. There was something he now understood. Leo just nodded in agreement to the silent revelation. Everyone else seemed to miss the exchange. He hadn't given it much thought since Kale had told him many moons ago that he would soar.

"So how's it feel to be a granddad, uncle?"

"I'm already a granddad as my real children have children. And I've been treating Lord Vardon's children like my inherited grandchildren, and it turns out they are real grandchildren. With the exception of Adwina."

"So the others are my real siblings. That's refreshing, with all the secrets I've had revealed this year," Leo said.

"I am excited. I've had the first child before any of all my siblings," Barton said. Indeed, out of twenty-three, none had had any children over the centuries. At least none born to both his mother and his father. The other God's children he wasn't thinking of in the count.

"It's officially the middle of summer. Six more weeks till the wedding," Lady Vardon commented.

"You sound more excited than us," Barton responded, smiling.

"Someone has to be. Everyone else is counting down like it's just another day."

Given the joy of the day, she didn't finish her thought: that after the wedding, there was a chance they would never see each other again. It was indeed a day to be excited about; the official start of what had been set in motion.

But today was about new life—and it wasn't going to be tainted by the trials ahead.

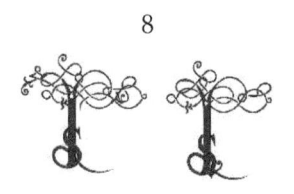

8

"I'm going to go talk to Garnter to see if I can get some free samples," Danais said. Then with baby Lynton, otherwise known as Lyn, he headed off the deck and into the store. It was just at that moment Barton, who was with them, received a mind-link from Adwina. He ran into the shop but was too late. He got in just in time to see Garnter and Danais disappear.

"What happened?" Leo once again dealing with a missing Danais immediately panicked.

"Calm down, Leo. The other group says they've captured the prince's Betave and have him alive. Me, you, Lord Vardon and Lady Vardon must meet the others now." Barton said.

Moments later they were at the edge of the woods with Torak, Mai'n and Adwina. Torak explained what had happened while Lady Vardon and Adwina seemed to be looking for something at the forest's edge.

"I was just talking to Adwina about Danais' love for pastries when I remembered I mentioned something to Garnter that he didn't seem to understand a while back." Torak spoke. "One of my sons and one of his are together, and he didn't seem to understand my joke about our two boys. I just thought he was overworked and didn't get the jest. But now that there's a shapeshifter, I realised it may not be him after all. It could've been nothing, but I didn't want to take the chance. I had Adwina link to Barton immediately. It was so long ago that it took me a while to bring that memory back. It's luck I got triggered to think about it."

"It's not all lost. I saw him when he recognised the stone Danais usually wears around his ankle. The one day it's around his neck is the day we go to Garnter's." Barton had made it just in time to see them disappear as well. "Besides, we were told to rethink all our unusual conversations. You would never consider one of your oldest friend's lapses—out of many he may have had—to be important," Barton said.

"Don't try to make it better, Barton. It was a big and obviously dangerous oversight. Chances are the real Garnter was killed, and now Danais is gone." Torak replied.

"Don't squabble," Mai'n interrupted the two. "We must concentrate. You and I are the Atorathians. We must track him. Just help us find him now. That is what we need from you."

Revelations

"I got it," Lady Vardon announced suddenly. "He landed here and walked into the woods."

Both Mai'n and Torak went to her. She touched them and let them know what they were looking for.

The hunt began. It seemed that every so often the Tyrant's son would disappear in an attempt to lose them. Luckily, Lady Vardon was extremely skilled in finding traces of magic, as was Adwina, so the plan did not work. They found the disappearing and reappearing spots with precision, and they advanced through the woods as quickly and efficiently as possible—both magician and hunters working together, as they should.

"We have a barrier up. He won't chance to use a long-distance mind-link or travel for fear of us detecting the magic. He will keep on foot until he thinks he is out of the range of our magical detectors before trying anything," Barton informed Leo as they moved.

It was a large barrier, so chances were they could be on the chase until nightfall. They didn't want a chance of someone trying to magic either Leo or Danais out of Atorath if they became suspicious of who they are. And the spells against sending information about them out of Atorath were even stronger.

"They're there," Adwina said as they reached the edge of the forest. She looked down on the river that Leo and Danais spent all spring and summer swimming in.

"There are hidden caves behind the waterfall," Leo explained. "He used to hide there as he did in the woods. He knows them well. I should be able to get us down the side of the river behind the waterfall without us falling to our doom. After nightfall, the rocks meld into each other and the entrance is concealed by magic and harder to find."

Everyone followed Leo. He was sure some mind-magic was used to garner this information about the caves and was worried as to what else was forced out of Danais. He was also worried about his child. They barely made it to the caves in time and realised it might be a hopeless task once inside. Somehow, the natural magic in the cave was making tracking harder for both Atorathian and Magician. Some of the oldest magics were quite powerful. Still, they had some idea of where to go.

After a few minutes of following the most obvious route,

they found something.

"Danais!" Leo exclaimed. If the situation weren't so dire, he might have shouted louder but as it were, he could only give it energy if not volume.

"What is it, Leo?" Mai'n asked.

"I taught him how to leave something for me should he ever be lost." Leo held up the rose petal. "The gift I gave him is some of the oldest magic, and it appears the cave wants to help us. There's no way with our limited abilities in here that we would just choose the right path." On the ground was a trail of rose petals. The undying gift was marking their way—something the Tyrant's son would never detect.

"How far ahead of us is he?" Mai'n inquired.

"An hour or so, but much less if we pick up the pace. They are moving very cautiously." Leo thought they finally had a chance at saving him.

"Adwina, take the front. Barton, in the centre with me, Lord Vardon, and Torak. Lady Vardon, hold the rear. The two of you keep up the light with as little magic as possible. We are all trained to see with minimal light. Can you survive with less light up front, Leo?" Mai'n returned to talking to him after giving orders.

"Not as you can, but I can sense the petals. I will be fine."

As he had predicted, they closed the gap in a mere thirty minutes. Leo sensed that around the next bend he'd find them. He began to run, and everyone ran after him, but none was able to stop him in time. As they turned the corner and entered a small empty section, he saw two people who looked like Danais sitting on a stone inlay.

Leo blasted the first one into flying limbs without blinking. It was only after he saw the rage in Mai'n's eyes that he realised he had done something wrong.

"You idiot! Are you positive you killed the right one?"

"Yes."

"Really?"

"He did not have the rose tattoo on his arm." Leo felt confident, but there was no way to know for sure. He was going to stand by his response.

"And you are sure beyond all certainty that this is true?" Mai'n demanded.

Revelations

"I am."

Mai'n had him against the wall with her sword to his throat faster than Leo had ever seen anyone move.

"If you ever lie to me again, mission or not, I will destroy you. Is that understood?"

"Yes, Mai'n."

Mai'n applied more pressure.

"Yes, First Commander!" Leo was, at this moment, the most terrified he had ever been. And he was certain this was nowhere near her full wrath. All five foot five of her managed to throw him against a wall and get her sword to his throat, looking up at him like a woman to be feared.

"I understand that you went on instinct. This time you were right. But you had enough time to assess the situation. He wouldn't have been able to disappear within the power of this cave. He didn't know how close we were. He had planned to sit and wait for us. If Danais is alive captured or not, we can save him. Dead, he is lost."

Mai'n was furious, but she contained herself. Leo wasn't nearly as trained in what to do—and not to do—like the rest of them. Still, she couldn't just let him off the hook.

"I believe in following instincts. But instincts are for when you have no choice: when the facts still seem off and when your skills have failed you. When there is no obvious answer, you must believe enough in yourself to make the right choice. This was not that time. As I said whether we ran or not, he was going to be waiting here for us. This was a plan to give him time to gather enough power to escape this cave. Our powers are limited, but for soldiers like us, soldiers like him, with enough time we can find a way. Come see what I saw."

Leo followed Mai'n and noticed that no one was inclined to speak or follow them. "Look amongst the remains and tell me what you see."

Leo looked, and his heart sank. He was speechless. There on a piece of arm was part of the rose he claimed he didn't see. The rose he said wasn't there was indeed there. He felt himself believing that this might have not been so bad if he admitted he wasn't sure. If he had admitted it was instinctual, Mai'n's berating would've still come, but she would've respected his honesty.

"Luckily, your instincts were correct," Mai'n told him.

"I should've realised after the first petal that he did not know how close or far we were. He would've needed a moment or two to stop and change, and if he had decided to disappear he would've just tried; not sit directly next to his hostage. All that you have said was obvious."

"Now that you see it, I suspect you'll be more careful or at least have the bravery of the warrior I need you to be to tell me the truth. Even some of the most advanced magicians can't hide their lies from me. Now I want you to witness something."

"Straight from scolding to lesson?" Leo asked, before thinking if a jest was appropriate.

"I'm head of an army. I take everything in stride. And I'm a mother now. I'm sure I'll be doing most things all at the same time, much like the army. Except it will be harder. My mother calls it multitasking."

"What is my mother doing?" Lady Vardon was beside Danais, who could not speak, moving her hands slowly and with immense concentration around his body, inches from touching.

"Since I will be training you," Adwina spoke, "here is your first lesson. Sometimes magicians leave behind touch spells. That means if you touch the magic, even without using magic, anything from explosion to vanishing of the object or whatever the intent of the magician, will happen. I suspect that if Danais is touched, he will go straight to the Tyrant's palace," Adwina said.

"What is she doing exactly?"

"Feeling for the layers. Sometimes there's more than one layer, so peeling of the first doesn't guarantee the spell is destroyed, though it may come close. Usually, each layer will explode. This type of reverse magic she is doing means she must give off a precise amount of magic to detect the layer. She must also draw it back in at the same time so as not to trigger the trap. One bad move and we can all die. If, and they usually are, set to explode as well." She gave him enough time to process the information then moved on.

"Many things are hidden this way. There are special teams of reverse magicians that work hard to ensure when we enter enemy territory that no spells or traps are there: to transport us

Revelations

to other enemy territory, or enemies to us, or weapons that can poison us and destroy the whole Alliance. It's a very dangerous job as most of the magicians have time for more than just the final layer when they make these traps. Sometimes people do get blown to pieces.

"Every new or strange place we discover gets a walk through just to be on the safe side and if anything seems off or suspicious reverse magic magicians are called upon."

"So how is it undone?"

"Once the spell is detected, the reverse spell must be done in a steadily growing, precise force. Like I already said the part of magic that touches things must be held back; no matter how strong the spell grows. It is probably the hardest thing to do magically: to cast a spell that pushes and pulls back simultaneously and hold it at a steady level of consistency.

"Unrelated but after the wedding, she will retake her role as head of that area. Being third in command was never really where she wanted to be, and the position was reappointed to her. She accepted."

"Okay," Lady Vardon interrupted. "It's going to be a while, but I've at least sorted out one problem. Shield yourselves in case this doesn't work. This will be the hardest part. I can't seem to break the final layer with the child and him together. Separating something from within a spell is always difficult. I'm going to need you, Leo."

Leo cautiously walked toward her. Not sure if any magical elements floating might trigger the spell. He also thought back to Mai'n saying for soldiers like them, they would find a way. That meant Lady Vardon had somehow managed to figure out the magic of the cave in order to exert the amount of magical control and power needed to perform in the short time they'd been here. Clearly that's what centuries of training could do.

"This spell is going to require your blood-connect to the child. I will assume control of your body and move your hands over the back of Danais, where the child is. When I say your name, the bond will be broken, and you must not hesitate; grab him immediately. Do not let yourself touch Danais under any circumstance once I release you from the spell. Understood? This spell is also a trap to capture you. We cannot afford to lose you both. I'll be concentrating on keeping Danais here once we break through."

"Okay," Leo agreed.

Lady Vardon wasn't the type to control other people by magic. However, she found that Leo made it easy by not resisting at all. It could be useful magic when needed but also quite evil when used the wrong way. She got to work, and it was just over an hour before she stopped moving his hands like they were her own and ceased the magician whisper. She called his name; Leo did as his mother told him and ran back as far and as fast as he could from Danais.

"Stop!"

Leo stopped instantly at the sound of his mother's voice.

"I have to be sure nothing will happen if you go too far." She looked to Adwina to check the child.

"It is safe." Adwina said and walked a safe distance away with Leo and the child.

Lady Vardon sighed. Even though this next step was slightly easier, difficulty was still high. "I must say I'm impressed," Lady Vardon said. "This is a pretty good bit of magic. And I'm sure he was working on it from the moment Leo found the first petal. He may have been evil to the core but a shabby magician he was not. This is a test for anyone's abilities. Each layer does something besides explode. Well, I better get started."

She stood after a few minutes and somehow managed to get Danais to float away from the wall, so she could circle around him as she continued to undo the spell. The air seemed to move much faster in the room and circle around the two in an awe-inspiring way. It was powerful yet reserved. This was what the best magical concentration created. Leo was in awe as was everyone else. They watched as she circled Danais: hair blowing lightly in the wind with sparks of lightning occasionally flashing around Danais' body.

After a long while, the last words were uttered, and all the collective concentrated force was sucked into Danais. Suddenly the force expelled, and it looked as if a globe had cracked around him, and the magical barrier, like crystalized glass, flew away. At that moment, Lady Vardon reached through the floating debris, grabbed Danais, and pulled him out just before the broken shield folded in on itself and exploded into nothing. The energy of the final explosion almost blew them all over,

Revelations

but soon the wind and the atmosphere returned to normal.

"As I said," Lady Vardon spoke, "an exceptional piece of magic. If that inward explosion touched him, this whole network of caves would've been demolished. I haven't been tested or seen anyone's skills tested this hard in a long time. The Betave?"

"Destroyed in a way that his secrets died with him," Mai'n said. "I'm surprised we caught him. Betaves are extremely hard to catch. Luck was on our side. And you—you never cease to amaze me. That was excellent."

"Thank you, first commander. They might need healing. I suggest one of our Keldonian healers see to them at once. I wouldn't have one of us try to heal them and get it wrong. Some of the magic may still be inside them. This is better left to the experts. Healing is what the mountain people do." She turned to her son. "Don't look so down, Leo. We've been doing this for years. And count yourself lucky. I've lost five ears, two left arms and my right hand to her rages," Lady Vardon said with a smile.

The healers did good work on her, Leo thought.

"It's not that bad. And it was only two ears. Besides Adwina is much, much worse than I am," Mai'n responded.

"Two left ears. Five total." Lady Vardon clarified as if that would make it seem worse.

"Details." Mai'n dismissed the clarification.

"Don't worry. With Adwina as your teacher, I doubt you will fail. I lost an arm to her too, by the way," Lady Vardon addressed Leo.

"Only an arm!" Mai'n exclaimed. "A healer had to reattach more of me than what you just said I took of you." Mai'n glared at Adwina, who merely shrugged in response.

Leo was glad that they were trying to cheer him up. He very well could've blown Danais to bits, and in their disappointment, even Mai'n was relaxed enough to laugh at the situation. Xan was right. It was his fate. He was going to succeed. Leo did, however, wonder why the Magician didn't shape-shift back to his original form after he blasted him. The broken pieces still looked like Garnter. But that was a question for another time.

It was a few hours later, in the very early morning, when Danais finally awoke. Leo was so content with feeding his child that he didn't notice. He was feeding the baby from the leftover mixture in the cauldron that birthed him. As long as the child needed it, the cauldron would remain full. The mixture was also used to feed the plant up until his birth.

"You almost killed me," Danais grunted.

Leo turned, relieved Danais was finally awake. "Yes. But I didn't."

"Mai'n wasn't too pleased. You could've lost your head. Why would you ever lie to someone like her?"

Leo walked over to the bed, and handed the child to Danais, and then sat in a chair beside him. "That's a very good question. Especially after Barton specifically warned me to be careful how I deal with her."

"This is going to get much harder than I thought," Danais surmised.

"Yes. But let's not think about that until after the wedding. It's clearly not affecting Lyn. He's already back asleep."

"Will you play for me?"

Leo knew he was an excellent guitarist, but Danais made him feel like more than that. He seemed to enjoy it on a level that made Leo feel like he played so much better when he played for Danais. Today he played something smooth and melodic. What amazed him most was that for someone who sang to himself frequently, Danais never made a sound when he played. Someone who loved to sing that much was deadly silent every time he played. If Danais liked when Leo said "Come," Leo, even more than liking Danais' pouty face, loved how much Danais loved to hear him play.

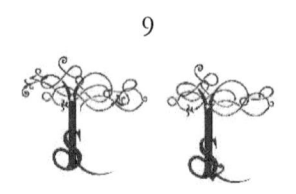

9

The wedding was beautiful. It was the first day of fall, and the weather was perfect. Outside at one of the chapels on the mainland, Barton's parents awaited, but Leo was perfectly sure they were magicians disguised as someone else. Well, at least one of them. He was unsure if his father or his mother was the god.

Danais thought much the same thing. It wasn't so much that he didn't believe they were his parents, but their appearance wasn't their true form. The same was said about Mai'n's parents. One was a magician not in his true form, and the mother was Atorathian, also disguised. He had a feeling that the people here knew, and it was only to keep Danais and Leo in the dark.

Danais was mingling with the friends of both families when Barton's father and Mai'n's mother came over to him. Leo was nearby, and somehow felt drawn to stand beside him.

"You are the two?" Barton's father stated.

"We are, sir," Danais responded.

"This is something the two of us have waited long to see," Mai'n's mother spoke.

"The start of the prophecy?" Danais addressed the woman who had spoken.

"That... and the two of you." she continued.

"Us?"

"Yes. You and Leo. There are only two people who would want to see you more than we do: the ones who sacrificed the most for the cause. But that will be revealed in due time."

Leo didn't know why, but even though he stood much taller than both of them, their presence made him feel small; almost as if he should bow his head and not look them in the eyes. Yet they seemed so polite, with their unexpected smiles and conversation. Who were these two?

It was at that time that Barton's mother came over.

"Barton has requested that I gift you a gift from him through me to you. Do not open them just yet. The gem in these leather pouches will give you strength of heart and protect you as a Dani weapon will, but only in the most extreme circumstances. If used correctly, it may save your life. When you need heart, the strength that comes from love will always be there."

The woman put the pouches over both their heads and instructed them not to take them off and remove the gem until safely on the start of their journey. She stepped back and admired the couple. "And now I must take my leave," she announced.

"We, too, must leave," announced Barton's father after the woman had left. He took Danais' hand in his and Danais felt a wave of energy, like a swift breeze, enter him, and then the same thing when Mai'n's mother touched him. It was the same feeling he felt at the meeting when both Mai'n and Dom had touched him. The two did the same with Leo, but nothing spectacular happened. He wanted to ask why but the two of them disappeared.

"So, how's it feel to be married, Barton?"

"Don't know yet. It's only been a few hours. I have something for you too, Leo." Barton took his hand, and this time Leo did feel the surge.

"You will feel this two more times. And Danais shall have one more. Then the parts of your full potential that are missing, that we had to take to keep you hidden, will have fully returned. Only your true identity other than those who know it will still be hidden by magic. It will be much harder to keep things secret then. But the two of you will feel whole."

"Have you both had enough drink and food? The sun will be up soon, and we should be across the river before sunrise."

"Then let's go," Leo said. He looked at Danais and hazarded a mind link.

"Did you notice something about Barton's mother?"

"I did," Danais said in response, *"The way she said Barton. He's not her son, but he is her son. It doesn't make sense. But his father was definitely his father."*

"His father is the God. And I sense so is his mother, but not mother. But which ones?"

"I don't know. Didn't you say a god child could manifest in any form, and not necessarily a direct link to how their parent looks? That means it could be any of the gods. Even Salinor herself."

"No. He said his earthly father. It's def a male god?"

"We both shook hands with gods. I hugged his father. I'm one up on you." Danais smirked at that.

Leo chuckled and started towards the river, a little further down than the spot where Danais and he usually swam. There was a raft waiting for them, and across the river, Adwina was already waiting with all the provisions and cargo needed for the journey. Barton was going to be part of the circling sentry, keeping a constant protective border around Adwina, Mai'n, Leo and Danais. The babies would travel in the centre with the four.

They took the raft across the river. Once on the other side, the others walked to the horses and cart while Danais stared back across the river. Not only was this the farthest he had ever been from home, but he realised this journey may claim his life. If not, it may change him so much that home would never have the same meaning to him. He was no longer the person in the blindless window of a small box of a room. All he knew about himself had to be left behind and stepping into the woods was the final acceptance of his new task in life.

He was terrified yet determined. He threw a rock into the water and watched it skip, making ripples on the surface. He took one last look across at the land that was formally his. He looked long enough to etch permanently on his mind the man he was to be no more, so he would never forget him; never forget where he came from. Then he remembered something Kale had said that made no sense before.

"'The journey shall begin at the drop of a stone,'" Danais recalled his words out loud.

"Danais," Leo said gently.

Danais turned and saw that Leo was looking at him. He seemed to fully understand what Danais was going through and waited for a response.

"I'm okay. Just thinking."

"Understandable. We are ready to go."

Danais dropped the second stone from his hand and realised that now the journey had officially begun. He paused and stared up into the starry sky.

"Danais," Leo said again.

Danais looked toward Leo, and the two of them shared a smile.

"Come."

Milton Keynes UK
Ingram Content Group UK Ltd.
UKHW031117231024
450133UK00015B/776